About the author

I was born in central London and raised in Camden. And then moved and lived in North London, Hertfordshire and then Spain. I now reside in Surrey with my partner. This is my first novel.

Bobbing for apples

Frank London

Bobbing for apples

Vanguard Press

VANGUARD PAPERBACK

© Copyright 2024
Frank London

The right of Frank London to be identified as author of
this work has been asserted by him in accordance with the
Copyright, Designs and Patents Act 1988.

A CIP catalogue record for this title is
available from the British Library.

ISBN 978-1-80016-563-2

Vanguard Press is an imprint of
Pegasus Elliot Mackenzie Publishers Ltd.
www.pegasuspublishers.com

First Published in 2024

Vanguard Press
Sheraton House Castle Park
Cambridge England

Printed & Bound in Great Britain

Dedication

For my children. Joe Max Ruby and Lily.

Prologue

She felt a sudden thrust on the back of her neck. It came from nowhere. She yelped. Something dug into her skin on either side. It was a hand – warm and sweaty. It felt like an act of aggression, like something she had never felt before. She twisted her head to try to escape the pain that she felt, but the arched clasp tightened around her skin.

She lifted and bent an arm to grab at the wrist that now had her at its mercy, and which was thrusting her forward. She felt an arm, an arm which was more powerful and dominant than her own. It was thicker than hers. She grappled with it but hardly managed to get any grip, to put up any kind of contest against it. Who was it? Who was doing this to her? Was it a game? If it was, she wasn't enjoying it.

She angled her fingers and scratched at its thick skin, then felt even more discomfort when the assailant's other hand thrust into her ribs. She flinched, pulling a face of pain and anger. She tried again with her fingernails to battle the terror that was behind her. She felt a nail dig into its skin. At last, she had made some resistance, but the clasp remained around her neck.

And then she was thrust forward and she felt the figure scoffing at her. Her feet were fumbling on the soft wet grass below. She looked ahead as she was being forced towards a large oak barrel. It had rusty metal hoops circling its flaky wooden exterior, reminding her of the side of an old galleon ship. She twisted her feet and tried to dig them into the ground to try to halt her forward movements. It made little impact.

She was now being frogmarched towards this large wooden object; she was taller than it.

What was going on? Who was this person punishing her? She hadn't wronged anybody, she didn't owe anything to anyone. Was it her controlling father, the man who had locked her in her bedroom on several occasions for failing to complete her homework on time? Had he caught up with her, and was also punishing her for stealing her mother's make-up, the make-up she now wore which made her look older than her twelve years? The make-up that made her attractive to boys. Would he do this to her?

Her face was a foot away from the smooth glass-like appearance of the still water. There was a reflection on its surface from the tree above, and objects rested happily on its surface. The force was still on the back of her neck. And then her head was forced forward and down. Her neck ached, and she stretched out her arms as she felt she was going to be plunged into the watery pool. Her palms gripped the sharp splintered sides of the barrel, her chest pressed against the edge of a metal hoop.

Her instincts kicked in and she squeezed her eyelids tightly together, hoping to stop the inevitable sting when the water would creep around her sclera. A pain that she had felt on her first swimming lesson. She also thought, how deep was this tub? Was her face going to be forced into the full depth of it, and be smashed on its surface? Her eyelids flicked open, taking note of how far away from the base she was in this cold abyss. Everything around her was black. She heard the faint sound of laughter, and the sound of a large object hitting a bell. Her lungs took in water as her lips parted. A long line of bubbles exhaled from her nostrils in tandem, looking like two bunches of Lupins. She shook her head violently, hoping that it would free her from the vice-like grip that her attacker held over her. Her view of what she thought was her world coming to a short end was the dark bottom of the barrel. Was this the last thing that she would ever come to see? She thought that only seconds ago she had been holding hands with her best friend, Mabel Taylor, revelling in the joviality and the excitement of the village fair. They laughed together and skipped hand in hand past the many colourful attractions that it had to offer them, without a care in the world, they were free to do whatever they liked on this sunny afternoon. Nobody was there to boss them around.

And as if her prayers were suddenly answered, the hold around her neck was gone. Instantly. Like it was never there, the pain turned to freedom.

She swung her head upwards, forcing the back of it against the weight of the water, the vacuum from her face drew waves in the pool. She saw an apple, bobbing wildly, and uncontrollably, trying to fight the sway of the wave, trying to stay afloat. She inhaled, as she gasped for oxygen, for air to keep her in this world.

She blinked rapidly to see if she existed. Excess water from her returned to the barrel, splattering down like heavy rainfall from a storm.

She heard hysterical laughter behind her, and on turning, saw the class bully, Danny Willard, a tall oversized incongruous figure, who lived on the Bush-Mead estate, an impoverished area of town. A place where you would turn down an invitation to visit after dark. His body was out of proportion for his age. He was giggling frantically with two of his sidekicks, at what he had just implemented. Picking on someone smaller than himself, for self-gratification. He was a creature of habit, showing off his might, just so he could get his kicks, just to show off what power he possessed to his cronies, and have his day in the sun, and knowing that no one could challenge him.

She shook her hair, dispelling as much of the unwanted water on her.

Everything else around her now went out of focus, as she narrowed her eyes towards the brute. Her small five-foot-two figure, in her pink gingham checked frock, with its white frilly laced edgings, was not going to match this tormentor of hers. She didn't possess the power to overthrow this thug, this lowlife of a human being, this person who cheats his way in class to get his results, and his marks up to standard. It's all he knew. She couldn't battle with him and win, she had no weight to take him on and defeat him.

Everything around her no longer had any significance. Her friend, the game, and the occasion had no meaning or bearing to her anymore. Except for one thing, the cotton twined rope with a noose, that dangled from a branch of a beech tree over the tub of water.

One

Halloween Night, Friday 2008

Christina pulled onto her driveway. She twisted the key turning off the purring engine and felt pleased to be home, or at least in her own driveway. It was a wet evening; dark, with a misty haze lying in the air. She heard party revellers laughing and giggling as they passed her house. Looking in her rear-view mirror, she saw the face of the devil. It curled its hands, claw-like at her, as their eyes locked on to each other's. She sat motionlessly. Then, in an instant, the face vanished. Its mother, pulling her son away from Christina's view.

Maybe she would be the devil tonight?

She draped herself against the seat and let out a long sigh, as she looked at her house through the smeared windscreen.

Her day had been long, she had skipped lunch again, and had one of the trainees pick her up some snacks.

It had been a tenuous and laborious day for Christina. With endless issues to sort out, and some things had got ballsed up. Her natural diligence meant that she hated it when things didn't go the way they were supposed to.

She had attended a meeting, that she felt only she could have dealt with as it needed her prowess and tenacity. She wasn't going to leave it to anyone else, *she* was going to the meeting. This woman never made mistakes.

And she had also had a resignation letter from her chief strategy officer, who had decided that he wanted to take up a position as "global strategist", with an investment company based in Paris, claiming that his French wife wanted to start a family back home. This would mean moving away from a land investment company into technology, Christina thought this to be a loss and summoned him to her office to convince him to stay, but it was all to no avail; he insisted his decision was final. Christina had been given no warning and was now left with the task of looking for a replacement. She demanded that her secretary fill the position immediately.

She also wanted the travel details for the meeting she had coming up in Atlanta in two weeks' time. Christina wanted to plan ahead, but her secretary, Hayley, had not yet been able to confirm the details. Hayley had been on the phone a few times during the day, negotiating times for pick-ups, transfers, and hotel accommodations, and had tried tirelessly to get them to her boss. But she hadn't received the correct details, as they still hadn't come in from America due to the yanks being unable to finalise the meeting across the pond.

Christina also had a party to attend, with her boyfriend, Antonio, in Ascot around the same time as the meeting abroad, and she didn't want to let him down. There could be some potential customers from his homeland, customers she was eager to meet, as this was an area untapped by Hammerson Shaw and of course, she wanted to see her boyfriend as they hadn't seen much of each other recently due to work commitments. Antonio was working away in northern Spain, and Christina had been working long hours over the last few months setting up a deal which her company was hoping to clinch in the land of Uncle Sam.

Christina was never going to become Mrs Garcia. They had been seeing each other for the last six months or so and he had asked her to get engaged, but she bluntly turned his advances down, claiming it was "too early". Yes, she loved Antonio, but something was missing... Maybe it was the thought of being with him for the rest of her life that just didn't sit right with her. He wasn't the one for her, even though her fortieth birthday was coming along quicker than her next pay cheque, besides, she had a dark side to her that she wasn't prepared to give up for anyone - not just yet - anyway.

She closed her front door and walked ahead and into the kitchen, putting her handbag and some documents onto the worktop. She grabbed a glass and ran the cold tap to fill it with just enough water to get her through the next hour or so. She then opened the fridge door, checked the contents and put her hand on a bottle of Pinot, making sure the temperature was to her liking. She closed it and smiled to herself, then headed upstairs.

She took off her work clothes, which ended up on the carpet, and entered the shower, naked.

As the water poured over her, she hoped it would help to wash away the issues of the day and ease her stress. She ran her hands through her long hair, hoping as she did so that someone else would be doing this for her a little later. She loved it when Antonio ran his fingers over her scalp and dug the tips into her skin. It soothed and relaxed her, it made her tensed up mind drift away, it released the tension and burden from her, and he got brownie points for it as well.

She washed off the lather and grabbed two fluffy white towels. She squiggled one over her hair, bending over as if to touch her toes, and wrapped it around her head turban-fashion. She stood up and glanced at herself in the mirror, stretching her body to try to give her more height. She ran a hand over her buttocks, thinking they could do with a bit of trimming, and a bit more jogging wouldn't go amiss, or should she be boring and cut out the wine? No, more jogging, she thought. There are just some things you can't give up.

She flopped down on her bed, leaned over and pulled open the bottom drawer of a side cabinet. She removed a mahogany box decorated on top with a pearl elephant. There was a small creased-up plastic bag inside. She opened it. She peered at it with mounting anticipation.

She then neatly sprinkled a thin line of the white stuff onto her glass bedside cabinet top, nudging it into line with a sharp razor blade. She reached over to her handbag, pulled out her purse and pulled out a straw that would transfer the line into one of her nostrils.

Christina was wary that she had taken a line of cocaine. It was not something she used regularly, it was purely medicinal, it was just there to get her out of trouble when she was down and wanted to feel good again, and when she wanted to be taken to another level, higher than a cloud in the sky, and it worked for her. She was too level-headed to get hooked on the stuff - she knew that it had its drawbacks. She had got it from a girlfriend, Rebecca Ansell. It was good stuff, not the best, and inexpensive. She had bought some from Rebecca before and had a small amount left, probably enough for two more lines. It took the tension away from her, it helped her unwind, and she didn't want to spoil the evening for her date. She was looking forward to it, it was going to be a new experience for her, something she hadn't undertaken before. It was a new fantasy she was looking forward to and was longing to fulfil. It was a good idea. She didn't want the day she had just had at work to play on her mind, but that's the way it went, it was uncontrollable, and she couldn't have planned how the last ten hours had gone.

She blow-dried her hair and left it slightly damp and rugged-looking.

Christina sat down at her dressing table and applied her mascara, making a pointed shape at the corner of her eyes, giving her a devil-like look, one to suit the mood of the evening. She applied some foundation and then ran a deep purple gloss over her lips, pursed them, and pushed them out toward the mirror. She sighed and rested her chin on her hand. Wondering when her prince charming would come along and into her life, she was waiting for that magic kiss. She hadn't been in love for years, or she *had*, but the favour had never been returned to her. 'How long am I going to be single, how many more years do I have to wait before he comes into my life?' she asked herself. 'I might want children… or do I?'

'Mirror, mirror on the wall… Oh, it probably won't work.' She squinted her eyes and then opened them but found herself still in the same place. She stood and investigated the mirror, wondering what might be wrong with her. 'Well, it leaves me free to indulge in this shit that I'm going through,' she thought.

She opened her wardrobe, removed a provocative red top and held it up, and then with little deliberation decided that would suffice as her battle dress for the evening. She accompanied it with a black skirt, which had a white pattern in the shape of a butterfly. Next, she pulled on a pair of black hold-up stockings, and then looked down at herself. She straightened her back and twisted her hips, thinking, 'Ah! It's OK, a little on the casual side… besides, time is against me.' As she flicked her head back, several strands of hair covered her left eye, and she thought, 'Well, I look hot at least.'

She sauntered into her lounge. Three of the walls were papered. They had blue-coloured flowers, surrounded by sparsely entwined leaves, with roots twisting around the petals. There was a picture of considerable size, hanging on the plain wall. It was a portrait of a dashing gentleman

– The Earl of Leicester, Robert Dudley. He was wearing a light grey suit and his collar almost covered his neck. He wore a gold chain around it from which was suspended a gold medallion. A sword hung from his thigh. The picture had been given to her by Robert on her 35th birthday. He had thought the name was appropriate. She looks at the picture practically every time she entered the room, and it had been tactically positioned for her to do so.

Christina stood looking for a place to put the two glass ashtrays she was holding, one in each of her hand. A small glass table sat at either end of her cream L-shaped sofa, and each table had a chrome art deco stemmed lamp placed on it. She decided that was where the ashtrays should go, but only put one down, keeping the other in her hand. She bent down to the beige carpet and picked up a piece of fluff. A male sparrow hawk would likely have missed it. She then knelt down in front of a cabinet, opened the door and carefully flicked through her CD collection, running a finger across the top of them looking for dust and checking that her daily had done her job correctly. Looking at her index finger, and then at the two-tone mark it had left, she winced.

'Maria will be getting a ticking-off the next time I saw her,' she thought. The plastic cases clicked against each other as she looked for some music to suit the mood of the coming evening. She picked up a plastic case and opened it, then pressed some buttons on the player, and a drawer slid out. She inserted the disc, pressed play, then twiddled with the volume control. She stood up waiting for the music to start, checked the clock, then turned on the two side lamps, switched off the main ceiling light and glanced around the room. Something was missing, but what was it? She frowned and headed into the kitchen thinking, 'It will come to me.' She returned the extra ashtray to a cupboard and then removed two glasses from a cabinet and put them on the marble worktop. They made a clinking sound.

'Candles! Of course.' That's what was missing; she removed two candles, two heavy glass candle holders, and a box of matches from a nearby drawer, and returned to the lounge. She placed the peach-scented ornaments onto the glass coffee table, lit them, blew on them gently and stood back to admire the effect as the flames danced from side to side. Satisfied, she smiled and returned to the kitchen.

Christina opened the door of the large refrigerator.

As she did so, a sudden instinct made her head turn and face the front door, which she could see from where she was standing. Through the opaque glass, she saw a silhouette, a blurred shape…Her face lit up with excitement. Her guest had arrived, while Mozart's Clarinet Concerto in A major played in the background.

Two

The Monday after the Friday.

Hayley Remington walked out of the lift on the third floor and smiled at a passing cleaner. Hayley was at work early today; she had a busy schedule ahead and didn't want to waste any time. She was carrying a folder full of documents that she needed for the day's task.

Hayley was conscientious, circumspect and thoughtful, and she showed sound judgment of people. She had worked for Mike Schreiber as his secretary for two and a half years. Mike liked the way she worked, and he told her so, giving her a raise three months before it was due.

Mike wasn't due in until 10:30 this morning, as he had a meeting at 9:00 with an American client in Kensington.

Hayley envied Mike's lifestyle and she looked up to him as a mentor, admiring his leadership. She would smile when he was around and this would set off tongues wagging around the corridors of Hammerson Shaw.

Hayley always dressed smartly; today she was in a black trouser suit, with a pink blouse and black shoes. Her blonde shoulder-length hair was slightly wavy and her original dark colour showed through at the centre parting. Today it looked like it needed further brushing. She was tall, and this gave her a look of credibility.

The office floor consisted of a labyrinth of desks, most of which were divided by partitions, allowing the workers to have a modicum of privacy. Although slightly dated, the large office had a spacious and airy feel to it, and wasn't overlooked by any nearby buildings.

The ceiling was high and the large windows let in light from two angles.

Helen Marshall walked in with a swagger, and in a confident and buoyant mood; she was holding a light-green leather handbag, with long straps. It looked new. She asked Hayley if she had had a good weekend.

'Very good thanks,' was the reply, and then Helen asked her if *she* was OK, she got the same reply but this time with a wry smile. Hayley thought Helen looked radiant and commented on how happy she was. Helen said that she had had a great weekend with her son and her boyfriend, thank you, and that she had enjoyed the time they all spent together over the two-day break.

And then, the junior worker Rebecca Ansell waddled out of the lift, looking tired. She was holding a distinctive white paper bag from the local bakers, part of which looked greasy, providing a clue to its contents.

Rebecca had worked in the offices for around a year. Hammerson Shaw had been asked by a local employment agency if they could take on an adult with mild learning difficulties. As they didn't want to upset the local community, they put her to work in their "running errands for anyone" department.

'Morning Rebecca,' Mars chirped.

'Morn…Morning,' she replied, looking at a confident Helen. Rebecca looked at Helen's new acquisition, now hanging from her shoulder. Rebecca's face took on a frown as Helen wandered off to her office.

Hayley opened the door to her room, put her bag down on the desk, took a long look around, picked up a framed picture of her daughter, and smiled at it fondly. She then picked up a folder and then headed out of her office to go down the stairs to the floor below.

On her way, she bumped into Jenny Ross.

'Morning Jen,' she said, sounding surprised.

'Hi darling, how's things with you, good weekend, get up to much?' Jenny said sprightly.

'Oh, I had a bit of a lazy one really. The mother-in-law came over on Sunday, but let's not dwell on that one, ah!' She pulled a face at Jenny. Jenny was in her late fifties and dressed like her nan, wearing skirts and tops with flowery patterns, all the time. They were cheap. She had been with the company since the year dot. Some sarcastically said that she had helped to build the offices they were in.

'Is Christina in yet?' Jenny asked.

'No, not yet, at least I don't think she is?' Hayley looked at her watch.

'She told me that she would be in at around half nine this morning as she had to wait for a new gardener to turn up and had to show him around. You know, tell him where things are, give him his orders, etcetera. Did you want to see her about something? She has a meeting at 10:00, but I haven't heard from her yet this morning. Do you need her for something?'

'No, I just wondered,' Jenny said. Hayley's face looked vacant.

'Are you okay lovie? You look worried about something… everything okay?'

'I'm fine,' Hayley replied. 'It's probably just because I haven't had my morning fix yet, you know. I need a coffee.' She smiled wistfully. Hayley moved away and headed down the stairs.

'Speak to you later, and enjoy your caffeine darling.' Jenny's voice faded away.

Hayley's office phone rung. She snapped it up quickly.

'Hello!'

'Morning Hayley, it's Mars.'

'Oh, morning Mars, what can I do for you?' she said resignedly.

'Er, can you just remind Christina that I'm leaving early today. I have to pick Tom up from school.'

'Yes, yes I will when she gets in.'

'Oh! Isn't she in yet?' Mars sounded surprised.

'Not yet, she's late, which is unusual for her, and she's got a meeting in four minutes,' Hayley said looking at the time on her computer screen.

'Oh okay, I'll speak to her later. Thanks, Hayley.'

'What time shall I tell her you're leaving?'

'Er, I've got another call coming in Hayley. I'll speak to you later, bye,' she said abruptly. The phone went dead. Hayley looked confused at the manner in which her work colleague had ended the call. It was unlike her as she was generally more considerate with her colleagues.

Hayley wandered around the offices, looking in bewilderment at the surrounding area. She had an instinct that something wasn't right. Unaccountably, her mood changed and she felt butterflies fluttering around in her stomach.

She knocked on the door of Christina's office and waited. She didn't try again. She acted not from reason, but mere caprice.

She phoned Christina's home phone, but there was no answer. She decided to call Mike. Christina had a scheduled meeting this morning with a regular client, who was now in reception.

'Mike, I'm worried! There's still no sign of Christina, and some of the girls are showing concern. This is totally out of character of her - she has never done anything like this before. A rep from Lansdown and Barrett is waiting in the lobby. I've rung her at home, and there's no answer. Just call it a woman's intuition, Mike,' she went on. 'Rebecca said that she phoned her last night, at around 8:00, then sent her a couple of text messages and emailed her, and she hasn't answered any of them.'

'OK. Who was the last person to talk to Christina, do you know?'

'No, I don't know Mike, but I can find out and let you know. I'll ask around the office. I suppose someone must be able to come up with an answer.'

'Yes, can you do that for me please, Hayley? I'm on my way in, so I should be there in about ten to fifteen minutes. If she's still not in by then, I'll get you a cab, and you can go to her address and see if she's there.' Hayley was disquieted by his remark.

'Where are you now?' asked Mike.

'I'm in the lobby with Jenny and Rebecca Ansell.'

'OK, I won't be long. Tell the girls not to worry - there must be a logical answer for all of this... Can you think of where she may be, Hayley if she's not at home?'

'No Mike I can't. She told me on Friday that she would be in half an hour late, as she was meeting someone at 8:30 at her home.'

'Who did she say she would be meeting Hayley? Can you remember?'

'She told me that she had a new gardener starting, and she had to show him around, and leave a key in a safe place for him.'

'OK. Maybe he was good-looking, and she eloped with him to a far-off land. Perhaps we will never see her again?' Mike said mockingly.

Hayley got out of the cab and stood apprehensively on the pavement.

The private car pulled away from her and drove through a puddle, making a splashing sound, as she glanced at it. She now felt cold and lonely, and wished that someone was with her. She shivered, and put an arm across her chest, still thinking that something wasn't right. Her instinct told her that she wasn't going to enjoy the next few minutes of her morning. The rain had finally come to an end and was quickly replaced by sunshine. The change made the air misty. She shook the rain drops off of her umbrella.

With a sense of foreboding, she walked up to the gate and pushed it open. It squeaked as it closed behind her. She wearily made her way up the path to the front door of the house. She looked down at the pathway and saw that weeds had begun to creep through cracks in the tiles.

Christina's car was in the driveway. Hayley knew that she took the train to work most days of the week, so she wondered if Christina had already left and she had missed her? She somehow doubted it. If Christina was running late, she would have driven to work, and the car would have been gone. Her intuition told her that was not the answer.

Hayley looked at the house. It was a large, semi-detached house, a grand-looking edifice. It had been constructed in the 60's and built in a Victorian style by its then-owner. It had weathered original stock bricks and sash styled windows which matched the houses in the street. The roof was a sharp apex, tiled in black slates.

The curtains in the lounge window on the ground floor were closed. Hayley looked up at a first-floor window, which she assumed would be a bedroom, but they too were closed. She pulled a confused face. Her eyebrows knitted together. Christina wasn't the kind of person to shut herself away from the world. Why was she all of a sudden shunning society? Was she ill, too sick to move from her bed? Or had she fallen over?

Hayley stared at the front door. She brushed her hands down the front of her coat. She slowly pushed a finger to the doorbell, touching it as if it were wet paint. She heard a ringing noise from inside the house and waited. She looked behind her, waited a few moments, and then rang the bell again. She tugged at the bulbous chrome door handle, but the door didn't budge. She cupped her hand and peeked through the frosted glass.

Then she walked over to the car and checked to see if any of the doors were unlocked. She walked around it, looking in through its windows to see if anything seemed out of place. She then walked over to the lounge window and peered through a crack in the drawn curtain. She walked back to the front door, then folded her arms around herself as a chill ran over her. She slowly lifted the letterbox halfway. She blinked her eyes rapidly. Hayley heard the sound of a fly buzzing around and tried to see where it was. It appeared to have come from out of the lounge and then settled on the wooden floor in the hall. She coughed at the stench coming from inside, pulled herself away and walked around to the side of the house. She gripped the black, heavily painted iron handle on the side gate and tugged at it in an attempt to force it open, but it only rattled. Frustrated, she returned to the front door and pushed up the letterbox again, now opening the flap wider this time. There seemed to be another fly…Her eyes followed its movements to where it landed. The air was fetid. Her eyes twitched.

She jumped back in fright. The metal letterbox closed with a dull thump, and she stumbled backwards, the heels of her shoes tapping on the tiles of the path. In vain, she held out a hand to stop her from falling onto her backside and it touched the car, but she continued slipping back until she composed herself. She stood up gingerly. Her face whitened as she put a hand over her mouth. Her lips had gone dry, and her breath became tense as she stared in disbelief at the door of number 14 Bollo Lane. Her stomach churned over. She didn't understand what she had just witnessed.

Three

'Her name gentleman, as you already know, is Ms Christina Zabrinski,' he said as he pulled back the white sheet which covered the deceased.

Richards and Sutton stood in the mortuary. The atmosphere was cold and melancholy. It had a hollow feel. Light entered through a row of opaque glass windows situated at a high level, giving the room an unearthly feel.

They were both eager to know how the vice president of a land company, Ms Zabrinski had met her tragic fate and what ultimately caused her death.

Richards had seen all this before, so his stomach didn't churn, his face no longer turned a nasty shade of pale, and he had no reason to run to the toilet to throw up. He had done all that on previous visits. He recollected one of his first as a rookie. He had witnessed a woman in her 70's, laid out naked, stripped of all her dignity and exposed for all to see with couple of tags tied to one of her toes. The woman more than likely had a family, a husband, and possibly children. But the rear of her scalp had been cut by a mortician, and then peeled over to cover her face so the pathologist could cut open the top of her skull. All because she had been involved in a hit-and-run accident with a car. The driver was never found.

The room was a mass of stainless steel. The body was laying on one of the steel post-mortems tables.

A row of fridges occupied one wall; Richards wondered whom they housed. Bodies were kept here until their cause of death could be determined, or until relatives had formally identified them.

'She was strangled,' Dr Waide said in a gentle tone, looking at the dead body. 'Before that she had been tied up to the post on the landing. She was wearing only one stocking, and the other missing. Strange!' he said, still looking at the body.

'When we found her, her eyes were wide open. And as you know, she had an apple forced into her mouth. It was a Golden Delicious, if that is of any significance to you gentlemen. I should imagine it was put there after the murder. By the assailant, probably.' He glanced at the detectives. Dr Ronald Waide had untidy grey hair which he wore in a parting and pushed over the top of his head. His eyebrows were thick and needed trimming. Several frown lines spanned the length of his forehead. He was dressed in a green plastic apron, and he was wearing Wellington boots and rubber gloves, his black-rimmed glasses pushed up. A large stainless-steel set of scales hung from the ceiling behind him.

'I have checked under her fingernails, and I didn't find any traces of fibres or DNA from her attacker. I only found traces of fibres from the sofa under them. I also found fibre traces from the sofa on her face,' said the pathologist.

'Any other clues we don't know about?' Richards asked as he wandered around the cold body placed on the glistening steel gurney.

'The cushions on her sofa have marks on where her face was pushed down as she put up a frantic fight to save her life.'

'Were there any…'

'Signs of sexual assault?' The sharp coroner cut him off.

'No, none, there weren't any,' he continued, looking at both detectives.

'She must have put up some defence against her attacker,' DCI Richards said, sounding metaphorical.

'She must have done just that, indeed, Inspector,' the pathologist went on.

'So, this makes me believe that she was murdered face down on the lounge sofa. That's where she must have met her death. There were mascara marks on the sofa cushions indicating that her face was being forced into them as she was being tortured and putting up a frantic fight against her attacker.

'There are also signs of bruising on her back and around her shoulder area indicating that her assailant was on top of her at some point, pushing down hard onto her.' He pointed to them. He paused. 'I suspect she was then turned over onto her back after she was dead. That's not all,' the doctor said walking around the body.

'So, gentlemen, she was found dangling from her left ankle by a rope. The knot around her ankle was a slipknot, quite an easy one to tie. But she has another mark. There is very mild bruising around her right ankle.' He gestured towards it. Richards glanced at the ankle.

'We concluded that she was dragged into the hallway, possibly by her feet,' Richards remarked. Dr Waide didn't like being interrupted and gave the detective a sharp look.

Richards looked at his colleague Sam Sutton, and then at the purple and white coloured body.

'Her eyes were painted with black mascara and there are long trailing lines moving away from them.' Dr Waide said pointing at her face.

'Her face looks like the singer, Alice Cooper; don't you think Sam?' Richards said, leaning forward, and peering closely at her face.

'Who?' said a confused-looking Dr Waide.

'He's a rock singer from the 80s and 90s. I think he's still around. He carried out an act on stage where he used to hang himself and had heavily painted black mascara on his face, when he performed on stage. She looks very similar to him.' He pointed to her eyes.

'Alice was a he?' said the doctor, still confused, and unsure of the detective's remarks.

'That's right, kind of,' said the DCI. 'She was a he.'

'Great. So, the murderer may have been a fan of Mr Cooper then?' replied Dr Waide.

'Or the victim may have been.' Richards replied as he tilted his head thoughtfully. Dr Waide looked lost. 'It's down to you two detectives to get to the bottom of that one – that is if your assumption is correct, detective,' the doctor replied huffily. 'We can only conjecture about what was in the killers mind.'

'It's just a thought.' The mood dipped. 'So, what else do we have to lead us to our killer?' Richards said looking at the doctor, then at his colleague, DI Sutton, and wondering if his hypothesis was the correct one.

'Well, the eyes were painted after Ms Zabrinski was murdered as the make-up was not smudged. She also has haemorrhaging under her eyelids. And a blood clot in her nose which was likely to have been a result of compression on the neck. There was also a lump on the rear of her head.' He pointed to it. 'She was hit by a heavy object, maybe an ashtray or a candle holder. Her head was cut, and we found tiny fragments of glass in it. She must have been hit with tremendous force gentlemen. This could have been the coup de grace.' He looked at the detectives for any reaction, but there wasn't one. 'We also found traces of cocaine up her nostril; it wasn't a great grade. This woman had the money to buy better quality.' The officers stared at the body.

'What was the time of the murder Doctor? Do you know yet?' Sam said.

'I've checked the potassium level in the vitreous humour and calculated from that.' He scratched his head. 'I would put the time of death Detective, down to no more than three days,' he paused.

'Making it Friday evening. The 31st of October.'

'Her letters which were delivered in Saturday morning's post weren't opened,' said the chief detective.

'Good call,' replied the doctor, 'but possibly Saturday morning, in the early hours. I'll carry out an internal examination later.'

'Any other leads Doctor?' said Richards, pleasantly.

'I found some white fibres on her stocking around the right ankle area. But I'm unsure at this moment in time as to how they got there, and why they are there.'

'How strange…Do you think she knew her murderer?'

'It's not my job to make that kind of judgement, detective,' the pathologist said, glancing at the detective. 'I only report on what's in front of me.'

'We have checked the fibres from the bath towels and tea cloths from the house and none of them match the fibres on the stocking. I find it rather odd,' said Dr Waide, looking at DCI Richards.

'We found carpet fibres on the back of her blouse and skirt, so we presume she was dragged from the sofa to the hallway.'

'Yes, we were thinking along those lines as well. Anything else, Doctor?'

'Yes, a few things. We found human hair which is a different colour and length to the victim, and some blue strands of cotton on the sofa in the lounge. Which we are checking on in the lab to see if we have a DNA match.'

'Let us know the results as soon as you have them, will you?' Richards mused.

'And her hands were tied with the same rope that she was dangled from, so, now, there are two pieces of rope. We put the cut ends under a microscope and found that they matched up. And, we haven't found any fibre fragments of any part of the ropes on any of the floors in the house, suggesting at this point that the ropes used on the victim were not cut in the house.' He moved two steps to a different position. 'So, the two pieces of rope that were used could have been cut somewhere else. We have vacuumed the carpet but haven't found any traces of rope fibres anywhere. And gentlemen, the rope used to strangle Ms Zabrinski is missing,' he said bluntly. 'There are fibres, from a different type of rope on her neck.' He peered at both of them.

'So, whoever killed Ms Zabrinski had a motive to kill her, they killed her and did so in a fit of anger. She was strangled with a rope, the killer then leaned on her back, and held her down with force while she was being strangled. They must have been strong as she had severe bruising around her shoulder area. She then grabbed at the only thing she could, due to her position. She dug her fingernails into the sofa cushions. In this position, she was unable to touch her killer, and her killer knew this. Once she was dead - as you mentioned Detective - she was then dragged to the hallway.' He peered up at the two staring faces. 'A rope was then tied around her left ankle, the kind of rope you can find easily in a DIY store. And you would have to be pretty fit to have then tugged a 138-pound body upwards with a short piece of rope, rubbing against the wood on the handrail. That alone would have made it an even harder task, gentlemen.

We are running tests on some footprints found on the wooden flooring in the downstairs hallway, and on the carpet on the landing. We have found fingerprints, and there are quite a few different sets. I'm guessing that this woman entertained a lot of people in her house?' DI Sutton nodded, as he took in what the doctor was saying.

'But there was one thing that I noticed, which I found rather odd Detectives.'

'Oh, what?' replied an eager-looking Richards.

The pathologist bent down and retrieved an object. It was a square wooden block, about three and a half inches long, and about an inch in width. He placed it on the edge of the gurney.

'I found this gentleman, under Ms Zabrinski's bed.'

Richards glanced at Sutton, thinking, 'How the hell did we miss that?' Richards picked it up. It felt smooth and was well lacquered.

'What do you think it is, Sam?' he said showing it to him.

Sam studied it. There was a short silence. 'It looks like some kind of toy building brick, from a set, maybe?'

'A toy, yes, could it be?' Richards said as he passed it to him. Sam caressed the wooden block in his hands.

'Does Ms Zabrinski have any children, Detective?' said the doctor.

'No,' said Richards, doubtfully.

'Do you think there could have been two people involved in pulling her up to the position she was found in?' Richards said. Waide pulled his face together.

'Quite possibly Detective, but whoever did this planned it meticulously. They, he or she took their time. Once they killed Christina, they then set out to embarrass, shame, and humiliate the woman. They left her exposed to whoever would find her. This woman had enemies. She must have had upset someone, and this someone was out to get her and destroy her and her dignity so she wouldn't interfere with their lives again. They wanted her out of the way so they could continue their own life in peace. Solve these parts of the jigsaw Detectives, then, you'll on your way to finding your killer.' Richards stared pensively at him.

The two detectives stood in the brightly lit corridor of the 1960s building.

'What do you think, guv?' DI Sutton remarked.

'Well, Christina was last seen at around seven p.m. on Friday 31st, leaving her place of work. We've spoken to many people Sam, and no one had seen her since she was found, and that's a long time,' said the DCI. 'If she drove straight home, she would have reached there at around 7:20 – 7:40 at a guess,' Sutton replied.

'Her mobile showed a call from a pay phone call box. We know that the call was made in Bath Road, at 8:31p.m. and we know that it was unanswered.' Richards scratched his head.

'I would say at this moment in time Sam, that she *did* know her murderer. We've found no signs of a break-in. Nothing was missing. There are no signs of burglary. The kitchen patio doors were closed and locked. The front door was also locked. We'll have to wait for the fingerprints to come back, that may tell us a few things at least. I think maybe the assailant had been in the house before. The length of rope needed to carry out this hanging must have been calculated and measured. The killer must have had a good idea as to how much was needed, so they must have done their homework,' Richards said as he stared down the gloomy corridor. 'They must have known the distance from the hallway to the top landing to be able to have brought along the correct length of rope. They must have known the geometry of the hallway.' Sutton looked thoughtful.

'And the handbag, which was in the bedroom wardrobe…The contents of the bag looked to be all jumbled up, as if they had been thrown in randomly. Some of the objects look like they should have been at the bottom of a woman's handbag, but in this case were on top. And it contained Jeff Turner's business card. How, and when did that get inside the bag?'

Four

January 16th, 2006

'I told you what she was like Jeff didn't I? I did warn you about her,' Mars said in a pleasant and unassuming tone, as she turned her diffident pretty face in his direction.

Their cab was heading towards Mars' house in Ealing. It was 11:20. The night was cold, and there was a mild fog in the air.

Hazy streetlights flashed past as they moved down the High Street. They were sitting on the rear bench seat with only a small gap between them, and their hands were perched on the vinyl upholstery with their fingertips unknowingly touching each other's.

The black cab drove past stragglers, on their way home from pubs, bars and restaurants. A police siren was howling in the background, making a piercing sound.

Mars looked ahead and found herself staring at two eyes watching her, from the cab driver's rear-view mirror. He was looking directly at her, glaring. It made her feel uncomfortable, and she wasn't sure how long these eyes had been focused on her, and for what reason. His face was creepy-looking, as if he was trying to intimidate her. She twisted her head sharply away, not liking what she saw. She found it spooky, and immediately decided that she didn't like this man, and shuddered with coldness.

'You did, Mars.' He turned towards her. 'You were right,' Jeff said. 'Is she always like that?'

'Like what? Like overpowering, domineering, do you mean?'

'Yeah, like she wants to take control of you, be in command, have you in her grasp, and own you,' he said slowly, looking oblivious, staring into space and seeming overwhelmed by the time he had spent in the company of these affluent people.

It had been a mixed evening, and a multitude of questions had been aimed at him, women eyeing him up, and there were lies and near misses. His thoughts were heavy. His face was pensive.

'She's like it all the time, Jeff. When she's right, believe you me, *she* is right. She can be a bit controlling.'

'A bit!' Jeff said surprisingly. 'That's an understatement.' Mars turned to him.

'She is very good at what she does, though. She gets results, you have to give it to her, she is on the move in the company, her bosses love her, she works bloody hard at her job, she works all hour's God sends, and she is a winner. Sometimes I hate her for it.'

'Oh, do you? But I bet she plays bloody rough,' Jeff said.

'Well, yes, I suppose she does.'

'Femme fatale?'

'Yes, you could say that, I guess,' her voice sounded hollow. 'And I want to get at her!' Mars snapped furiously.

'Sorry!' Jeff sounded startled as if he had been caught off guard, as he turned to her.

'I want… her job, Jeff! And her position in the company.' She grinned cunningly at him, her face changing from a dignified, mild-mannered look, to one of hatred as she flicked her head. Jeff looked at the colour of Mars' eyes. They were darker than he had thought. The pupils looked black. He looked away from her and around the vehicle as he tried to think if he had said something wrong to upset her. He cleared his throat.

'Yes… It's something that I want Jeff,' her voice sounded bitter. 'I have made up my mind. I may have to fight for the position, but I'll go all out for it. I'll work towards the post in the coming months, I think I'm worthy of it.' Her voice trailed off to a softer tone, more like the usual manner it had been earlier in the evening, and since the time that he had known her. Jeff looked confused by her sudden outburst. It had come out of the blue and surprised him, it wasn't her. Even the driver looked worried for a moment. 'Why did she do it? She wants this job that she goes on about, but why kick out at me? She hardly knows me.'

Helen Marshall had had a good evening with her new date, the charming Jeff Divine, and at times it had been a somewhat challenging one. She had felt this evening that she had gained some ground in the battle to win over her boss' vote for the vacant vice president position coming up in the company purely by having this charming and appealing date on her arm. It had worked out to be a good choice.

Her hair wasn't as immaculate as when he had first met her, her make-up wasn't as sharp, and she had a giggly, girlish smile brought on by the copious amounts of alcohol she had consumed throughout the evening. She wasn't going to drink much tonight she had told herself, but the activities of the last several hours had taken their toll on her. Still, at least it had panned out better than she had imagined. She had started the evening nervously, not really knowing how she would get on with Jeff, and then not knowing exactly how her date would get on with her officious boss. It was a strategy that she had worked on, and she was somewhat content with the conclusion.

As he was staring out of the cab window, watching the world pass by in front of him, Jeff felt somewhat relieved to get away from the clutches of the domineering host. He felt that the tension had been removed from his nervous shoulders as he ran the palm of his hand across his chin. His silk tie was rumpled; his legs were stretched out in front of him as he stared down pensively at a mark on the vamp of one of his once immaculate shiny black shoes. He now knew that he had a bigger problem than he had first expected, now that he had met, and come face to face with his predator.

Although he felt that he had learned something about her, he wasn't sure if it was a good or bad thing. At least he now knew what she was like, and had also learned from how she had been described to him intermittently by Mars. But he now knew how hard it was going to be to beat her; she was going to be a tough cookie to crack, and it was probably going to be tiring to break her down. Could he run from this tyrant of a woman, and escape her grasp? It was something for him to work on. Food for thought. 'Still, she has a lovely pair of pins at least,' he thought.

'You were chatting to her a lot this evening, weren't you?' Mars said, turning and trying to coax an answer from Jeff, using her pretty smooth face to do so. 'I noticed that she didn't want to leave you alone. What were the chats about, may I ask?'

'You're not getting jealous now are you, Mars?' Jeff said in a sarcastic tone.

They had just left Christina Zabrinski's party. Christina had been intrigued by her new guest, Jeff Divine, brought along by her work colleague this evening – so intrigued, in fact, that she wouldn't leave him alone from the moment they first met. She had followed him around, like a tiny lap dog, like a new puppy following its owner.

Whenever he would move away from her and talk to Mars, or any of the other guests at the party, she kept a watchful eye on him. She would monitor him, scrutinizing his movements with the eyes of an eagle. She didn't touch a cigarette all evening; if he didn't smoke, then she would respect him and be polite, and she wouldn't smoke either.

She would make sure that he wasn't showing interest in anyone else; if he did, her jealousy would get the better of her. She would move swiftly, like a leopard shifting through the jungle to interrupt the conversation and break it up.

She would pretend to offer her guests another drink and butt into their discussions, offering them some hors d'oeuvres in order to take over the conversation they were having, without her.

Her party food had been arranged by an outside catering company, and they had been at Christina's house for most of the afternoon preparing it. The kitchen table was centred by a large crystal glass bowl full of crab and vegetable dip. This was surrounded by various platters consisting of such tasty morsels as stuffed crepes, grilled shrimp skewers and chocolate-covered strawberries. There was also a large helping of French pink champagne on offer served in the finest cut glass. Tall scented candles flickered as the guests breezed past.

Christina would change conversations and steer them in a different direction to stem the flow between Jeff and her guests. She had the power to do this. She was devious. No one would tell her off for it. She was the boss, and it was her house that they had been invited to. They were the fortunate few. They were lucky to be in their boss' house - these people were privileged.

'We spoke about this and that, Mars. Triviality. She said that she liked my aftershave, and asked about my roots. I just told her the truth – oh, she also asked where we met. I told her, and she asked what job I did for a living, and did I own my own company. She was very interested in my existence.'

'Yes, that sounds exactly like her, prying into everyone's business affairs. I had a suspicion she would be interested in you.' She narrowed her eyes.

'Well, it goes with the territory Mars,' he said in a conceited voice while trying to adjust his tie. She gave him a doubting look, and thought, 'What a big head! But I like this guy, he can be a bit of a charmer.'

The taxi slowed down and stopped.

Mars stepped out as they reached her house.

'I'll ring you, Mars,' he smiled .

'That would be nice of you Jeff. And again, I can't thank you enough for supporting me tonight, you were great company,' she replied, and she blew him a kiss.

'Thank you.' He stared as he closed the cab door whilst looking at his date for the evening as she wandered in the direction of her house. He rested against the back of the seat and reminisced for a second. Thoughts of the evening's events circled his head. The good-looking Mars, her smooth skin, her tasteful sense of dress, her rich perfume, her immaculately painted fingernails…I'm sure she had blue eyes? Why did she suddenly snap like that? He thought. It was totally out of character of her. And the dominant, "look what I've got" Christina, showing off to her work force, and looking down on people.

'Where to guv?' came a familiar voice, sounding like it should be selling fruit at a market stall.

'Home, back to Acton mate.'

Five

Spring 2004

The sun shone through her bedroom window. She lay there, on her bed, in a semi-comatose state, with the duvet up to the back of her shoulders and her arms stretched out, in her normal sleeping pattern.

'I hope it isn't there, I hope it's bloody not there, but it was before I came up here last night. Maybe I was seeing things, and it righted itself and disappeared in the middle of the night... I can't bear it, I can't bear seeing it there!' Christina thought to herself in annoyance. She turned over and lay on her back, pushed the duvet down and looked at her body, realizing that she needed to do something with her life. Her stomach needed trimming, or perhaps she just needed to cut down on the alcohol and take more care of herself.

'Huh, I worry too much! She pulled herself out of bed and glanced at the leftover contents on the small square mirror on her bedside cabinet.

As Christina strolled down the stairs, her steps were heavy – her body hadn't quite yet come to terms with the idea of entering a brand-new day. She was yawning and at the same time tying the rope around her flimsy silk dressing gown.

She glanced at the front door mat to see if the postman had been. She then meandered through the opening and into her newly extended palace.

Recently her kitchen had been extended and tastefully decorated. She had spent a lot of time and effort getting it to the way she wanted. She could still smell the paint drying on the walls, a slightly musty smell but nonetheless it smelt like perfume to Christina. She loved the openness of it, she marvelled at the extra space and comfort it brought to her way of life. The previous kitchen was too small and too cramped to work in, and the units that had belonged to the previous owner were from a different era, as if they were stuck in a time warp. It wasn't up to her high standards. But the kitchen had now been completely transformed. The original kitchen space had been completely gutted, and a new room built onto it, extending it outwards into her garden, and creating an area now three times the size as the old one.

She enjoyed the quality of the marble floors and worktops and liked the sparkle of the shiny chrome and the mystery of the deep oak wooden cabinets.

Christina looked around for her cigarettes as she ran a hand across the cold silky marble worktop. She picked up the half-empty red packet, and then hesitated, reconsidering. It was too early in the morning for her and she wasn't a big smoker anyway - she just had one occasionally to be sociable.

She leant over and flicked on the switch of her chrome kettle to try to get the morning off to a start, and at the same time heat yesterday's water. She placed one of her white bone china teacups onto its matching saucer.

She glared at her unwashed wine glass from last night as if it were a crystal ball. Noticing her reflection, Christina went into a semi-conscious state as the glass captured her mind for a few seconds of her morning. She became oblivious to all that was happening around her and floated off in a surreal dreamscape. Her eyes became relaxed, as did the tension on her shoulders, and she drifted into a world that didn't exist, a world which held no worries, no fear, a world consisting of soft clouds, bright flowery colours and a shining sun. Green fields in the country, waves rushing up onto the shore…

Click! The silence was broken; her dreaming and her escape from this world for a minute of her life were shattered. The sound of the kettle coming to the end of its boiling process had brought her back to reality.

She looked at her freshly decorated kitchen wall, which appeared to have a greyish, wave-like line, starting from above the patio doors, and making its way neatly up to the ceiling of the room. It was too neat for her liking.

As she poured the boiling water into her teacup, her attention turned to the newly formed wall.

'The cleaner was only here yesterday,' she thought again. 'She should have rid of the cobwebs. I remember reminding her of some of the finer points of the cleaning chores when I employed her. Besides, she's quite tall, with a feather duster on a stick. Reaching up and grabbing a cobweb near the ceiling should have been an easy task for her. What was on the girl's mind?' Christina frowned. She didn't like it when people were told to do something, and then disregarded it.

She knelt on a chair, placed a fingernail on the wall and began to slowly move it towards the odd shape. As it scraped along the surface, her nail was halted by a hairline fracture in the plaster of the wall.

'A crack—a crack!' she said out loud. 'How come? What the bloody hell is a crack doing there, what is it doing on my kitchen wall?' She wondered how on earth it could have formed. And where it had come from.

'So how did it get there? Was it supposed to be there?' she thought. 'Don't be stupid Christina,' she said back to herself, 'Of course it isn't supposed to be there, stupid.' She didn't like the look of it, or it's mere presence.

She picked up her mobile phone and pushed the buttons to contact her builder, Mr Jeff Turner, but there was no answer, so she phoned her architect, Harrison Blake.

'Harrison. It's Christina, I can't get in touch with Jeff Turner. I've tried to contact him, but he's not answering his phone.'

Christina employed Harrison to oversee the project on her new kitchen as her schedule at work was always full, and she probably wouldn't have been around for too much of the time anyway. She didn't want to get involved with the builders; it wasn't quite her style. She was far too busy with work.

Jeff Turner had been introduced to Harrison by a friend of Christina's.

'I'm sorry Christina, I'll try him myself. Is there a problem, or do you need to speak to him about something else?'

'Harrison, listen, it may not be anything, but when I woke up this morning and went into my kitchen, I saw a mark on the wall, above the new French doors, and when I went over and investigated it further, I discovered it was a crack. A small thin crack, but it was there, on the wall. It was also there last night. Is this normal Harrison? Is this correct? It's only been around four months now since the building work was completed, and already there's a crack in my wall.'

'A crack did you say, Christina?'

'Yes, that's right,' she said with concern.

'It could just be building movement,' Harrison replied.

'What is building movement Harry, are you implying that my kitchen is moving and if it is, where is it going to?' Christina said not understanding what building movement meant. She used Harrison's nickname on occasion.

'Building movement dearie is just what it says. The building must settle. Sometimes the walls move a very small amount, the foundations have to settle and sometimes cracks appear. Things like this are quite normal. It's not uncommon in new builds Christina, and you'll find it's probably nothing to worry about.' She cringed. She didn't enjoy the name "dearie"! It was cheap to her, and unladylike. But she had learned to put up with it.

'But why above the French doors, and why not anywhere else? I hope it's normal and everything else is OK Harrison, but I would still like you to speak to Mr Turner and see what he has to say about the matter. Could you get in touch with him? And then get back to me please, as soon as possible. I would appreciate it.' She sounded concerned.

'Sure, I will Christina, not a problem. I'll do that.'

'And then can you let me know the outcome and let me know if everything is OK. Could you call me later today please?' she said anxiously.

'Of course I will Christina, as soon as I speak to Jeff, and we get something sorted out. I'll let you know, I'll call you, don't worry—and enjoy your day.'

Jeff Turner and his team had only undertaken the work on the main structure of the building. They had dug out of the trenches, and laid the concrete for the foundations of the extension and carried out the brickwork. They had also built the framework for the rooftop of Christina Zabrinski's kitchen.

Christina had then employed a separate company to decorate the walls, a bespoke fitting company to carry out the installation of the kitchen, and a specialist tile company to finish the work on the floor.

She wasn't much impressed with the idea of dealing with holes for foundations, mud, cement mixers, hairy - arsed builders running up and down ladders. She wasn't thrilled by the wolf whistles and having to make numerous mugs of tea each morning and supply them with a lorry load of biscuits. It just wasn't her style. She couldn't imagine getting her hands dirty. Harrison recommended Jeff Turner to Christina, but Christina had never met Mr Turner, as she preferred to deal with a very good friend of hers who was a professional architect.

Before Jeff had started the work, he had warned Harrison that a lot of his time would be taken up on a job near his home, and that he had to stay there and complete it as he was running behind schedule due to bad weather. But he would oversee the work in her kitchen.

Six

'What do you flipping mean you can't make it? Plus *Mr* Turner, you are also a day late. You were supposed to call me yesterday. I waited for your call, and now you are telling me that you can't make it today. Why can't you make it, Mr Turner?' she said angrily.

She slammed the side of a pen on the table. Jeff had phoned Christina at 9:15 to tell her that he couldn't make the appointment; Christina was also eagerly hoping to meet her builder for the first time.

'Christina, I'm sorry to upset you but I have so many other engagements now. It's the time of year, it's just the way it is right now. I have so many things on my plate, customers seem to come at you from all sides this time of the year, they want everything done, sort of, now. What if you leave the key in the usual place, and I come around later to sort out the problem?'

'Do you think you can treat my house like a hotel?' she barked. 'Like you can come and go as you please Mr Turner?'

'Er, no Christy.'

'Ms Zabrinski to you. *Mr* Turner,' she said forcefully.

'Er…OK.' Jeff was now being pushed back by his angry client and felt that he had to solve this problem fast, get out quickly, and move on to his next project.

'*If,* you are planning on coming around later Mr Turner, at what time later, if I may ask, please?' she snapped.

'Erm, I will be round at 12:00?'

'You are becoming very unreliable, Mr Turner. Is this how you treat your customers?'

She was in a foul mood as she stared out of her lounge window. She looked up and down the road and wondered why there was a grubby van parked across from her house. She was dressed in a dark business suit, and her face was stern. Not waiting for Jeff's answer, she carried on.

'And my patience is wearing thin.' Her voice was gathering strength and determination.

'Do you think that I have the time to wait around for you,' she said abruptly. 'I have appointments to keep. By the way Mr Turner... the crack is now wider, and longer. I do really, really hope you can solve this matter; I have to be at work by 10:30. Are you sure you can't get here any earlier?' she said furiously, as she stomped around her lounge.

She began to pace the floor of her room, her face pointing down, and her mobile tight against her ear.

'I'm sorry; I have to pick up materials for—' Christina abruptly interrupted the conversation.

'I do not want to hear your feeble excuses Mr Turner. I am fed up with them, and they are pissing me off. I will leave the key in the usual place, under the mat outside the French doors, near to *where* the crack is, Mr Turner,' she said scathingly. 'And when I get home this evening from work, I will expect the problem to be solved and the crack to be gone, out of my sight, forever! For good!' Her voice was forceful and dominant. 'Do I make myself clear to you?'

'Er...' Jeff tried to reply but again Christina gave her builder no time to answer.

'You have been to my house twice this summer to try and remedy this fault, and you have failed, so you can understand my annoyance Mr Turner, can't you?'

'Well, yes, I can,' said Jeff, as if he was hiding from her, and cowering in a corner. 'Don't worry, the problem will be solved, I guarantee you.'

'I have to go now, I have an incoming call that I have to attend to,' she said impatiently, Jeff looked at his phone as he suddenly got cut off.

'Hello, Christina Zabrinski here,' she said looking around her lounge.

'You owe me!' came the voice. It sounded scruffy, like a Mexican in a cowboy movie.

'Pardon? Who's this? Who am I speaking to please?'

'You owe me Ms Zabrinski,' the voice sounded muffled and untrained, and slightly anxious. The caller then cut off. Christina fixed her eyes on the mobile. She had an idea as to who the caller could be, although he had neglected to himself.

Seven

Jeff stood on the floor of Christina's new kitchen, and stared up at the wall above the patio doors where the crack was located. His face was filled with concern, and his thoughts were empty and bare. It looked too large in his mind to fill in and paint over. He couldn't quite work out why it was so large. It didn't look like building movement to him. It seemed to be the wrong shape of crack, and it looked too deep. He'd seen building movement on many an occasion; it was common in his work, but this one looked somehow different and his experience said it was far too wide.

He flicked on the switch of Christina's kettle and decided to make himself a cup of tea. As if he owned the place, he sat down and reminisced about his antics with his date of last night. This was the real reason he had found it difficult to get up early and keep his appointment with Christina this morning, but he wasn't about to tell her that. His mind wandered off for a second. The kettle had boiled; he searched around for the tea bags. He took the milk from the fridge but wondered where the main ingredients were hiding. Feeling that someone was looking at him, he looked over his shoulder. He felt a twinge of guilt as he remembered to cure the fault and not to be snooping around his client's premises. He dismissed the fault and decided to look through the kitchen drawers, thinking that as he had never met the ferocious Ms Zabrinski before; he would try to find out a bit about her. She was certainly a fiery character, and certainly a tempestuous woman. He'd found out that she lost her temper quickly, but she may have had a point too. He was standing in a woman's kitchen, a woman who he had never met before, but who had allowed him to enter her property to carry out work. He felt the situation certainly unusual.

Feeling a little uneasy, he pulled out a drawer. 'Nice feel,' he thought. He then came to some paperwork - a mass of Waitrose and Selfridges bills, and instructions for her new kitchen appliances. Then he found a glossy photograph of a man. He took it out and held it up in front of him for a closer look. The man looked to be in his mid-thirties and he was a handsome-looking figure. It reminded him of someone, but he couldn't think who. The man had dark, wavy hair, and was about thirteen stone; he was a good-looking male, with an olive-like complexion. He held the photo closer, studied the picture, squinted, smiled and realised that the man had the same characteristics as himself. He put it back in its rightful place like it was her prized possession, and then he pushed the drawer shut. He shuddered.

'Where are the bloody tea bags?' he thought.

Jeff filled in the crack with some plaster, which he had mixed up, knowing in the back of his mind that this probably was not the answer; he stood back and scratched his cheek, but couldn't quite put his finger on why there was a crack the size it was, and also being so deep. He walked around the kitchen, closely examining the plain smooth walls, searching to see if there were any others; he ran his builder's hand over the smooth surfaces. His main man, Donal, had been back a couple of times to fill in some minor cracks over the summer months, but now this one was larger. It seemed that every time they repaired the wall, a crack appeared to open up some months later.

He then went outside, looked around the extension, and checked the outside brickwork. There was a small, hairline crack on the rear wall at high level. It was barely visible, and he didn't take too much notice but he still wondered about it. He could fill it in with a bit of cement, he thought.

He walked back inside the house and left a note for Christina, saying that the plaster was wet, and that one of his workers would be around Monday morning and was going to paint the whole wall for her. He didn't mention the crack outside due to fear of her boiling up at him, but he would tell his colleague to make it good, as he couldn't be bothered at this moment, he had too many thoughts racing around his head.

She held her drink with zeal and headed towards the garden. She eased open the left side of her new patio doors, and went outside, pushing the door closed behind her. Pulling up an iron chair, she dropped herself down on it and leant backwards.

A robin disappeared into a nearby bush. She held out a hand and ran it through a nearby cyclamen bush.

'I wish I had brought a cardigan out with me,' she thought, as she sat there in a cotton shirt.

She then leaned over from where she was sitting and stretched out an arm which was just in reach of the door.

She jolted it towards its closing position. It seemed

that this time it didn't want to move with the ease that she was accustomed to. Something wasn't right. She screwed up her face. Was it her imagination? She tried to think back, and wondered if it had ever slid back to its rightful place with ease in the past. She stood. Something caught her eye, there was something unusual on the kitchen floor, just in from where she was standing on the patio. It was dust. She stepped into the kitchen to take a closer look; she then looked up at the wall inside the room.

She grabbed her mobile from the worktop and walked back out into the garden.

She sat down on the garden chair, tilted her head back and took a sigh.

She pushed resolutely at some buttons on her phone.

'Jeff. It's Christina,' she said with annoyance in her voice. 'Can you please call me at your earliest convenience, I know it's the weekend, but it's regarding the patio doors that you installed for me at my extension, there seems to be a problem with them, they seem to be sticking, and not opening and closing correctly. Plus, the crack above the door has also opened up again. I'm getting fed up Jeff. Can you call me please? It's Christina Zabrinski. 14 Bollo Lane. Thanks.'

Christina was trying her best to keep her calm as she left a message on Jeff Turner's voicemail.

Her arms were folded, her hand clutching her mobile as she stared imperviously at her builder's workmanship. She was unhappy and boiling with rage inside and she desperately wanted to talk to the very elusive Mr Turner.

Eight

Christina jolted sharply; the room was black as if she were lying inside a coffin. There was a soft thud, as if something light had fallen from her bed and onto the carpet.

She lay there motionless face down, spreadeagled across her bed.

One of her eyes was covered by her pillow, while the other was wide open and staring in the direction of her bedroom window as she tried to work out what time it was and what had suddenly woken her from her sleep. The fingertips on one of her hands were touching the outside of the mattress, and she felt heat moving from her arms and swirling around her back as if someone was running a burning hand over her skin. This was accompanied by a tingling sensation. It was a reaction of fear. She was tense, and her stomach was churning and twisting with anxiety. Her head felt like a lead balloon. She couldn't move it. Her neck was rigid, and her heart rate increased twofold.

She tried to look through the curtain to see if there was any light. Her clock was behind her on her bedside table but she found herself unable to move in fear of making a noise and disturbing the silence. She didn't want to disturb the silence. She didn't know where this noise had come from.

She lay awake staring at the same curtain, listening for the slightness of noise - a creak of a floorboard, a foot on the stairs, a movement of any sort, but there were none.

Terror crept over her body. She was perspiring, her neck was moist, and her veins felt like they were pumping. She had never felt like this or been in this position before, and she had no idea how to get out of it.

It was at a time like this that she wished a man were lying in her bed next to her. She needed someone strong to turn around and hold, and cuddle, and to tell that she thought she had heard a noise downstairs, a strange sound, something she found hard to deal with herself. She wanted that person now, so she could say,

'Can you go and investigate the noise downstairs please honey,' and then go back to sleep while they clambered out of bed and did the dirty work for her. But Christina was alone in the bed. And in the dark of the night. And she was by herself – she hoped.

She waited and tried to plan her next move. 'Should I turn over and face the door or do I stay staring at the same wall?'

What seemed an eternity had passed before she realised that she couldn't stay in this position all night. She wasn't going to be able to go back to sleep, she was too wide awake, and she wasn't going to relax.

Eventually, she would have to do something about it. She had to make a move, but what if someone was in her room, staring at her, possibly wearing a balaclava, or something else sinister covering their face, and was holding a large sharp instrument in their hand ready to pounce on her and kill her or, worse, rape her…

She didn't hear another noise for some time. She tried to think what time she had fallen asleep. It must have been about 10:30. She had felt drowsy. She remembered trying to read her book, and then that was it, that was the last thing she could remember. Had her book fell on the floor? She thought, 'Please be the book, please! Was that the thud that I heard?'

Then, her eyes flicked open wide, faster than a light turning on, as she heard a strange noise, a bang, then a kind of scraping noise which soon followed. The noises seemed to have come from downstairs. She was even more scared now. She squirmed. Her eyes had stayed open ever since, they were fixated on her curtains, and she was unable to close them.

She waited which seemed to be for-ever. When she hadn't heard any further sounds for some time, she felt that she had to do something.

Christina slowly lifted her head from the pillow, leaving a deep imprint. Slowly and anxiously, she twisted her head around toward the bedroom door.

Her eyes surveyed the dark room. She could only see distant shapes. She lay back down on her warm pillow. After what seemed like another ten minutes, she lifted her head again to look at the clock. It displayed the time as 3:51 a.m.

She guessed that she had been awake now for around half an hour. She looked toward her bedroom door. It was slightly ajar, open just a crack, and there was light in the hallway outside, and it was coming in from an outside streetlamp shining through a window. Was anyone out there in her hall? Was there anyone else in her house? Why had she not heard a sound now for some time? Was she in a dream?

Her clock said 4.07 a.m. She began to hear the sounds of birds chirping. Should she just lay here and wait for daylight? She could still get attacked in the light and, besides, it was Sunday. No one was around on a Sunday. The street came to life only at around 10:00. Why were there no further noises? she thought. The first sound was so obvious, it was a sudden thump, like a flat wooden object landing on something firm, like a solid surface. It had been followed by what she could only describe as being a soft material rubbing against a hard surface. Whatever was downstairs had made that sound. She tried to think.

Another ten minutes elapsed; she looked again at the bedroom door. She eased a leg out from under her bed clothes and onto the carpet, trying to be as quiet as she could, trying not to make a sound. Then the rest of her body followed. She stood up hoping not to make a noise so as not to attract the attention of any intruder. She looked around her dark room. It had a ghostly feeling. Everything was quiet, as silent as the grave...

'Where was her mobile? In her bag. Shit. Where was her bag... downstairs, of course. Bloody great!' she thought.

She stood up straight. Her body was naked and trembling. She leaned down and retrieved a sweater from the floor and put it on. It covered her down to her thighs. She noticed her book from the previous evening was still on the bed and she sighed. She looked toward the opening of the door to determine if anyone was on her landing, but there was no noise, no shadows.

She looked around to see if there were any weapons that she could use to confront the evil that may be in her house. She picked up her glass from the bedside table and pulled a tissue from a box.

Christina eased herself toward the door, walking like a pensioner who has just left the hospital after having both their kneecaps replaced.

She slowly eased her face out of the crack of the door and looked down the hallway. She was trying to use all her senses. She felt like the girl in the bathroom in the film *The Shining*. She was scared, and she felt that she was being hunted.

She found herself standing at the top of her stairs and looking down, a glass in one hand for protection. All she could see was a dimly lit hallway with wooden flooring. Words entered her head. 'You owe me.'

What was she going to do, was she going to walk down that set of stairs? No way, like hell she was! Should she wait until daylight?

There was no noise, no movement of any kind, but there was one thing, something strange which didn't feel right. She crossed her arms, the glass still in her hand. She thought she felt a draught against her legs. She stood there nervously, pondering her next move. A car passed by outside and momentarily flashed a light into the downstairs hall, throwing a shadow across the wooden floor.

All of a sudden, her body turned to ice, and her head throbbed, then what felt like electricity raced through her veins as she became rooted to the spot where she stood. The shadow was in the shape of a person. It seemed to be standing motionless in a waiting position and appeared to be that of a small man. It then vanished as quickly as the light disappeared. She wondered if she had been seeing things and it was just a figment of her imagination. She became increasingly unsure of her thoughts.

The air was chilly, and she shivered. Should she retreat into her bedroom and lock the door and wait? Maybe the intruder wouldn't come up the stairs and into her bedroom not knowing who else was in the house. Could they know who owns the house, or is this a random attack? Maybe they won't even attempt to come up the stairs at all.

What did she once read on a food tin? *Keep cool, do not freeze*.

She sat down on the landing floor and rested her back against the wall, pulling her knees towards her chest as she focused on the downstairs hallway.

Her head again jolted, her eyes slowly opened, and she found herself lying down with her head on the carpet. 'The man in the shadow, the silhouette, where is it?' was her immediate thought, 'And how long have I been asleep?' She looked at the carpet, then pushed herself up and looked down the stairs. There was a change in the light, there was a glimmer of brightness creeping through and, at last, the night was beginning to turn into day.

What time could it be? Christina stood up and held the glass in her hand. There was a creepy silence. She mustered up some courage and stepped forward and then onto the first step. She felt tired.

'Hello,' she said… She waited. Would an intruder answer her anyway? Were they likely to reply? This person could beat her to a pulp, maybe murder her. So where were they, and why were they not answering her call?

'Hello! Is anybody there?' Her voice was pensive, musing, and she shivered. She looked behind her and then took another step down - she wasn't going to stay here all night. She wondered why, since she had been asleep, her hunter hadn't made a move and attacked her.

'The first thing I'm going to do Monday morning is get an alarm fitted,' she thought.

Christina sat on a step and waited for more daylight. She sat there for about half an hour, her eyelids heavy, as she ran a hand over her forehead. But she still heard nothing, although she could still feel that draft. 'Where's it coming from? There must be a window open. I can't remember leaving a window open… maybe I'm thinking too much, maybe I forgot to close one of the windows…'

She walked down the remaining steps towards the hallway, gripping the glass tightly, all the time waiting for someone to jump out in front of her. She found herself at the bottom of the stairs. To her left was the kitchen, to her right was the lounge and the front door.

She stood on the bottom step. One more then she would be in the hallway, and exposed, and in the open, where she could be seen, and become a target. She gripped the glass tighter, and she wrapped the tissue around it to protect her hand, just in case it shattered.

She lowered a foot onto the wooden floor. The wood creaked and she flinched. Her heart was pumping, she could almost hear it, and her pulse raced. Her other foot touched the floor, and she stood still, waiting to be pounced on at any moment. She winced and waited… She was built of steel, but she was not prepared for a moment like this. She wasn't about to give into this coward, this person who hadn't shown their cards, this person who had been silent, for hours. Her confidence was beginning to grow, although she still felt tense and nervous.

She stood in the hallway and turned to her left. 'Oh, my God,' she thought. Fear was on her face, and she stopped, motionless. Then she turned to her right and looked at the front door, and then glanced toward the lounge and saw that the door was open. She could see most of the room, but not all of it from where she was standing. She observed that the room was how she had left it and the curtains were closed. She looked back in the direction of the kitchen, it was now beginning to brighten up, and she began to gain courage, realising now that there was possibly no-one around after all, as there were no further noises.

She walked cautiously into the kitchen, moving slowly as if she were at a funeral, and saw that some of the drawers were open. She looked at the patio doors in front of her. One of the panes of glass had been removed and was standing upright in the garden against her table. This was when she realised that someone had indeed been in her home. Her handbag was on the floor, upside down. She leaned down, picked it up and looked inside. Her purse was missing and there was no sign of her mobile phone. She looked behind her.

She then concluded that she was finally alone, which was the only comfort she had, unless someone was in her lounge…

She pulled a bread knife from its wooden block on the kitchen worktop, it made a mild slicing sound, as the blade rubbed against the inside of the holder. She moved toward the front room and stood at the door.

'Oh shit,' she blurted.

She looked at the space where her television would normally stand. The space was empty, and all that was left was the black cable snaked across the floor. Who had been in her house? Was it the two males that she had seen in the van opposite her house?

She could hardly phone the police seeing the amount of stuff she had purchased from this supplier of hers; there would be too many awkward questions to answer, and it would get back to her company. What would happen then was that her reputation would be left in tatters. And she couldn't let that happen.

Nine

'Morning, Donal, how are things going today. Well?' Jeff said as he walked into the gloomy surroundings of his new environment. Donal stood with a tool bag in his hand. He wore a red and black lumberjack shirt; it was unbuttoned at the cuffs. He looked surprised, thinking that his boss generally got in later than this.

'Aye, I'm OK. Cold, but not to worry, ugh,' he went on.

'Donal… tell me something, mate,' Jeff wanted to get what was on his mind off of it as quickly as possible. Something was bothering him, so he got straight to the point.

'Aye!' Donal pulled a frown.

'Can you remember that job we did, the extension, for that woman in Chiswick, Ms Zabrinski? You know the one, don't you?' Jeff said, knowing full well that Donal did, as he questioned his fellow worker, having arrived ten minutes after his colleague.

'Sure, boss,' he said. Donal had worked for Jeff now for almost two years. He was reliable and hardworking. He was five foot six tall, with dark wavy hair, he was muscular, he wore a short beard. They got on well with each other, liked a laugh and a joke, and were of similar characters. Donal had come across the border to England from Stranraer with his parents when he was young. His mother had got a job in London as a schoolteacher while his father worked as a car mechanic and hadn't looked back since.

'Well Donal, I've received a letter from her, and I'm not bloody happy! She's looking for answers and she wants them *now,* not tomorrow, or next week, but now mate,'

Jeff said, waving the folded piece of paper in his hand. Donal looked at it in despair, as if Jeff were holding a live snake.

'We've been back there a few times now. I don't really want to keep going back, as now she is really getting pee'd off with me, and you know where I'm coming from, don't you?'

Donal had carried out most of the work on Christina Zabrinski's kitchen extension, along with two labourers that they had employed at the last minute, as most of the work consisted of digging out earth, removing rubble and debris, which turned into mud when it rained, and loading it into skips, mainly throughout the cold, wet weather. It was dirty, messy work, and it had been in the middle of a harsh winter, and Jeff hadn't wanted to get involved with the mucky side of this building project.

'So, what's happening, Jeff?' Donal said.

'Well, now the patio doors are sticking,' Jeff was leaning his back against a wall, running his hand over his head, and his mind was thoughtful. 'Well, I was around there last week with the architect. I was trying to adjust them, but I couldn't. I even phoned the manufacturers and asked them for some advice.'

'What'd they say, boss?' said Donal, scratching his chin and looking out of the window, then back to Jeff.

'Well, I told them what I had done with the doors,' he said, explaining the situation to Donal with his hands. 'And I told them how they were fitted, and that they had been working and in use for around ten months. They said that there couldn't be anything wrong with them. I then asked them if they could send a rep down to take a look at them, but they said what I had explained to them on the phone was all OK, and that they couldn't see the point of sending anyone along to take a look, and besides, seeing that we fitted them, and not themselves, most if not all the responsibility was down to us.'

'What does the architect think the problem is then Jeff?' replied Donal, looking sheepish.

'Well, he wasn't impressed with what was going on. He said that it may be more serious than we think, he said that if the cracks kept appearing the way they do, then we may have to consider that there could be a fault with the foundations and that they may have to be investigated further. I told him that it couldn't be the foundations as we used a reputable company to supply the mix.' Donal had a worried look.

'When you fitted the patio doors, did everything go OK?' Jeff looked him in the eyes and waited for the required explanation as he bit his bottom lip.

'Aye. Yeah,' he hesitated. 'No problem, Jeff - good as gold boss. I can't think of anything that went wrong with them mate, they fitted nicely. They were opening and closing just fine mate when we finished.'

He bent down in order to conceal his expression, opening a large bag of dusty pink plaster, which was lying on the wooden floor. He was just about to start working on a room that they were going to decorate.

'Well, mate, the crack above the door is also still there. Each time I go back, it seems to get bloody wider,' Jeff said, running a hand down over his face; he was looking concerned as he walked across the floor.

'Maybe the bird fancies you, Jeff?' He chuckled, tipping some of the plaster into a bucket. 'Maybe she likes you, didn't you think about that?'

'Fancies me?' He looked startled. 'I haven't even met her yet. What's she like?'

'What'd mean, you haven't even met her?' he sounded shocked. 'But she's a customer of yours, isn't she? Surely you know her, don't you?'

'Yes, I do, but it's… it's a long story, Donal, as to why I haven't met her yet…I may meet her one day, that's not what I'm asking. Anyway, what does she look like?'

'I am surprised that you haven't met this customer of yours, ha! Well, I think she looks a bit like, er…' Donal tried to get a picture of this woman, the woman whom Jeff was working for, and who, through a twist of fate, he had never crossed paths with.

'Aye, mate, I know – she looks like that Jane Bullock girl; you know the one, the one on the telly, in all the big films, the real pretty one.' Donal had left the room and was filling a bucket with cold water from a tap in the bathroom.

'Who?' Jeff said with a raised voice.

'That Jane Bullock girl,' he said in an echoing voice as the water was splashing heavily into his bucket. 'You know who I mean, she was in that film, called, er…' Donal couldn't think. He stared at the dragon tattoo on his forearm, turning off the tap and lifting the weighty load. 'With, what's his face, Matt Damon.'

There was a pause.

'Sandra Bullock?' Jeff said, frowning, and looking confused.

'That's right, isn't that what I said?' Donal returned to the room, walking past Jeff, putting the bucket on the floor and shrugging his shoulders in defence of his answer.

'You idiot, Donal. It's Sandra.'

'Oh yeah.'

'So, come on, tell me - why are the cracks still there?' he said, holding out the palms of his hands. 'And don't say it's building movement, we've been down that road before. It's something else, it's not building movement, Donal.'

'I don't know, Jeff, I just can't think what it could be right now.' He scratched his eyebrow.

'I'll give it some thought, and let you know. How about that?' He was stirring the ingredients of the plaster and water with a wooden stick, crouching down and glancing up pensively at Jeff, wondering what his next question may be.

'No, I can't wait, Donal.'

'Oh. So, what have you done about these cracks, Jeff?' he replied, still stirring the pink mixture.

'The cracks just keep getting filled in, but I bloody need to find the cause of it. I need to find the root of the problem, Donal.'

Donal looked up. Jeff was flicking through Friday's addition of *The Mirror* newspaper which had been left on the windowsill in the room. 'When they get filled in, they open up again. You did put the correct lintel above the opening, didn't you?' His head turned rapidly towards Donal.

'Aye, I did, Jeff.' Donal hesitated for a moment, coming to the end of his stirring when something clicked in his mind.

'Course, the one on the drawing, the one specified by the architect. Besides, the building inspector was there on site when we were bricking up above it, he witnessed it. I think he wanted to be there that day so he could see it going in. He was a nosey sod,' he said, not looking at his boss.

'They have to be sometimes. So come on Donal, come on, what's been overlooked? You were there,' he said, forcing over a page of the wrinkled paper in irritation. 'What were the two labourers like? Were they good workers? What were they like? Tell me.'

'Sound mate, aye, OK. They did what was asked of them. One of them, Petrov, he was good, but he kept going on about the rich bird, with the flash silver Audi with the spoiler, and how well off she was,' he said, grinning and scraping off the contents of plaster mix on the side of the bucket. 'He did go on a bit! Some days he wouldn't bloody stop.' He lifted a trowel from an assortment of tools from the large heavy-looking cloth bag.

'She was a good-looking girl, but there was something about her.' He ran the edge of his trowel on the stubble of his chin, 'She was a bit too bitchy for my liking, a bit dominating. She took no shit!' he said, pointing the trowel at Jeff. 'You know what I mean?' Jeff didn't answer.

'She used to leave early most mornings. She used to just wait for us to turn up, make sure we had arrived and that. Then she would smile and disappear. And then sometimes she was abroad on business, and we didn't see her for days.' He leant the tool in the bucket. Jeff stared at it, whilst turning over the last page of the tabloid, searching for an answer and looking agitated.

'Chase,' said Jeff, sharply.

'What?' Donal looked baffled.

'The film that Sandra Bullock and Matt Damon were in was called *Chase*. That's the one, isn't it?'

'Aye, it was,' Donal said, looking at the contents in the bucket. 'That's right, it was that one!'

Donal stood up and stretched his legs. He arched his back, pressed his hands on the base of his spine and let out a heavy sigh. It was cold, and his breath was full of condensation.

'So, what's missing Donal, come on,' Jeff said, wandering towards the door, his hand scratching away at his forehead, desperate for an answer. Desperate to get to the cause of this problem he had with the work and find an answer so he could get the marauding Ms Zabrinski out of his life and move on.

'Come on, Donal! Think bloody harder - you were there, you've had time to think.' His voice rose a decibel. 'What about Petrov, would he know?' He turned and looked back at Donal, who had his back towards Jeff and was scooping up the first contents and launching it onto a section of the wall, which needed the attention of the new, fresh compound.

'Wouldn't have thought so, mate,' he said, stretching up and laying the pink stuff on the bare brickwork and feeling slightly under pressure from Jeff's questioning.

'OK,' said Jeff. 'Let's start at the top.' He removed a red pencil from the front pocket of his scruffy blue jeans and drew a bad picture of a set of patio doors with a concrete lintel on top of a space on the kitchen wall.

'The cracks are appearing from around the patio doors.' He sketched a wavy line above his artwork.

'You have already told me that you put in the correct beam. Is that correct?' he said, turning to Donal, and looking for an immediate answer to his question.

'Aye, it's the correct one mate,' Donal replied, tilting his chin up and agreeing with the picture. 'The building surveyor was there when we were putting it in. I told you that.' He stared ominously at the pencilled drawing.

'What about the engineering bricks supporting it, were they the correct ones?' Jeff said, pointing his finger back to his sketch and gulping some of his now cold tea from his takeaway cup.

Donal's face moved towards the concrete floor of the kitchen that they were standing in. He was thinking about the concrete at Bollo Lane and beginning to feel some pressure whilst listening to Jeff, and he began to recollect the day that the concrete mix was poured into the trench that had been dug out to take the foundations last year. Donal knew that Jeff was going to raise this issue with him during this talk, and he tried to search for answers. He folded his arms and looked at the drawing. The back of his head became itchy and uncomfortable as he thought,

'When is he going to get to the foundations, which support all the structure of the building and the weight of the walls? How shall I answer his questions and what shall I say? I need to somehow distract him…'

Turning to his boss, Donal said, 'Jeff, the architect came along at the end of the day. He saw the brickwork, he was happy. When we finished, he then left, and then we cemented it over.' He glanced at his reflection in the window as if hoping to find a better answer to the one he had just given. He was beginning to repeat himself.

'What are we going to start on first in this kitchen, Jeff?' Donal said, looking up at the ceiling, and spinning his head around the room as he ran his hand over one of the walls, making a rubbing sound.

Jeff looked around the room as well; he hadn't fallen for Donal's tactics of trying to change the subject.

'What… So, what about the footings, what were they like?' He continued to question Donal.

'What'd you mean, what were they like?' Donal growled as he flicked a hand.

'Did you check the ballast that went into the ground?' Jeff shot him a stern look, 'Were you there at the time it was being poured? Were you happy with what the company, Harding's, that supplied it? Think back Donal or I'm fucked pal. Don't you get it? I feel like I've got a shovel in my hand and I'm about to dig my own grave,' he said in a rage, banging his index finger at his drawing. 'Something's wrong, and it's me they'll come after. Not you, Donal' he said, pointing towards his work colleague.

'Aye, of course, Jeff,' Donal said anxiously leaning away from his pointing finger. 'It was sound.' He brushed his forehead with a hand, turned away and walked over and leaned against a wall as if for support; he was feeling tense, uncomfortable, and alone.

'I was there all the time. We waited for the concrete to settle before the brickie started work on it.' He shrugged his shoulders, looking just past Jeff, trying to hide the deceit on his face.

'Well, something's bloody not right. You are being honest with me aren't you, Donal?' he said holding out a hand.

'Aye Jeff, why shouldn't I be?' His face said he was distorting the truth. Jeff took a breath.

Ten

Jeff was unexpectedly woken at three minutes past seven by the sound of his mobile phone. He appeared to be in a dazed and confused state. A hand moved out from the side of his duvet and grappled with his phone. It was a ring tone he was familiar with. 'What the fuck!' He fumbled at it before it dropped to the floor and then when he'd retrieved it, he put it to the side of his head. His eyelids were still locked together. He guessed which was the answer button and wearily pushed it.

'Mr Turner?' The voice was subtle, as if it had come from a figure standing in the still, darkened room and only the whites of the eyes could be seen. It had a disturbing tone to it. The voice repeated, 'Mr Jeff, Turner?'

Jeff wearily sat up in his bed. The room was dark and gloomy. First, he looked at the window, and then he looked at the door. He wasn't quite sure what day it was. He scratched the back of his head whilst yawning.

'Er...Yeah, it's me,' replied Jeff. 'Who's this?' The voice waited for him to gather his senses for a few seconds.

'My name... is Christina Zabrinski. Mr Turner, we haven't met.' Her voice was chilling and creepy. The curtains of the bedroom window were slightly ajar, and the room was cold. The window had ice on the inside of it. He heard a car drive past. The sky hadn't quite lit up yet. It was a chilly winter morning. Jeff hadn't planned on getting up for at least another hour, and he felt aggrieved at losing some of his precious sleep to this voice issuing from his mobile.

He pulled up the duvet and covered his shoulders to keep himself warm in his icy prison.

'I'm sorry, Mr Turner. Have I disturbed you?' she said sarcastically.

'Er... no, no you haven't, Ms... Zabrinski, it's OK, I was awake anyway,' he said, not wanting to be caught out by his customer and feel embarrassed.

'Good. I'm so glad you know who I am, Mr Turner.' She sounded acerbic. 'We need to talk.'

'Oh, we do?' he said, sounding unsure, and slightly humble. She moved straight on, wanting to get to the point sooner rather than later.

'I understand that you met with my architect, a Mr Harrison Blake, at my house yesterday. Am I correct, Mr Turner?'

'Yes, that's correct, Ms Zabrinski,' he agreed to her words as it was too early to find his own. His voice was incoherent.

'We…we went over a few points regarding the problem with one of the walls in the extension and we took a look at the French doors.' He sounded jaded.

'And what did you conclude, Mr Turner?'

'Er…Well, we found several points that need to be addressed,' he said, sounding ambivalent.

'Oh, did you now! And?'

'Well, yes, we spoke about a few issues.'

Christina stopped Jeff dead in his tracks.

'That's not an answer Mr Turner, and it's certainly not the answer I was looking for.'

Christina was a ruthless businesswoman. She worked hard and played hard just the same. Once she had got her teeth into you, she wouldn't let go until she had succeeded in her aim. She was working hard to get to the top of her company and she wouldn't let anyone get in her way. And she was furious at this man who had failed to complete a project for her - a relatively straightforward task for an established builder, and a man that had been recommended to her and was apparently held in high esteem. Yet he was a man who had failed in his duties toward her, even after she had trusted him with the freedom of her home.

She always had busy work schedules and didn't need this extra load to deal with, but she would deal with it, and she would deal with this man. She spoke without rancour.

'Let me tell you, seeing that you do not appear to know the answer.' Jeff looked concerned and began to feel that his client was starting to get the better of him. His words had fallen short of their duty.

'You haven't given me time to finish my sentence, have you? You tend to try and take over the conversation, don't you?' Jeff said wearily, slowly waking up and getting used to the situation.

'No, I haven't let you finish because I received some very significant news when I spoke to Harrison yesterday. He said that the problem may be a serious one, and because they couldn't find any other reason for the cracks to continue appearing, there may be a fault with the foundations of the building, that's the only logical reason it could be, and that's why your repairs have been fruitless. He also said to me that he would need to take along a structural surveyor to examine the way the extension was built and that the area outside would have to be dug up to expose the ground beneath the walls, and this may be the only way to find out where the weakness was, and that this could possibly be the main cause of the problem I have, the problem being beneath the walls, my *walls,*' she said as she emphasised the point to him. 'They will be coming along to see me this Friday, that's why I didn't let you finish what you were about to say Mr Turner. What are your views on what I have just told you? Do you have any?' She was out to get this man, this man who she felt had dented her character, embarrassed her and shamed a woman who never made errors. And what were people going to think of her? What were they to think of her reputation? Christina was someone who was an organizer. She was astute, clever, articulate and precise in what she did and what she carried out, and this person had deceived her, cheated her into believing that she had purchased a state-of-the-art product, only for it to fall flat in her face. She had spent thousands on this new venture of hers. She was going to grind him into the ground. She had the backing and the ammunition to do so, and she was going to use it. She knew important people who could deal with him and deal with the mess that he had caused. It was just a matter of time until she found out the real truth as to why her newly built palace was crumbling away in front of her. She would soon find out the reason why her newly built kitchen was cracking up, and why the walls were becoming irreparable.

Jeff cleared his throat. 'Ms Zabrinski, first off, you can call me Jeff.' He felt that his client was trying to demoralize him. He was being taken to task by this woman for how he had treated her. And he was probably right anyway.

'Can I put a point across Ms Zabrinski, or shall I call you Christina.' Christina blatantly ignored Jeff's last comment.

'*What* is your point Mr Turner? I find it very difficult to imagine that you have a point to make! But I am intrigued to find out what this point is going to be. So, tell me, what is it?' Her voice was snappy.

By now Jeff was sitting on the side of his bed. He looked behind him at the bedroom window, hoping that it was getting light outside, hoping that some light may brighten up the conversation. He was looking for any help that he could find around him, but it was only 7:16 a.m. and there was no sunshine in his life at this moment.

Ms Zabrinski was on a mission. He knew there was a major issue with her extension, and he knew that she knew it as well, and since he had left Harrison. He knew that she had had a long and intense meeting with him and that he had told her about the problem. She had also spoken to other contacts about the faults.

Jeff knew that he didn't have too many answers to her questions, but he had to stick up for himself, at least until the problem had been solved for certain. He was innocent - for the time being at least. He was leaning forward. His thumb and index finger were sliding from side to side across his closed eyelids. He was feeling pressure from Christina's voice. It was too early for him.

'Well, first off, I was not on-site to oversee the construction of the foundations, or the pouring of the concrete, or the initial laying of the brickwork once the foundations were in place.'

'Ah,' interrupted a feisty Christina. 'Then perhaps you should have been there at these important, and crucial stages of the project. Surely, it's within your remit as the owner and boss of your company and the supervisor of your team to be involved in major issues such as these, is it not?' She listened in askance to his story. She began not to call him Mr Turner so much. She knew that she had made her point.

'Yes, it is, but I had good men on the project to run it for me, and to see that things went smoothly—' he began, but she butted in.

'It appears that these so-called, good men failed in their duties to carry out the work correctly. Do you agree with me, Jeff?' she said intensely.

'We don't know the outcome yet, do we?' Jeff said. 'Isn't it best that you hear from the surveyor first?' He knew he was verbally being pushed back by Christina.

'We will wait for his report. I have instructed the structural surveyor, who is coming here, to my premises this Friday, and to which you are *not* invited Mr Turner to this important meeting, as you have always found it difficult to meet our appointed times in the past. Do I make myself clear?'

Jeff found it hard to find words to defend himself from the rampaging Ms Zabrinski. He felt like a boxer on the ropes being pounded by a barrage of blows to his head with nowhere to run or hide.

'I have also outlined everything that has occurred on this project, Mr Turner. I have already sent you one letter stating that you have failed in your duties as a professional to correct the faults that you have brought on by yourself.' Her voice was prevailing. 'And also, I do not expect any good news for you from the meeting on Friday, after which you will receive a second letter from me stating what my plans will be to resolve this issue. This will depend on the scale of it. But should I think the situation to be out of your control, then further communication will be through my solicitors, Greenfield and Lewis. So, I do not think that we will talk again. On that point, do you have anything to add?'

Jeff thought, Christ, what has this woman been doing over the weekend since coming back from a business trip abroad? She's spoken to her architect, and she's also spoken to, and arranged an appointment with a structural surveyor, doesn't she take any time off work? I couldn't get hold of any of my guys over the weekend. They aren't interested in talking. They are all out, doing their own stuff. The word bollocks came to mind, but it was one that he could not use at this moment in time. He stared at the clock on his bedside cabinet. He was looking for some form of solace. It wasn't there.

'No, I think that you've made your point quite clear. I will wait with bated breath for your letter,' he said mockingly, thinking that he would have a moment of glory himself.

'Pardon?' Christina quickly sensed his sarcastic quip.

'Oh, nothing.'

'Please, Mr Turner; I hope that you will take our conversation seriously because if not, it will have severe consequences for you.' Jeff pulled his mobile from his head and glared at it in astonishment. 'Who the bloody hell does she think she is?' he thought. He decided now to have his say.

'Listen, Ms Zabrinski, I don't think you're in a position to chastise me at this moment in time.'

'Mr Turner!' Christina tried to butt in.

'Don't "Mr Turner" me, Ms Zabrinski, or talk down to me. I'm not a juvenile, *Ms* Zabrinski, and I won't put up with you trying to talk to me as one either, so I suggest you get your surveyor to send me his instructions to put the matter right, and as I said Ms Zabrinski, I will wait with bated breath.'

Jeff had now decided that attacking this ferocious woman would be his best form of defence. He could no longer put up with her domineering voice, and he wasn't going to take it on the chin any longer.

The temperature was finally rising in the room. OK, she was probably correct in her assumption, but until it was final, he thought that she should be more respectful towards him.

'Mr Turner, let me say, you have made a grave error of judgment at my premises. First off, I have a room that I cannot use due to your lack of professionalism and skill, a wall with a crack in it, a garden I cannot use for fear that it will be dug up, a kitchen in which I feel uncomfortable, and have no confidence working in, and now, I will be facing an extra bill for your incompetence, and possibly more work to rectify a possible fault for which you and your company are responsible. And I also paid all your invoices on time, and without hesitation. I think, Mr Turner, I have a right to have my *say* as an unsatisfied customer, don't you think?'

Jeff ended the call and threw the mobile against the wall. He leaned his head down and supported it with the palms of his hands.

'Fuck,' was the only word he could think of.

He picked up a pair of blue denim jeans that were lying on his bedroom floor, put them on, and gulped down a drink that was on his side cabinet. He wandered into the lounge, sat on the sofa, and finished by pulling a sweatshirt over his head. He stretched out his arms and put his hands behind his head.

'How the bloody hell did all of this happen, and how did I manage to get into this mess?' Malicious trout, he thought. 'I need to find out what went wrong, and where.'

Eleven

It was raining hard and the falling drops made a crackling sound on the ground outside. It was a wintry morning - the kind of day when you thought the rain was never going to stop.

Donal was in a room, by himself. The client had left for work over three hours ago. It was cold. He was well wrapped up, but could only just about feel the tips of his fingers, and there was a peculiar feeling around him today. A strange silence covered the bleak grey lounge. All alone in this chilly environment, he was feeling the pressure. He knew that his boss, Jeff Turner, was going to meet the architect, Harrison, at Bollo Lane to discuss the problems with the cracks in the wall, and they were sure to come up with a solution. After all, they were professional people; Jeff, Harrison, and the surveyor would solve the problem once and for all and get their client the answers that she desperately wanted.

Donal had not slept well Thursday night - things were bothering him and his mind had been far too active to surrender to seven hours of sleep.

He was working at a slow pace, knowing that soon his mobile would ring. He had glanced at it many times that morning, thinking, if it did ring, and it was Jeff, what would he say? And how was he going to give him an answer? He wouldn't have a plausible one for him.

When they had found out the reasons for the cracking on the wall, he would either have to fabricate an answer, or feign ignorance. But it wouldn't solve the problem, and he would be in serious trouble. The consequences would be catastrophic for Jeff - this could ruin him financially, and his reputation would be in tatters. His friendship with Harrison would deteriorate, and work would stop coming his way, a good source of work, quality work from respectable clients, people with money, who didn't mind spending it. The money would all dry up in one fell swoop.

Christina would find it demoralizing, and it would put a dent in her reputation of being something of a perfectionist. She would want to have

Jeff Turner's guts out. She would feel that by employing an inferior builder, she had made a mistake, a gross misjudgement of error on her side, as she felt that she didn't make mistakes, she always made the correct decisions, and that was the reputation she had strived for.

Donal knew he had no way of getting out of it. He had even considered not turning up for work today, and he wondered if he should quit the job and just say to Jeff that he had found something new elsewhere…

He was becoming agitated and wasn't working well as his mind was elsewhere.

The rain was easing off and the flat was quiet, except for the sound of the radio and the irritating tapping noise of rain drops on the window ledge in the lounge.

There was no one around. He glanced at his phone; it had just gone 11:30.

He was thinking, 'Why hasn't it rung yet?' and staring at it as he scratched the back of his neck.

He thought, 'Jeff had met Harrison at around 10:00, like he said he would be doing, by now the hole would have been dug out, even allowing an extra 15-20 minutes leeway for this rain to have slowed things down, by now the concrete would then be exposed.'

So where was Jeff? If he found the problem and he wasn't happy, he would have been on the phone straight away. That was his nature, that was usually the way he worked. He would always relay information as soon as possible to whoever needed it.

If they hadn't found a problem, then Jeff would be happy, and he probably would have driven straight over, maybe phoning on the way to let Donal know of his whereabouts and to see how the job was going.

But there *was* a problem. A major issue had occurred at Bollo Lane, and a costly one as well; the repair work would run into the thousands. 'Who would ultimately pay the price for the mistake?' thought Donal. '*Jeff.* I shouldn't have done it,' he thought. 'It was only eight hundred bloody quid, and besides, he's not a bad bloke.'

Donal slowly pushed his hands across his forehead and took a deep breath. 'I'm in trouble,' he mumbled.

He looked out of the window as if for an answer, then he twiddled with the control on the radio, trying to find a different station just to pass the time. He could see the top of St Paul's Cathedral. 'I wish I was there,' he thought. 'And not here.'

Unable to find an answer, he turned and looked anxiously at his phone, then pulled his head backwards and moved it from left to right as he felt tension build across his shoulders and a pain in the crown of his head. He felt a tingling sensation running down his legs. It was 11:46 a.m.

Still there was no call. He thought, 'OK let's work out another theory. Let's say that he's found the problem and was enraged by it. What else would he do?

What would I do in that situation? So, you've just been told by your architect that there's a major fault with the foundations of the building, and you've been told to correct it, at your own expense - that is if the architect hasn't lost faith in you, and also if his client lets you on her premises again, and allows you to continue the work.

You would have to deal with a woman like Christina Zabrinski, who would want to tear you limb *from* limb and try to financially cripple you.

How could she tell her friends that her new kitchen, with all its bone China crockery, chrome electrical appliances delivered from Harrods, and Italian marble floor tiles imported from Perugia, were sinking into the ground? She would feel embarrassed. She would be furious.

So that's why Jeff hasn't phoned me yet, because if he had done, and told me this, that would have given me the chance to pack up my tools and disappear. So, he's probably on his way to me now.'

Suddenly, his mobile rang. He leaned over and looked at it - the name on the display read 'Jeff'. *No,* he thought. 'So, what the fuck do I do?' He didn't answer it, he just let it ring. It must have rung for about ten rings. When it finally stopped, for a split-second Donal was relieved. But then the mobile rung again, only this time for even longer.

Donal looked anxiously at the time. it was 11:52 a.m. his head was aching, and his skin felt warm and clammy. He looked out of a window of the flat, thinking that he might see Jeff approaching.

'So, then let me work this out…An hour and a half for the meeting, plus the journey from Chiswick to here, he pondered for a moment.

Probably forty-five minutes. Jeff should be here around 12:15 p.m. He looked at the time again. 11:54 a.m.

'I have to leave and get the shit out of this place. If he's in a bad mood, which I'm sure he will be, especially being faced with a large bill, he'll batter me. He's a fit bastard. If he's in a foul mood, he'll drive faster, you drive faster when you're angry. He's probably got his foot down on the gas pedal right now, gritting his teeth, with blood pressure rising… Maybe he'll be here at 12:00?' His mobile told him it was 11:59 a.m.

Time was moving on. Four beeps sounded from the radio which sat on a kitchen unit. The newsreader was announcing that it was midday. His decision had been made.

Donal gathered his tools together as beads of sweat formed on his forehead. His hands were trembling and his breathing became uneven. He looked around to check he wouldn't leave anything behind and found himself making sure the windows were locked. But then why should he care?

He headed out of the kitchen and towards the hallway holding his bag. The floorboards creaked as he moved across them. The palms of his hands were sweaty as he looked towards the glass-panelled front door of the flat. Although he was high up, on the third floor, he could still hear the sound of car engines from the road outside, and they made him nervous as he thought who might be driving them. He stopped, turned around and went into the front room, then walked towards the window which looked out onto the road. His van was there, parked about fifty yards away. He edged the curtains to one side and peered up the road, both directions, looking to see if Jeff was in sight.

Turning away from the window, he headed towards the lounge door. His stomach rumbled, but he wasn't hungry. Food was the last thing on his mind. He entered the hallway, his heavy bag pounded against the wooden door frame. He opened the front door of the flat then stopped. He had heard the main door to the 1930s apartment block open downstairs, a few floors below where he was standing. It was a grand old building, built with the best materials available at the time. He heard the sound of hinges squeaking as the heavy door swung open. The hallway sounded hollow, it had a slight echo and he heard the shuffling of feet on the elaborately tiled floor. He stopped for a second, waited, and then peered over the bannisters. He saw a hand on the railing below, a couple of floors down. It appeared to be man's hand, and it looked powerful. Veins were pushing out from his skin. Donal jerked his head back as he thought he saw the figure look up at him.

'*Donal*,' came a commanding, booming voice. It began moving up the extravagant spiral staircase like a tornado. 'Donal.' He then heard Jeff's feet pounding the oak stairs. Donal had nowhere to run - he was on the third floor of a mansion block and there was no escape route for him, no way out. He stood on the cold marble floor. He couldn't go back into the flat, there wasn't anywhere in there for him to hide, and there was no fire escape. The tiny kitchen balcony was a sheer drop to the ground. He looked up at the floor above. He had never ventured up there, and he didn't know if there was a route out of the building. The footsteps became louder as they moved up the stairs towards him. He heard the gripping, twisting movements of Jeff's hands against the shiny wooden handrails as he pulled himself upwards and nearer to him. Donal's heart raced and he could feel the tension in his chest.

He noticed a door on the landing, close to where he was stood. It looked like a cupboard, but what was inside it he had no idea. He noticed a lock on the door, which looked fully closed. He looked quickly at the front door of the flat, then back at the cupboard door.

Jeff reached the flat.

'Donal!' he shouted; the door creaked as he pushed it open. 'Donal!' he called again, as he moved angrily into the hallway, walking wearily, and thinking that he would soon bump into his mate, the mate that had stitched him up and let him down badly. He was listening out for any movement from his now so-called work colleague. The only sound he heard was that of a gravelly-sounding folk singer, telling us that, 'the answer was blowing in the wind,' from the radio.

Jeff moved through the hallway and walked into the kitchen. He immediately sensed that there was no one around, he looked for Donal's tools, but they were nowhere to be seen. The only signs that he had turned up for work this morning were an empty coffee mug and a screwed-up tabloid newspaper. Jeff picked it up and checked the date, then threw it down with rage.

'Fucking bastard,' he said, as he cut the grainy-voiced singer off in full flow, pulling the radio lead from the socket in a violent temper.

He put the knuckles of his hand against his mouth.

He considered biting a chunk out of them, but thought better of it, clenching his fist and leaning an elbow on the top of the fridge. 'Why do I do this bloody job?' he thought. 'I should be a full-time gigolo. If only it were more regular, if only the income was better, better than this crap.' He looked around the place. He knew Donal was gone. And he now knew that Donal had made a mistake at Christina's house and used an inferior concrete mix for the foundations. 'Why did he do that? I always looked after him, I looked after him for years. The bastard.'

Donal used the cheaper concrete to make some money for himself, pocketing the difference in price from the usual brand. Jeff had given him two years' work, paid him on time, all the time, loaned him money when he was short of it, and had never said anything to him if he arrived for work late. Jeff knew that he was drifting down a river on a raft, without a paddle. His business would suffer a major setback, recommendations from his main contacts would stop coming in, his phone would ring less, and people would just not want to use this man anymore. His finances would suffer. Bills would become harder to pay.

He stared at the new window that Donal was asked to fit. He pushed two buttons on his Nokia and scrolled down to Donal's name. His eyes were fixed on his phone for a second. He hesitated, then tapped a further button, which made the sound of a ringing tone. He moved the mobile slowly to his ear. As he waited, he gazed out of a window, staring at the Islington rooftops - smoke was billowing from chimneys below a featureless sky. It was quiet, and there was a slightly odd feeling in the room.

Jeff thought he heard the faint sound of a mobile ringing. It was a muffled tone, and it sounded like it was coming from somewhere in the flat. Maybe from the lounge area, he thought. It was ringing in tandem with his phone. Was he imagining it? He then heard a noise which sounded like a shuffling movement. He moved resignedly down the high-ceilinged narrow hallway. An art deco lightshade hung above him. He moved cautiously, not knowing what to expect. He peered into the lounge, then continued moving slowly towards the front door, stooping as he went. The sound now just a couple of feet away from him, and he was unsure of what was going on.

He moved out to the black-marbled landing area. There was a noise, and a cold feeling in the air. His eyes directed him to an open cupboard door. There was a bag of tools on the floor inside, below some fuse boxes. He heard a scraping sound. He leaned over and looked down the staircase where he locked eyes with his enemy, who was now on the ground floor looking up.

'You bastard Donal! Come here, you bastard!' he yelled, his voice was piercing.

Jeff charged down the three flights of stairs. He sounded like a herd of wildebeest being chased by a hungry lioness, his feet only pounding on every third stair. He had a frantic look on his face, like his prey in front of him.

He reached the front door of the lobby and nearly slipped on a pile of mail on the floor. He pulled the door open towards him – glanced both ways up the busy London Street. A double-decker bus went by and he studied the faces of the commuters on it. He then looked fifty yards down the street, only to see the door of a van being closed as he watched helplessly. It screeched off, its engine being thrashed, as it crossed in front of moving traffic. Jeff watched as it got smaller and swung around a corner and out of sight.

Jeff sat motionless in his vehicle outside number fifty-two Chiswell Road. One hand resting on the steering wheel, a thumbnail from the other was digging between two of his teeth. He had just phoned Donal three times, but of course he hadn't answered.

The sky was a cloudy grey. Traffic whizzed by; taxis taking smartly-dressed businessmen to their meetings, commuters walking to their place of work with mobiles stuck to their ears, cars speeding up the road, all hurrying to get to their destinations on time.

He pondered his next move and looked at his mobile on the passenger seat. It gave him an answer. He picked it up and made a call.

Petrov had told Jeff that Donal had used a company from the *Yellow Pages* book. They were from somewhere in Essex and they turned up in a very large lorry, but it wasn't a cement mixer. There were five of them and a couple of children. He thought that they were gypsies. Donal must have found a much cheaper company than the one that Jeff had specified.

Donal would have kept the invoice himself and printed out a fake one. He would then have got the work done at an even cheaper cost and pocketed the difference. Donal could then afford the holiday he so dearly wanted to go on with his girlfriend, for a week at Christmas.

Petrov remembered that he had once seen Donal and Christina arguing, and he had noticed Donal handing something to her one morning before she went to work. Whatever it was, she had put it in her handbag. Jeff had suspected that Donal used some sort of drugs, but he didn't know what type or what kind of quantity, and he hadn't known that he sold the stuff.

Twelve

The office workers poured into number 211 Fulham Palace Road. It was a five-storey building in the heart of W6. Some were late, some were early, and mobile ring tones were sounding out all kinds of tunes. It was a busy morning. There were sounds of high heels clattering on the tiled floors. Some workers were heading up the chrome and glass staircase, whilst others loitering around the lobby, waiting for work colleagues to turn up.

The dinging of the lift sounded as it arrived on ground zero to pick up staff and transport them to their destinations on various landings. It was the first day back to work after the Christmas break for the staff of Hammerson Shaw. It was cold outside and drizzling with rain – a typical January morning.

'Sherry!' came the cry of a woman's voice cutting through the mix of suits as they shuffled their way past one another. 'Sherry, I'm over here!' Sherry looked around and saw a hand waving in the air as if flagging down a plane. She moved towards it, bumping into a passer-by holding a cardboard cup full of tepid coffee.

'Whoops, sorry,' Sherry said, squinting her face up, and hoping that she hadn't upset the elderly gent.

She walked over to Mars with a smile on her face.

'Morning, Mars, how are you? Did you enjoy your Christmas break?'

'Fine thanks. Have you heard?' Mars said with an air of eagerness in her voice.

'What? Please put me out of my misery. Heard what?' said Sherry, looking disillusioned, and out of sorts as to what was going on. The two girls stood together, away from the rush of bodies.

'Mike is standing down in six months' time,' Mars said with glee, resting a hand on Sherry's arm, and leaning towards her.

'Oh.' Sherry was surprised.

'Well, you know what that means don't you?' Mars said excitedly, straightening her back.

'What does it mean Mars? Tell me more! I'm all ears, darling.'

'Well, Christina will probably take over his position, right?'

'Well, of course, I guess...' Sherry hesitated, and studied her excitement, while adjusting her scarf over her bag, and wanting to hear the gossip.

'Then that leaves the door open for me to take over Christina's job, right?' Mars said, holding her hand out as if wanting a reply.

'Well, right, that's assuming that she wants you to take over her role. She's a very pedantic woman, you know, Mars. I wouldn't have thought that it would be that easy. I doubt it's going to be a shoo-in, my love.' Mars edged her head back from Sherry.

'Why not?' she said, a little taken aback. 'She must want her position to go to someone she knows, someone she can trust, and there can't be too many applicants, can there? We all know that she's always wanted to move up on the board. She has done for years. So, then that leaves the next person in seniority, and there's no- one else who knows her job as well as I do,' Mars said, concentrating on her friend.

'Don't count on it, Mars, she may look around. She may want to bring in some fresh faces to the company You just cannot tell with that woman, she's unpredictable. Some love her, some despise her, and few are ambivalent about her.' Sherry glanced down at her watch, then looked around, giving a wave and a smile to a fellow work colleague who was heading up the stairs. Mars stared away from Sherry for a second, thinking hard.

'Is it down to her to choose who takes over *her* position or down to the president?' Sherry said.

The president was Mike Schreiber. He had been with the company for sixteen years. He virtually ran the operation, and his decisions were quick and final. He'd often turn up for work on a motorbike in the summer months. He was on your side if you were fair with him. He would complement you and support you, should you need it. Mike had graduated from the University of Cambridge, and gone straight into banking, working for Atlas group, an American merchant Bank in the city. He had left and joined the Royal Air Force for a brief spell before returning to the City.

'Well, he's the boss, so it would probably be down to him but seeing he is outgoing, I would expect that Christina would figure largely in the decision somewhere along the line, wouldn't she?' Mars said with an anxious look.

'Well, I'll have to think about it. Do you think they will choose you?'

'I don't see why not Sherry. She's made me work hard the last two years, and I've responded well to her demands. She's put me through my paces enough times and I've helped her out on many an occasion.'

'But you have clashed with her as well. Haven't you?'

'Sometimes. Maybe. But she understands my values and my commitment to the company.'

'Well, if she likes your guile, hopefully, you'll get the position, but be aware, Mars, you can't tell her friends from her enemies. It's a thin line.' Sherry leaned towards Mars, touching the back of her hand with her fingertips, 'I'm just telling you as a friend,' she said, as if she didn't want anyone else to hear. 'I've known the woman for some time. She's changeable, unpredictable, you know. It could go to her head, knowing that she was the head honcho in the company. I would rather work under Mike than under her - at least he's predictable.' Mars looked bemused; Sherry moved away. Sherry had known Christina Zabrinski longer than Mars had known her. Sherry looked at her watch again. She had a look of empathy on her face.

'Mars, look, I'm sure you'll get the position. I don't see why not. I'll keep my fingers crossed for you darling.' She looked around. 'And I'll put in a good word for you. You have worked hard, and you deserve it, lovie.' Sherry smiled politely. Mars looked concerned. 'But I must be moving on, I've got a meeting to attend to soon,' said Sherry, leaning forward to peck Mars on the cheek.

'Thanks, Sherry, I will take in what you said, but I'm not going to worry. I'll get the bloody job,' she uttered, as Sherry left her and headed for the stairs. She pondered a while, her scheming eye's scanning the lobby. The walls were marbled from floor to ceiling, the windows faced the busy road outside, and exotic plants grew in large, heavy-based terracotta oblong pots that decorated the flooring. The crowds were thinning out and there was a moderate amount of movement in front of her now. Many thoughts were turning in her head. Not many people got on with Christina Zabrinski. She could be cold and selfish, but she was also a master tactician and a perfectionist, who had received a top education, at a girls-only school.

Mars reached into her handbag and checked her mobile. 'Somebody loves me,' she thought. But it was just a text message from her mother telling her she was out of beans. Her son Tom loved beans. 'Is that all she has to worry about?' thought Mars. She realised it was time to start her day's work.

Hammerson Shaw's offices were situated on the third and fourth floors of the building. The more careless workers took the easy option and used the lift, whilst those eager to lose as many calories as they could shift after the Christmas break took the stairs.

This time Mars took the latter.

Thirteen

Mars stood at her computer and checked an incoming email. it was 2:50pm.

"I hope you all had a lovely Christmas, and an enjoyable New Year. I am holding a drinks party at my house, in Bollo Lane, on Monday, January 16th, at 7 o'clock sharp, and you are cordially invited. It will be a light gathering of work colleagues. You are welcome and *must* be accommodated by a partner".

Mars was at her desk; she had just digested the generic email when her desk phone rang. She jumped as it caught her by surprise.

'Helen Marshall.' She knew who it was from the screen on the phone, but still decided to announce herself.

'Did you get the email?' the quirky voice said.

Dave Palmer was from sales and had been for the last two years. Dave was in his early forties.

'Yes, I did Dave, what's it all about?'

'Well, she's odds on to get Mike's job,' replied Dave. His voice went into a whisper. 'And I expect she wants to flaunt it. Plus, you know she's had this new kitchen fitted recently, and she's had loads of trouble with it, but now it's all finished. She's spent loads of dosh on it, so now she wants to show that off as well. You know what's she's like, don't you? I bet its chrome this, expensive marble that, and, *ooh,* look what I've got!'

'Yes, I do, I know what she's like,' Mars said cantankerously.

'Still, if she gets Mike's job, then that puts you in the running to take over her job, doesn't it?' he said chirpily.

'What do you mean "in the running", Dave?' Her voice deepened. 'I cannot think who else she would choose, or do you have anyone in mind. Have you heard anything? You haven't heard any rumours, have you?'

'Hmm… I haven't, no Mars.'

'Who would you think would take over her job? You know her reasonably well, don't you, Dave?'

'She hasn't said anything to me, Mars,' his voice sounding defenceless.

'You don't sound too sure, Dave. You don't sound convincing enough for me.'

'Mars, she wouldn't let it slip this early, would she? You know her. She wants to be in control, she wants the limelight, she wants all the attention, and she wants people to grovel up to her. If she let her guard down, then she wouldn't have anyone sucking up to her, would she? But no, I don't know who it is that is taking over her position. She'll be tight-lipped about the whole thing, I'm sure.'

'True statement, but don't worry, I've already had this conversation with Sherry this morning. I don't need it again, but if you hear anything, let me know... won't you? ... As quick as you can, please,' said Mars. Dave hissed.

'Wash your mouth out Miss Helen Marshall. I work for the majestic Christina Zabrinski, remember?' Dave said in a half-hearted voice. 'Anyway, moving on, if she's invited you, you had best be there. She won't take no for an answer. She's also looking for you to be coupled-up as well. She says it will create a more balanced out atmosphere. She doesn't want a load of giggling girls in one corner, or a bunch of guys getting pie-eyed in the other.'

'Bloody snob!'

'Sorry?' said Dave.

'I said, OK.'

'There's only going to be about twelve or thirteen couples there, mainly close work colleagues. You know - Sherry Hill, Jenny Ross, Morgan Cable, the beautiful Helen Marshall, and whoa. And I expect some of her high-heeled friends. It's going to be a regular *soirée*, I expect there will be nibbles and champers on offer on the night.' Dave's voice was formal, to the point, and not entirely on his boss' side. Jenny worked in marketing, while Morgan was in finance.

'I need names, Mars. Like, who will you be taking along on the evening in question?'

'I can't tell you right now, Dave. I don't have anyone in mind just yet. It's come along all too sudden, but I'll let you know, soon. And thanks for the compliment, it was sweet of you.'

'My pleasure. You mean you have too many admirers to choose from?' 'Bloody no admirers at all,' she thought. She leaned back in her chair and glanced at the large picture of Van Gogh's sunflowers on the wall.

'Well, Christina's theory has gone right out the window, then, hasn't it?' She smiled at herself, fiddling with a paper clip in her fingers.

'What do you mean "gone out the window"?' Dave sounded bemused.

'Well - Morgan.' She lowered her voice as if someone might be listening. 'Doesn't he bat for the other side?'

'There may be a touch of ambiguity there, I'm sure my love, but it's going to be interesting viewing at 7 o'clock on the 16th.' His voice suddenly sprung to life. 'You've now have got something to look forward to, haven't you? It may even make the evening a tad more exciting.'

'Yes, it may do, plus we can all look at her new kitchen. I *did* hear through the grapevine about the saga of the building work. I'm sure we will get the full run-down of what happened.'

'Yes, Helen, she did, she had loads of bother with it, but it may be in our best interest not to mention it too much, eh?' You know you need some brownie points, don't you?' Dave said.

She gazed out of the office window at another office opposite. Already the day was giving itself to the gloom of the darkened evening. She saw people walking around and wondered if their life was the same as hers. 'Were they better or worse off? What time do they work until? Do they work harder than me? Who am I going to take to the ball?' She bit her pen hard in annoyance.

She thought of her last boyfriend, Johnny Scotland. 'He dumped me for... who the hell did he dump me for? It must have been for someone with black hair. He told me once that he liked dark-skinned women with dark hair. Why the bloody hell did I go out with him? I must have been crazy, or desperate.

It only gives me nine days to find a date. Not long,' she thought. She leaned back in her black leather chair and spun it halfway around, facing her desk.

'That nice computer engineer asked me for a date two weeks before the holiday when he came around to fix Dave Palmer's laptop. He left me his card, I remember.' She reached down to the floor and retrieved her handbag, rifled through the contents and pulled out a creased white business card. She looked at it. It read, "ACL computers". The name on the card was Alan Barwell. It had his mobile and landline phone numbers, and his email. She looked sternly at it and flicked it on the side of her chair. She took another look, and thought, 'Why did I not agree to a date with him there and then? I'm single.' She pondered for a while and put a corner of the card between her lips. 'He was, well, OK... He was well dressed and had a sense of humour; he was tall and presentable. Where did he say he lived?' She was in deep thought. She glanced around and looked at the office opposite. The night was drawing in, and lights from the neighbouring buildings, offices, shops and apartment blocks were flicking on.

'Sod it,' she thought. 'I can't ring him, it's against my principles. I'm a woman, and women don't do things like that. Perhaps I should phone him and say my computer doesn't work... but he'll know it's OK, it's his business to know.' She crossed her legs, tilted her head backwards and looked up at the ceiling. 'It needs a coat of paint,' she thought. She looked at a photo of her son, Tom, which was on her desk, and smiled. 'I must pick up the dry cleaning on my way home. Is there food in the fridge? Is there any milk?'

She tapped her index finger on her keyboard and glanced at her bare ring finger, then scratched her forehead and let out a deep sigh as she cracked off a square of chocolate from a bar. She put the business card on the table next to the PC face upwards, and then went on to a search engine. She hesitated a while and then typed in the words: 'escort agencies.'

Fourteen

'Hello, you must be Mars?' he said, joyfully, with a warm smile.

Jeff had had a call from the escort agency he did occasional work for, around a week ago, informing him that there was a client interested in his services. The client lived in west London, and she had to attend a business drinks party on the evening of January 16th, and would he like to take up the invitation.

Clients would choose an escort from the agency's portfolio, either going to the agency's office or choose from the internet. Once the client had made a choice (in this case, Mars), there would be some minor forms to fill in and a fee to pay. Jeff would receive his percentage from the company, while it would be down to the client to pay for Jeff's expenses for the evening ahead. What they did on their date would then be entirely up to them. They wouldn't meet until the arranged time.

Mars had chosen Jeff for his looks, his height and his physique, and to impress the host. Mars had sent Jeff some photos to give him some insight into her and to see if Jeff liked her looks. However, Jeff wasn't bothered about the looks of the women he went out with. He met all kinds of women of all different ages in his work. He was only really interested in the financial side of the arrangement but, nonetheless, he had taken a shine to the women he saw in the pictures even though it meant working late on a weeknight. It would generally mean him being very tired the next day at work, but at least it boosted his income, and he would get to meet a lot of new women and perhaps get to sleep with one or two of them, should the situation arise.

Mars worked under the host of the forthcoming event. She was a single girl, thirty-seven, had been married before, but was now divorced, and had a nine-year-old son. She had straight, blonde hair, and was five foot six inches in height, with blue eyes. She was slightly nervy about meeting Jeff, so she had a few drinks at home to relax before going out. They had spoken a couple of times on the phone to arrange details of a meeting place and to get to know each other, and discuss what the evening would be like, what was required, as well, and times, etcetera.

The party had been arranged for 7:00 in the evening, and Mars had received a formal invitation by email, although she worked in the same office as the host.

The drinks party was to be a general get-together, and an opportunity to chat about the forthcoming changes to the company, which the host was very excited about. And she also wanted to show off her brand-new kitchen to her closest work colleagues. Christina wanted to make sure they saw what she had achieved, and in which direction she was heading.

Mars had arranged to meet Jeff at a wine bar a ten-minute cab ride from the house to where the party was being held. Jeff had politely phoned Mars before he left home to let her know his whereabouts. He had jumped into his truck and headed for the meeting place. He was in a confident mood and felt good, sure that he was going to get on well with his new date this evening. He liked the look and sound of Mars. She looked attractive to him - she was his sort of woman; classy, smart and eye-catching. He liked her eyes. He was ready to go.

At just before 6:00, Jeff sauntered into The Slug and Lettuce on Chiswick High Street as if walking down the catwalk at a fashion show in Milan. He had decided to give this date his best shot. He was wearing his best dark-navy Hugo Boss suit, adorned with a thin checked pattern. His trousers were pressed, razor-sharp, and he wore a crisp, white Paul Smith shirt, the cuffs of which protruded about one and a half inches past the sleeve of his jacket, showing off his nine carat gold cufflinks. He had carefully ensured that his left wrist was sufficiently exposed to show off his Rolex Milgauss watch. He was wearing a deep-mauve tie, loosely knotted at the neck. His freshly polished shoes could have brightened up the dimly lit wine bar for the rest of the evening.

He wore sunglasses and expensive aftershave. His hair was gelled, combed back and wavy, and he donned a cheeky, warm smile, with a "look at me, I've arrived" swagger.

Nature had been very good to Jeff and had endowed him with good looks.

He had noticed an attractive blonde-haired woman sitting on a stool against a table. She was by herself. He had walked over to her.

'Hello… and you must be Jeff,' Mars said, apprehensively.

'Pleased to meet you,' he said leaning forward and politely pecked her on the cheek. She observed his smooth olive skin, in full and direct focus, and drew in a breath to smell his fragrance. She thought that on her first viewing of this man, she had made a very good choice indeed. As he drew away, she thought to herself, 'Where are you going? How many times in your life does someone get an instant attraction for someone? Twice, three times maybe?'

Their eyes met and they smiled at each other, both thinking that their dates were as good a choice as they were going to get.

Mars had recognised Jeff from his pictures on the internet. She had been in the bar for ten minutes and was holding a large half-full glass of Merlot. She appeared to be impressed and slightly overawed by his presence. For this reason, there was an air of nervousness about her - as she had never done this sort of thing before. Meeting a date over the internet was something she never did, although it was second nature to him, so he was the more confident of the two.

Jeff took off his sunglasses, which were only a fashion statement, and not required on a grey, dark evening in the middle of an English winter in a poorly lit wine bar. Nevertheless, Jeff felt they gave him the look of an Italian film star, which was the image he had been aiming for and besides, they matched his Mediterranean complexion, upon which he had built his character.

'Pleased to meet you. My name is Jeff Divine, I must apologise for being a little late.' Jeff used Divine as a pseudonym for a second name. He didn't want to use his surname and thought Divine suited him. Mars cleared her throat.

'No, I'm early. I've been here for about ten minutes. Pleased to meet you too. You look like your photos.'

'Thanks,' Jeff replied.

'Can I get you a drink?' Mars asked uncertainly. She had to ask as she had to pay for the expenses for her evening.

'Can I have a coke, with ice please, is that OK?' Jeff said as he winked at her. It was second nature to him to answer a woman's question as to what he would like to drink and watch them walk to the bar, stand there and wait to be served. That would normally be considered what a man should do on a date, but it was not that kind of date. In reality Jeff had no reason to put his hand into his pocket all evening - the expenses would be paid fully by the client. She was the employer, and he, the employee.

As Mars stood waiting for the drinks, Jeff's eyes took a tour around the establishment he was in, a place entirely new to him. He found the clientele to be a charming bunch - young thirty-somethings, he thought. Relaxing with their partners, drinking a latte, or pinot, and they were at home in their environment, having earned their six-figure salary for working hard, five days a week in the City.

'Good luck to them,' he thought. 'It's a sight better than being a builder and having to work nights for a living.'

Just then Mars arrived back from the bar with Jeff's drink, and a sparkling water with ice and lemon for herself.

'Thank you very much, that was very kind of you,' said Jeff, as Mars gave him his drink. He gave her a mischievous smile.

'I must say, you look stunning tonight.'

'Thank you,' she replied, coyly. They both took a seat and sat at a high-raised wooden table. 'I thought I'd ask, as the agency told me to, but do I owe you anything for your travelling expenses for this evening?' Mars said, courteously and naively. She had still not settled into the fact that, in reality, this was a blind date, and she had never been on a blind date in her entire life before. She was nervous, but thankfully the alcohol was kicking in. She had ordered the water so as not to completely make a fool of herself - better to have a break from the strong stuff, and move on to something to get her on a level footing, to neutralise her body now that she was over the awkward part of meeting her man for the evening.

'Well, thanks for asking, Mars - by the way, I love the name Mars.'

'Oh, thanks.'

'Anyway, I got a cab here this evening.' Mars looked up from taking a sip of her water; she had half expected Jeff to have driven. 'I saw him walk into the bar, but I didn't see any sign of a cab pulling up outside, and there's enough space outside for a car to park in front of the bar,' she thought. Mars now became suspicious. She wasn't tight with her money, her income was comfortable, and she had enough disposable cash for a quality social life, but she was a businesswoman and didn't like to pay more for something than she had to.

'If he did get a cab down here, wouldn't he have asked the driver to drop him outside the bar? And why is he only on soft drinks?' she thought. 'He looks fit, so maybe he doesn't drink, maybe it's part of the job. Perhaps he has to stay sober for the evening?

'Where do you live, far?'

'Er, Ruislip, Mars.' He sipped his drink and turned, looking around the bar. 'Ruislip, Middlesex.'

She waited with bated breath for the cost of Jeff's journey, and knew that this was going to be an expensive evening for her, probably the most expensive in some time. She knew Ruislip wasn't nearby. She had stopped off at a cash machine earlier in the day to top up her purse.

'Ruislip to Chiswick,' she thought. 'Well, could be thirty, maybe thirty-five pounds?'

'Oh, that's a fair distance to travel?' She looked at him as he grinned.

'So, how much is that then?' she said, sounding a little nervous.

'Forty-five pounds,' Jeff said buoyantly and with a smile on his face.

'Oh, OK,' she replied. 'Is that return?' Mars thought that she might as well try her luck. She may be lucky, or unlucky, but thought she should ask and try to throw some guilt his way.

'Wish it was Mars,' he said audaciously, and with a deep look on his face. 'But unfortunately, that's just one way.'

'OK. That's fine,' she said thinking, 'Bloody expensive! has he bumped up the figure? And how much did he give that cab driver?' She unzipped her handbag and delved for her purse. Jeff couldn't help noticing the quality of the leather, the class, and the stitching of the bag. He had been on this scene for some time, met a lot of wealthy clients, and was no stranger to fashions, and had a good judge of what the client was worth, where the evening was heading, and if he would spend the evening sleeping with his customer.

He fancied Mars - she was a good-looking girl. She looked after herself and had a good body, and if the chance arose, he would go to bed with her.

She clearly appreciated the good things in life. But she seemed to lack a bit of confidence in this field. Maybe, he thought this dating scene was new to her. Jeff knew that this was the first time she had used this agency, as they had told him so, so he was going to make allowances for that.

While Mars was retrieving her purse from her bag, he carried out some detective work. Unbeknown to Mars, he was scanning his eyes over her handbag looking for a label or a brand name. He finally spotted the word 'Prada'. 'Very smart,' he thought. Jeff decided to give himself a raise for the evening.

'Plus, a tip,' Jeff said to Mars, beaming his charm at her, and giving her a wry smile.

Mars had a wad of notes in her hand, which she pulled out, ready to hand over to her date.

'Oh, and of course, a tip…' She coughed. Mars looked up at Jeff with a look of condemnation in her eyes, and thought, 'Is he hiding something from me, is he telling me the truth?'

'I'm a generous chap, you see. I like to tip the cab drivers as you never know when you might meet them again.'

Yes, I bet you are, she mused.

'So, how much is that then?' she said.

'Err… Forty-five pounds for the cab,' he said with slight hesitation in his voice knowing that a cab would have only cost him thirty-five pounds. 'With a five-pound tip, I make that an even bullseye.'

'Sorry!'

'Fifty pounds Mars, one way.' He looked her in the eyes.

'So that's one hundred pounds return then, is it? You like to travel in style, don't you?' she said with a hint of sarcasm.

'Yes, I like style Mars,' he said with a cheeky grin, looking at her. 'I'm sorry, but that's what they charge.'

'No. That's OK,' she replied. 'Do I get a receipt for that?' she asked, knowing that she had more chance of seeing Brad Pitt appear at the bar.

'Sorry?' said Jeff, with a surprised look on his face, 'I didn't think I needed to get one?'

'It's called business expenses, you know. No? Well…' Mars looked at Jeff and thought, 'I knew that answer was coming.'

Jeff looked blankly at her.

'And, well, the fare goes up to time and a half after midnight,' he said with a smirk in his eyes.

'Does it?' she replied. 'I think it is due to end at around eleven.' She didn't want to give this man any more money than she had to. She needed to get one back on him, and not give him any more cash than what she had in her hand. She felt she was beginning to be fleeced by this playboy.

'Besides, people have work commitments, and have to get home early. Seeing it's a weekday, some of us have to be up at the crack of dawn.'

Jeff looked at Mars, knowing that he had her cornered. He knew she couldn't prove the cost of his journey. But her face told him that she knew he had bumped up the price, but what could she do about it? She had no choice, but to hand over the five newly printed twenty-pound notes to him. That was on top of the two hundred pounds the agency had taken from her credit card for hiring "Mr cocky git". 'I wonder what his cut of the two hundred pounds was? Fifty percent maybe?' she thought.

'Thank you,' he said, gracefully. 'Do you have any hobbies then, Mars?' He thought he should quickly change the subject. Jeff looked her up and down, provocatively. He was undressing her in his mind. He liked her style. She wore a ring on each hand and a thin gold bracelet on a wrist. He found her pert up nose attractive.

'Er. No, I don't actually, Jeff.'

'Everybody needs a hobby, Mars,' he said, making a joke.

'So, what is a pretty girl like you doing having to phone an escort agency to find a date for an evening?' Jeff continued trying to steer the conversation away from the subject of money in order to melt the coldness he had begun to feel emanating from her. He knew she was no mug. She couldn't have reached her position without at least a grammar school education, and she may well have gone to university and earned a degree. He had been given some information on his client from the agency but only said that she was a businesswoman working for an established company in London, she had worked overseas in the past, and at present, lived in Ealing West London. The rest of the puzzle had to be put together by himself. He had made a habit of finding out something about his clients. He felt it put him in a more comfortable position for the evening ahead.

Mars took a deep breath and glanced at Jeff, looked away in a different direction, and then looked back at him again. Jeff wondered what was going on in her mind, as well as what she was going to say to him. It looked as if she was going to tell him that someone had just died, but surely not... Jeff didn't know this woman he was with, and he certainly didn't know her family. Was she hiding something?

'Well, OK, Jeff, it's like this. I'll get to the point as to why we are here this evening, and as to why I called up an agency to hire you, and it's not easy.' *At last,* Jeff thought. He leaned back away from the table, relieved that Mars was going to come clean and confess to the point of this meeting between the two of them. It really didn't bother Jeff what her plan of attack was. He was going to get paid for the evening. He was in the company of an attractive woman who he had just successfully financially conned. If she wanted to get up and walk out of the door and not meet him again, that wouldn't bother him either, he had earned his money already this evening. But he did want to hear what she had to say, and he was all ears.

'We are here because, well, it's about my boss. She is a very clever lady, you could say...highly astute, very intelligent... she generally gets what she wants in life, and doesn't let up at any expense, she can be a bit like a rottweiler, as they say, she can be ferocious. She *does* do very well in her work, and the CEO admires her a lot. She is looking to move up in the company, and her position will become vacant in a few months' time.' Mars' conversation was now in full flow, but Jeff cut in at this point.

'Sorry, to interrupt, but what is your boss' name?' Jeff was only trying to slow her momentum down, as he felt that she was beginning to get a bit flustered, and in need of a sip of her drink.

'Call her Christina when you first meet her, can you? It will be best,' replied Mars. Jeff's eyes twitched. She continued where she had left off and didn't want to stop her conversation. 'It's a position that I want *badly*,' she said with menace. Jeff was slightly surprised by her swift change of nature. 'I've done enough to deserve it, but I feel at the moment I'm being ignored. That's where you come in, Jeff.'

Mars paused, sighed, then finished off her other glass, the remains of her wine, as if it were the first of the evening for her, and briefly closed her eyes, feeling that Jeff was becoming a good listener. Her face relaxed. Jeff joked.

'Well, I don't know much about the fast, frenetic world of business Mars. I use the odd designer hair gel and I like quality aftershave sold to me by glossy ads, but apart from that, I'm not a high-flyer myself, I'm afraid. I don't think I could live in the world you pacey movers live in.' Mars looked at Jeff in confusion.

'I'm just teasing, Mars.' Jeff leaned forward and stroked her arm to console her. Mars looked at Jeff with a pleasurable, 'thank you' smile.

'I like your watch,' she said. 'It suits you.'

'Thanks. It was given to me.'

'She must have liked you?' she said, smiling through her eyes.

'How do you know it was a she?' He smirked.

Mars looked mystified.

'Well, I just assumed that it would be from a female. I just couldn't see a bloke buying it for you, you don't look that type.' She threw him a cunning grin.

'It was, Mars,' he said, looking pensively at her. 'You're right, I was only joking. I'm sorry,' he paused. 'It was from a Middle Eastern woman. She's older than me - she's in her late forties, and she's quite attractive, although not as attractive as you,' he said leaning towards her. Mars looked smitten by the remark.

Mars glanced at his watch and realised that time could be moving on.

'It all sounds very intriguing! You're obviously in demand by the rich and wealthy women of the world, I can see that.'

'They are not all rich.'

'Ha, I bet.' She moved away from him. 'I just have to go and powder my nose, Jeff. I'll only be a couple of minutes.' Mars stood up. 'Will you excuse me?' She headed in the direction of the ladies. He watched her as she wandered off.

'Hello, can I have a cab please?'

'Where from, please, miss?' came the voice at the end of the line.

'Oh, from the Slug and Lettuce Bar in Chiswick High Road, W4.'

'And where to, madam?' came an Asian voice.

'We're going to Bollo Lane, for 6:50. My name is Mars. Thank you.'

'It's 6:50 now, miss!'

'Is that the time?' she said, looking worried.

'OK, for seven then, or as quick as you can, please.'

'It will be twenty minutes miss.'

'Erm…OK, thank you. *Hold on!*' she snapped at him. The hapless taxi controller must have thought her hand was going to appear from his end of the phone and grab him around his neck.

'And also, how much is a cab from the Slug and Lettuce bar, to Ruislip, please?'

'What part of Ruislip, miss?' said the Asian voice from her mobile.

'I don't know what part of Ruislip, just Ruislip.'

'So, you don't know where you're going to, miss?' the voice said calmly.

'Yes, of course I do,' barked Mars. She was becoming uptight.

'It's a big town, is Ruislip. There are different tariffs, you know.'

Mars looked at her watch, and knew Jeff would soon be wondering where she had got to. 'OK. The centre of Ruislip then, how much would that be?'

'OK,' said the voice. There was a moment's hesitation. 'That will be thirty-five pounds, miss.'

'How much did you say?'

'Thirty-five pounds,' mumbled the voice from Mars's mobile. The voice continued, 'Would you like to go to the centre of Ruislip instead of Bollo Lane, miss?'

'Er… No, it's OK,' she said. 'I'll stick with Bollo Lane for the time being, for seven, is that OK?'

'About seven-ten,' came the reply

Mars grinned bitterly as she ignored the man, thinking, 'OK so he's done me out of twenty pounds, what can I do now? Not much, but it would have been nicer if the two figures matched up with each other.' She didn't like to be done out of twenty pounds, knowing just how much she had paid for his services in the first place. She snapped the lid of her small silver powder case shut and wandered back to the bar.

'So, Mars, talk to me, where do I come in?' said Jeff as if he were standing on a pedestal. She had to step up a gear.

'I need to be at the forefront of her mind, so what I plan is… You don't mind being used as a pawn, do you, Jeff?'

'Mars, that's what I'm here for,' he held out his hands. 'Use me.'

Jeff nearly added, "and abuse me", but held back. 'I won't be too forward, just yet,' he decided. 'Let me know more. Tell me what you've got on your mind for me for this evening. What are up to? You are the client, Mars, you're the customer. It's your evening and I'm here for you. I'm here to please you and to make your evening comfortable, so, please, don't hold back, tell me what you want.'

'OK. Thanks, Jeff, thanks for that.' She paused. 'So, you are my new boyfriend, I've recently met you, tonight would be our third date. We met in this bar three weeks ago. We're getting on very well, and we are happy with each other… Sorry, Jeff. I forgot to ask you, is this your full-time profession, or do you do anything else for a living? Do you work in the day, I mean?'

'I do work in the day,' Jeff smiled, and thought, 'I'm in the company of a professional businesswoman here, so I'll up my credentials, just because I can.'

'I run my own construction company,' Jeff said. Besides, construction sounded more professional than building, and he could have got away with saying anything he wanted to. He wouldn't be seeing Mars again. He knew she only wanted him as a trophy for the evening, someone to pose with and someone to show off. He thought that he and Mars wouldn't hit it off sexually anyway. And as for her governor, 'Well, I'll just say what I have to say, nod when I have to nod, smile when I have to smile.'

'I take it you are going to be asked lots of questions tonight, aren't you?'

'Yes, I am. She will probably grill me, and dissect my every word.'

'Why?' said Jeff.

'Well…Well…,' hesitated Mars. 'She just absolutely adores Italian men, or at least good-looking men from the Mediterranean. She loves their looks. You see, her last boyfriend, Robert, left her to work abroad. He was of a similar shape and style to you, and I think she is still in love with Robert. She hasn't quite got over him, and I think she is on the lookout for someone like you. And I would like her to think that I have something that she doesn't. I want to make her jealous. Does that make sense to you, Jeff?' He nodded politely.

'I hear what you're saying.'

'She's like an onion, she has several layers - you peel one-off and find a different layer and a different personality. What you see is not always what you get. There's a job coming up in six months' time, and I want it. She's taking over at Hammerson Shaw, where we both work, and I could be in the running for her position. It will give me more stature in the company, plus there's a salary increase, and some other perks.'

'I see,' said Jeff. 'God, what are you girls like? And what's it like to be in the fast lane in the business world?' he said with an interested look on his face. 'So, who am I? What's my role in all this? I'll need to answer a few questions here. I get the impression she's likely to ask me a number of them as well?'

'Oh yes, you're right. You'll be asked several questions, Jeff, don't you worry about that, so what I have worked out is…,' she paused. 'OK construction, right, you own and run your own company, and you have qualifications in engineering. That's an area of business I hope she knows nothing about.

Your income is good, you live in Ruislip. You also have a Villa in Menaggio, Lake Como, in Italy.'

Jeff raised his eyebrows, pushed his lips together, and spoke. 'Wow, you've done your homework Mars, haven't you?' he said with a smile. 'Lake Como sounds very nice. Does it have a swimming pool?' Mars looked at him, and thought, 'He has a sense of humour.'

'Well, if you want it to have a swimming pool then yes, and yes, you're right. I have done some research. You have to, Jeff, believe me, you have to. Once she gets her claws into you, she doesn't let go. If she wants something, she generally gets it, you will see.'

'So, what if I fancy this woman, Mars, have you thought about that?' Mars' face showed a look of bewilderment. 'I mean, I'm single, and she's an unattached female, affluent…' Jeff leaned towards Mars, 'And she's on the lookout for, a…' Jeff leaned back, pulled his chest inwards, straightened his shoulders, flicked his neck left to right like a peacock showing its feathers of to a prospective mate, and grinned, 'A good-looking bloke in her life and you never know. I may be the one. I may be the one she's looking for.' Mars frowned.

'She isn't your type,' Mars said quickly as if to move on with the conversation and try to forget what he was saying. Jeff detected a hint of bitterness in her tone.

'And how do you know that, then? You don't know me, you don't know what sort of women I like, do you?' There was an element of mockery in Jeff's voice. Mars was beginning to see his point, and his words got her thinking, but she thought that he was only pointing something out to her. Despite knowing him for the little time she had, she felt that the two wouldn't go together. She knew her boss, and knew she would only go for someone with money, someone in a good financial position, and who had a future in a well-positioned job.

She had concluded that Jeff fell short of her boss' standards. Maybe if he had pulled up in a two-door Porsche, or a top-of-the-range Mercedes, and bought *her* a drink, instead of making her go to the bar and queue up, but he hadn't. Her boss wouldn't go for the type that had to carry out a full-time job while doing part-time work on the side to make ends meet. She was a sapiophile, so she was safe. Robert had met all her requirements, but he had left to work in Dubai for a salary increase and a more secure future with a global investment bank. But in the back of her mind, she remembered Jeff's words that he might be the one she was looking for. Maybe they could get on?

'Have you ever been to that part of Italy Jeff? Just in case she asks any questions,' she said, looking at her watch.

'No, I haven't,' his face was thoughtful. 'I'll just have to make it up as I go along, I'm sure I can manage it. I'll sweet talk her,' he said, grinning at Mars.

She turned and looked out of the window saying, 'I think our cab has just turned up, and it's ten minutes late.'

'So, onward we go. And into the battle zone,' said Jeff as they headed out of the bar and onto the street.

Fifteen

Mars and Jeff eased their way into the back of the private cab. It had a smell of glass cleaner. They both sat at the rear of the car, feeling comfortable with each other. Mars felt relaxed.

'Where to, sir?' said the driver. He was an Asian man and in his fifties. Jeff's arm was draped across the top of the bench seat, and his redundant fingers began to fondle the back of Mars' hair. She appeared to enjoy his playmaking and flirting, and she grinned and glanced very briefly back at him.

'Bollo Lane, please,' Mars said to the cab driver.

'Bollo Lane!' Jeff looked in amazement. 'Bollo Lane did she just say?' He coughed. His face looked confused and distant as if he had just been told that he had been sacked on the spot from his work. Thrown out of the company. His chest tightened. He released his fingers from Mars' hair.

'Bollo Lane!'

'Pardon?' said Mars.

'Oh, nothing,' replied an empty-looking Jeff.

The cab pulled off and made its way down Chiswick High Street. It made a left, and then a right turn. Jeff swayed gently with the movements of the taxi. He had gone quiet and looked out of the window, he felt that he was in a dream.

'Everything OK, Jeff?' Mars said, thinking that all of a sudden he wasn't saying much anymore, and wondering, 'Why the sudden silence?'

He flicked his eyes. 'Oh, yes. Fine, Mars, just admiring the views I'm not from around here, you see, so I'm taking it all in.'

After a few minutes, the cab drove down a quiet street and its brakes screeched.

'We're late. We'll have to make some kind of excuse.'

'Yeah, sure. Blame it on me - say I got to the bar late, say that I was working and fell behind and didn't realise the time.'

'I'll make something up, she won't like it,' Mars replied.

'She likes punctuality.'

'It's nice around here,' he said, his anxious face peering out of the window, his eyes squinting. A woman was tugging her small dog away from the wall of a terraced house.

The cab rushed down a one-way street, and then turned and made its way down the infamous road. The driver was moving slowly as if expecting to receive his instruction to stop in a microsecond. He had obviously done this before.

The houses were Victorian and the street was narrow, with few parking spaces. If you were unfortunate enough to get home after seven in the evening, you were probably going to have to drive around the block a few times or park a hundred yards away and walk back to your house.

Some areas were dark; the road wasn't very well-lit.

'Just here, on the left,' said Mars pointing to a house. The cab pulled up.

'Thank you,' she said. Mars looked at Jeff with a smile and said, 'We're here now Jeff.' His expression of puzzlement said it all.

She leaned forward to pay the driver. Jeff opened the door and gradually eased his way out. He stood on the road between two parked cars and stared at the house in disbelief. His head moved slowly around to his left; he stared in amazement at the front of a house. It was built in the 1960s and it was noticeably different to the Victorian houses. It had been built in a different era, probably constructed on a piece of wasteland, or perhaps the owner of the house next door may had sold off some of their land to a developer.

It had been constructed of light brickwork, on two levels and was one of the few houses with off-street parking.

Jeff's face was pale and his body felt like it had lost a stone in weight. His eyes were in a hypnotic state. His face slowly moved to the number on the door. As he stared in disbelief, his fears were realised.

'Bloody hell,' he said to himself. He turned and looked at the car on the driveway in horror; it was a silver Audi, just like the one Christina Zabrinski drove. He looked at the number plate.

'So, what the fuck am I doing here?' he thought as his heart raced. He twisted his perspiring neck to release it from his shirt collar. For a moment, Jeff thought he was in a dream, and all this was a figment of his imagination. He blinked, hoping that he would wake up. It was a cold night and he felt very chilly. This was a nightmare, and he was in it. He had thought that he might be the star of the show tonight, the centre of attention, and maybe some new women would take a liking to him. He had hoped to flirt with a few of them as well. So, why was he here? 'What am I doing on this Road?' He was a little bemused. 'Why?'

Mars closed the car door with a thump and walked wearily towards him. She thought that he had changed his mind all of a sudden, he looked so unusual. Was he now having doubts about the evening? Had she given him too much to do, too much to think about, and speak about? Could he remember what she had told him? He had seemed to be full of confidence in the bar, fifteen minutes ago, but now he appeared to be a different person. He now looked on edge.

'I've settled the fare, Jeff,' she said, as she was rearranging the change back into her purse. She looked at him.

'Are you OK? You haven't changed your mind, have you?'

'No. No,' he said in bemusement. He stepped onto the pavement. The cab pulled away, its tyres scratching on the tarmac surface.

'OK. Shall we go in now?'

'Go in. Err... Yes. Of course, Mars.' Jeff needed some time to work things out. His head was spinning faster than a carousel at a fairground. For a second, he felt dizzy. There were so many thoughts turning around inside his mind. He was thinking. 'Christina Zabrinski is inside that house, she is the host.' Mars had mentioned that her boss' name was Christina. "Just call her Christina", she had said to him. 'I owe that woman sixteen thousand pounds or more, and she's inside that house. How do I explain that to Mars, and that I now can't go any further, and the evening may have to end here, right now?' Jeff looked at Mars as she was moving towards the front door.

'Mars. I have to make a quick phone call to the office, is that OK? I need to let them know my whereabouts.' Jeff needed time to work out how he was going to tackle this situation. He removed his mobile from his jacket, pretended to push some of the buttons, held it to his ear, and pretended to make a call. He turned around and took a few paces down the street, away from where she was standing. He was only trying to work out the situation. What was he going to do?

He thought, 'OK. I'm going to walk into that house, and she's going to be there, but does she know me, does she know who I am? Maybe someone has described me to her, maybe they have. Possibly Harrison, or maybe Donal could have done, or someone else. But I will never know. No, we haven't met, have we?' He doubted himself and questioned his theory. 'I don't know what she looks like, but does she know me? Could she know what I look like? Donal said she looked like Sandra Bullock. Does she know me?' He questioned himself again. He turned and looked at Mars. A hand was tight against her chest. She had lifted her shoulders towards her neck, and was tapping her long black leather boots on the pavement as she was trying to keep warm on this cold night. A thick cloud of air was coming from her mouth. Jeff knew he couldn't keep her waiting much longer.

'One minute please, Mars,' he said, smiling at her, with his mobile still pressed up against the side of his face.

'No, we don't know each other,' he reiterated to himself. 'We have never met, so she will not know who I am.' He appeared puzzled; he scratched his head.

Mars looked at her watch as she walked towards the door of the house, then looked around, and saw Jeff begin to walk slowly towards her. She rang the doorbell. It was twenty-five past seven.

'She will bloody kill me,' Mars said.

'What the fuck is she going to do with me, then?' he thought.

After several seconds, which seemed a lifetime to him, they heard a figure move the other side of the door. Jeff stood strong, his face tensed up. He braced himself for the door to open. A blur appeared through the small glass window. A creaking noise came from the handle. The door opened.

Sixteen

'*Mars!*' They hugged, then pecked each other on the cheek.

'Sherry. This is Jeff.' Mars introduced her date for the evening to her work colleague. She looked him up and down, scanning him all over in order to give her friend her honest opinion.

'Very nice,' she said, in a soft voice, looking at Mars and acknowledging her choice of man. She pouted her lips. Jeff looked at her in confusion and smiled.

'Sherry, who's Sherry?' he thought. He shook her hand. 'Is that her, but changed her name?' He began to get paranoid. He pondered for a second.

'Come in,' said Sherry. 'It's cold out there, isn't it?' They walked through the hallway of the house. Two couples were engrossed in a heated conversation with each other. One of the men was pointing a finger as he was making his point. Mars momentary touched Jeff's hand, pleased with her friend's approval of him.

'Come through,' Sherry said as if she owned the house herself. Jeff walked across the wooden floor behind the two girls as if he were hiding from someone. He still felt unsure about the situation that he was in. Although he was a confident person, he felt uncomfortable. They walked through a set of double glass doors to the kitchen area. Jeff stood at the threshold. It felt surreal. His breathing quickened and his heart rate increased as Mars stood slightly in front of him. Sherry wandered into a crowd of people.

They were clutching glasses of wine and some were holding china plates containing neatly cut sandwiches filled with caviar and salmon, and some with deer's tongue.

Jeff's eyes crept towards the kitchen wall to an area above the rear patio doors, the point where Christina Zabrinski first told him that a crack appeared after he had finished the work on her extension. He'd been in this kitchen before. The wall was now painted a different colour to the one he left it in, a slightly deeper neutral colour. He quickly moved his thoughts away from the wall, thinking that Christina Zabrinski could be looking at him. As he had never met this woman before, the woman whom Mars had explained to him in detail, he was also unsure if she was in the room.

Somehow he just didn't get around to meeting this, ex-client of his for various reasons, adversity was one of them.

He scoured the room, nervously, and noticed the guests were all well-dressed businessmen, and women. They made passing comments toward one another, some were nodding their approval. He could smell the money in the air.

He wondered which one might be Christina and looked for a woman fitting the description that Donal loosely described to him.

He noticed a tallish figure standing near a glass dining table. She was holding a flute glass full of pink champagne and making small talk with a male, around the same age as herself. She had long, straight auburn hair, and was around five-eight in height. Her lips were immaculately glossed in crimson red, and she was wearing a black Karen Millen laundered shirt, the top two buttons of which were undone.

'I'll get you a drink, Jeff and introduce you to Christina,' Mars said. His heart skipped a beat. 'You may need it in that order, what's your poison?' Jeff thought that the comment was so true, it was an understatement.

'A very large Bacardi please, darling,' he said almost in a daze. 'Now, where's that Sandra Bullock lookalike then, she must be here somewhere. I once read that she was the fourteenth richest female celebrity.'

Christina turned her head toward the direction of her new guest. She pursed her lips and her pupils widened.

Christina Zabrinski? thought Jeff, as his eyes locked onto hers like a guided missile. He took an inward breath, and his shoulders tingled. And, for a second, everybody and everything else in the room went out of focus.

He glanced towards his employer for the evening as she handed him his large drink. He looked at it with vigour and gripped the glass. Mars turned back toward the kitchen worktop, near to where she came from.

which was full of wine and spirit bottles and Waterford Crystal glasses. As she fetched a drink for herself, and thought, 'Ah, he does drink then!'

Christina strategically flicked her hair forward, left her friend in her wake, just barely touching his arm, and moved towards Jeff like a lioness in a field moving in on its prey. She squeezed past a young girl, in her mid-twenties, her back towards Christina, brushing the palm of her hand over the buttocks of the girl's tight skirt. When Christina came face to face with Jeff Divine, the young girl glanced around at her. A few other eyes in the room noticed the subtle move. Christina's eyes lingered on him, she held out a hand. This guy was magnetic - he wasn't intimidated by women, he had patience and charm.

'Good evening,' she said, her voice was suggestive, redolent. She stared at him confidently, like a temptress. Her face was provocative. She was in awe of this man's presence. Inside, her heart was beating like a drum. This was déjà-vu. She looked him in the eyes as she raised her arm and offered Jeff the back of her hand.

'My name is Christina… Christina, Zabrinski.'

Seventeen

The alarm sounded, Jeff wished that it didn't go off as early as it did. It was 6:30 a.m. He'd been awake for about an hour in the night, when he was woken by the neighbour's washing machine, which was spinning, or trying to spin at 3:30.

'Why the hell was that machine going at that time of the night?' he thought as he tried to open his eyelids.

'Can't they put it on during the day, or early evening, why in the bloody middle of the night?'

He somehow eased himself out of his bed a few minutes later, and headed reluctantly to the bathroom, yawning on the way.

The palms of his hands gripped the sides of the wash basin, his arms were straight and taut. His face was pale. All that covered his dignity were a pair of Calvin Klein boxer shorts and a creased-up Guns 'N' Roses T-shirt.

He found his reflection staring back at him from the oblong mirror. *Who's that?* he thought. His once black wavy immaculate hair had disappeared and unrecognisable after his short night's sleep. He felt like he had just got into bed. It was one of those mornings, and he had had many like this in the past.

His pupils were unfocused and his stubble needed clipping.

He twisted the head of the cold tap and cupped his hands together like a beggar praying for food on a street corner. He filled them with water, some pouring out through the gaps in his fingers, and he lowered his head, forcefully splashing the contents onto his face. He let out a long sigh. It had helped his cause.

He sipped his hot tea, not waiting for it to cool down. He leant against the kitchen worktop as he stood tall. He gazed out of the small kitchen window from his flat. It was still dark outside as if it were 11:00 at night.

His mind was twisted. He had thoughts dancing around his head. Just twelve hours ago he had met with his predator for the first time. The imperious Ms Christina Zabrinski.

'Not bad looking? She was different to what I had imagined. Lovely eyes, nice, a bit too bossy for my liking though. That Mars girl was right, we're not a match, ha! I don't know if I could put up with her domineering me. And constantly asking me questions. I imagine that she would want to control you, tell you what to do all the time. What sort of bloke would put up with that? No wonder she's not married. She appears a little obsessed.' He thought as his mind wandered.

'What am I thinking? I'm not going out with her. Still, she has a good job, and I bet she's loaded. She looks as though she is.' Thoughts continued going round in his head.

'Nice house she's got there… shame about the kitchen wall! Nice party, full of snobs, but great food. What a bloody coincidence—me, turning up at her house.

Quite unbelievable. How ironic is that! I just couldn't believe I'd been invited to her party, of all the people.

Why did she paint that wall a different colour? I quite liked it in off-white. It opened the room up and gave it a sense of space. Now it looks closed in with that shadowy deep stone emulsion colour.

That Mars girl is lovely. Fantastic eyes. What colour were they?' He sipped his tea. 'Lovely blonde hair, a right good-looking girl. I might be in there? Yeah, and what a coincidence, I'd never thought that I would see Bollo Lane again. I wonder if she knew who I was?'

'The Jeff who she employed to build her extension for her. Surely, she couldn't have. Could she? Incredible. Fantastic kitchen units. The girl's got taste, you have to admire her for it, although she's a bit stuck up. And the way she shook my hand when we met, she held on to it for some time. I don't think she wanted to let go.'

After snapping out of his deep thoughts, Jeff had his shower and jumped into his truck. Material receipts were strewn across the top of the dashboard, and his empty sandwich box was on the seat next to him, with his mobile phone's on top. One bleeped. He looked at it. Mars had sent him a text message, thanking him for the evening. And for being a good "boyfriend" to show off to her boss.

His attire was not quite the same this morning. He had donned a pair of scruffy jeans instead of a sharp pair of cotton trousers, a zip-up fleece instead of an immaculately ironed designer shirt, and a pair of tan-coloured boots instead of the shiny Gucci shoes of last night.

'Jesus,' he thought, as he stared, winding down the window. His hair wasn't like it was last night. The leftover gel was quickly pushed through and rearranged with his hands.

'I've got one auburn-haired woman who's single and loaded and wants me. And there's also a stunning blonde woman, who's also single, sending me a thank you text. Can't be bad!' he thought. He twiddled the knob to turn up the radio volume, then turned the key and started the engine.

Eighteen

Mars ambled into Mario's, and ordered a drink. She made her way over to where Christina was sitting. Sherry arrived soon after and approached the empty counter and ordered a coffee and a toastie. Christina had two seats waiting for the girls. She had arrived a few minutes earlier, she had made sure of that. She had just ordered a coffee. Dave Palmer was sitting at an adjacent table and tucking into a large ciabatta. Christina was wearing a leather jacket, which she removed when seeing Mars and Sherry arrive.

'Wow, like bloody wow, he's gorgeous, Mars. Where did you meet him, and how long have you been with him for? You kept him a bit of a secret, didn't you? Where have you been hiding him?' Christina said, cooing and looking a tad jealous.

'OK, calm down! He's quite good looking I know,' she said, looking a trifle smug.

'Very good looking if you ask me!' replied Christina.

It was lunchtime, and the coffee shop was bustling with the usual workers from nearby offices. A queue was now forming at the till. The three girls had a seat next to a window, and the large pane had a splattering of raindrops. Christina had arranged the meeting this particular afternoon, emailing the girls early in the morning to find out more about the date Mars had brought along to her party the previous evening. She had taken a certain interest and couldn't resist finding out more about this tall, charming, suave male, one that you would find on the front of a men's glossy magazine. She had met this man at her party only the night before and was looking to get to the nitty-gritty of the relationship, to dig into Mars' private life - she just needed to know who this stranger was.

The three girls rarely lunched together, but today was different.

Just then a ringtone came from the direction of Mars' bag. She retrieved it, looked at the screen and turned the volume abruptly off.

'Not answering the call then, Mars?' Sherry said, staring at her friend and being nosey.

'Not your new bloke, is it?' she continued.

'Ha-ha, no, it's a number I don't recognise, actually - probably someone wanting to sell me double glazing, or telling me what a fantastic customer I am, and do I want to upgrade my mobile contract,' she said sheepishly as she returned the phone to her bag.

'Come on then, dish the gossip girl,' Christina said eagerly.

'Jeff, you mean. Oh, I've known him for a few weeks now,' Mars said lying through her teeth.

'He's brutally handsome, isn't he?' said Christina, looking at Sherry.

'Thank you.'

'You've never told me that you had a new man in your life…' Sherry said quizzically. 'So, where does he come from, where does he live?'

'He lives in Ruislip, not too far,' she replied, looking at the girls as they began to bombard her with questions.

'He's in construction, isn't he?' said Christina, butting in.

'Yes, he runs various building projects around the southeast of the country with his business partner, how do you know that Christina?' replied a startled Mars.

'Well, I spoke to him last night.'

'Yes, I saw you spend some time with him,' Mars said wryly. 'What else did you prize out of him, then, when you were pinning him to the wall?' Christina smirked.

'Oh, I just asked him a few questions, like where he works and stuff like that. No harm really, just small talk.'

'Did you take a shining to him then?' Mars said, wanting to get one over Christina. She knew she would like Jeff - fancy him, in fact - but how much, she didn't know. She was looking to get one over her boss, get something that she hadn't got, make her jealous, have a competitive edge over her, and have a tool. It was beginning to work, and she started to feel eminent for once. She felt the momentum was moving in her direction.

'We had a good talk, yes, he was quite interesting, easy to get on with,' Christina said in a defensive voice. 'he told me he has a niece, and his sister lives in Pinner, I think, wherever that is, that's all… oh, and his mother's Italian. She's from Viareggio, its near Pisa, and he hasn't been to visit her for nearly two years. And that he has a house overlooking Lake Como, with stunning views of the water.'

'Oh, has he now!' Mars said with concentration.

'It doesn't have a swimming pool, though, it didn't bother him, because it was only a short stroll down some steps to the Lake.' Mars looked quizzically at her.

'You seem to have asked him a lot of questions Christina. Did you ask him anything else?' Mars said with an air of jealousy.

'Yes, I did as a matter of fact.'

'Somehow, I thought you may have.'

'I asked him when he was next free,' she said fluttering her eyebrows.

'Pardon! Excuse me.' Mars stared at her boss with contempt. She thought, 'Is she winding me up, or is she telling the truth about asking her so-called "boyfriend" out on a date behind her back?

'And!' she said abruptly.

'You have a good man there, Mars - he politely said that he was unavailable and that he was not in a position to meet anyone else whilst he was with you.' Mars smirked.

'He's bloody good-looking though, don't you agree, he's my type of bloke,' Christina acknowledged to Sherry.

Christina began to describe Jeff to Sherry, even though she had met him herself, as Mars looked on open-mouthed.

'Did you notice him, Dave?' Christina said turning around to their male colleague, who had his back to them. He was too busy with his lunch to understand what the girls were gabbling on about.

'Notice who?' Not waiting for answers, she went on. Dave turned and faced the girls and took some notice.

'He has Olive skin, he's tall, he dresses tastefully, and looks after himself, and he smells good. Oh, and he works out at the gym. When you've finished with him Mars, let me know.' Christina began to taunt her colleague.

'I may pass him on Christina, but it won't be just yet, I've only just met him.' Mars pulled a face and forced a half-smile.

'When are you seeing him again?' asked Christina nosily.

'I don't know yet. I may meet up with him this weekend if he's not busy.'

'You don't seem too sure,' said Dave, feeling dragged into the conversation. Just then, the waitress brought over the girls' order.

Mars stared into oblivion through the window, her eyes followed a raindrop trickling down the windowpane as she went into a daze knowing full well that she had no plans to meet up with Jeff. She knew Christina fancied him, insatiably, she had told her several times now that he was a good-looking guy and Mars knew that Christina had no real interest in her current boyfriend, Dan. But she was uncertain exactly how she could use this as a weapon against her boss in order to snatch her job, which would soon be up for grabs.

'I have something that she wants. I can use Jeff as a chess piece if I want to… I can dangle him on a piece of string, if I want,' she smiled to herself at her own ideas. 'At least I'll have some fun doing it, and I have the bait.'

'Are you OK?' said Sherry. 'You look miles away, darling,' she said, looking at her mate.

'Yes, good, Sherry, thanks. Sorry, no, I'm not sure, we don't have any concrete plans for the weekend just yet. Why? What are you two girls up to, then?'

'I'm off shopping for wallpaper. Got to get hubby to decorate the lounge in the near future,' said Sherry.

'And you, Christina?' Mars said, not caring what she got up to.

'I haven't made any arrangements yet; I may travel down to Amesbury to visit my parents on Saturday night and treat them to a meal somewhere.'

'That sounds exciting!' said Dave sarcastically as he got up to leave, and grinning at the trio.

Christina said nothing.

Sherry grabbed her jacket. 'Dave, I'll walk back with you.'

Christina Zabrinski had had an academic upbringing. Her father had globe-trotted for years, spending his late twenties travelling to South America, progressing from consultant to senior manager of commerce and technology divisions in Brazil. He used to rack up air miles by taking flights when airlines ran special promotions, earning himself double points. Her mum still worked as a part-time paediatrician, having entered the profession after graduating from the Imperial College of London.

'What about your man, Dan, are you not meeting up with him?' Sherry said, adjusting the buttons on her coat. Christina had a male friend who she only saw occasionally. She kept him at a distance as she didn't want to become too involved with him, and she used him solely to be seen with to show that she had a man around. A bit of a puppet on a string was Dan, the relationship was solely on her terms. He was eager to become closer to Christina he had phoned Mars on at least one occasion to find out some information about her boss and try to discover her true feelings, and whether she just thought of him like a lapdog. Mars found it difficult to provide answers to his questions; she was on his side but didn't want anything getting back to her boss should things go wrong between them.

'Not this weekend,' Christina said sounding tired and looking solemn as she took a sip of her coffee.

Sherry sensed that the mood was dropping, that she saw that she had something playing on her mind and seemed to not want to talk about Dan. She had a distant look on her face. Maybe she was thinking of the striking Jeff Divine as she made a point of describing his looks so admiringly.

Sherry and Dave said their goodbyes and left the girls to their own devices. Christina watched them leave.

'How are you getting on with chasing that builder who carried out the work on your kitchen extension Christina?' Mars said, breaking a small silence between them. She felt a tad guilty for asking, thinking that it might spoil Christina's lunch break.

'Oh, that. Well he had thirty days to pay from the date of the court case in December, but hasn't so far.' She pulled a face of apprehension. 'So I've sent a threatening letter. Let's hope he reads it and is intelligent enough to respond. I'd certainly like to get it sorted out sooner rather than later. I want to see him hung up!'

Christina suddenly changed the subject.

'We'll have to meet up, just the four of us. You'll have to bring Jeff along one night to meet Dan, so we can go out as a foursome. How's that sound then?'

'That would be nice,' Mars said, cautiously, looking quickly away from Christina in order to hide her lying expression.

'OK, I'll book a table at a restaurant in Chiswick, then.' Christina seized the moment when Mars briefly agreed. 'What's best for you, a Friday or Saturday night?'

Mars had to think quickly. Did she want Jeff to meet with Christina again? It could be to her advantage, it could be dangerous. You couldn't tell her friends from her enemies. She had a lot of the latter.

Nineteen

Jeff eased open the front door of his flat and noticed something lying on the floor. He bent over and picked up his morning mail. He pulled out the letter he was dreading. Carefully tearing the top of the brown envelope with his front door key, expecting nothing but gloom inside.

He opened the court letter and stared intensely at it. His fears were answered. He knew this was coming, he had felt it for some time. He sat on the stairs and read it through. It was the final demand to pay damages of £16,182. He looked at his mobile phone. It was just after six in the evening.

He felt that there was no way out of what he had just read. He was cornered, stuck, trapped. He felt lost and isolated. There was no one around, he was all by himself with no one to talk to.

He made his way into his kitchen and opened the fridge door. He pulled out a cold can of lager, flipped up the aluminium ring and poured the majority of the contents into his throat in one fell swoop.

He was holding a piece of paper that told him. "You can't afford to pay this". He couldn't afford to pay it today, tomorrow or next year; he just didn't know how to cover the cost. Maybe he could take out a bank loan, but that would be a loan hanging "around his neck" for some considerable amount of time, and that was the last thing he wanted. He only wanted to maintain his life the way it was - debt-free, with no hassles and no big bills. The debt was a demand for payment and it couldn't be ignored.

'I need to speak to some people,' he thought. 'Firstly, my solicitor. I'll do that tomorrow.

'Sixteen thousand pounds!' exclaimed Martin. 'How the hell did that happen then?'

'It's a long story, Martin,' Jeff said feeling stressed by his reaction.

'Well, explain it to me, son?'

'It was a building project that we carried out in Chiswick, an extension, and one thing led to another. I employed a couple of guys. I thought that they knew what they were doing; in fact, they probably did. They made a mistake with part of the work, and then took advantage of me, took advantage of the freedom they had without me around. Some things happened that I didn't expect. They used an inferior mix of concrete for the foundations of the building - they got a cheaper company than the one that I specified to lay the mix. They fabricated the invoice to steal some money from me, and then a few months later, cracks started appearing down the inside wall.

I didn't supervise the job that well as I was trying to finish off another job I was behind on. I had an architect looking after some of it for me. Anyway, they left me in the crappy stuff, big time, without a shovel, know what I mean? And one of them had worked for me for some time, he was a sort of a mate,' he said looking concerned. 'Things went belly up, and here I am now with this bloody debt. I know it's a lot, but somehow I just have to find the money to pay it.' Martin wiped the perspiration from his forehead with a towel while he listened to his friend's woes.

'This is becoming serious. I found out who her bloody solicitors are,' his voice sounded restless.

'So, go on, - who are they then?' said Martin.

'They are Greenfield and Lewis, they once won a case for Richard Branson against British Airways on route fixing, so you can see what the bloody hell I am up against can't you? What bloody chance have I got, eh?'

Martin was sitting on a workout bench in the gym, his face full of remorse. There were people next to them on running machines, panting and sighing. There was a clanking sound of metal weights.

Martin was a friend of Jeff's - they got to know each other from attending the gym. He was twenty years older and somewhat wiser. Jeff found him easy to talk to and on occasions, they would go for a beer after the gym. Martin was married, so he never stayed out for too long but was always up for a chat.

'So, how much was the original cost of the construction, then?' he said philosophically, trying to put some figures together in his head.

Jeff ran a hand across his forehead, and then through his hair. He peered at Martin, then hesitated before replying.

'Well, it was around about twenty-five grand. And now it's about sixty percent of that to put it right.'

'How come?' Martin's face showed concern. 'What the hell went wrong to cause that amount for the repairs?'

'She's doing me for the lot, mate, lock stock and effing barrel. The underpinning, the bloody foundations, she's had the majority dug up and redone.' He was waving his hands, showing Martin the shape of the building. 'She's doing me for rebuilding a flank wall, plastering, new patio doors, and roof tiles. She employed a structural surveyor and a company to put the lot right, and then sent me the bill. I tried to correct the problem, but without the correct information from the guys who carried out the work and the backing, I didn't know where the problem was. I ran out of time, and she ran out of patience, and now I have this bloody bill.' He ran a hand down his face.

'Can't you get hold of the guys who worked for you, and who put you in this mess, and let them pay for some of the damage?'

'Chance would be a fine thing Martin, but the main one has disappeared. He's moved away from where he lives, and he's changed his mobile number. Besides, he won't pay up, he hasn't got the money, and he likes a bit of coke now and then, so that's where his money goes. I've been out looking for him - I went to his flat where he lived, but the bastard has just disappeared, he's moved away. He made some money out of the job, and spent it. Besides, he knows I would kill him if I saw him.'

Jeff turned away and ran his gaze around the gym, noticing that a number of the people seemed intent on looking like they had just flown in from a beach in California.

'Did you go to court with this woman, Jeff?'

'Yeah, sure I went to court to put my case over, what bloody case I *had*, and to meet her face to face, once and for all. It was hardly the right sort of circumstances, though.'

'And?'

'And she wasn't there, she didn't turn up. She sent along a solicitor in her place to fight the case. She was smart enough to know that she had too much evidence against me, and I really had no defence. She had no reason to turn up - she knew that she'd won the case already, so she probably didn't want to waste her time. Very clever, I thought. When I walked out of the court, her solicitor gave me a reassuring smile at the end. And a smirk, great! The judge also seemed happy to see a dodgy builder on the losing side as well.'

Jeff knew that he had not been dealing with just anyone here, he was dealing with a woman intent on winning. So, how was he going to get out of this mess he was in? He knew that he could not pay the debt outright. He knew that she would come for him if he didn't pay for it. Still, it wasn't going to defeat him, he wasn't going to lie down without a fight.

'So, what do you think then, Martin?'

'What do I think?' He pondered. 'What if you make her an offer, maybe offer her half, see what she says. You can only ask. There can't be any harm in trying, can there?'

'Good idea, but I don't even have *that* amount, mate!'

'Well, I think you need to find yourself a bloody good and expensive lawyer. I hope you've got one, haven't you?' He looked thoughtfully at Jeff.

'Well.' His face said that he didn't.

'Or one of those rich women that you meet, and that you go on about, preferably a generous one, one with a few pounds in her bank account.'

Jeff looked thoughtful. 'My life is boiling over. It's happened before…' he said to himself. But a few names came to his mind.

Twenty

A Day Later

'Hi there, Jeff, what a lovely surprise! Good to hear from you. To what do I owe the pleasure of this call Jeffery? I'm flattered,' came back Shabina's sultry answer.

'Oh, I was just driving past your house, Shabina,' he said, knowing that he was nowhere near her. 'I thought I should check up on a good-looking girl.'

'You are as enchanting as ever, Jeff Divine! You don't change, you know,' she said in surprise. 'I was thinking of you recently - what have you been up to?'

'I've been working my butt off, Shabina, as usual. You know how it is.'

'Ah, I'm so upset for you, Jeff,' she said mocking him.

'And be careful of that butt of yours.'

'I thought you would have some sympathy for me, Shabina?'

'Of course I do, darling. So, you haven't met yourself a young wife yet and swept her off her feet then, have you?'

'No, not yet. Anyway, who would take me on?'

'Ha-ha, very funny, Jeff! You have a good sense of humour. I know a few people who would take you up on that offer, darling.' Jeff decided to seize the opportunity.

'Oh yeah? Anyway, seeing I was in the area, what are you up to? Are you free for a coffee, sometime in the future maybe – only, of course, if that wretched husband of yours lets you?'

'Funny, Jeff, you know I would love to meet up. I have a soft spot for you, Mr Charmer. My wretched husband, as you call him, doesn't come into the equation,' she said, with a joyful sounding voice.

'Don't you think that's a little bit harsh, Jeffrey? Murder a woman because you owe her sixteen thousand pounds, darling, isn't that overstepping the mark a little bit too much? Have you not thought it over enough? There must be another solution to this, an easier way out. I didn't realise that you had that amount of anger inside of you, Jeffrey Divine!' she said in an understanding tone. 'She's entitled to chase you for her money, isn't she? If you undertook work for me in the same manner, and you messed my building work up and caused a major issue, I would want compensation, Jeff, wouldn't I? It's only natural. I can see this woman's point of view. She's severely out of pocket, and she wants compensation for it. Your issues are with the labour force that you employed.' Shabina was offering her perspective on the situation that Jeff had just told her about. 'I mean, what sort of woman is she?'

'She's a bloody she-devil if you really want to know, Shabina, believe you me, and I doubt that I would be the only one wanting to afflict harm on the bitch. Besides, it's probably over sixteen grand I now owe her, with the interest.'

'My word, Jeff, that's an awful lot of money to owe someone, isn't it? It's a fantastic amount.'

Shabina stood in the doorway of her bathroom with a towel wrapped around her. Her long black hair was dripping water on the carpet, as the steam dissipated behind her. She had just finished her shower, when Jeff had broken the somewhat disturbing news to her that he felt the only way to prevent Christina Zabrinski from pursuing her claim against him was to shut her up once and for all, even if it meant ending her lifeline. She wasn't too pleased with what she was hearing. Shabina looked him in the eyes, and she felt that he meant what he had said. She didn't want to become involved with what he was thinking, and the scheme he had, even though she loved this man, and would have done anything else for him. She understood his plight and she would stand by him and support him in any way she could, but murder was not on her list. There was no way she was going to be involved in the killing of a woman and become an accessory.

Jeff lay on her bed with a sheet covering most of his masculine body. They had just spent the night together. Shabina stared at him as she tilted her head back and rubbed her hair with the towel.

'Why, do you know of anyone else who doesn't like this woman?'

'I can think of a few, darling.' His face was full of bitterness.

'When do you have to pay this—debt to her by. Is there a time limit?'

'Yes, Shab. It's overdue now, and she's on my case, sending me threatening letters, you know the stuff. She wants access to my bank account, and she's talking about putting an order on it so I can't use it - not that there's much in it, anyway.' Shabina cringed at her name being shortened.

Jeff twisted around on the bed as she listened.

'She's threatening to bankrupt me, but there's ways to get around that. I can talk to my accountant on that point.'

'You need to talk to someone. Can you pay in some kind of instalments?' Jeff looked up at her.

'It's too far gone for that. She wants the lot, like, yesterday.'

'I can lend you some of the money, Jeff, if that's any help, but I can't lend it all to you.'

'You're a star, Shabina, you really are, and I may just take you up on that one.' He pondered for a moment. 'But I was thinking of a way to avoid paying for all of it. Maybe I'll just have to kill the bitch myself.' He laid back on the bed, and put his hands behind his head as she disappeared back to the bathroom, not wanting to hear about his murderous intentions.

Jeff stared at his reflection in the mirror on the ceiling and pictured seeing Shabina in it last night. He grinned, a long grin. 'Filthy cow,' he thought. 'Who would have a mirror on her bedroom ceiling - does she think this is some kind of brothel? Am I just one of her pretty friends? I wonder who else lays on this bed, then? I can't be the only bloke she sleeps with.' He turned to look at her, but she had gone.

They sat in the kitchen. They had spent the previous evening at a majestic wedding in St John's Wood. The bride was a niece of Shabina's, and she needed a man at her side. Jeff had called her at the right time. Jeff was intrigued by the grandeur and wealth on display at the function. Shabina liked Jeff, but knew he was only after her money to pay off his debt. She was his rich woman, as Martin calls her. She was tactile, generous, and a mature and gifted person. She continued to carry out some work for her rather wealthy and elusive husband, who was always away on business with what she described as one of his "other wives". She had accepted that they were no longer in a meaningful marriage. Her husband paid for her house and gave her an income, and she looked after their son in London.

She brought Jeff a coffee and placed it down in front of him as he sat at the kitchen table.

'Thank you, Shabina.'

'So, what's your next move going to be then Jeffrey darling, in this battle with this, so-called devil of a woman?' Shabina stroked his head with a hand as she returned the small silver patterned coffee pot back to its base.

'I've been thinking, thinking real hard. This woman doesn't know me, well in one guise she doesn't.'

'Pardon?' She sounded surprised by his remark. 'I don't understand, Jeff, what do you mean you do not know this woman. I was on the understanding that you undertook some work for her at her home. Surely you had some meetings with her whilst the work was going on?' she said, looking confusingly at him.

'Come and sit down and let me explain, Shabina.'

Twenty-one

Mars was faintly cautious of the night ahead; she had realised Christina was on a mission. She thought Christina was out to move in on her so-called "boyfriend" to try to see if there was any kind of strength in their relationship, to see if she could open them up and get between them. Mars could sense an air of consternation - she had to tread carefully with her boss, and she had to be on her guard. It could be an uncomfortable night ahead.

'Can I get you any drinks, please?' said the waitress. Mars ordered a soda water with lime.

'Not having a drink tonight, Mars, darling, that's rather unlike you, isn't it?'

'Maybe I'll have one later, Christy.' She pulled a customary grin, and thought, 'Nosey bitch.'

Jeff glanced at Mars as if to say that she needed to get herself into a comfortable mode. He felt a slightly nervy atmosphere, and he also felt Christina was getting herself in control. He knew things were going to happen and there would be some uncomfortable moments in the hours ahead. When Mars contacted him, he had felt that he couldn't let her down, as he became curious when Christina's name was mentioned, despite feeling that he should avoid her. He wondered how Mars was going to play it. He sensed an atmosphere.

'What business are you in, Dan?' Jeff asked as he pushed back his jet-black hair. Christina shot him a look.

'I design aircraft engines Jeff. I work at Heathrow.' Dan was tall, five-eleven, with dark-brown hair and a craggy complexion. His attire wasn't like Jeff's - he wore a plain mauve V-neck jumper with a white polo shirt beneath it.

'And how did the two of you meet, then?' asked Jeff, looking at Christina, then back at Dan.

'We met at a business lunch on exporting, in Chelsea, just over a year ago,' Christina said, hijacking the conversation, making sure that she answered the question. Jeff seemed a little surprised at her, thinking that she appeared to be jealous already. Dan sat silently. He wasn't going to challenge her - he knew that Christina was a feisty character.

'Daniel was there as a speaker on the trials of selling products abroad. Identifying opportunities for UK businesses and the understanding of local rules, cultures and preferences so you can make informed decisions.'

Dan seemed slightly annoyed at Christina's bolshie attitude as she answered Jeff's question. He was Christina's on-off boyfriend, he liked her a lot, but found it difficult to get close to her. Their relationship ran purely on her terms - she made the decisions and called the shots, and it was she who wore the trousers. Jeff was slightly surprised at her officious attitude. Mars sat there calmly but inwardly annoyed by Christina's overbearing mannerisms.

'Are you from around here then, Jeff?'

'Not too local, Dan. I live in Ruislip mate,' he said, lying through his teeth.

'And how do you earn your pennies, then?'

Christina smiled assertively at Jeff as the two became embroiled in conversation. Mars sipped at her fizzy drink and waited for the conversation to become more intense. She had met Dan before and was thinking about how she could unload Jeff onto Christina.

'So, are you two going strong together?' Christina said, butting in again, as she looked at both Mars and Jeff. She was resting her chin on her propped-up hand, waiting for their reply.

'Yes, we are,' replied Mars quickly. 'It's been about four weeks now,' she said, smirking. To Jeff's astonishment, he felt Christina's foot rub against his leg. He didn't flinch, and managed to keep his cool.

'You look familiar to me, Jeff. I'm not quite sure if we have met in the past... Have we met before, Jeff?' He blushed slightly, something he rarely did. He picked up the jug of water from the table and poured some into his glass, took a mouthful and glanced at her as she kept her focus on him.

'No, I don't think so, Christina. I would remember if we had. Jeff grinned at her. Mars stared at Christina, thinking that this was probably one of her ploys as she was trying to coax Jeff away from her. Mars was unaware that someone had described the builder, Jeff Turner, who had carried out the work for her on her new extension, to Christina. Mars had to butt in to stop her in her tracks.

'Maybe it's Robert that you're thinking about, Christy.' She picked up the jug of water.

'Anyone else need lubricating?' She smiled.

'So, you like each other, then?' Christina said with suspicion, her eyes peering at them both. She knew that something wasn't quite correct between them and could sense an uneasiness in their relationship. Mars didn't like the question - she found it impertinent and decided to change the subject to avoid further intrusions.

'Where do you live, Dan?' she said with haste, glancing at Christina, and then moving onto him. Jeff gave Christina a cunning look. Mars felt that her boss was beginning to bite too early, and she didn't want her prying into her private life. Anyway, it was nothing to do with her. Jeff also felt some pressure as he found her questions too profound.

He thought, 'How the hell does she not know who I am? I'm sitting here, two feet away from the woman, an influential woman, and someone to whom I owe sixteen grand? How come she hasn't worked it out yet, how come she hasn't joined the dots together? But I suppose tonight I'm Jeff Divine and not Jeff Turner - that's the missing link, the surname.' He felt he was walking barefoot on broken glass, but he also found the circumstances very intriguing. Yes, he liked Mars, and liked her company, and found it a fascinating coincidence that he was in this situation but, overall, he loved the adrenaline rush. He felt a sense of power and control, and that Christina liked him, and he knew that she was trying to entice him away from Mars. He loved the attention of this very Amazonian woman.

They were eventually sliced apart by a glossy Thai menu shoved at Dan's chest by a marauding Christina, intent on bringing them back into their evening. 'It's time to order now, darling,' Christina said, sardonically fluttering her eyelids at Dan and thinking, 'Wow, I would like to go home with Jeff.'

Twenty-two

She stared up at him to see his roguish grin. His Mediterranean complexion matched his tousled wavy black hair. Beads of sweat trickled from his brow, easing their way down his temple and finding the grittiness of his cheek. The perspiration anoints her skin.

Moonlight shone in from the window and onto his bronzed torso, giving it a two-tone effect, that accentuate his olive skin making him look like a Roman emperor in a film. He was her hero.

A current of electricity ran down the length of her body and she felt a fire in her groin as she licked his skin, tasting the salt in his sweat.

She glanced at the protruding veins in his supple but muscular arms that were pushing his skin outwards as they held his naked, powerful and masculine body above hers. She groaned as she shook her head from side to side, her hair flicking across her face. His breath blowing onto her skin, like a breeze from an autumn shore. It was cool and invigorating. His voice was moaning with gratification. It was a sound that she had missed - she hadn't heard it for some time, at least not from someone whom she loved. It had been too long, and her life had been baron without it. Her past lovers had done nothing for her, unlike this Casanova of hers.

The feel of his skin against hers sent a pulsating sensation through her, it was like she was travelling through a swirling vacuum with him, spinning and twisting together through a dream. She felt honoured to be in this man's company. She kissed and sucked his moist lips, and her tongue explored his teeth as she ran the tip of it around them. He returned the delight, pushing his to the roof of her mouth, swirling his tongue in revolving movements.

She felt his hips pushing against her hips. His hands caressed her body, fondling, stroking and teasing her. She felt the heat from his body and cried out as he framed her face with the palms of his hands while he thrust down harder on her. Air oozed from her lungs like a small explosion, air that she thought she never had. She closed her eyes. She forced her pointed red fingernails into his soft supple buttocks in unadulterated pleasure. She saw darkness behind her eyelids as she remembered what it had felt like with Robert some years ago. The man of her dreams, who had never been far from her thoughts since he departed from her life. This man was more athletic, more tanned; he was taller and stronger, but just as passionate and sensual.

He paused his movements, and then she opened her eyes just in time to see him opening his. That was a sign of endearment for her. They didn't speak, they just gazed at each other. His blue eyes looked like diamonds.

She felt his warm breath and breathed in his fragrance. He tilted his face and looked down at her chest as she enveloped her legs around his and plunged him forward in passion. She felt physical joy and pleasure. She smiled to herself.

Moments later, his back crashed onto the crisp cotton sheets. He felt heavy. He lay there, panting deeply. Christina twisted around and faced him as she lay on her side. She touched his smooth skin and stroked his arm with the tips of her fingers. She began to scratch at his flesh with one of her painted nails and felt pleasure run through her body. She admired him - this was the sort of man she wanted in her life, this was who she wants on her arm when she walks down the street, or into a restaurant together. She wanted him to show off to her friends, work colleagues, strangers, anyone she could. She wanted to flaunt this person. She wanted to smile and say, "He's mine".

She pulled the sheet up to her shoulder. There was a chill in the air. The bedroom curtain flapped in front of the open window. Her eyes caught her clock on the bedside cabinet. She pondered for a while. It was dark, apart from a small light shining over her from the outside.

He murmured as he fell asleep. She felt somewhat disappointed that he had left her alone, but she was also satisfied that she had finally got to go to bed with this charming and delightful person. Christina slowly turned over, glanced back at him to make sure it was true, and that he was still there. She smiled, turned away and lay motionless.

Her eyelids became heavy. She was weary, and she drifted off into a deep sleep.

Christina was rudely awoken by the clanging together of glass milk bottles, sounding somewhat like a poor musical instrument, as the milkman showed no respect for the sleeping inhabitants of Bollo Lane.

'Why can't they use cardboard cartons instead of glass bottles? It's so annoying,' Christina thought as she cracked her eyelids open. The clock read five-forty-two. She twisted around and peeked at him, He was still there, lying stationary, the sheets covering him up to his waist. There were only soft breaths coming from his mouth as he slept in silence, like a baby.

Dan lay there, oblivious to the world, his arms stretched above him, and his head resting on the pillow. She turned back. 'Not quite my Italian caballero, but hey, anyone can dream, can't they?' She smirked and squinted her eyes, and it was a fantastic dream. 'If only,' she thought. She smiled to herself as thoughts ran through her head. She pulled the sheets over her and drifted off.

Daylight eventually crept through the side of the curtains, disturbing Dan. He turned over onto his side, taking most of Christina's warmth with him. He said something alien to himself and grunted, but he was still asleep.

She eased her legs out of the bed and rested her feet on the floor. She sighed, and turned and looked at him, then picked up her shirt and headed towards the door, and the shower.

Twenty-three

She got out of the shower, her long legs stepping onto a small mat as some droplets of water covered the tiled floor. She held up a towel, and wrapped it around herself before heading along the hallway and towards her bedroom.

Mars sat at the dressing table, then began her daily routine of applying her make-up and choosing her clothes for the day ahead.

But this day would be a little different in several ways. Her make-up had to be applied with a little more grace and skill, her clothes had to be some of the finest in her wardrobe - only the best would do today. Tom had been dispatched to her mum's last night, so that she could be alone and plan for the following day by herself. She didn't want her little soldier interfering with her precious time this morning. He was going to be spoiled by his nan, maybe even get his favourite meal of 'spag bol' cooked for him, followed by a dessert of chocolate mousse, if he was good, but then he was always good. Even when he was bad, he was good.

She had plans to prepare, tactics to work out and she had to go over some last-minute paperwork and make some final preparations for the meeting she was about to have with her boss.

She was in a confident mood, but not assured that the vacancy was going to be hers. She had worked hard for this day to come along and end up to her advantage. Christina had dropped numerous hints that the job was hers. They had had their differences along the way, but Christina enjoyed the tension between them. She liked the way Mars stood up to her on occasions and admired her business acumen. She had the fight and determination that Christina wanted from her staff. Although her boss always seemed to come out on the winning side and have the last word. Mars enjoyed the challenge. She had been Christina's apprentice for far too long. Now it was time to step up into her boss' shoes.

But she had a small problem – Morgan Cable, he was the sticking point. She remembered her friend Sherry's words, "Don't count on it

Mars, she's unpredictable". She had thought about those words long and hard, and they stuck in her mind for some time.

She looked in the mirror as she ran her best, "made in Paris" pink lipstick from left to right across her top lip, squeezed both lips together, then parted them. She sighed audibly. It wasn't the right colour.

Mars buttoned up her blouse. It covered the top of her black stockings. She wasn't happy with what she saw and noticed a ladder on the left one. She swore violently as she rifled through the top drawer of her dresser and pulled out the only pair of tights fit to be worn. She held them up and said, 'Bloody passion killers,' throwing the laddered stocking onto the floor in disgust.

She stood sideways in front of the long mirror, practising a look of authority. She looked at herself and pushed her hands down both hips to straighten her black skirt. She couldn't feel her suspenders and felt that she didn't feel dressed enough.

'Maybe I'll pick some stockings up on the way into the office.' She opened a slim cardboard box, pulled out a foil packet of tablets, pushed against a tightly packed capsule and released a caffeine pill. She threw it down her throat, then repeated the procedure with a second, and then a third one. She took a drink of water and washed down the tablets.

Mars looked at the time and then quickly sprayed on some of her favourite perfume from a dark glass bottle.

The early morning train was packed. It was almost full as she stood gripping onto a steel handle. Mars was travelling the four stops from North Ealing to Hammersmith, her place of work.

The carriage was unusually crowded. Most days were generally not as busy as this.

She had found herself staring at someone, someone she recognised. 'I know that face, she thought. I've seen him somewhere... Where on earth could that have been? She turned away and fell into deep contemplation, then turned back and moved slightly closer. 'Yes, it is, it's him, it's Silvio Berlusconi, *ll Cavaliere!* The former Italian prime minister. He looked happy enough, but then again, he always looks happy, and he was wearing a broad smile.'

He wore a dark jacket and a white shirt with a thin cotton tie. He was on the front cover of one of the passenger's broadsheets. His face was so close to hers that she could smell the print. It said that he was the third richest man in Italy. Mars continued to read on about the billionaire prime minister. It stated that, in 1996, a mafia informer declared Berlusconi and Dell'Utri were in direct contact with Salvatore Riina, also known as Toto Riina, head of the Sicilian Mafia in the 1980s and 90s. 'Still, I wish I had some of his money. That reminds me, I wonder if Tom had his favourite meal of spaghetti Bolognese at Mum's last night. I'll ring her when I get out of this sardine-infested capsule. But Mum's probably too busy at the moment, getting him ready for school.'

The train moved off from its second stop and jolted nearly everyone standing in the carriage. Regaining her composure, Mars continued to read the front of the free newspaper. The owner seemed to be oblivious to her - he was probably a sports enthusiast, and appeared to be enthralled by the back page, allowing the front to be on view to all and sundry.

A column on the right of the front page said that there had been a murder in Moss side, Manchester. A young man had beaten his wife to death, and all because she had failed to let him see his two daughters, aged eleven months, and two and a half years, purely to spite him because he had had an affair with an ex-school friend of hers. She was twenty-three years old, and her husband was twenty-seven. Mars became fascinated with the horrific story. 'Those poor kids,' she thought. It went on. "The husband had stormed into the marital home after being out all day on a drinking and drug-consuming binge. He had beaten up his estranged wife, tied her with some rope to the bannisters, and then beat her again until she lost consciousness". At the time of the murder, he was fuelled by crack cocaine. She couldn't quite believe people like this man were walking the streets. The husband had been found guilty of first-degree murder and was looking at life in prison. He was to be sentenced the following week.

The owner of the paper moved it away from his face, and flicked it to straighten the top, making a crackling sound as he did so. As he turned it over, their faces met, and he threw Mars a polite grin, then turned the paper around to view the front page. Mars was now forced to read about the sport events that had happened the day before, the article that the man had been engrossed in. She learned how South Africa had shattered Australia with a record 438-run winning chase.

'That's a lot of goals to score in one game,' she thought. Mars didn't understand the rules of cricket and couldn't work out how it took them days on end to finish a game. She turned away from the daily paper and focused on the carriage.

Some people were coughing, some were reading books, and others frowning at their mobile phones.

'I bet that bastard of a husband gets life. He deserves it, and I will be intrigued to find out.'

Mars wanted the position, she had decided that it was for her, she was sure she could do it justice... and she was ready, she had determination flowing through her. But she had a rival in Morgan Cable, who was a sharp, no-nonsense talking realist. In his late thirties, he was also expecting to get the nod from Christina.

He had been a Walmart retail manager in America for six years before moving back to the UK and working for a large insurance company claiming he had moved back because he was homesick. The only blot on his CV had come from being a witness in the trial of an ex-boyfriend who had fleeced thousands of pounds from his victims by pretending to be an MI5 agent. He had also stolen nine thousand pounds from Morgan. When Zurich insurance had stated that he was unreliable due to his own experience of being duped, Morgan had taken it upon himself to part company with them.

He carried a wealth of financial managerial experience. Christina was leaving her position, and Mars had had a phone call from her the previous Friday, late afternoon, asking her to come to her office at eight-thirty this morning. 'OK, it was short notice,' she thought. 'But that's life at the top.' And it meant dropping any plans that she might have had - work had to come first.

Christina had decided who was going to succeed her at Hammerson Shaw. Mars was smartly dressed in a black pencil skirt and an off-white blouse but she was on edge as she stood outside waiting for Christina. She removed a piece of fluff from her shirt as she entered the office.

Twenty-four

'I am sorry, Helen I have made my decision. You are well-educated, worldly, and hard-working, but not exceptional. Morgan Cable has more financial experience, and that's what the company needs at this precise moment in time. I'm under no further obligation to tell you why I haven't chosen you,' Christina said, in a qualified voice.

'I'm sorry, and I can understand your annoyance. It shows your tenacity. I wouldn't have expected you to turn around and walk straight out the door.'

'You know how much I wanted this position, Christina.' Mars said fiercely, pointing a finger at her boss. 'We both know that Morgan is a slime ball. We've spoken about him before, haven't we Chris? How he has enemies in the company, and how at times he causes unrest. I cannot believe your decision.' Her voice was aggressive, as she looked blankly at her boss. She was shaken by Christina's decision.

'I have made my mind up, I'm sorry. I also have a meeting at 9:00. It's a closed book, Mars.'

Christina glanced at her sparkly watch. She was sitting on the side of her heavy wooden desk next to some immaculately laid out paperwork, a pen was placed evenly next to it. Her thigh was taking most of her weight, one leg snaked around the other. Mars looked out of the office window at the traffic moving methodically along the A4. The grey clouds appeared to be moving faster. A devious thought began flowing through her mind. Should she say now what she had begun to think? Was she courageous enough? What would the reaction be from her superior? Would Christina hold it against her? Would she condemn her, would Mars find herself in the position of no longer working for the company, and be told to leave, on the spot, today? She could find herself without a job and a severely dented track record. But she had no alternative but to say what she was thinking, she couldn't walk out the door without expressing her feelings and her thoughts, and she wasn't going to leave the office knowing that she had something to say, something significant, and something that just may turn things around and get that bitch of a woman to wonder if she had made the correct decision this morning.

The two women looked at each other with sharp eyes. Mars had a plan waiting, an alternative strategy, but she had not decided when it should be put in motion. Maybe this was the right time. Perhaps it was the only time.

'Christina,' Mars said carefully, in a thoughtful voice. She scrutinized her boss, interlocked her fingers and squeezed them together as she sighed, looking down at her shiny leather shoes. 'What's the worst thing that can happen?' she thought. 'How is it going to pan out? Thoughts spun around in her head, and the palms of her hands became clammy.

'Yes, Mars, what is it?' Christina replied sharply, in a strained tone. 'Is there something you want to say?' If so, it must be quick!' She looked musingly at her work colleague.

'Yes, yes, there is something that I want to say to you,' said Mars in a measured manner. She paused for a moment; the atmosphere was tense. Christina moved from her position off of the desk and stood up. She ran a hand down the side of her dress as she stayed silent, waiting to find out what her work colleague's words would be. She was slightly mystified. Was Mars going to try and twist things around and convince her that she should be the chosen one? She couldn't imagine what her argument could be. Time was running short, but she would make an allowance for her.

Mars's eyes moved up to Christina's, then down, and then back up again. She cleared her throat. This was a big moment for her, probably the biggest in her working career. Here she was, an understudy to this powerful and influential woman. She was facing her boss of several years and she knew that she wasn't as ruthless, but she was tenacious. And she had a secret weapon.

'It's about, Jeff, Christina.'

'Jeff! I'm sorry?' exclaimed Christina, sounding shocked.

'And how has Jeff got into this conversation, Mars, can you please enlighten me? I am intrigued to know.' She appeared startled and thrown off guard by the subject. She scoffed.

'I've seen the way that you look at him.' A sneering look entered Mars' face, 'I know you quite like him, and I've seen you flirt with him. I've seen *him* flirt with you.' She hammered the point home to the woman who was now her nemesis.

Christina was astounded by what she was hearing. She felt a little off balance, but wanted to hear more. Yes, she liked Jeff Divine... She focused on Mars, eager to hear what she was going to say about this enigma of a man.

'Well?' she demanded, her voice prickly.

'He appears, on the surface, Christina, to be your sort of guy.'

'Pardon!'

'*He's* the type you go for. I noticed it from the first time you set eyes on him at your drinks party, at your house, in January. You couldn't take your eyes off him, and your bottom jaw was nearly touching the floor. You knew at the time that he was with me, but you continued to flirt shamelessly with him in front of me, and in front of the other guests. Anyway, it was very good viewing at the time. I laughed. You probably didn't realise how engrossed you were with him. You were all over him.' Christina stood silent. Mars had her full attention now. She ground her teeth in annoyance and bitterness but remained still.

'Even when we went out as a foursome to that restaurant the other month... Poor Dan, he couldn't get a word in edgeways, could he? I saw the way you were looking at Jeff. You hardly took your eyes off of him, didn't you? You seemed mesmerised by Jeff. You certainly made sure that you sat opposite him so that you could touch his leg.'

'Who told you that?' she growled.

The two girls were looking at one another. Mars knew, through her stillness, that she had her boss pinned into a corner. She became more relaxed now that she had said what she wanted to say, and had got it all out in the open, knowing that Christina had no defence. Although that wouldn't stop her trying to deny everything Mars said to her.

'I am at a loss, Helen Marshall,' snapped Christina her voice sounding bossy. 'What are you trying to tell me? Is this all relative to our conversation, and the decision that I have made? Because if it is, it isn't working. If you want to walk out of this office now and forget what you have just said, it will be fine by me, and I will scrub it from the record, so long as nothing else is said about the matter, and it is not repeated to anyone. I will forget everything and I will pretend that I never heard it,' she smiled at her. 'I will say this conversation never took place.'

'Maybe it is relevant. Let me tell you something.' Christina breathed a long sigh, thinking, 'Do I want to hear what's coming next? I'm the boss here. She should be listening to me; I am the one in charge. But if I kick her out now, perhaps I will miss something significant. I need to know about the luscious Jeff Divine. I could go on to regret not hearing what she has to say about him. It may play on my mind, the not knowing, and why is Jeff entering this conversation anyway? I've just told her that she hasn't got the job, and she brings him into the fray. Is he her boyfriend? Or what, what's she about to say?'

Mars helped herself to the water on Christina's desk, pouring herself a glass from the large, half-full decanter. She didn't offer her boss any. Christina threw her a wily glance as some of the ice cubes splashed into the glass.

Christina said nothing as Mars took a healthy mouthful as if she were drinking a chilled beer on a hot summer's day. Christina felt a modicum of pressure. She looked at the top drawer of her desk.

'We are not an item, and we never really have been.' Mars looked Christina in the eyes. 'We are not joined at the hips, he's just someone to go out with, a bit of male company, do you know what I mean? He's, yes, bloody good-looking, tall, articulate, witty.' Mars turned her back on Christina and paused. 'And adventurous,' she said with a grin.

Mars had felt for the first time since knowing her superior that she was the one in control of the situation. Christina seemed in awe of her and had nothing to say. For once in her life, she was speechless. At heart, she wanted this man and she didn't want to let on to Mars that she wanted him this much. She perched herself against the edge of the desk and listened intently, with mounting jealousy, eager for the conversation to move on. She wanted to know more – was there a bad side? Was Jeff married? Was he going away, never to be seen again? Mars was going to get to her. She felt the atmosphere thicken with tension and she could sense that Christina wanted to know more – she could feel in her stomach that the balance of power shifting towards her. She could feel Christina's anxiety - she could almost feel her heart beating.

'So! What I want to suggest to you… is a deal.'

'A deal. Huh.' Christina blurted, 'I don't do deals. I make the terms. How the hell does Jeff Divine become a bargaining chip in getting this position? I don't quite understand your mind-set.' Christina was showing open resentment toward her work colleague. She pulled open the top drawer of her desk and fumbled at her box of Marlboro Lights. They were next to an opened box of flupentixol. She picked away at the cellophane wrapping with a fingernail, then decided not to light one. She threw them down and forced the drawer shut.

'Well,' Mars said with a pang.

'You just might be interested in what I have to offer you.' Mars was now standing some distance from her boss.

'And *what,* precisely, have you got to offer me, Mars? Time is pushing on, and you are running out of it. It's almost nine o'clock and, like I said, I have a meeting to attend.' Christina poured herself a glass of water from the jug, wishing it contained something stronger. She walked towards the window, gazed out at the morning light, and then turned to Mars.

'Your meeting can wait a few minutes, Christina,' Mars said, plucking up the courage to unleash her deal on her boss.

'Well, out with it, what is it?' Christina stormed.

Mars stood firm, she glared towards her rival, the sky was behind her, and she drew a breath.

'I can get you Jeff's mobile phone number. I am sure he'll be willing to talk to you – he's easy to talk to, easy to get on with… You know that don't you?' Christina had a startled look on her face. This answer had come out of the blue. 'And I am sure *you* would be pleased to talk to him, on his own, all alone, just the two of you, a quite meeting together.' Mars turned away from her boss momentarily; she walked towards the door of the office, then turned back and looked at her, waiting for a retort. Christina looked taken aback. She said nothing. She waited.

'When, or if I give you his number, I will walk away from Jeff, and leave you two to your own devices. I will take no further interest in him, and not see him any longer. I will tell him that we are finished and then erase his number from my phone. But… but it comes at a price - you do realise that, don't you?' Her voice was firm. Christina folded her arms.

'And what's this price, Ms Marshall,' she said arrogantly.

'The price being that you hand me your position in the company, and not Morgan Cable.' The atmosphere thickened. Christina looked angry.

'Huh! You are joking, aren't you? It can't be done, Mars. I have made my mind up as to who will take over my position in the company and my decision is final.'

'Who *else* knows?' Mars snapped.

'That's not for you to know. It's confidential, you should know that. And have you thought this through? I'm not too sure that you have.'

'Oh yes, I have. I have thought it through, Christina. Long and hard.'

'I don't think you have. Let's look at the situation, shall we?'

'What situation?' Mars snapped.

'If we went through with this, and if I became Jeff's girlfriend, we would still be working in the same office, and how could we face each other on a daily basis, me knowing that I had handed you a position purely in exchange for your so-called *boyfriend*?'

'He's not my boyfriend, Christina,' Mars replied. Christina peered suspiciously at her.

'How could we work in the same environment together? I can't see it working, can you Mars?'

'We could always work on different floors and occupy offices as far away as possible. Remember what I said, Christina. I will break all ties with Jeff, I will move on. I won't be marrying him, he's all yours, and I will be very professional about it.' Christina was expressionless. Her thoughts were swarming around in her head. She wanted Jeff, and knew he could be just a phone call away, but she didn't want to renege on her word. She was in charge and no-one told her what to do. Especially her understudy. Especially someone lower down the company ladder than her.

'I'll tell you what I'm going to do, shall I?' said Mars. Christina again stopped in her tracks and waited impatiently for the answer.

'I am on tenterhooks as to what it will be, Mars.' Her voice was acerbic. 'I *am* all ears.'

Mars pointed towards the office door. Her arm was straight and firm as if directing traffic. It was time that she played her ace card and called Christina's bluff.

'I'm going to walk out of here and get back to work. After work, I will be in The Empire bar. At six. By then, I will have already spoken to Mr Jeff Divine about the two of us. I have a feeling Christina that he would enjoy meeting up with you, and I will have his phone number waiting. If you don't show up, then I will understand, and wish you good luck in your new position. We are both adults, Chris. We both know what's going on, don't we? And I will accept your decision on our meeting this morning.'

'This is blackmail,' she raged. Mars could feel her vanity coming to the boil. Christina went to open her desk drawer in a temper.

'Call it what you want.'

Christina looked angrily at Mars. Thoughts were turning around her head, faster than a spinning top. Their eyes locked onto each other for a second. There was an awkward moment in the air.

The door sounded like the vault of a bank closing on her. She was locked in, on the inside, in the dark, and all alone. Christina looked contemplatively as the sound echoed in her head. She pulled open the drawer and removed her packet of cigarettes. She turned and gazed at her reflection in the window, lit one, and blew the smoke out rapidly. It billowed in front of her as she stared at the shape of the clouds. Her index and middle fingers were gripping her cigarette, pushing in its sides, as she drew on it, searching her mind for a response to her associate's underlining's demands. She realised she was in a dilemma, but she hated the idea of giving into Mars. If this ever got out, she would be ridiculed for it and embarrassed to have let herself be blackmailed by someone with less authority than herself. If the chairman found out, she would be told to resign.

There was a buzz from her desktop phone. She pushed a button to answer it. And heard her secretary reminding her,

'Mr Cable is waiting for you, Miss Zabrinski.'

Twenty-five

'Hi stranger! If it isn't the return of the Red Planet!' Jeff greeted her mockingly.

'Hi, how are you? Sorry, what's this Red Planet thing?' she replied.

'Mars, it's the Red Planet. That's what they call it, isn't it?' Jeff replied.

'Oh, ah, I see.'

'Sorry, Mars, I was just trying to kid you. It can't be working, so let's change the subject. What are you up to? Did you get the job that you were after? Did you topple your boss from her throne, then, knock her from her perch?'

'Not quite, Jeff, not quite, it's all ongoing. It's still to be decided.' *If only,* she thought.

'Oh, I see, it's one of them is it, it's still ongoing?'

'Yes, it is. Are you OK to talk for a few moments, Jeff?' Mars was on her lunch break. It was twelve-thirty, and she was sitting at a table outside a coffee shop. She was huddling up inside her fluffy jacket, wearing large, dark sunglasses, more to keep the wind out of her eyes than the sun. She only had a large latte as company. The sun was out. It was hardly giving her any heat, but at least the worst of the winter had passed.

'Jeff, I'm looking for a favour, a very big favour.'

'Oh, I thought you would never ask, Mars,' Jeff said sarcastically. He liked what he heard. He so much wanted to get to see more of this girl - he felt that the time he'd spent with her just wasn't enough.

'So, what's going on there between you two high-flyers then? I sense a problem somewhere in the camp… with that bitch of a woman boss of yours,' Jeff said in annoyance.

'I thought you liked her, Jeff! You do surprise me.'

'I do, oh yeah, sometimes. In a certain guise that is.' Jeff was trying to hide his anger at the Christina he owed a substantial sum of money to, and also try to pacify Mars about Christina, her boss, all at the same time. He was provoked by the question. He felt that he had come close to carelessly revealing his secret to her and was angered by the Christina who was chasing the debt he owed her.

'So, there's trouble, is there?' Jeff said, moving the conversation on.

'You may well be correct. There is a small problem, you could say that.'

'Well, out with it, girl. What is it, what have you got to say?' came the chirpy voice from her mobile.

'Jeff, it's… well, Christina Zabrinski would like to meet up with you.' Jeff tensed up, thinking, 'What Christina does she mean?' He was hoping it was the one he'd met.

He took a chance. 'Tell me something I don't already know, Mars,' came back an alert-sounding voice.

'Good. I'm so glad we are on the same wavelength, Jeff.' She now felt that her next question may become easier. She took a sip of her coffee, then clanked the cup back onto the saucer. 'So, how about a date with her? She's eager to meet you face to face. What do you say? There may even be romance in the air for you,' she joked.

'I bet she's flipping eager to meet me on a couple of accounts,' he said under his breath. 'Well, that was a bit upfront Mars. It was very forward of you.' Jeff was both flattered and somewhat disillusioned with the proposal offered to him. He thought hard.

'Well, I suppose the word "yes" comes to mind. What's going on between you two? Tell me more, darling. Are you up to something?' he said, thinking that one of them must know his true identity. He was unsure if they knew him as Jeff the builder or as Jeff the escort. He thought that if he walked away and refused the invitation, then he would never know. The temptation was far too great for him to turn down, and the buzz that he would get would be too great to miss out on. A great power rush was waiting for him. Was this the moment it all came out?

Mars told Jeff about the outcome of the meeting she had had with Christina that morning, and that she had lost out on getting the position she so desperately desired to Morgan Cable. She told Jeff that she would have to break ties with him if he were to go ahead with meeting Christina, that they were the terms which Mars had laid down to her, although nothing at that moment in time was set in stone, it was all assumption. Pure supposition. She had to hope that she could get these two people together at the same time and the same place. It wasn't going to be easy for her. She knew Christina was more than eager to meet Jeff by himself, but not under these circumstances. Christina would shudder if this episode got out to anyone. She would be outraged and would want Mars's blood if she ever let on to anyone or if anyone found out about their secret rendezvous. Mars was hoping that, at the same time, she could lure Jeff into the trap that she was setting. She had to play her cards very carefully - time was short, and there was no room for errors.

Jeff saw an opportunity and tried to seize it. He had spied an opening, one that he couldn't let go of. He had something on his mind. Something cunning.

'Oh, I get it. I'm a pawn, am I? A piece of meat for you two businesswomen to haggle over, to barter with. Now I get the picture,' he said, trying to lure Mars into *his* trap.

'No, Jeff, it's not like that.'

'Oh, I think it is!'

'Let me explain…'

'So, you're dumping me, are you? I'm heartbroken.' Jeff said butting in.

'Sorry…'

'Mars, I truly am. I don't know how I'm ever going to get over this moment, Ms Marshall' he said continuing to tease her.

'Look, Jeff, we are not exactly an item, are we? Come on, let's be honest. We have been on a few dates together, and we've shared some jokes and laughs, but you have your career and things and I'm a single mum trying to juggle bringing up a young child and furthering my career, and going out with a playboy is, well, not on my agenda at the moment. I'm sorry, Jeff.' A sniffing sound came from Mars's phone as if Jeff were in tears.

'You've hurt me and damaged me as a human being, Mars! I'm shattered.' Does she know something? he continued to think.

'Oh, come on, Jeff. You're winding me up a bit, aren't you?'

'Yes, Mars. I'm only joking with you, sweetheart. I can see your point. We've had some interesting times together. I love your company and I'm not stupid, I know Christina has a crush on me. I suppose I can fit her into my already packed diary somewhere.'

'I knew you could, big head,' she said half- heartedly.

'Pardon.'

'Er, nothing, Jeff, it must be a bad line.'

'So, when does the Amazonian woman want an answer by?'

'Thanks, Jeff, you're Divine,' she quipped. Jeff sniggered.

'I've told her I'll let her know by the end of work today.'

'Bloody hell! You don't hang around, do you?' Jeff replied.

'Well, she's leaving her position and moving up, and she wants it filled by next week at the latest. That's the pressure she's now under.' There was a slight pause.

'OK, Mars, on one condition.' Mars knew him well enough to know that there would be terms attached. She tried to play it down.

'What do you mean, on one condition?'

'Well, it's a quid pro quo, Ms Marshall. A date,' Jeff said.

'What do you mean a date?' Mars responded sharply, sounding somewhat surprised by his proposition.

'I've told her that if you agree to meet up with her, I will no longer see you, or have any contact whatsoever with you. I've just told you that, Jeff.' Her voice sounded slightly bemused.

'It's a case of, you scratch my back, do you know what I mean?'

'No, I don't know what you mean, Jeff. You said that you would like to meet her, and I've agreed to no longer be involved with you, and now you're asking for some kind of date. I don't understand. It has to be a clean break between us if you agree to meet Christina.'

'Mars, darling, you are not hearing me properly, are you?' Jeff said forcefully. 'One last date between us, Mars, and then that's it, you go your way and I will go mine, or this pact is off, finished, over, do you hear me? Do I make myself clear?'

Mars huffed.

'This isn't fair!'

'I'm afraid life is a bit like that Mars, isn't it?'

'So, what's next?'

'OK, a date this week. It's Tuesday today, so let's say, erm, Thursday, this Thursday.

'Thursday… Er… I can't make it this Thursday, Jeff, it's kind of short notice. You see, I've got a manicure after work.'

'*Change* the appointment,' he said firmly.

'Pardon me?'

'Mars, darling, you do so want that position, you do so want to become a vice president, don't you? Tell me you do.' She held her phone away from her ear and looked at it. His voice had become eerie.

'Yes, but…'

'No buts, Ms Marshall, if you want to dispose of our relationship, and you want me to take Christina off your hands for your career to grow and prosper, then I think it has to be a favour for a favour, don't you agree? I can't go lightly from you, Mars, you're far too nice a woman for that.'

'What does he mean, I can't go lightly?' She became puzzled by his comment.

Twenty-six

The saloon was brisk with locals, and passers-by. She retrieved a bottle of perfume from her bag and gave her neck a mist full of the fashionable perfume, she returned the bottle to its temporary home.

Christina was looking towards her, from afar, she was a shadowy figure, and she sat motionlessly. She looked creepy, as if she was mourning the loss of a close friend.

A bottle of white wine was tilting in a large silver patterned wine decanter on the table that she was sitting at. There was an extra glass. Mars noticed her, and she was drawn by the vacuum of her dark eyes. She looked like an old-fashioned movie star in a black-and-white picture. Her hair looked different to what it was like this morning.

Mars flung the strap of her bag over her shoulder, in an act to gather some courage. She stared at Christina, and moved resignedly to where she was sitting, not knowing the reception that she would receive from her feisty boss, assuming it would be a hostile one. She feared the worst but hoped that she was wrong, her thoughts were contradictory.

'Evening,' Christina threw her an indulgent smile.

'Been here long?' Mars said, studying the half-empty bottle of wine, and thought, 'Long enough to get through one and a half glasses of the French stuff'. The label told her it wasn't her usual order. She wondered why this was, was it a stronger vintage?

The modicum of friendship they once had had seemed to have frittered away when Mars walked out of Christina's office, eight hours and forty-eight minutes ago. There now seemed to be a barrier between them. They hadn't been the best of friends before, they were always clashing with each other. But Christina admired her ferocity, she liked the way Mars tried to stand tall in front of her, even when Christina had the upper hand in their battles. Mars would always say what she had to say, even when she knew Christina's decisions were final, and when Mars wasn't sure about them. Christina liked her for her astuteness. She couldn't remember Mars having a day off for being sick or ill, she was always in on time, she was punctual, she had full knowledge of the company, the way Mike liked to run it. But now the barrier was slightly wider. Since their meeting this morning, there was now hostility and betrayal between them. Christina had had little time to digest her thoughts and how she was going to resolve the feelings between them, Mars seemed to have thought out her strategy for some time, she had thought through her plan before entering Christina's office this morning, and caught her off guard.

Christina raised the cool bottle of wine, and poured her counterpart a glass, without asking if she wanted it or not. The air was as frosty as the side of the wine decanter.

'Thank you, Christina.' She picked up the glass, and took a sip, as her eyes scanned like a radar, looking around the bar, ignoring Christina's tantrum-like appearance, and waiting to hear her boss' next sentence, her heart rate increased. She felt stressed, because of what she had said to her boss this morning. She felt that now, it was down to Christina to do the talking. It would be up to her to start the next sentence. Mars didn't know what Christina was going to say. It could well be the end of her working time with the company. This could be her last day. Tonight, she could be fired, she could find herself having to look through the papers or on the internet tomorrow morning for another job, and she would have no answer to her boss's decision, seeing that some hours ago, in her boss' eyes, she had tried to blackmail her.

Loud sounds of laughter came from a bunch of blokes, standing at the bar. Mars smiled as she thought, I'm glad someone is happy this evening. 'Well, at least she turned up! What is she going to say?'

'Well, let's not sit here like a married couple having a domestic, Mars. How's the wine?'

'Good Christina, and thanks for the drink.' Mars thought that she would try to be as professional as possible, and would start by using her name in full, and not just Christy, even though they were now technically out of working hours. She was going to think that they were still at work.

'You've been with us now for some time, haven't you, Mars?'

'Uh, yes, seven years, I think?'

'Six!' came Christina's brusque reply.

'OK, six it is,' she said feeling belittled.

'You were angry this morning when I didn't choose you to succeed me as vice, weren't you?' Mars didn't answer. 'What makes you think you deserve my position over Morgan? Why do you think you can run the company better than him, is there something I don't know?' Her voice was domineering as if it were continuing from this morning's meeting. There seemed to be no let-off from Christina. Mars thought she would be in the driving seat, seeing that she had the ace card, that being Jeff's phone number, but it wasn't to be. Christina was still letting her know who was the boss, and she gave the orders, and that Mars was not in the driving seat. She took another sip of wine and looked at Christina.

'To be honest Christina, it's a fine line between Cable and myself, I understand that, and I understand how difficult it was for you to decide between the two of us. But now, I live for the job, you know that. I have youth and energy on my side and want to give my all to this company, but we've gone through all this before, haven't we?' She was becoming tired of Christina's interrogation of her.

'He has the experience,' Christina butted in.

'I know that, but since your position came up, everyone in the company knew it was going to be a two-horse race between Cable and myself. I've picked up some negative vibes about him.'

'Oh, and what are they Mars, tell me more please... about this negativity.'

'Well, I'm not going to dwell on the issue, I don't think it's fair to him, as he is not here to answer, only to say that he talks about people behind their backs.'

'Don't most people do that, Mars?' There was silence.

'Let's change the subject,' retorted Christina.

'Yes, let's,' came a sultry reply.

'So, where do you see yourself in five years' time? Could you still stay dedicated to the company for that amount of time, do you think? Could you still maintain the momentum?' she said, gazing at her understudy.

'I don't see why not!' came a nonchalant reply. 'I hope that the skills I've gained will help the company reach its goals, and I can take it forward in the coming years. I can continue to learn, take on additional responsibilities, and contribute as much value as I can.'

Christina had not formally interviewed Mars or Morgan Cable for her position, but only assessed them on their CVs which had been updated, and emailed to her recently, and she knew their capabilities, seeing as they were already employees of the company.

'Tell me, Mars, what is your weakness?' She paused.

'Well, I never want to be a loser Christina,' she cleared her throat. 'I still have ambitions in life that I want to fulfil, I have too much energy, and sitting around doesn't work for me. I would say that I can be too much of a perfectionist in my work. Sometimes, I spend more time than necessary on a task, or tasks personally that could easily be delegated to someone else.' Christina twisted in her chair. She raised her hand and called the waiter over; she had noticed the bottle of wine was beginning to become shallow.

'Another drink, Mars?' Christina was gearing herself up for the grand finale. She still had another somewhat tricky question to ask her antagonist. She needed to feel lubricated.

'Er, only a weak one please, Christina, white wine and soda will be fine, thank you.' The waiter disappeared.

'How's your son Tom these days is he enjoying his school?'

'Oh, he's good, thank you, he's getting on fine, and growing up fast, too fast I think.'

'Do you have anyone to look after him while you're at work during the day?'

'Yes, I have Mum, bless her, she's retired and doesn't live too far, and of course Silvia, my nanny, they're both around when I need them.'

'What about your ex, does he help you out at all?'

'He's around, occasionally, he's moved to Suffolk now, he's bought himself a small holding to rear sheep. He's also found himself a new girlfriend, so he's decided to stay in the area. We don't talk that much any longer, only about Tom.'

'He's rearing sheep is he, interesting, what kind of sheep if I may ask, not that I know much about the farming industry.'

'Suffolk sheep, believe it or not. He's always been into the great outdoors, he has around five acres now and makes a good living out of them. It's now one of my son's favourite sketches, drawing sheep.' Mars peered at her.

'Really,' Christina replied drily. 'So, you think that you can handle the burden that this job carries?'

'Yes,' Mars said tersely.

'It isn't a routine nine-to-five, Mars, it has its drawbacks. You would need to take work home and be required to drop engagements that you have made for the sake of the company.'

'I understand…'

'But it does have its perks,' Christina said, cutting her off. 'You get to travel first class.' She grinned ingeniously at Mars.

The slim waiter returned, he was dressed all in black, he placed the new drinks on the glass table. Christina handed the waiter a twenty-pound note. He thanked her.

'So, Mars. What do you think of your boss?' she said with a stern grin on her face. Christina sipped her drink and peered at her, waiting anxiously for the correct reply. It had to be good.

'I think that's an unfair question to ask Christina under the circumstances, don't you think? It's a question that I won't answer. You can gladly ask me another, and I'll consider it.' Christina contemplated her counterpart. The atmosphere was tense and there was an uneasy silence. There were sounds of clinking glasses, and people chatting with each other in the background.

'Well, Mars. You'll be pleased to know, I have reluctantly suspended my search for a replacement for my, favourable position.' Mars looked startlingly at her.

'You have!' she said with amazement. Although Christina was in the place where Mars suggested meeting, Mars still didn't know what decision she was going to make. She knew that she could be there to tell her that she had refused the deal, plus it would be an excuse to have a drink after work, and she wouldn't turn that down either. She was known to enjoy the odd glass or two of wine, as there was no one at home to share it with.

'Yes,' said Christina. 'There are one or two points that are still outstanding, and there are a couple of issues that need ironing out, so you see, my job is still open.' She threw a cunning stare at her rival.

'You're right, Morgan Cable *is* a slime ball, but that's not the only reason. There's other stuff that the staff have mentioned to me, but that's my problem. Plus, I want the phone number you have for me please,' she said hastily.

Mars put her drink on the table, she held the stem watchfully as she studied the colour of the drink in front of her, she spun the glass gently. She looked up at Christina.

'Jeff has told me to tell you that it would be a pleasure to meet up with you.' Christina listened with awareness.

'And, that he could possibly meet up with you in the next day or so. I have told him that I hope it goes to plan and that I will give you his phone number. I've said that no matter what happens between you both, whichever way it goes, I will no longer be involved with him any more… I wish you luck, Christina. I hope it's all plain sailing for the both of you, and that romance is in the air.' Mars finished off the remains of her glass, opened her bag, pulled out a business card and handed it to Christina. It had Jeff's mobile phone number on it.

'Thank you,' said Christina, as she looked at it imperiously. Mars picked up her handbag and moved triumphantly towards the door of the bar, and out onto the street. She realised that Christina hadn't given her an answer about the job that she was looking for.

The light was dimming, the pavement was damp. She raised her hand and hailed a black cab. She knew she still had one more obligation to fulfil before becoming vice president of Hammerson Shaw.

Twenty-seven

'You have reached your destination,' said the conservative female voice from the dashboard of Mars' car. She peered out of its window. The flats on the Ruislip housing estate looked oppressed. The blocks were square and uninteresting, and a tad shady, and it didn't appear that there were too many people around tonight.

A man appeared on the street, wearing an anorak, he was walking along the path on the perimeter of the estate. He was carrying two rather heavy plastic shopping bags. His shoulders looked like they were feeling the strain from their weight. His shoulders were arching over, and he looked as if he had walked a long distance from the supermarket, unable to pay for any form of transport to lighten the load, to make his journey easier.

Darkness was settling in. Mars looked up at a second-floor window on a balcony, it appeared to be in the direction to where Jeff had loosely described it to her, to meet him. She pulled the cuff of her jacket back. The time was 7:28pm.

She pondered a while. She heard cars revving in the distance, and wondered why the hell Jeff has invited her here, to this shabby place. 'Maybe he wants to get his wicked way with me?' She thought as she grimaced.

'He wants to get me alone, that's what this date must be about, he's invited me to his flat and he hasn't even mentioned that perhaps he'll be cooking a meal for me, the selfish git, he's getting nothing from me. But what about the job?'

Mars leaned over to the passenger seat, put her hand in her bag, retrieved a silver flask and spun open the metal top. She tipped some of the neat Jack Daniels down her throat. It instantly relaxed her. She looked out of the car window to see if anyone was watching her. The flask was then left on the passenger's seat. Again, she looked at the flats with angst.

She was feeling nervous about what may be lying in wait for her. She thought that maybe he lived somewhere more to his character, homely, cleaner, and tidier at least. This was tacky, and with a dead-end feel.

Her mind was made up, it was time to go. With her bag in hand, Mars opened the car door and began to move out.

'Christ!' She winced. A sudden, high-sounding noise of a car horn broke the silence. 'I should have looked. She felt foolish, and for a second scared, as a car whizzed past her. She shook for a second as the boy racer continued on his way. She felt the vacuum of the car pull at her. 'I wish I was at home, with my feet up, watching Emmerdale, with a nice glass of wine.'

Mars gathered her senses. Her black gloss high heels clacked on the grey concrete stairs as she headed up towards Jeff Divine's abode.

She moved up the grimy steps with caution, this was a place that she had not ventured to before in her life.

The paint on the thin wrought iron bannisters was flaky, grubby and sticky. A bicycle with its seat missing was chained to the black metal stair railings. The first door she passed had a large dent near to the bottom of it, it preceded a rubber scuff mark.

There was a smell of rubbish. A cat appeared from

nowhere and then shot out of the open lobby door. She thought that this was a baptism of fire for her. Graffiti donned the grimy walls. A blob of chewing gum stuck to a handrail.

Mars moved out of the stairwell and arrived on the second-floor balcony. Her immediate view was of a block of flats opposite, the same as the one she had just climbed. 'Déjà vu,' she thought. She looked down and saw her car.

There was a sound of a baby wailing from the adjacent block. 'How do people live this close to each other? I don't want to be here.'

She walked along the balcony passing other doors until she reached number forty-one. It had a green plastic door. She looked for a bell, but there wasn't one. But the door looked like it hadn't been closed correctly. Slightly ajar. The atmosphere around her seemed somewhat odd. She tapped the metal letterbox and glanced back down the balcony. After a minute Mars reluctantly eased open the door. She thought that maybe it could have been left open for her.

'Jeff!' She cried timidly. She peered inside, and down the short hallway. There were stairs to the right of her leading upwards, and a door to the left, which she presumed was the kitchen. She looked up, the bulb was missing from the ceiling light socket. Music was sounding from the room in front of her. Music that she hadn't heard before and certainly wouldn't want to have in her collection. It wasn't her taste, it sounded deep and heavy.

Jeff! Jeff, are you there, it's Mars,' her voice had more venom, she moved along the short magnolia painted hallway towards the door.

Suddenly, it flung open. She recoiled, and he stood, there in a silhouette.

'Sorry darling, I was miles away, how are you? You look terrific. Welcome to the pleasure dome.' He bowed gracefully.

'You frightened the life out of me Jeff,' she said infuriatingly. 'You took me by complete surprise, it scared me.'

'Oh, I do apologise sweetheart, I'm so sorry.' He leaned forward and pecked her on her cheek, 'Come here.'

Jeff embraced her. His arms engulfing her. Her face pointed towards the room, it was unnerving, with only a table lamp to light up the place. Through some half-opened curtains she noticed a razor blade sitting on the windowsill, and an opened can of beer on a cheap wooden table just below the window. There were some glossy magazines on the carpet. Without being a snob she thought it looked untidy and it lacked a woman's touch. It didn't seem to be his usual surroundings. He was always smart, sharp, well groomed. He always presented himself well, his shoes were always immaculate and well-polished. His clothing looked tawdry. This room didn't match his image, and he seemed agitated.

'Come in and sit down darling,' he said. 'I'll get you a drink.' He wore a cheap ten-pound pair of jeans, looking like they came from a supermarket, and a brown T-shirt, advertising Adidas. She removed her jacket and rested it on the sofa.

'No, not for me, thanks anyway.' Jeff took no notice. He picked up a glass from the table and poured some Chardonnay into it, from an already-opened bottle. He handed the drink to Mars.

'So, Jeff, is this where you live? I thought you lived, well, somewhere different?' she said looking around the out-of-date lounge. The cream wallpaper had mauve and amber stripes running lengthways. In some areas the paper was peeling away from the seams where it met the ceiling, making a V shape pattern.

'Er, no, well yes, it's my sister's flat actually, she's away at the moment, she's in Norfolk visiting our parents for the week, she hasn't seen them for some time, she's taken her little kiddie with her as well, so I'm staying here for a few days, while my flat is being decorated.' His voice was hesitant. 'Do you like it?' He held out a hand.

'Yes, very nice Jeff, it looks well, well lived in, I suppose you could say.'

'Anyway, thanks for taking up my offer Hel. So, what are you two girls up to then, are you still fighting with each other?'

'You could say that. There are a few things that are going on now at work, it's all getting a bit messy.'

'Messy ha! You want Christina's position don't you?' he said with a devious look on his face. 'She's moving up, isn't she?'

'She is moving up to Mike's position, that's right, and you know full well I want it. I've been after it for a long time.' She continued looking around the lounge. There was a cobweb in one corner of the ceiling.

'Jeff.' He raised his brows, 'I couldn't help noticing that I saw a razor blade on the windowsill over there.' She pointed her head in the direction of the item, as she took a sip of her drink.

'Blade?' he said sheepishly. 'Oh really.' He looked over at the window. 'I don't know my love, it doesn't worry you, does it? I can move it if you want?'

'No, no it doesn't, I just wondered what it is there for.'

'Maybe sis left it there, it must be hers, I guess.'

'With a kid around,' she thought. 'No, I don't think so Jeff Divine?'

The carpet was flowery, and out of date. The two main long walls of the lounge were painted caramel. There was a large cheap picture on the wall of a bridge in San Francisco, in a silver frame.

151

A cupboard formed one corner of the room, it was fronted by badly painted white glossed louvred doors, with cheap brass handles. It looked very nineteen-seventies. There was a large antiquated grey television embedded in the corner. A DVD player was on a shelf under it, Mars wondered if this was his sister's flat, it looked untidy and dated, and it lacked a woman's touch, but then Mars had never met Jeff's sister. She felt that he had come down in the world. She just wanted the evening to end.

Mars turned back around and noticed that Jeff was observing the gap between the two top buttons of her black lacy blouse. He spun his head sharply towards the music centre when she noticed him.

'What music do you like then Mars, anything in particular, I've got a selection of music here.' His back was now pointing to her.

'Not this,' she frowned. 'What the hell is it?' she quipped.

'It's something I found. It's rock music, it's OK, don't you like it Mars, is it a bit too deep for you?'

Mars looked at Jeff, he appeared to look wayward, as if he'd been drinking, but without the smell on his breath, he seemed spaced out as he sat down on the sofa beside her.

'I love your hair,' he commented. 'It's all neat and golden,' he glared at her. His blue eyes were wide and with a contorted look.

'I need it trimmed a bit but thank you for the compliment Jeff.'

'Do you have any desires, Mars?'

'Pardon. What do you mean, "desires"?'

'Do you have a dark side, you know, do you do anything out of the ordinary, any interests, you know, needs.'

'I don't understand you. I don't understand what you are saying,' she said sounding confused, feeling anxious, and not liking his questions.

He twisted around and moved his body towards her direction, he leaned closer to her, she tilted back with an astonished look. He gracefully pecked her cherry-red lips. She blinked a few times. He repeated the procedure, only this time the kiss lingered longer. He put a hand on her waist and squeezed it.

'Jeff. What are you doing?' She said all ladylike sounding taken aback. She didn't want to show him that she was easy prey for his advances.

'Relax, Mars,' Jeff said, thinking that this was the obvious reply. 'Just relax a bit.' He looked contently at her.

He then ran his four fingers of a hand down the side of her temple. She blinked. He then slowly dragged them back, bending his fingers so that they dug into her skin. He then pulled his fingers through her hair. Mars became relaxed, she began to enjoy the free head massage she was receiving. She let out a diminutive groan.

'Is that nice,' he said smiling. 'Do you like that?' She breathed in, hoping to take in his usual waft of expensive aftershave, but it wasn't there.

'It can be,' she said, her eyes slowly closing and waiting for the next movement he was going to perform. She felt slightly anxious and cautious of his actions. She would have to give into some of his demands, but not to all of them, she had to somehow balance what she was going to do for him this evening, to please him, and draw him into her as he said that he, "wanted a favour".

He then repeated the procedure. Her head was tilted backwards, and leaning against the sofa, her eyes were closed, and her face had a tranquil look. He ran his fingers through her hair again and then pulled it. She murmured. She also felt some of the wine taking effect.

And then, without warning he climbed on top of her, he embedded his knees into the cushions, and his legs now straddled her. She quickly flicked open her eyes and glanced up at him, he looked a powerful rigid like figure. Like a stone statue. His T-shirt was too tight for him, it looked a size smaller than his body. His two hands then slid down her temples, he arched his fingers and then dug harder into her skull and dragged them back.

'Thanks Jeff, this was a bit out of the blue, wasn't it?' She groaned with delight and was also becoming wary of his moves. He didn't answer her. He repeated the manoeuvre. He then released his hands from her head. He eased up, leaned over and turned up the music a notch. She watched him. He then pulled his T-shirt up, raised his arms, and flung it to the floor. His hands returned to Mars, only this time to the inside of her short black skirt, he slid them upwards towards her waist.

'Jeff!' She shrieked. 'What do you think you're bloody doing?' Her voice sounded startled.

'Everyone needs a hobby, Mars.' He leered.

'What!'

He ripped at her panties with his strong hands and tore at them.

'What!' she yelled. 'Christ Jeff, what the crap do you think you are doing?' Her eyes widened and she had a startled look. She tried to move forward but his large hands forced her backwards, and her head hit the sofa. A hand loosened a button at the top of his jeans.

'Jeff! What the shit is going on, what do you think you are doing, I'm not liking this, please get off me, please?' she tried to plead with him.

Then out of nowhere, and like a flash of lightning, a rope appeared in his left hand, faster than a magician producing a rabbit from a hat, it was twisted and worn. Trepidation entered her face. He had a look of deceitfulness. He had an evil look in his eyes.

She stared at it. 'What, what's that for Jeff, I don't like it!'

Like a cowboy he looped it around her neck, there were small ringlets at either end of the rope, just large enough for his wrists to fit into. He used them both. His hands were now resting on the back of the sofa, he eased them apart. The rope started to bite into her neck. She moved her hands towards it and tried to force her fingers to its inside and to protect herself from the rope going any deeper into her skin.

'Jeff,' her voice sounded gritty like it was full of sand. Her eyes opened wider than a deer in the dark staring at an oncoming headlight.

'Stop! I can't... breathe... Jeff, stop!' His debauched face was looking down at her as she tilted her head. He ground his teeth and her pupils dilated, as she began to perspire. She shook her torso from side to side.

'Please Jeff,' her voice was muffled. 'What are you doing to me... you're... hurting me. Please stop!' Her voice became strained.

She now felt trapped, her mind wandered as if she were drowning in an ocean all alone, and with nobody to turn to.

'Please,' she moaned. His eyes were full of provocation, she lifted her knees and tried to position them in a weak attempt to hinder his movements and to slow him down, but it did little good. The rope bit deeper into her neck as he tightened the grip. She twisted her head trying to wriggle out of his actions. Her skin was stretching and lines began to appear on her porcelain skin. Her face became pale and she began to weaken, and her skin looked flaccid. Her eyes moved up into her head.

He felt her body begin to weaken; life was draining from her. Her knees flopped back down and her legs shook, she gave up trying to defend herself, she was too weak and her attempt to stop him was in vain. His strength was too powerful for her. Her lips slowly closed, they were sapped of moisture as they stuck together, the music swelled in her mind and she was defenceless. She couldn't compete with his power.

'No,' she said in a timid voice. It sounded distant. She weakly shook her body, trying to stop Jeff from going any further.

She was unable to defend herself any longer and could sense that the end of her life was inevitably in sight. Objects spun around in front of her eyes as she weakened, some she recognised, and some she had never seen before. Strange shapes. Pictures of her childhood whizzed through her mind, her, sitting at a desk in her bedroom. Horses with wings, a picture of a wooden barrel, with metal straps. A sky that turned green. She saw Mabel Taylor in a white striped frock, smiling, with a gap between her teeth. A boy standing on top of a building, which looked like her son, or was it her primary school bully?

Was she dreaming, when was this going to end, or was her life slowly disappearing from her? Should she give up trying to fight, and hope that it would suddenly end?

Jeff was panting heavily as he began to release his grip. The coarse rope slackened from around her skin, he sighed as he looked at the limp figure of the woman whom he once called gorgeous in front of him.

He relaxed his grip, and the rope which dug into her skin began to loosen. He shook his arms trying to release the pressure of it from his wrists. He pulled at the knots to remove his wrists from the cord, his skin bore the marks where the rope had dug in.

He straightened up, still on top of his victim. His reddened face was perspiring as he ran the palms of his hands over it. He stared down at her white complexion, of her once beautiful face, her eyelids were shut, and the room was silent apart from his breathing and the needle scraping on the vinyl from the turntable as it continued revolving.

The sardonic music had come to an end. There were two people in the room, but he felt alone.

He gaped down at her dishevelled body, tilted his head up towards the ceiling and blew a long lingering sigh. He wasn't sure if he was happy or relieved at what he had just gone through. He had just performed an act that he had wanted to carry out for some time, it was a fetish that was on his "to-do" list, and he was unsure as to why he wanted to carry this act through. It had been a ludicrous fantasy of his for some time. He wanted to live on the edge of life at some point, to see what it was like to be a taker of someone's life. He stared again at the ceiling, and for one short moment he felt victorious, he felt influential, he felt that he was the lead role in a movie. Pleasure oozed over his body. Sensations ran through his veins. He felt in total control. Here, he had a victim beneath him, someone lifeless and someone that couldn't answer him. He wasn't sure if this was the correct victim as he had met other people whom he wouldn't have minded murdering, but this was this time, and the situation just arose. Maybe the killing of a beautiful woman had a creative purpose to it. The lust associated with erotophonophilia was too great for him to control. The fear of getting caught, or not getting caught was a risk worth taking, an ultimate adventure, maybe? But he felt that the time was here, and it was now, so that's why he continued with the feat. He wanted to kill Christina, but the situation hadn't arisen. 'Maybe next time,' he thought. 'Possibly, I'll get that ogre next time.'

There was a sound, there was a timid purr, he shot his head back towards her faster than a bullet from a rifle. Her parched arid lips pierced open, saliva had formed on them and had stuck them together.

Breath rose from the sigh she gave out from her mouth. Her pale-coloured face began to darken, she slowly moved her head to one side, and she let out a weak cough.

Her fingers slowly stretched as if she was searching for life. She moved her hand up and ran it around the front of her neck, feeling for indentations of the rope, it dropped back down like a lead weight. Her tongue moved across the edge of her top lip. Her eyes were still closed, she wasn't sure how long she had been unconscious.

Jeff's face looked relieved, he leaned across, put a finger into his drink returned it and ran it over her droughty lips. She shook her head aggressively from side to side. She breathed out and coughed again.

'You bastard… you're fucking perverted!' her voice was weak and coarse sounding. 'What are you up to… you could have killed me. There's something wrong with you.' She coughed a kind of splutter, as she struggled for air.

She opened her eyes and she flicked them, she was unsure as to what to do next. Her skin began to regain some sense of colour, and redness began to appear on her once-pale face. Her body was still weak.

'Get off me please… Jeff.' Her head was tilted to one side, she was feeling used and embarrassed. He smiled at her.

'I'm so pleased you're still with us Mars, darling.' He flung himself up to his feet, as he stood there, he scratched his chin with his fingernails, just as quick, she flipped over and crouched like a frightened lamb on the sofa. Jeff zipped up his jeans and took a final swig of his drink, it was warm. He looked guilty. He turned and walked towards the window, his hand moved the curtain to one side, as he stared out into the darkness, and he observed the bright lights in the distance. He was not sure as to why he carried out this dreadful act on a beautiful woman, a woman he liked and admired, a woman who was a friend to him. He'd realised it was the wrong person who he wanted to strangle, but the moment just arrived, suddenly, in front of him, it was all set up for him.

'What have I done?' he thought, his head was pounding. He could go to prison for this sort of attack on someone, on a person who was unwilling to participate, he could be locked up, put behind bars.

'Are you OK, Mars?' His voice was guilty, his back turned to her.

'No, I'm fucking not OK,' she coughed… 'OK, you nearly suffocated me just then, what the bloody hell do you think you were doing to me, is this what you got me here for, was all this planned?'

'No Mars, it wasn't planned, I just… I just got carried away with myself. It wasn't meant to be, trust me.'

'Carried away! I want to go now.' She sounded lost. Her head was pressed into a cushion, trying to hide her face from him. 'I feel dirty and used.' She wriggled around trying to find life, making sure that she still existed in the world. She eased her weak body up and stared at the spot where it happened, and then she glanced at the sinew of Jeff's naked back, he was clenching his fists, and she quickly looked back to the spot again. She adjusted her blouse and buttoned up the ones that came loose.

She gradually stood up, she wobbled like a new-born calf as she tried to steady herself. Her thighs felt sore and tender.

'I need air,' her voice sounded tired. 'I'm going outside.'

And instantly, she turned and disappeared, holding onto whatever would support her weak body.

Mars' head was slumped over the railings of the second-floor balcony. Her arms abreast of her, she was gasping and drawing in the night air, and she was staring at the street below. She felt bile in her throat, she spat out the contents of her mouth. She then spewed, sick, downwards, towards the ground. It tasted like a mixture of the last drink she had had and fear. She felt dreadful, she was a respectable woman and this shouldn't have happened to her. She was draped over the balcony and was dribbling out the remnants of her evening. There was a line of saliva hanging from her mouth.

'Take this,' Jeff said as he appeared holding a glass tumbler of water in his hand. She turned and snatched it from him without a thank you, and with the other hand she swung it at him, catching his face with her fingernails. She made contact with his skin, and it drew some blood, she went to repeat the action, but he caught her wrist and held it tightly, they stared at each other.

'I should bloody report you for this.' Her face was filled with torment, she tugged her hand from his grasp, and he let go and felt his cheek. She turned back and faced the night.

'I'm so sorry Mars, you don't deserve what I just did to you in there,' came his pathetic answer.

She gulped down the water, as if she'd been lost in a desert for days and flung the empty glass from the balcony in temper, it flew through the air. She was angry and betrayed, it's all she could muster up; she couldn't fight him as he was too large a figure, she thought about reporting him, but it would probably ruin her job prospects, an employee with a court case to fight. Her boss wouldn't take too kindly to that, or did she really care, her dignity came first. The glass thudded on an area of grass below, she gazed arduously at it.

'I didn't expect that of you, you of all people, Jeff. I always saw you differently, more of a clean-cut person, someone that I could rely on, a bit of a charmer. Tonight you changed my expectations of you. You enticed me in, and you made me cheap in there,' she said pointing to the flat. 'And I felt like a two-bit whore. I should report you for attempted murder, I never agreed to be part of your sick game.'

'Come on,' Jeff cried defensively.

'I don't think I ever want to see you again. You've hurt me, you've taken my self-respect away,' her voice softened. 'And you took advantage of me in there,' she said still slumped against the railings, her back facing the front door. There was a noise from a closing of a window along the balcony as if someone had been listening to them.

'That's harsh Mars, isn't it?' his hand pleading with her, his chest was bare. 'You agreed to come along to a place you've never been to before. To meet me.'

She twisted her neck and faced him, 'Don't you dare blame this on me,' she said indignantly, her black eyeliner was becoming blurred.

'You have no right to have done what you did, I didn't consent to this, this crap.' Her head twisted around at him.

Jeff stood motionless. He looked like a guilty schoolboy.

She stood up straight, her back still facing him.

'But why Jeff! Why do what you've just done in there to a friend.' Her voice was sounding bitter.

'I... I can't really say Mars,' he sounded incriminated, he looked around, and then to the floor. 'Maybe it was, frustration, maybe a degree of compulsion, maximum joy I suppose?' He looked at her with disdain.

'Maximum joy, you're sick Jeff, you need a doctor.' She pushed past him.

'I need to get my jacket, I'm feeling cold.' Displeasure was in her voice. 'I want to go home, *now*, I need a bath, you have made me feel dirty and cheap, and you disrespected and insulted me, you have taken my dignity away.' Her voice was fuming.

Twenty-eight

Mars gazed wearily at the dazzling street lights at the side of the carriageway, as she headed eastbound towards home. She felt weak and tired.

Her memory was full of the last few hours of her 'date' with the warped Jeff Divine. Pictures of a rope flashed in her eyes, stripes in the curtains appeared in her memory. Maybe because these were the last things she had been picturing, as she clung on for her life, they remained in her vision. She had found it hard to breathe, as his malevolent face reigned terror over her, when she was trapped by him, defenceless against his supremacy, pinned down by his strength and dominance. She was thinking, what the hell had she just been through?

'Here I am, a single mother, trying to raise a son and put him through a good education, and this happens. I'm not a player in a three-way tryst. I'm decent, fresh-faced and clean. She peered in the rear-view mirror, her eyes became moist. Was this what he wanted in return for me setting up a meeting with Christina, surely not, it couldn't be. Why did I just go through that shit?' she thought. 'I didn't expect that would happen. It took me by surprise, it was totally unexpected, and it was certainly unforeseen. But was it all worth it? What now, will he show up and meet Christina, as part of the deal, he now doesn't have to, he's done what he wanted to do, does it matter to him?'

Her mobile phone vibrated and interrupted her thoughts, and signalled that she had received a text message. She became agitated and wriggled around in the seat of her car as she looked down at her handbag, nervous about the contents of the text message inside. She glanced at it and at the traffic ahead. She was curious, so she fumbled inside and retrieved her mobile. She held it aloft, at the top of the steering wheel. She was looking at both the phone and the road. She squeezed a button. Jeff's name was on the screen. Mars looked around her, wondering if she should read it, or return it to her bag. At that moment she found herself behind a white car at a set of red traffic lights, the polite female voice from her dashboard told her that she was on the Western Avenue, and she felt she was getting closer to home, and her salvation.

Curiosity got the better of her. She decided to read it, what he would have to say to her, she really couldn't imagine, or possibly gave a damn. She pushed a button.

Hi Mars,

I know you hate me for what I've done, plus I'm sorry about this eve: plus I wish u good luck. It was followed by a mass of x's.

'You bloody misogynist!' she screamed. Tears welled up in her eyes. She had to remove them with a finger as they ran down her cheeks. Her hand adjusted the mirror as she took another look in it. Black mascara became abundant, and it spread around her eyes, thin black lines formed, and she thought it reminded her of a rock star. 'How can someone who seems so nice be so bloody awful?' she thought.

She had run her bath. She dipped a toe into the foaming vanilla essence and then slid down beneath the water level. Her eyes began to fill with water and only her head was on show. She couldn't believe the ordeal she had just been through. 'Should I tell anyone?' she thought. She had taken a shine to Jeff Divine and thought at one time there could be something going on between them. She had enjoyed his company immensely, had started to get feelings for him and was beginning to love the man. He was the best bloke she had met since the breakdown of her marriage, she enjoyed his laughter, his jokes, his cheeky smile, his stature, and his bloody dashing looks. But she hadn't seen enough of him to form a relationship, and she was wary of what he got up to when he went out on his liaisons in the evening with other women. She was unsure what he had said was true, but tonight changed her perception of him. If she reported the incident then Christina would null and void the 'so-called' contract they had. She wouldn't employ someone with a legal trial hanging over them, it wouldn't look good. It would go against the reputation of the company. She would have to go on "gardening leave". Her boss would then employ someone else to take her position in the company, probably Morgan.

'Was that bastard going to penetrate me when I was dead? Was he going to perform necrophilia on me? What was he going to do with me?' she shuddered as she recollected the past evening. She fiercely kicked out at the bathwater in a temper. She was enraged and felt hatred and disgust towards Jeff. She felt dead inside. She closed her eyes and wondered to herself if she should get him back for what he had done to her. Could she get her revenge on him for carrying out this vile act on her?

Twenty-nine

Christina pushed back a curtain in her lounge. She heard the tremor of a car engine outside in the street. She waved thinking that Jeff hadn't seen her. He parked the car and got out. By then she had left her house and was walking down her path, making her way towards him.

'Evening,' he said, as he leaned forward and pecked her on the cheek, as they stood outside her garden gate. 'You smell nice.'

'Evening to you too, and thanks for the compliment, Jeff.' They chatted for a while.

'The restaurant isn't far from here, is that OK with you?' Christina said. He held out his arm and pointed it in the direction of his car and bowed a little like a chauffeur.

'Your car awaits you, the world is your oyster Ms Zabrinski,' he quipped. Christina smirked, as he glanced at the house. Christina slid into a squeaky leather seat, the car pulled away. The light was just starting to fade in the sky, and their evening was just beginning.

'I must say you look stunning tonight, Christina.'

'Thank you, Jeff,' she said coyly, with a sultry expression. 'That's very kind of you, you're a Gent,' she said tilting her head towards him.

They walked into Buon Amici restaurant in Chiswick Road, a popular eating house in the area. Booking was essential. Christina had seen to that earlier with a phone call.

There was a very large aquarium in the lobby, filled with exotic tropical fish. Some large, some tiny. Piped Italian music made them feel as though they weren't in west four, on a chilly March evening, but somewhere in Tuscany.

The atmosphere was vibrant, and the staff were polite, charming, and friendly. It was filled with local clientele, the mainly thirty-something set, casually but expensively dressed, and on good incomes. They were discussing the issues of the day, and how they could put the world to rights. Glasses knocked together and plates clanked.

They both sat on stools at the bar, Christina ordered a large Merlot, Jeff a Bacardi and coke. Christina asked the waiter to put the drinks on the bill for the evening.

'Oh, but it's my honour to pay for the evening, seeing as I asked you to join me tonight,' Jeff said politely.

'Please Jeff, it's on me, this evening, let's not have our first argument,' she said modestly. 'Besides, I'll put it on expenses, it isn't a problem.'

'Now you're very kind.' They tilted their glasses towards each other, and laughed. Jeff didn't insist on paying any more, he'd become used to women treating him to meals, and evenings out.

Christina crossed her legs and brushed a hand over the split on the side of her black cotton dress. Jeff shot her a glance. It was a reflex action, one he'd undertaken a thousand times before.

Christina was out to impress him. She was attracted to him, and his subconscious, and hers had been waiting for some time for this moment to arrive. She felt that now, against the odds, she had got her way.

She wore black leather high-heeled sandals that make her five-foot-ten, and around two to three inches shorter than her date. They had silver sequins scattered over the straps. She wore a silver Cartier choker around her neck with a matching wristwatch. Perfume oozed from her pores, wafting mainly in his direction.

Jeff was feeling a little more relaxed this time round, and the first drink had helped him, although he thought he might need another. He also knew that this woman didn't realise who he was, didn't grasp that she was owed over sixteen thousand pounds by this handsome, tall man, whom she was out to enjoy herself with. Jeff wondered if he was out of his depth with her, he wondered if she knew anything. He knew she was after him for his affections, and that she was trying to seduce him. He wasn't worried about her advances. He'd been here before, many times. This was easy for him, but what was unsettling was the position he was in, a case of double jeopardy. He was going to play along with her, he enjoyed the fear it gave him, he knew something important between them that she didn't.

He was attracted to her, and he knew he could get her into bed, it was a formality for him, only a matter of time, but was that something he wanted to do? He had to develop the situation between them and work Christina out first. He had been in this situation many times before. He had been with rich, wealthy and powerful women on many occasions. Women had taken him out on dates as their trophy to show off to clients and friends at receptions and parties. Jeff had once been flown to Monte Carlo by a wealthy American client from Texas a couple of years ago, whose husband couldn't attend the lavish function which was held on a yacht moored in the harbour a day before the Formula One Grand Prix, he then stayed on to watch the race. The client's husband turned up on Sunday, a few hours after he had left the woman.

A very rich Turkish client had invited him to the diplomatic resident's home in central London when the place was almost empty. They were chauffeured around and dined at a top restaurant as part of the hospitality. He never once had to reach into his pocket to pay for anything. She wanted him to propose to her. She was a stunning ex-model in her early forties who was married to a diplomat and millionaire telecoms tycoon, ten years her senior. They had a penthouse flat in Regents Park, but they spent too much time apart he was always away on business, and their relationship was beginning to go sour, and she felt lonely and vulnerable. She wanted Jeff's hand in marriage.

He'd seen this situation before. If he bedded Christina, and she found out later exactly who he was, what would her reaction be? Probably one of rage, anger, embarrassment, and disgust, but he could use it to his advantage to bribe her and get her to drop the debt against him. What would she say, how would she face the world? This woman never made mistakes. This would come as a massive blow to her ego and pride. Maybe it would work in reverse and go against him, she would use her power to humiliate him. Would she contemplate dropping such a large debt for anyone? He somehow doubted it, but it was on his mind.

The situation was becoming complex, but it was one he was thriving on. He loved the adrenaline rush it gave him, women wanting him, the flirting, the chase, he loved the attention of it all, he loved the game, and he loved playing it.

He knew she was a powerful and ruthless businesswoman, a formidable figure, and a very clever individual, but would she realise who he was? Would she be able to figure him out? This evening, or at any other time? Jeff thought she couldn't possibly put the two together. The only thing that connects them at this moment in time is the name, Jeff. And possibly his job, construction.

He wondered exactly what she wanted from him. Was she a player? She couldn't be, could she? 'I'll find that out later, ask some questions,' he thought. 'Could she be a gold digger? She hardly knows who I am, or what I really do for a living.' Jeff knew he couldn't compete with her financially, and he wasn't going to either.

He thought back to the remark made by Mars on his first meeting with her, that, 'She's not your type,' she said. 'What did she mean, why wouldn't she be?

'So, Christina how was work today?' he said with a gleeful look. He was leaning with one elbow on the bar. He wore a deep-grey suit with a light mauve shirt. 'What is it exactly you do?' Jeff said, sipping his drink, he swirled it around as he returned it to the bar.

'Well Jeff, seeing that you have asked, as it's not my favourite "out of hours topic" at all. I work for Hammerson Shaw, in Hammersmith. I'm head of sales and marketing, and finance, strategy, and everything really. I run a tight ship. I control a workforce of around a hundred enthusiastic, spirited staff. We buy land, as much as we can get our hands on, and we have just purchased five petrol stations to add to the others that we own. We have also invested in property in Dubai and Atlanta recently, and we also own around fifteen employment agencies. I make sure my staff work hard, today, and every day, they know who's in charge. The better they perform, the more I get excited.' She pointed her perfectly made-up eyes at him.

'If they burp, I *need* to know about it,' she said formidably, running her hand down her thigh. 'If they screw up, they have to deal with me. I'm a bit of a piranha in a goldfish bowl.' Her eyes glared venomously. Jeff looked in awe at the way she described her position in the company. He would have thought she would be more subtle, seeing this was only a date and not a sales lecture.

'I *hate* it when things go wrong, don't you?' She put a hand in her bag and withdrew a screwed-up packet of cigarettes. 'I'm not the only one, am I?' she said, fluttering her eyebrows at him. 'You don't mind do you, Jeff,' she said subtly, holding the packet in his direction, and referring that could she have one, she felt stressed by her last speech.

'Be my guest Christina,' he said, holding his hands out.

'Would you like one yourself, Jeff?'

'Thanks Christina, but I don't.'

'Can't say I blame you, it's a nasty habit. I will pack it up one day and actually I don't smoke that many a day, and I'm sorry I don't usually smoke in the company of non-smokers, but the subject stresses me a little, and this will calm my nerves.' But she decided to return the packet to her bag, knowing full well she shouldn't smoke inside. She also received a cutting glare from a waiter, but she didn't appear to care.

Just then, the barman placed two small dishes of green and black olives in front of them. At last, she had something to do with her hands.

'Thank you, sweetie,' she smiled at the barman.

'Yourself?' she said, her face looking bewitching, and her black mascara pointing from the side of her eyes, giving her a vampire look. She sipped her drink, waiting for an answer.

'You once told me before—I remember, construction, isn't it?' she said with apathy.

'You remembered.' Jeff looked buoyant.

'I remember most things,' she said conceitedly, looking around the restaurant. Jeff stole a glance at her black low-cut top before she returned and looked at him.

'What do you mean you hate it when things go wrong? Work not going to plan Christina. Trouble in paradise?' He grinned.

'Not work Jeff, work always goes to plan darling, well most of the time,' she said mordantly. 'Sometimes things just don't work out, do they?' She twisted in her seat.

'Tell me something Jeff,' she slanted her eyes and looked at him. 'You're in construction, aren't you?' He sipped his drink.

'Yes... I am,' he said hesitantly.

'I'm not going to dwell on it, it's neither the time nor the place, we're both out to have some fun together, but the subject has now arrived, and you may be able to answer a simple question for me?' She moved straight on. 'It's that I'm owed seventeen thousand pounds by a builder.' Jeff's face was stoic. 'He worked at my home. Funny, his name was also Jeff.'

Her eyes narrowed at him. He coughed. 'He made a dreadful error of judgement, and so, I sued him for the work that he undertook.' She sipped at her drink; Jeff looked on intensely, nervously scratching an eyebrow.

'But now, even though I won the court case, I'm still owed the bloody money.'

He put his hand to his mouth, cleared his throat, took another large gulp of his drink, and turned his head away from her. 'She can't possibly know who I really am, he thought. It's impossible, there's no real link, there's nothing to put us together, nobody knows, do they? Balls.'

'Are you OK, Jeff?' she said, leaning forward and gently touching his leg with her painted fingertips.

'Just fine,' he said, looking at her almost empty glass of wine. 'Would you like another drink?' He held his glass up to the level of his face, 'And I'm nearly empty as well. I think I'll order another round.' He raised an arm at the overly grinning face of the barman. 'Same again please Sam.'

'Thirsty are you, Jeff?' she said readily.

'You could say that. A little Christina, I'm in need of lubrication. It's been a long day, a long week, in fact. Thousands of things to sort out, and it all starts again Monday!' She peered at him.

'So, what do you intend on doing about your outstanding debt Christy, sorry, Christina?' he said rubbing his chin.

'How are you going to get your money back from this company?'

She stared at him, with a look of guilt.

Jeff got up from his stool, flicked at the creases in his trousers and shrugged his shoulders backwards. He caught her looking at his torso as she put her wine glass to her lips, whilst not taking a drink from it. She pulled at the end of her long hair.

He needed to be comfortable for Christina's answer to his telling question. He had to ask it, as it was playing on his mind. He wanted to know how she was going to be able to force the debt on him, and he needed the information so he could outmanoeuvre her. He wanted to know her thoughts and schemes. The more information he could extract from her the more power he had and the better chance he had of dodging her movements.

'Tell me, Christina, what plans do you have?'

'Do you work out Jeff? Do you go to the gym?' she said completely changing the subject.

'Yes, I do, I try to go a couple of times a week,' he said frowning at her. Her changing of the question had baffled him.

'Why do you ask?'

'Oh, I was just thinking of joining one myself. I jog a lot, but I need a different angle I need to tone up more.' She got straight back to the conversation at hand. 'Well, it's like this, now Jeff, he appears to have vanished. He's out of sight, and he simply doesn't live at the address any more to where the court papers have been sent. I've frozen his bank account, and any other accounts in the future that he may open,' she said resignedly. 'I have somebody working on the case, someone very good at tracking people down. This person is living somewhere, and he has a surname, so I *will* recover my debt from this man. I tend to get what is owed to me,' she said with a bitter tone in her voice. 'He won't escape me.' She momentarily hesitated, 'Jeff.' He felt a quiver run over him.

He rapidly took hold of his fresh drink, the moment they had been passed to them both by the smiling Italian barman.

'Do you have any ideas?' she said pertinently. 'You appear to be in the same industry as each other.' She leaned forward and gently brushed the arm of his suit, something was annoying her. There was a piece of cotton she just had to remove from it. 'Nice watch, Jeff.'

'Thank you,' he said glancing at it. 'Er, have you been to his address to see if he lives there by any chance?' He gulped.

'Yes, I have, I sent a girl from the office to the address to take a look around for me.'

'And?' he quickly said.

'She just confirmed that the place was empty, letters were piling up on the inside of the floor of the flat, and it looked like it hadn't been lived in for some time.'

'Well, what if he's changed his name for instance, what if he's staying at a friend's, or a relative's house,' he said with an innocent look.

'OK, look,' she said pushing her glass slowly along the marble top bar and in his direction.

'Let me ask you this.' He stared at her. 'Your company undertakes some work for a customer, yes?' He nodded.

'And that customer doesn't pay you,' she said pointing at him. 'You take them to court and win the case, and that customer *still* won't pay the debt, what would *you* do Jeff Divine?'

'Well Christina.' He looked uncertainly at her, as she sat waiting for his reply. 'You're telling me that he's moved away, there's not a lot you can do, is there?' He looked away from her and then back, he shrugged his shoulders, 'What about a private investigator then?'

'Good idea, Jeff,' she said as if she was chastising him.

Jeff looked away from her again searching the depths of his mind, to try and find the missing link between them. 'I feel like Clark Kent being questioned by Lois Lane, asking me do I know who Superman is?' he thought.

'We have the registration number of his van. It's black, or dark grey, something along those lines,' she said with firm intention. 'He must pick the documentation up from an inhabited address at some point, I know people in high places, *Jeff.*' Jeff looked astounded as she bent down and lifted her bag to her lap. He looked at the window of the restaurant and thought how lucky he could have been. He had pestered his friend Martin into lending him his car tonight, saying that he was taking out a "classy" woman. One who had money, a woman who he wanted to charm this evening and that it would have been inappropriate to pick her up in a truck! Martin was reluctant to loan out his Jaguar, which was his pride and joy, but Jeff promised to return it with a full tank of petrol. 'If I had turned up in that four-wheeled truck, I would have been screwed!' he thought. 'Found out and done for.'

A cold sweat prickled over his back. He felt his skin turn crimson. 'Who the shit gave her my registration number?

Harrison was the only one. The slimy two-faced git. He took some interest in that vehicle when we had our last meeting on that fateful Friday in January. How would he have known that would be our last meeting together and that I would have disappeared soon after. He couldn't possibly have thought that far in advance?' Jeff pulled his index finger and his thumb down his cheeks searching for clues, he threw a look at her.

'She asked him to, I bet. And she hadn't told him yet if she had employed a private eye.' He needed to find this out.

A waiter appeared with a happy look, they looked at each other.

'Christina,' said Jeff, raising his brows. 'Our table is ready,' they got up and headed towards their port of call.

'So, you see, the problem will be solved in one way or another,' she said with an air of confidence, as she took her seat. Jeff's face was following her every move. She looked at her glass as it was becoming empty, she wiggled it.

'You don't know him, do you?' she said ironically.

'Pardon!'

'I just wondered. Well you never know do you. It was a long shot darling, take no notice of me.' Jeff rubbed a hand around his perspiring neck. He loosened the knot on his dark tie, and undid the top button of his shirt.

'Very good, Christina.' He sighed, a sigh of relief.

'I thought I would ask, no need to take it to heart darling,' she said with a cunning smile on her face.

'Anyway, cheers Jeff.' She clanked her almost empty glass onto his.

'So, Christina, did you engage a private investigator,' he said with caution.

'You didn't ask me what went wrong Jeff, at my home, with this builder.' She scrutinised him. 'I thought, you, being in the same line of work, you might be interested?'

'Oh, I didn't?' he replied, sounding surprised by her question.

'It doesn't matter now. But in answer to you, it's a route I may well want to take,' she said, as a waiter brushed the tablecloth with his hand.

Jeff pulled up outside Christina's house in Bollo Lane. The evening had gone well, and Jeff thought she was attractive, loquacious, and intelligent, although she could be difficult sometimes, and she had a wickedness about her. He would like to get more information out of her, he felt a frisson of excitement, he found it intriguing, playing two roles in one, and seeing Christina's reactions, however clever she was, she had still been unable to track down Jeff Turner. He would like another shot at this woman.

Thirty

'No thank you, I'm OK, in fact—I'm waiting for my friends.' Mars stood alone, as she fended off an admirer, a tall male, six feet in height. He was asking a single girl standing by herself if she was OK, and did she want to chat.

Her eyes were glazed beneath her dark sunglasses, and her body was impervious. As she was staring at the street and the passing traffic, she saw a faint reflection of herself in the office window. Vehicles were making their slow journey home for the evening, creeping inch by inch along the Broadway.

'Maximum fucking joy,' she thought. 'What a bloody bastard.' The sky was lifeless, the clouds were slow moving.

She dug her hand into her bag, and took out her mobile. She looked at it, checking that she had not missed any calls or messages, she then flung it back in her bag again. She then pulled out a half-size bottle of Jack Daniels. She turned her head to see if there was anyone looking at her. She cracked open the lid and then slurped some of the contents into her mouth, then returned the bottle faster than a speeding rocket, swallowing the whiskey, enjoying the warmth it gave her.

Life didn't feel good at the moment for Mars. Christina had done an astonishing U-turn on her this morning, going against her word, and telling her that she had had a change of heart overnight. She had reneged on their private "contract" that they had had, and that Morgan Cable would become vice president.

She felt betrayed by her, and let down, there was nothing she could say or do to change the situation. She had virtually blackmailed her boss earlier in the week. Christina could terminate her contract if she stood up to her.

She couldn't even turn to Jeff for affection, as she felt that he had also betrayed her. She felt that she had been tortured by him for his perverted pleasure. She felt used and cheap and wasn't sure if she could face him again.

'Hiya darling, been here long?' said the bubbly Sherry walking up to her, closely followed by her young workmate, Rebecca Ansell.

'Are you OK, darling?' Sherry said, looking slightly confused.

'Fine, good now you're here,' she replied.

'Do you know Becky?' Sherry said introducing the young girl, she was wearing a red patterned dress and matching top, and her cheeks appeared to have too much foundation on them.

'Hi. Yes, we've met once or twice. How are you?' said Mars.

'I'm good, thank you,' she said, with a reticent smile.

'Have you been here long?' Sherry said, her eyes looking up the busy road.

'Too long,' she thought. 'About, fifteen minutes,' Mars said, looking sulky.

'Where are we off to?'

Mars was gripping her handbag between an arm and the side of her body. Rebecca was standing behind her, her five-foot-two frame, daydreaming.

'I'm so sorry to hear that you didn't get the position you were after, Mars.'

'Thank you, Sherry.'

'There's a bloke over there staring at us!' said the youthful blonde-haired Rebecca, as she opened her bag, and took out a box of ten Number Six cigarettes. Neither of the others replied, their conversation was far more intense than taking notice of the young trainee's comments.

'How are you Sherry, have you had a busy day?'

'Oh. I've had busier days, sweetheart. I've been wrapped up in the Greybull saga, who recently went into administration, nightmare,' Sherry said with a solemn smile. Mars gazed at her movements. Becky was lighting up her cigarette, whilst looking at the two non-smokers. She looked over at the staring male.

'The thing is Sherry, I thought I was in line for the job, I needed the pay increase to put Tom through private education. I'd found a school for him not far from where we live. I'd received the paperwork from them, and now I have to bloody cancel it. Tom got all excited about it, and I had to tell him that's it's not going to happen. You should have seen his sad face,' Mars said, leaning towards her, and pointing her finger in Sherry's direction. 'I ticked all the right boxes, and she even hinted to me that I would get the position. She's a bloody bitch,' Mars said with displeasure, looking at her through her sunglasses. Rebecca's attention moved away from the suited chap. Her brow's flickered, as she realised that the conversation was suddenly heating up. It became better than ogling over at the single man.

Sherry glanced at Rebecca, and just as quickly back to Mars.

Mars couldn't tell them that she had bribed her boss. Sherry was friendly with Christina and always got along well with her. She liked her personality. She was friendly with Mars too, and couldn't understand why Mars was so bitter, and showing so much resentment towards Christina.

'I don't know if I can face her at the moment,' Mars said furiously. She swung her head back, she needed more alcohol. 'I may take a couple of days leave to get away from it all, they owe me some. I'll probably go down to Cornwall or Devon for a few days. There's an important meeting next week for all of us, isn't there?' she said with her eyes locking on to Sherry's. 'I'll take it then, to get away from that cow, at least.'

'What do you see in her Sherry?' Not waiting for an answer. 'I know she's good at her job, but she thinks she's God's bloody gift. No wonder her last bloke had it on his toes, there's just no appeasing her,' she glanced at the road, and her eye caught a builder's van. She turned back to Sherry, 'I now know why, to get away from her. She's nothing but a bitch.'

'Who was her last bloke then?' Rebecca said naively, with a fresh cigarette between two of her fingers, trying not to be left out of the conversation.

'It doesn't matter, Becks,' Sherry said with an irate look.

'I know you get on with her Sherry, but at the moment, I flipping well don't! I'm off her for the time being.'

A vibrating sound came from Mars's bag, she opened it up, removed her sunglasses from her face, and sifted inside for her phone.

'Nice bag,' commented Rebecca, as she was flicking her cigarette.

'Thanks, how's work going Becks, settled in?' Mars said smiling and looking into her bag.

'It's good thank you, I'm enjoying it, and it's not too far to travel.' She shot Mars a look. 'You've got a mark on your neck, Helen,' she said, pulling the skin together on hers with her fingers.

'Have I?' Mars glanced at her, sounding off guard. She covered the mark with her hand and answered the mobile with the other. Sherry gave her a sideward glance.

'Sorry girls, I must answer this. Hi Silvia… is everything OK?'

A muffled eastern European voice came from the phone.

'I will be about an hour Sylvia if you can hang on for that long? I'm in a meeting now, when I'm done, I'll jump straight into a cab. How is everything, is Tom OK?' It was Mars's nanny calling her. She was looking after Mars's son, and saying that she wanted to leave, and go home earlier, if she could.

Mars was packing her phone back into her bag with both hands, her chin tilting down over the skin on her neck. Rebecca was still eyeing her.

'Is Tom OK?' Sherry said politely.

'He's just fine, Sherry thanks.'

'So, Rebecca, do you have a boyfriend?' She veered the subject away from the mark she thought she had hidden well with foundation and also thought she would include Rebecca in their conversation, as she seemed a little lost. Sherry looked at Rebecca waiting for an answer.

'Er no, no I don't Helen,' Rebecca said cautiously and turned her head from the question, to hide her blush.

Sherry looked carefully at Mars, thinking that she was going to pry further into this new girl's private life. Mars buttoned her jacket.

'So, what's your next move then? Don't let it get you down, sweetheart,' Sherry said with a silken look on her face, she had a humble look about her.

'Don't feel so downhearted, Mars.' Sherry embraced her. Mars stared at the male from over Sherry's shoulder, and then closed her eyes.

Maybe I should have said yes to the guy. He's good-looking, clean cut and probably meant no harm. But she just wasn't in the mood for conversation right now. Instead she needed a friend instead, someone to console, someone to talk to.

Thirty-one

Around Two Years Later

'He's looking self-righteous, happy and he has a smug look on his face. He looks proud with himself. And comfortable with his find, stroking her nose with his finger.

She's looking smitten. She must be about five years his junior, slim. Slim petite with blonde hair, and a young, fresh face. They look so much in love with each other. He has the nerve to bring her in here. Why here, does he live around these parts now? I thought he lived in Middlesex, or was it Buckinghamshire, or somewhere near there. What's he doing in here then? He's miles from home, that's the second time I've seen him around these parts recently. Is he showing her off? If so, who to?

He's bloody good looking though. She's a lucky bastard to meet someone that handsome, and with a good sense of humour. And who are the elderly couple? Are they his parents, or hers? The older woman resembles her, she also has blonde hair, the same length, and her cheekbones are the same shape, a well-looked-after appearance. It's her parents. They must be her parents. They may live in this area, or she might live around here. Maybe she lives with her parents. The elderly couple look affluent. He dresses well for a father, he has a large stomach though, that may be from years of contentment. His clothes look expensive, not sure what make his shirt is.

His wife looks well-dressed. The outfit that she's wearing looks like it comes from Marks or Selfridges, but I could be wrong. Even so, they too look happy. Good luck to them, it's no good being cynical, or jealous. Bitter probably?

I hope they all have a wonderful evening together. Or do I? I haven't been that happy for years. Is that what love brings, two people gazing into each other's eyes, oblivious to their parents' whereabouts, unaware as to anyone's thoughts. They're starting to look around. Sugar, did she just catch me out staring at her? No, she's looking at someone else. Thank God. At last the waitress has brought their drinks over.

The lovey-dovey couple will somehow have to prise themselves apart from each other. How, I do not know. It's going to be a difficult task. But of course, they still have to hold hands, they just can't let go can they! How are they going to pick up their drinks, perhaps their parents will drip feed it to them. Oh, fuck! I'm just jealous, aren't I? I wish I was there, with him, I wish I were the one having my nose stroked. I haven't had my nose stroked like that for years. In fact, I haven't had any part of my anatomy stroked for years, come to think of it. I just can't remember. Think, perhaps it was, bloody years ago. But he is still handsome.

Is that a ring on his finger?'

'Boo!' Mars's bottle of Smirnoff Ice went crashing to the ground, bouncing on the stone tiles, and then spinning like a wheel, before coming to a stop.

'You *bloody* frightened the life out of me, Jenny.' People in the bar turned their heads at the noise, breaking an otherwise still atmosphere.

'I'll pick it up then, shall I,' Mars said in a hushed voice trying to hold back a sneer.

'OK. Bossy. Leave it to me.' Jenny was leaning down attempting to pick up the bottle from the floor, giving out orders to her.

'You just stay there then.' Mars had the menu from the table covering her face, she peered around from it. Her eyes were covered by her large dark sunglasses, they were rounded, and it made her look like a bumblebee. The people at the table she had been spying on were looking over at them. A waitress appeared from nowhere, five-foot-tall, with black bobbed hair, as if she had been beamed down from the ceiling.

'Let me help you, please.' she said in her Scandinavian accent.

'It's OK, there's no damage done,' Jenny said. Mars was straightening up on her chair, still with the menu covering her face, and peering at the table with the four happy occupants again to see if they were still looking over. 'They had turned back, they had much better things to do,' she thought. 'Like gaze at each other!'

'You weren't wearing those sunglasses before I went to the loo, were you? If I'm not mistaken Mars. Who have you got your eye on?'

'No, I wasn't, you're right. And I haven't got my eye on anyone Jenny,' Mars said defensively. 'Where have you been? You've been some time, haven't you, been pushing some white stuff up your nose have you then?' She was trying to get Jenny's thoughts away from her, and on to a different subject.

'Ha, ha! Very funny, it's women's problem.' Jenny Ross worked with Mars, she was of a stocky build. 'So where is he, who are you eyeing up then?' It didn't work.

'Jenny you're so, so meddlesome, there's no one in here to bloody look at!'

'Temper! You just looked in dreamland when I came back from the ladies.' Jenny waved her head around the bar. It was thinly dotted with customers. A couple of middle-aged women chatting at one table, three suited males at the bar interested only in discussing the events at work, and a young couple in their early twenties slouching on the leather sofa near the window, with two short drinks on their table. Her head finally came to a standstill.

'You could be right, Mars, you won't pull this evening. The barman is quite dishy though?'

'I don't believe you, you just don't give up, do you?' Mars said abruptly, shooting a look at the tall thirty-something barista, who had a tea towel squeezed into a pint glass, twirling it around trying to get it to glisten. Jenny was finishing off her wine.

'Can you not take a joke, Mars? I was only teasing you. Anyway, I must say, you are looking fitter these days, are you working out?'

'Do you think so?'

'Yes, I noticed that you looked leaner when I met up with you earlier.'

'Oh right, yes, I joined a gym some months back now. Thought I might try to lose some pounds now that summer is on its way and try to get into some new outfits.'

'You kept that one quiet, didn't you?' Jenny said with an air of suspicion.

'You never asked, plus I don't think it ever came up in a conversation anyway. It's a local gym that I use, not far from me. Sometimes I pop in there on my way home, and sometimes I go there on a Sunday morning. It's good, it makes you feel alive. What's the time anyway?' Mars said deliberately digressing from the subject.

'Oh, nearly eight' she replied.

'Have you had enough, do you want to go then?'

'I've still got half a glass left,'

'Well, hurry up, I'll wait for you' Jenny said, checking inside her handbag, and making sure she had all her contents for the evening with her.

'There's no rush, really, you go on I'm going to stay here and finish off my drink. Mother's staying with me for a few weeks, or it may turn into months, who knows. She's looking after Tom for me, and dropping him off at school tomorrow, it's great,' she enthused. 'So there's no urgency.'

'How is Mum these days since your dad passed away?' she said solemnly, with an air of sadness in her look. Mars showed no sorrow. She hadn't got along with her father, and wasn't upset at his passing. They argued when she was young. Her dad used to lock her in her room when she was naughty. He once waved a rope at her and threatened to tie her up if she tried to get out. She was mildly pleased now that he was no longer around.

'Oh, she's OK, bearing up, you know. Happy I think that she has Tom for comfort, pain in the backside at other times. And she's always wondering what the worlds going to be like for her grandchildren when she's not here anymore. Plus, it's good for her to get away from the house, it holds too many memories for her.'

'There's something up with her,' Jenny thought, looking at Mars with apprehension. There seems to be something on her mind, something deep. She took another view around the bar, there was no one looking in their direction. The suited males at the bar had deserted the place. They had been replaced by a rather large middle-aged chap, with a baggy flannelled shirt, hanging out, probably to hide his beer belly. He has a newspaper tucked under his arm. Three young Asian males were sitting at a low table in the middle of the drinking establishment, all with coffee in front of them, laughing out loud. A foursome, a couple out with their parents for the evening perhaps, sat at a table nearby. The younger male with his back to her. 'Well, I've asked,' she thought.

'OK Love, I'm going to depart then, him indoors will be pleased to see me. I'll leave you to your own devices. Are you sure you're OK?' she said cheekily, tilting her head towards her.

'I'm fine, I'll finish my drink and catch the train. It's still light outside... Just.' The girls both stood up from their stools at the high table and embraced each other. Jenny wandered arduously into the direction of the door, turned and threw a retiring wave.

Mars' attention turned immediately to the happy foursome at the table in front of her.

She continued to ogle at the jollity between them. They were all content with each other. Her mind wandered, and devious thoughts raced through her head. She sipped her wine, there wasn't much left as she placed it back on the table.

'The bloody sick bastard,' she thought, as she stared at the younger of the two men. 'This is where we first met, about, two and a half years, maybe?' She ran a hand over the front of her neck, she could still feel the indentation of where she was strangled by him. The memories were still there. 'I wonder if he strangles his petite, doting wife, the way he did me. I bet he bloody doesn't, but what do I know?'

'Now's the chance for revenge,' she thought. The ascendancy is with me. I'm going to make him wish he hadn't chosen this bar for his evening's entertainment tonight.'

At that point the petite girl moved from her chair, pushed it back, got up and headed towards the toilets. 'I know, I'll follow her, and find out who she is. I'll be inquisitive.' She watched as the girl walked past her. She waited a few minutes, looked around, and then headed towards the toilets.

She walked in and stood nestled up against a wash basin. She gazed at the mirror and fumbled in her bag, pretending to retrieve some make-up. Just then the girl appeared from a cubicle. Mars's eyes glanced at the mirror and watched the girls movements as she stood there, next to her, looking at her reflection.

Mars turned towards her.

'Hello! Sorry, do I know you?' she said with a startled look. 'Do you work at the NatWest building, in town?'

The girl looked perplexed.

'No, sorry, I don't. I work for Honda.'

'Oh, I'm so sorry, you reminded me of someone. I thought I knew you. I do apologise.'

'That's OK,' she replied diffidently, looking at Mars, then back at the mirror. She turned on a tap and adjusted her eyeliner with a finger.

'So, whereabouts are Honda based then, if I may ask?'

'Oh, I work at their West Drayton branch, in Mill Lane,' she smiled. 'What about yourself?'

'I work at,' she hesitated. 'Coopers and Taylor, in Ealing. I like your skirt,' Mars said.

'Thank you, I got it in a sale, I think.' She smiled at Mars as she wandered over and grabbed a paper towel. She quickly dried her hands and threw the paper into an adjacent bin.

'I must go,' said the girl. 'I've got family waiting, nice to meet you though,' she smiled wryly. She headed out.

The door eased itself shut on its closure. Mars peered at the mirror, flicked her thumb on her bottom lip, and also departed to regain her position at her table.

A waitress arrived with two plates of food, placed them in front of the respective diners, and then disappeared, supposedly to collect two more dishes of cuisine for her customers.

'Well, they're going to be in here for some time,' she thought, as she spied at them through her tilted sunglasses. At that moment the younger man swung his head around, and in her direction. Before their eyes locked on each other, Mars grabbed the menu and held it in front of her to cover her face from his stare. She peered at it, tapping it on the tip of her nose. Her heart was thumping, and she wondered how long she should keep it there, covering her face. How long would he be peering over in her direction? Did he recognize her?

Mars heard the sound of the waitress, saying, 'Scampi?' 'He must have looked back by now,' she thought. She eased the menu down to see the foursome enjoying their meal and chatting with one another.

'OK, so when shall I make my move? When shall I embarrass him? When shall I throw the cat amongst the pigeons?'

Mars opened her handbag and pulled out her mobile. She scrolled along to the letter J, and found the name, Jeff Divine. She was making sure she still had his number. She placed the mobile back into her bag, and retrieved some lipstick and a small mirror. She applied the makeup, and checked it, squeezing her lips together, and then checked again. As she gulped back the remainder of her wine, she noticed the red smudge mark around the top of the glass.

She stood up, straightened herself, took a deep breath, picked up her bag, and began the slow, methodical, and slightly nervy walk towards their table.

Jeff's back was towards her. The petite blonde-haired girl to his right, the elder woman was facing Mars and a diamond formation was made up of the elder man facing the younger girl, and towards the window of the bar.

There was a roar of laughter at the other end of the bar, the younger girl glanced over at the noise, as she dangled her fork in mid-air.

'Hello!' Mars said in an uncomfortable voice, removing her sunglasses from her face. 'Jeff, how are you doing darling? I haven't seen you since, well, it must have been, a couple of years, I think? What a surprise this is, you haven't changed much, how are you?'

Jeff was holding his knife and fork and gaped at her in amazement, his lips were apart and not moving. He looked startled by her presence. His olive skin was beginning to lose its colour and lighten. The other three members of the party all looked at her in wonder.

'Are you still living in that archaic second-floor flat, in, erm, Ruislip, was it?' Mars thought about how far she should go with the torment of him. She started by letting him know of their last meeting together. The other three members of the table were looking between Mars, not knowing who the hell she was, and Jeff's startled look.

'Er, no I'm not,' he mumbled, as he cleared his throat.

'Need a large glass of water, do you, Jeff?' She looked at him with a sneer.

'No, I'm fine.' He looked shaken by her presence.

'So, are you going to introduce me, *Jeff?*' she said with a gallant stare. By now he had a look of fright on his face. He looked cornered, not knowing what to do or say. Was she going to continue with what happened on that fateful night, or will she leave it. Was she bold enough to mention the incident? She hadn't mentioned it yet and it cannot be proved. If he told her to leave, then she just might become agitated, and just bring the subject up, to spite him.

'Who are you?' said the petite girl, in a clear and precise voice, resting her cutlery on her plate. 'That was you just a minute ago in the ladies, wasn't it?' She felt uncomfortable with Mars's presence, she'd noticed from Jeff's body language that he didn't want her around. She could also tell by the look on his face.

'Helen Marshall,' she held out a hand but didn't receive a reply. She glanced at the elder couple and gave them a courteous smile.

'Sorry. Your name is!' Mars asked.

'Annabelle.' Annabelle turned to Jeff, 'Is she a friend of yours darling, do you know her?' she said discontentedly. Jeff hesitated.

'She is a friend, aren't you?' he threw a half-hearted grin at Mars. Both the elder couple looked slightly startled at Jeff's look and this girl's approach to him. They had an inclination that she was an ex-girlfriend of his, and had probably been dumped in the past by him, at the wrong time. Annabelle looked her up and down with jealousy and disdain. Who was this woman who suddenly appeared from nowhere, the woman who spoke to her in the cloakroom? She tried to work out the difference between the both of them. Jeff knew he had to say something to please Mars. He couldn't upset her at this point, it was the worst thing he could do. He could tell from her body language that she was bitter towards him, and he really wished that he was somewhere else tonight. He felt that she was ready to implode, should she be ignored and not be recognised by him. He had to use some of his charm.

'How have you been? Have you been keeping well? You look good anyway,' he said politely. Annabelle looked pensive.

'I'm keeping well. Thank you for asking. It's kind of you, Jeff.'

'So, are you local?' Mars said looking at the elder man.

'Yes, we live in Dover Gardens, just around the corner,' he said, raising a hand, a finger pointing towards the door.

'What about yourself then?'

'I live in Ealing, but work locally.' Mars smiled at Jeff.

'We met in this bar… some time ago, *didn't* we, Jeff?' She touched the front of her neck in view of him, her eyes delving into Jeff's weakened stare. He noticed the move and gulped. He picked up his glass of beer.

'We did indeed. But if you don't mind now Mars, it's been a pleasure meeting and seeing you again, but we need to move on. I'm out with my family for the evening, it's a small get-together, you know, so we'd like to carry on. We have things to discuss.'

'Who's Mars?' Annabelle said.

'It's, er, a nickname for her,' Jeff replied. Mars smirked at the bewildered-looking Annabelle. The elderly couple gaped.

'I'm sorry, yes, I must be moving on myself. You're very good at getting rid of people aren't you, *Jeff?* When you need to.' She smirked. Annabelle threw her a reflective look.

'Anyway. It's been a pleasure meeting you all, and you *Jeff.* I just wish that I had more time and could have stayed a little longer,' she said sarcastically. 'However, I hope you all enjoy your evening, together, won't you.' Mars said glancing at all of them, and finishing by simpering at the man she once knew as charming.

'It's a shame that it ended the way it did, wasn't *it* Jeff?' she said sharply. She got in the last word, hoping that when she left, the evening would turn into a night of questioning and embarrassment for the suave Mr Divine. Mars hoped that his relationship with his new wife would become tense and strained. She hoped that they would argue that evening, over her, and that Annabelle would walk out on him, and that the love between them would dwindle, causing the marriage to hit a sour note. But of course she would never know.

Annabelle looked quizzically at her man. Mars donned her sunglasses, flicked back her hair, and headed outside. She stood on the pavement, and lingered a while, with her back towards them, in view of them all. She knew they would still be looking at her, she felt that she had made a statement to him, she wanted to make her mark, disturb Jeff's evening, and unbalance him. She thought that she had done a good job.

The evening air was turning to a chill. She turned and wandered towards the station.

Thirty-two

It was a glorious spring morning. The sunshine battered against the window of Mars's office. She was kept cool by the office's air conditioning unit. She was running over a legal document that Hayley Remington had handed to her just as she should have arrived in for work this morning. There was a noise from her handbag. It was her mobile. She looked at the screen. It was a number she didn't recognise. She picked it up and pushed the answer button.

'Hello. Helen Marshall,' she said chirpily, whilst holding the paperwork.

'Hello. Do you know who I am?' said a sedate voice. She looked at it.

'No I don't. Should I know who you are? And can I help you?' she said, seeming a bit puzzled.

'You shouldn't have done that last night Mars. You were out of order, you disrupted my evening.' Mars moved the phone away from her ear and looked at the number.

'Jeff is that you?' she said with a startled voice.

'Yes Mars, it's me.' His voice was intoned.

'So, you've changed your number then?'

'I changed it ages ago; does it really matter?'

'And to what do I owe this privilege, Jeff Divine. What can I do for you? I'm at work and I'm very busy, I don't have much time, so can you be quick please.'

'You shouldn't have interrupted us last night in that bar. We were all out enjoying ourselves. You messed up the evening. Can you believe the questions I was asked when you left? It was so embarrassing, my wife was fuming. She thought I was having an affair with you.'

'Oh, it was embarrassing for you, was it Jeff? What a shame.' She snorted, as she walked towards the window of her office, the phone pinned to her ear. She looked down at the road.

'Not as half as embarrassing as it was for me, having a fucking rope tied around my neck while being nearly choked to death, can you remember that *Jeff?* Mr Suave Divine, can you remember that, can you, that lovely evening we spent together. You didn't even attempt to make it a romantic evening, did you? You didn't even attempt to cook for me, or suggest that we go out somewhere. It was all planned, wasn't it?'

'No. No, it wasn't planned Mars,' he said lying.

'Do you tie a rope around your wife's neck, Annabelle's neck, each time you go to bed with her, do you?' she said with a steely voice, turning and walking towards her desk.

'So that's what it was all about, was it? That evening, years ago, and you haven't got over it?'

'You haven't answered my question, have you? And it takes a damn lot longer than a few years to get over it, something as shameful as that.'

'I don't need to answer your questions,' he snapped.

'Besides, you didn't even report it, so it couldn't have been that bad.'

'You bastard, you bloody selfish bastard. Maybe your pretty little wife needs to know what you're really like.'

'I said, it wasn't planned,' he replied. Mars sighed and wondered where this conversation was going to end up.

'Oh, I see, you only do it to me then, do you? Some kind of perverse fetish of yours is it?'

'No, it's… not,' he said, trying to defend himself.

'Did it not cross your mind that perhaps there was the smallest of chances that you may have bumped into someone like me, or Christina, seeing that we use the place on occasions. Did you not realise that? Did you not think?' She turned and paced the floor, she felt in control of the situation and felt she could belittle him.

'Are you some kind of idiot, leaving yourself open to what and whom you may have bumped into? There are hundreds of places you could have taken your pretty wife to, don't you think, Mr Divine?' she said with disdain. Jeff remained silent. 'So why there then, hoping to bump into someone, were you?'

'Hardly, why would you think I would want to bump into someone?' he said smugly.

'I don't know, you tell me, I'm confused, mystified in fact.'

'I was there because Annabelle's parents live local, and they suggested it. She's now not talking to me. I hope you're pleased with yourself; I hope you feel happy now!'

'Are you having a go at me? Because if you remember, Mr Divine, *you're* the one who's done wrong. I should have reported you a long time ago, I should have gone to the police. I still can, as a matter of fact!'

'Well...' Jeff hesitated.

'Well, what?'

'I love it when you get angry Mars, and you're still as attractive as you were then.'

'Jeff, I really do not bloody care for your mind games,' she said in a tiresome voice, twisting her head from left to right to relieve some stress. 'It was just strange seeing you there after all these years, and if you weren't bothered, then you wouldn't be calling me now, would you?' The phone went quiet.

'What do you want, Jeff? Why are you calling me when you are the guilty party in all of this?'

'I don't know Mars, it just seemed strange seeing you after all this time as well. It brought back a few memories, you know, well it would do, wouldn't it? How's the rest of the crowd, how's that bitch Christina? What has she been up to?'

'Why do you want to know?'

'I'm just asking, I'm curious, it's natural, seeing you again brings it all back.' Mars realised he was not going to go that easy. Even if he is a bastard, he has some kind of panache, bloody git.

'Yeah, she's the same, no change in her, never will be, still bossy and single. She dumped Dan, and now she has a new squeeze. She's now seeing, surprise, surprise, a Spanish guy. Antonio. You know how she loves her Mediterranean men don't you? And she keeps going on about that debt that's owed to her, and how long it's been outstanding for now.'

'Oh, really, that's interesting. What about yourself then, is there a man in your life?'

'No Jeff, there isn't, I don't seem to get the time,' she said, wishing that there was a man around.

'So, where are you living now, the same place?'

'No, I'm living in Chesham, why are you asking?' Mars didn't answer his question.

'Jeff, I must go, I have to, I have to get on with my work, I'm running a little behind.'

'OK, it's been good talking to you again, after so long. Can I call you again sometime?'

'What for Jeff? You're sick.' Mars was angry, and at the same time confused.

THIRTY-THREE

Mars entered the lobby of the Honda building. It was four-storeys high, it had that "built in the eighties" look.

White oblong slabs were placed vertically, with clear glass and grey cladding in between them. The roof was squared off with wider horizontal blocks, giving it a compact look. She was smiled at by a tall male, of a similar age to her, wearing a sharp suit, and walking as if he had an appointment. She smiled back, as she removed her sunglasses. She liked tall men.

She edged attentively through the large lobby, and towards the reception area, acutely aware that she shouldn't be here. She could hear her footsteps as she walked over the large off-white marbled tiles. She glanced around behind her, the male glanced around at the same time, and just as quickly she looked away, 'Telepathy?' she thought.

The receptionist sat behind the front desk. She was a young girl. She had long blonde hair and was in her early twenties. She wore far too much make-up on her lips and above her eyes. She had two silver rings on the middle finger of her left hand. She gave Mars a genial smile.

'Can I help you, please?' she said merrily, with a "I'm putting on a false smile" grin on her face.

Mars smiled, and glanced around, making sure Annabelle wasn't in the lobby area, or in sight anywhere.

'Erm, yes. I'm looking for Annabelle Divine, is she in today?'

The girl looked confused.

'I'm sorry, we don't have an Annabelle Divine Miss. We do have an Annabelle Turner though.' Mars quickly thought. She looked at the girl with scepticism. She had to make a hasty decision.

'Erm. Is she petite? And does she have blonde hair?

'Yes, that's Annabelle.'

'Ah that's right, she's recently married, hasn't she?' she said, trying to digest the surname.

'Er, yes to Jeff.' The receptionist didn't hesitate; she tapped away at her keyboard.

'She's off today. She's back in the office tomorrow at nine,' she said staring at a screen with a smiley face.

'Oh, thanks. Thank you, you've been so kind.' She turned in the direction of the doors and pondered her next move.

'Is she expecting you, Miss?' Mars turned back; she liked what the girl said.

'Yes, er no,' she said as she stumbled over her words.

'She's a friend of mine, and I'm trying to contact her.' The girl looked at her computer screen.

Mars gathered her thoughts. She investigated the girl's fresh face, and thought 'this girl looks new.'

'I love the colour of your top. Where did you get it from?'

The girl glanced down, her face lit up with a smile.

'Thank you, do you like it?'

'It's unusual,' Mars said conceitedly. She knew it was a cheap brand, and that the girl hadn't spent much money on the blouse.

'I bought it in River Island, in Slough. I've had it for some time, it wasn't expensive.' The girl was delighted by the compliment.

'It's lovely.' Mars smiled. 'Have you been working here long then?' asked Mars, again looking around, keeping an eye out. She knew she shouldn't be in the building. She felt a sense of fear come over her. Time was moving on. She was on the lookout just in case someone with any seniority came along and started asking her questions.

'Oh, sometime now,' she said with the same smile. 'Where do you work then?'

'In town, I used to work here some time ago, with Annabelle' she said deceitfully, not waiting for an answer from the girl. She went on. 'Who was that tall chap with the sharp suit who just walked out a moment ago?' Turning, and gesturing towards the exit.

'Oh, that's Matt Robson. He's in charge of... well, most things around here,' she said not really knowing his position in the company.

'He's good-looking, isn't he?' Her smile got wider. 'I thought I recognised him' Mars said, not telling the truth.

'He's been here for some time, hasn't he?'

'About five years, so I'm told.'

The young girl's inexperience in life was playing into Mars's hands. She had her right where she wanted her. Mars lifted her shoulder bag and rested it on the counter, the long straps flopped down, the bag was on full view, so the girl could see it. Mars slowly unzipped it, while she studied the girl's expression. She could see that she was drawn to the item, her face was gaping at the expensive Prada design, with its gold ringlets, and a large gold buckle. Its name was advertised above the side zip, pointing towards the youngster.

'What's your name?' Mars said as she looked inside the bag.

'Maxine,' she said gladly.

'Mine's... Ellen,' she said hesitantly, almost saying Mars, and thinking that would be too complicated to explain to the young office junior. She noticed the girl studying the leather bag with curiosity, moving her head gently as she looked at it.

'Is that one of those fake bags, or is it a real one, Miss?' the girl said inquisitively. Mars's arms stopped fumbling in the bag and went rigid for a second, like a statue. She shot the girl a dagger of a look, her eyes looked mortified. 'Bloody charming,' she thought. 'I spend three hundred and fifty bloody pounds on the genuine article, and this stupid little upstart, with her poxy River Island top decides to say to me, "is it a bloody fake?" 'No Miss cheap top, it's bloody not a fake,' she said under her breath.

'No, it's a real one,' she grinned a long grin.

Mars decided to keep her cool, she thought, 'She's young, and still learning her trade. I'll give her the benefit of the doubt.'

'Have you got Annabelle's address, Maxine, for me please, I can't seem to find it, in my fake bag,' she said gritting her teeth and smiling cynically. She looked up at Maxine. Maxine turned to the screen and typed on the keyboard, it made a tapping sound.

'Twenty-one,' she hesitated. 'I don't know if I'm supposed to give out addresses of workers here.' Her face looked puzzled as she looked at Mars. Maxine looked around the lobby area to see if there was anyone with seniority, anyone she thought she may know. She knew that she would be doing wrong by giving out the address, but she knew this woman was a friend of hers, so why couldn't she give it to her?

'Maxine darling, stand up a minute for me will you, sweetheart,' Mars said, waving her hand in an upward movement. The young girl obeyed and stood almost immediately. Mars leant over the reception desk and handed the young girl her handbag.

'Put it over your shoulder for a moment, let us see what it looks like on you, Maxine.' The young girl did as she was told. 'Now that looks good. How does it feel. Tell me, does it feel good? It suits you anyway.'

'Wow, it's fantastic. Great Miss!' she said looking at the expensive item. It was probably the most expensive fashion item she had had the pleasure of holding. Mars let her investigate the bag for a few minutes to make her feel good, she knew the girl would like the feel and the experience of such a fashion item, she could tell. She would let her friends know of the time she had had this morning, holding such a grand and stylish item. Mars knew that she should be moving along soon, she didn't want to continue playing games with this inexperienced youngster.

'Wow, is that the time,' Maxine came to her senses and returned the bag to its rightful owner, not letting it out of her sight.

'Nice isn't it.' Mars smiled.

'Yes, very.' She replied excitedly. 'I would love one of those.'

'Well, I'm glad you liked it, I thought you might, Maxie, darling.' Mars said affably, her eyes widened, her arms resting on the reception. 'I must be off now; time is moving on. Oh, sorry, I almost forgot Maxine, what was Annabelle's new address, twenty-one?' The young apprentice of life looked at her monitor. Mars thought she wasn't a person of integrity and initiative.

'Twenty-one Alexander Street, Miss. Chesham.' She bit her lip, still not knowing if she had done the right thing.

'Alexander Street, that's the one, it was on the tip of my tongue.' Mars grinned and zipped up her bag, Maxine took one last look at the article, and then smiled up at Mars.

'I love your handbag.'

'Thank you, Maxine, it's been nice to meet and talk with you.' She said, placing a hand on the waist-high counter. Maxine smiled and said nothing. Mars turned to walk towards the doors of the office. There was a Black delivery driver, with dreadlocked hair. He was wearing a red polo shirt and wheeling in a trolley of office stationery. It looked heavy.

She turned back towards the young girl, their eyes locked on to one another.

'You are probably right Maxine, I'm not too sure you are supposed to give out confidential information to people who just ask for it, I could have been anyone.' The girl's face looked fearful.

'Oh, am I not,' she sounded startled as she moved a hand towards her mouth.

'No, I don't think you are, it's all about data protection you know, all that stuff. But anyway, not to confuse things, I won't say a word to anyone in seniority here, if you don't mention it, us, having this little chat with each other, OK.' She winked at the anxious face.

'Thank you, Miss,' she replied as if Mars were her headmistress at school. Mars turned and headed towards the door with a shrewd look on her face, her place at the reception was now filled by the delivery driver. She now knew where Jeff lived. 'What would be her next move,' she thought.

She glided out through the heavy double glass doors, she looked up. The sun was high in the sky. Mars squinted. 'What shall I do now, now that I have Mr Turner's, or Mr Divine's address?' She ran a hand over the front of her neck. She pulled a frown.

She was still after revenge for what Jeff had done to her on that fateful evening. The memory still hadn't gone away. She was angry at herself for not reporting it. She was bitter inside. She knew it was a crime and she hadn't agreed to it. She did meet him on her own accord. She wasn't taken to the flat forcefully, she wasn't dragged there, she was invited, and she took up the offer. Although she had known Jeff was up to something at the time, she didn't know exactly what. 'It's probably too late now, I would get asked too many derisive questions and my personal life would be dragged through the courts.'

She felt that she still also needed to talk to someone about it. She needed to get it out in the open, to relieve some of the anxiety she was feeling. If she had spoken to anyone that she knew they would have all said the same thing, "report it". Maybe she didn't want to report it? Perhaps she enjoyed the thrill of it and maybe it was an excuse to seek her revenge on him.

She skipped down the steps from the office, opened her bag and withdrew her sunglasses. She had a scheming look on her face. Mars put the glasses on as she headed across the car park.

'Hello!' The male voice came from the open window of a parked car. It was a surprise to her. Matt Robson got out of the sporty vehicle and closed the door. He stood and adjusted his jacket.

'Oh, hello,' she said as she cleared her throat, her voice startled by his sudden appearance from nowhere.

'How long had he been there for?' she thought. 'He looked in a hurry when he passed earlier.' Her heartbeat increased. She thought he was very good-looking.

'I haven't seen you around here before, are you new?' Matt said as he strode towards her. He stood a couple of feet away. He was just over six-foot tall, with dark hair, and a medium build, slightly tanned, with a healthy complexion.

'That sounds like a chat-up line if I've ever heard one,' she thought. 'Still bloody good looking though.' She glanced at his left hand. 'And he's not wearing a ring, this could be my lucky day. You wait for ages, and like buses they come along in pairs, only this is different. I find two good-looking guys in the same morning. How should I answer his question. He's been here for five years so Maxine told me. If I mention Annabelle's name it may get back to her, if I don't give him a correct answer, he may ask the receptionist what I was here for.'

'Oh, I was just passing by, and popped in to see an old friend, but she's since left.' She wasn't a very good liar, her voice sounded unconvincing. She had to move the conversation swiftly away from her visit today. He may want to help her further by asking for the name of her so-called friend.

'I don't know you, do I?' she said, thinking, 'Christ, is that the best I can do?'

'Matt, Matt Robson,' he held out his hand, smiling.

'Director of sales and marketing. I saw you earlier, in the reception area,' he said, twisting his head towards the building. His voice was smooth, it sounded like Timothy Dalton in James Bond.

'That's right,' she laughed at herself as she removed her sunglasses. She glanced over at the office waiting for his answer.

'So, who was your friend, perhaps I can help in finding them?' She didn't want to hear that question.

'It doesn't matter, I think I may have found where she has moved on to, but thanks all the same.'

'Oh, okay. So, are you from around these parts, do you work local to here?'

She looked at him as she pushed her fingers through her hair.

'No, not quite, I'm from Ealing, and I work in Hammersmith, for Hammerson Shaw.' Thinking, 'Was it right to give him the name of the company?'

Matt liked this girl, she was smartly dressed, she had bobbed blonde hair, and he could tell she looked after herself. She looked like a classy woman who enjoyed the finer things in life. Her clothes were expensive, he could also tell by her body language she was a bit nervous but wanted the conversation to last.

They made small talk.

'What time do you have to be back at work? If you work in Hammersmith, you're only a few miles away aren't you? It shouldn't take you much time to get there.'

'Oh. I'm OK, my boss is flexible. He's no bother as long as I look after him.' She scratched her cheek with a finger. She felt a pang of nervousness creep in as they briefly looked into each other's eyes.

'Would you like a lift back to work? I don't mind dropping you off, I'm going into town myself,' he pointed behind him at his car.

'I'm OK thanks,' she became edgy. 'My car is parked just around the corner from here, besides I've got an appointment in Richmond this afternoon, at one.' She looked down at her watch, it told her it was eleven-forty-five. She looked back up at Matt, eagerly waiting for his next sentence to begin, and she looked at his blue eyes.

'Well OK, if I can't give you a lift to work, can I take you out for dinner one evening? If you're free, that is?' He raised his eyebrows, although she was waiting for Matt to ask her for a date, it still came as a shock to her. She was surprised by his asking.

'Er, that was a surprise, that would be nice, thank you for asking.' she said with a hint of bashfulness.

'I'm sorry,' said Matt, holding his hand out, and looking apologetic. 'I didn't catch your name?'

'It's Mars.'

'Pardon?' Matt jolted his head back slightly and looked perplexed at her answer. He cracked a smile. Mars looked shyly at him.

'Oh, it's a long story, it's a nickname you see, and it's kind of stuck with me. My surname is Marshall, hence the first part broken down. That's where Mars came from. My ex gave me the name when we first met, and now everyone, well almost everyone calls me it. It's OK, I'm used to it.' She looked seductively at him.

Thirty-four

'What the hell am I doing here? I feel like a bloody stalker.

Twenty-one, twenty-one twenty… Ah! There it is.'

Mars was in her car driving covertly down Alexander Street, looking for the address given to her by the receptionist at Honda. It was a warm sunny afternoon. Number twenty-one was a cottage, with a blue front door. It had two steps leading up to it, the numbers were in brass, and it also had a brass letterbox. Parking in the street was a luxury but she found a place about thirty yards from the house. She got out and wandered up to its front door. She looked at the front of the house. There was a side entrance, and she noticed what she thought to be long pieces of wood, which were probably for scaffolding lying parallel to the side wall. She took another look at the house. There was a wheelie bin. She opened the lid, and took a look inside. She moved a plastic bag, and grimaced. She closed the lid. She walked back to her car and sat surreptitiously inside it and waited. She had to make certain that Jeff lived here, at this address, the one that she had been given. She couldn't rely solely on the information given to her by, "miss cheap top", she had to be a hundred percent correct, or her plan wouldn't work. Mars needed to see either Jeff or Annabelle go in, or out of the house to prove that it was theirs.

She pulled out her phone from her bag and pushed a button to retrieve any text messages. There were no new ones so she returned it to its home. She glanced up at the house, and then down the street. A mum was pushing her child in pram, a man with a large PDA machine in his hand was taking readings from electric meters outside some of the buildings. She looked back down inside her bag, and at the phone, it had a text message. It was a new one, from Matt. He said that he was looking forward to their date tomorrow night and that he would phone her in the day to make the arrangements, it was followed by an x. She got all excited over the message and stared at it profusely. Matt told her that he would take her for a meal, and she too was looking forward to meeting him again. She told her friend Jenny that she had a date with a tall dark stranger. Jenny was impressed and happy for her and wanted to know all the gossip the next day.

Mars looked at her watch, it told her it was four-twenty-five p.m. She pulled out a company document from her bag and glanced over it for a few minutes, checking her forthcoming work schedule.

Her mobile rang, she jumped slightly, as it surprised her. She looked at the screen and recognized the number, she pushed the green button.

'Hi Morgan, how are you?'

'I'm fine, Mars thank you, lovely weather don't you think? What's it like where you are?' came the voice from the mobile.

'Er, good, good,' Mars said in a guilty tone. She shouldn't be where she was, so she was trying to cover her tracks. One of Morgan's virtues was that he didn't hover over you. He was phoning her to change an appointment in her daily schedule for tomorrow. It was no big deal, in a way, he was just keeping her informed and up-to-date, and just being a boss, letting her know he was around.

She moved in the seat of her car and looked around at the street. She was getting irritated, and she glanced at the clock on the car instrument panel. She folded her arms and became cosy and snug. She lent her head back on the headrest and closed her eyes.

Two young girls, in their early teens, walked past the car, one of them tapped on the window and was laughing at the other and she pointed at what she saw inside. Mars stirred, her eyes came to life, and then she jerked upwards, not quite knowing what day it was, or where she was. She twisted her head around and saw the girls walking away from her, happy and skipping, hand in hand, they were good friends, she thought. She pulled down the sun visor and looked in the vanity mirror. Now realising that she had dozed off. She looked at the clock, and it said ten past five, she worked out that it had been just under ten minutes. She looked back at the mirror, checked and adjusted her hair, and pushed the mirror back to where it belonged. 'I could be here all night,' she thought.

She waited another fifteen minutes. Then opened the door of her car, got out and stretched her legs, 'I'm going straight down to the gym after this. I desperately need a workout.' The neighbour at number twenty three was pulling some dead leaves from her hanging basket. She noticed a blue car turning into the road and heading in her direction, she jumped back into her seat. The car found a place near the house she was stalking and parked. A slim petite girl got out, holding a Tesco plastic bag, Mars watched intensively at her every move. The girl then lifted the boot of the vehicle and retrieved another bag. She headed in the direction of number twenty-one, she put down the shopping bags, pulled out a key and opened the door.

'About bloody time.' She waited until Annabelle had gone in and closed the door, she started her engine. 'Gymnasium here I come.'

Thirty-five

A police officer was standing at the front door of the house. There were a couple of police cars outside parked in the road, plus a few onlookers, standing and staring. They were neighbours, who were eager to know exactly what was going on. They were pushing up against the yellow police tape, which was there trying to keep observers away, but these people wanted to find out what was going on inside the house, a house in their street, on their doorstep. Things of this nature just didn't happen around here. They were interested to know what was wrong with the resident of the house.

The hallway had a somewhat creepy atmosphere when the two detectives entered it, there was a pungent smell.

'Jesus, what the fucking hell is this?' said DCI Richards, looking slightly stunned, whilst looking up at a deceased, grotesque body as he entered the hallway of number fourteen Bollo Lane. He coughed at the stench in the air, burying his mouth in the arm of his jacket.

'Bloody hell, how the crap did she get up there?' replied DI Sutton, following him in, whilst squinting his eyes.

Christina Zabrinski was dangling, upside down, in mid-air. She had a rope tied around her left ankle, it was biting into her decaying skin, and in turn the other end of the rope was tied around the wooden handrail on the first-floor landing. Her eyes were wide open, and she was staring into oblivion. She had long lines of mascara trailing from her eyes, downwards, and over her eyelids. Her hands were tied together, behind her back. Her long wilting hair hung straight, and towards the floor. It was frizzy and matted. It looked dry. Her face was pallid, and morbid looking with almost a witchlike appearance.

Strangely, and mysteriously. She had one stocking missing, from her left leg. The leg with the rope tied around it. But even more bizarrely, she had an apple, stuffed in her mouth, her teeth gripped into the green skin, and maggots were climbing out of the crevices.

Richards stood almost rooted to the spot in amazement. A bemused look was on his face, his mouth was slightly open. DI Sutton was close behind him, he looked faintly stunned by the scene. They hadn't seen anything quite like this before, nor had witnessed a scene remotely like the one in front of them during their time in the force.

It looked like a scene from a horror movie. It looked surreal, fictional, it looked like a picture, but it wasn't a picture. It was real, and it was in front of them. A grotesque figure, beaten in a fight, with someone, someone possibly stronger. Strangled, poisoned, drugged, who knows. And then hung out to dry, hung upside down, from a rope, and humiliated for all to see.

Like an exhibition, she was on view, on display for anyone who would next enter her home. She wasn't hidden or covered over. Was this the way it was meant to be? Was this how the culprit or culprits meant for it to look like, and if so, why?

'Who knows how she died? Who knows how she got into this position? Why was she put where she is?' There were so many questions, Richards thought.

'Her name is Christina Zabrinski,' the voice came from behind them. 'She's thirty-eight, and works for Hammerson Shaw in west London Sir,' said the young fresh-faced officer. He had arrived on the scene first, with his colleague.

'Thanks.' Sam mumbled, forcing the words out, and looking halfway around at where the voice came from. Richards didn't take his eyes off the body, whilst ignoring the young officer.

'How long do you think she's been dead for Sam?' Richards asked his partner, whilst gulping at the figure.

Sam shot him a look.

'Tough one guv?' His mind was making a calculation, the question came to him too quickly, he felt he was still in shock. He moved forward and felt the body, her skin was soft. He paused, the room was quiet. 'Well looking at her complexion, her flaccid skin, and the blue-bottle that's on her face.' He leaned around and looked in further detail, coughing at the odour that it emitted.

'The white of the apple is now brown, it looks dry and flaky. Blood is beginning to form in her mouth, and she's starting to bloat. I would say it's been there for.' He looked thoughtful; he didn't want to give his answer too quickly. 'Say two, maybe three days.' Richards moved towards the body. Sutton took a step back and stared up at the handrail on the first floor.

'Yeah, I was thinking the same.' As he examined the texture of the corpse. His eyes ran up and down the disgusting-looking figure as it hung upside down. He gaped at the top of Christina's hold up stocking and wondered why she was only wearing one. It was two- tone. A thick black band followed a thinner one as it reached the top. The nylon had a sheen and he wondered what the material was made from. It looked to be an expensive brand. There was a crease near to her knee. The stocking must have dropped down in the struggle with her attacker.

'Her body looks dusky.' he said, running a finger over her flesh.

Sutton moved towards the body.

'It looks bizarre, a bit of an overkill. It reminds me of "bobbing for apples" guv,' Sutton replied.

'Sorry!' came back a startled voice. Richards turned and looked at his colleague in amusement. The lines on his forehead rose out.

'Tell me more Sam, I'm bloody intrigued.' The young, uniformed officer pulled a face of astonishment.

'Well. It's a Halloween game guv. It's called, "bobbing for apples". It's just a thought?'

'Right.' He glanced at Sutton in astoundment. 'Go on, carry on.' He looked back at the body.

'So, you see, it's a game guv, you put apples into a large bowl of water, or you tie an apple to a piece of string, and then you dangle it. It's a lover's game, girls would try to bite them, and they had their hands tied around their backs, so as not to cheat. If they got them quickly and bit them, then they would get the chance to marry, early.'

Richards gasped at his counterpart.

'Really?' he said, sounding confused.

'Yeah that's right. Looking at her, she has a rope tied to her, which denotes the string, and an apple in her mouth, which you try to bite, and she's dangling, like the apple on the string.' Richards looked and listened interestingly at his colleague, as he stroked his beard. He complimented him.

'Clever.' he said, not understanding the game.

'Well, if she was murdered, three days ago, that's Friday, right?'

'OK.' Richards replied, looking agog.

'So, I thought that seeing it was Halloween night on Friday, just gone, the culprit may have had that on their mind. The dangling body, and then the dangling of an apple, maybe the two might be linked with each other, I mean.' Richards still looked perplexed at Sutton's logic. He stood as rigid as the deceased.

'Are you thinking that was where the killer got the idea from, the dangling of an apple on a piece of string?' Richards said looking up to where the rope was tied to the wooden rail.

'Just a thought guv, or maybe they were into the occult, it being Halloween. It all ties in… Sorry about the pun, a Freudian slip guv. But it all adds up, doesn't it?' Richards didn't answer. Sutton then stupidly pushed the side of the rigid body slightly with his hand. The bannister creaked, like the sound of a large wooden ship sinking. The weight of the body moved with momentum, and they all immediately looked up with trepidation to where the noise came from, expecting something to give way, thinking that the body would come crashing down and hit the floor.

Sutton cringed, thinking that wasn't the right thing to have done. Richards winced at the moving body, he pulled at his pointed beard.

There was a sudden silence. The young police officer flinched as he swung a hand at a blue-bottle. The body swayed gently, like a pendulum, and it began to twist around in a circle, as the rope gravitated, making a tightening sound. Her eyes were dark. They appeared to be looking in turn at each of the officers as if she knew them. The officers looked at the revolving corpse.

She was wearing a short black skirt, it was hanging down, exposing her black underwear. Richards sighed with relief and was pleased when the deceased body slowed and came to a halt. He breathed out, trying not to show his anger at the idiotic move that Sutton had carried out. He thought that would be the last thing he wanted, was for poor Ms Christina Zabrinski to crash to the ground. The forensics would be unimpressed. He scratched his head. He sighed and looked at Sutton and the young officer in relief.

He decided to move on from the foolish act.

'Does she have a ring on her finger? Is she married?' Sutton walked around the body and checked Christina's hand.

'She doesn't appear to have anything on the wedding finger. She has a gold one on the middle finger though guv, with a couple of diamonds in it.'

'Have you preserved the crime scene officer? I mean you haven't moved anything since finding the deceased, have you?' he said, turning away from the body, and asking the young officer as he looked around the hall for clues.

'Well, no guv. We took a look around the lower part of the house when we got here. We checked her pulse as she wasn't breathing. Which told us that she was dead, and probably had been for some time. Plus, we gathered by the flies, she had been here for days, there were so many of them when we got here.' the officer said. Richards threw him a mordent look.

'If something dies, they'll find it. Were you the first here, at the scene,' Richards said, glancing at his shoulder, and his badge number.

An older officer then appeared and butted in.

'Yes sir.' He cleared his throat and glanced at his notepad. 'We got here at eleven fifty-two a.m. My colleague, officer Davies and myself forced the front door open, as her work colleague, a Ms Hayley Remington was concerned that Ms Zabrinski had not showed up for work this morning, and wasn't answering her mobile phone, or landline, and this was out of character of Ms Zabrinski. Ms Remington looked through the letterbox and noticed a fly buzzing around, and a strange odour in the house, and witnessed the deceased, hanging up, from the rope.' DCI Richards glanced at the officer.

'Have you touched anything?' he said, glancing up the stairs of the house.'

'No, sir.'

'Very good, any signs of a break-in then?'

'No. We've taken a look around and cannot find any signs of forced entry. There doesn't appear to be anything out of place.'

'What do you think Sam? What's your perspective on this crime,' he said, looking up at the pivotal point.

'I haven't quite seen anything like it before, guv.'

'No, neither have I. It appears that she invited the killer in.'

'It does, guv.'

'I've seen people hanged by the neck, from the rafters in the loft space. I've seen people hanged from trees, strangled and tied up, and put in bags, and boxes. Seen them tied to all sorts of devices—but not upside down. Why do you think the killer hung her in this way? What was the reason in the killer's mind to hang her upside down? I'm thinking that she was probably dead first, and then put in this position afterwards, what do you think?'

'I have to agree. It would have been difficult to get her in this position if she were alive, it would have been one hell of a struggle to get a kicking and fighting woman up there,' he said looking at the point where the rope was tied.

Richards moved away. He strolled into the lounge, and just as quick, the young officer followed him. Richards walked over to the window and looked outside. He could see the crowd of onlookers getting thicker. He looked around. He pulled out a tissue from his coat pocket as he noticed a glossy magazine tilting upwards, with possibly something underneath it. He walked over to a cabinet, moved the magazine, and picked up a mobile phone, he took a gleeful and interesting look at it and pressed the buttons until he found the list of incoming numbers. His heart raced. He then did the same to find a list of text messages.

'When do forensics get here?' he said as he looked at the officer.

'They should be here very soon guv. I called them at 12.12 p.m.'

He glanced at the officer, who was scouring the room with optimism.

'Any luck with the numbers on the phone sir?' the young officer said, looking at the DCI who had a wry smile on his face.

'The last text message was this morning from, Hayley, saying, "Chris I'm on my way over to you now be bout fifteen mins x". I take it that's the girl from her workplace, who informed us about Ms Zabrinski's disappearance isn't it?'

'Yes, it is sir.'

'Found anything of interest, guv?' DI Sutton said as he walked into the lounge.

'Yes, I have Sam. I've found her mobile, and it has a couple of interesting phone numbers and text messages on it.'

'And?'

'One text is from a Bill, at 9.01 a.m. saying that he can't make it this morning, his wife was poorly.

'And one from, a Becks. "Have a lovely weekend darling x".

And one sent to Mars! This is interesting,

"Looking forward to our private meeting xx", timed at seven twenty-two p.m. on Friday the 31st. It was the last time she used her phone.' He looked with delight at Sam.

I think we need to speak to these people,' he said with gratification.

Thirty-six

Mike Schreiber leant on the desk. His arms were folded and his face bemused. Sherry stood staring out of the window, utterly motionless. Her back facing towards them both. Hayley had just returned to the office after being interviewed at the police station.

'What do you think is going to happen now, Mike?' Hayley said with an anxious tone in her voice.

'Well Hayley, the police told me that they will be back here in the morning, to take some more statements with everyone who came into contact with Christina.' He looked at both the girls.

The air was tense, 'We will have to accommodate them and they are going to be here early.' Mike brushed his forehead with a hand. 'Who the bloody hell could have done such a horrifying and degrading thing to Christina?' Hayley shook her head.

'How long were you at the station for, Hayley?'

'I was there for at least four hours, Mike.'

'Christ. What did they ask you?'

'Well, I told them that we were all worried for her because we'd been calling her, and that we hadn't got an answer from any of her phones, and that she also hadn't returned any of our text messages that we'd sent. We all agreed that someone should go to her house, to see if she was there, and to see if she was okay. I said that you had ordered a cab, so I went to find out why she hadn't shown up for work, as it was strange of her to do such a thing, and that it wasn't in her nature to be late. I told them that she's a punctual woman. They asked me how long I'd known her for, how long I'd worked here for. They asked me what time I left the office on Friday, and what time I'd arrived home.'

'Oh,' Mike replied. Sherry turned around.

'Because there was a space of over two hours. Me, leaving here at five-forty-five p.m. and got in at just after eight, they thought that was enough time to commit the crime. They looked at me as if I were the murderer, because I was the last one, apparently to have seen her alive.'

'What did you say to them?' Mike said.

'I said that I just happened to take a long walk home that evening, that's all. I just needed some fresh air. I said that I got off the train at Tooting Broadway and picked up a bag of shopping, before heading home. They asked me for the receipt. Well, of course, I didn't keep it!' She sighed.

'They are going to look at my bank statements, plus any CCTV that the shop has.' She looked emotional.

'Don't be concerned Hayley, you will be alright, they are only doing their job.' Mike walked over to her and stroked her arm. Hayley went on.

'She had arranged to meet a gardener before nine that morning, I remember Christina mentioning this to me on Friday. Someone was sitting at the station. He looked at me when my name was mentioned, it may have been him.' She sniffed. He moved his conversation to Sherry.

'Did she have any enemies that you know of Sherry?' Mike said with a straining voice, as he looked around the room, running a hand around his neck.

'No, well not that I know of, or at least not anyone I know of, to want to have killed her,' she replied. 'I think she had some fierce rivals in business, but no one that would have taken it further.'

'What about you Hayley.' Sherry butted in.

'Mike. I just have to mention something to you both.' They looked anxiously at her.

'Well, I once overheard a blazing argument that Rebecca Ansell had with Christina, over the phone.'

'Oh, and?' Mike said, eagerly waiting for her reply.

'Yes, it was nasty Mike. It was late one afternoon when a lot of the office staff had already left. I was here until six, I was sitting at my desk, and Rebecca was standing at the end of the corridor.' She was gesturing to the position. 'She was on her mobile speaking to Christina in a foul and disdainful manner, her attitude towards what was her boss was unjust, and I don't remember Christina ever reprimanding her for it. The conversation went on for some time… it sounded like a lovers' tiff to me, if you want to know. Rebecca sounded angry.'

'Right. What was she angry about Sherry, did you hear anything substantial?' Mike became interested in the argument the girls had had, he unfolded his arms, he wanted to find out more.

'It was as if,' Sherry hesitated and touched an eyebrow with a finger, she swallowed. 'It was as if they were seeing each other, going out with each other, in a relationship, if that makes any sense.' Mike looked at the expressions of both girls. 'It seems hard to believe, well I don't know what Christina's sexuality is, or was,' she corrected herself. 'It was as if Christina was ditching Rebecca, and Rebecca was not too pleased about it at all. She said, what it sounded like, under her breath, something like, "I'll fucking kill you".' Mike raised his eyebrows. He opened his bottle of water and took a sip.

'Well,' he replied. Hayley put a hand over her mouth in disbelief at what she had just heard.

'Did you tell the police this?'

'No, no I didn't, I didn't think it to be relevant. Is it?' Mike sighed and stared at her, thinking it was. She paused. 'I'm not saying that Rebecca killed Christina.' She lowered her voice. 'But the anger was there in her voice.' Mike looked pensive. He looked down at the floor, then back up again.

'I didn't think that Christina was bisexual. When did this argument take place? Can you remember a date at all?'

'No, I can't Mike.' She frowned. 'I was staying on until six-thirty one evening, as I was going to meet Steve after work.' Steve was Sherry's husband of ten years. She pulled out a diary from her bag and flicked the pages backwards. Hayley looked on with trepidation.

'It was, I think, around six weeks ago, possibly?'

'I think you need to mention it to the police tomorrow when they show up. I believe they need to know this information. It may be vital for their investigation, although quite unbelievably at the moment.' Mike looked astounded. 'Is there anything else to add, Sherry?'

'Only that,' She paused. 'I saw them talking together on various occasions in the past. The sort of discussions that couples have when they have problems with each other. Intimate discussions, as if they were sorting out personal issues, you know, things that you sort out when you're seeing someone. I don't think Rebecca would be able to get that close to Christina to sort out business matters, or certainly wouldn't be allowed to talk to her in that vein. She would have to go through the correct channels to get her point across without confronting Christina directly.' Mike looked absorbedly at Sherry, he then wandered around the office looking for an answer. 'I'm not saying Rebecca was the culprit Mike, I'm only saying what I saw.'

'I understand. It would be hard to believe that one of her work colleagues could contemplate doing such a thing to her. It doesn't make any sense that someone from this company would want to kill Christina, and in that gruesome fashion. Still I'm getting ahead of myself, aren't I? We don't know the answer yet, let's all hope we find out though.' He then turned to Hayley.

'Hayley. What are your views on what Sherry has just said, seeing you worked close to Christina. Have you seen anything unreasonable between Rebecca and Christina, recently, anything indifferent between the two of them? Anything you think we here, or perhaps the police need to know.' Hayley took a long sigh.

'Well, I have seen some goings on between the pair of them, but I thought nothing of it. I thought, perhaps they were talking business. Although, I did see Christina peck, Rebecca, on the cheek once, at a time when they thought that maybe no one was looking. I thought that was rather peculiar. She stroked her arm rather longingly as well, what could I say.' Hayley shrugged her shoulders, 'She was my boss, I worked for her, and I wasn't about to spread malicious rumours everywhere. It may have been nothing. Christina always had a boyfriend around, somewhere, mainly casual. So, it was hard to believe that she could fancy a woman. Since the break-up with Robert, she found it hard to hold down a relationship, possibly she was too hurt over the split. I think she's been seeing someone new now, a Spanish guy. I think. I'm not sure for how long though?'

'Listen, I don't think we are going to solve this tonight' said Mike, glancing at his watch. 'What I think we will do, when we have all been interviewed tomorrow I will call a meeting between everyone who worked closely with Christina. I'll get us all around a table and try to get some answers for our good, for the company's good.

Thirty-seven

A Day Later

Mike's office door was slightly ajar, there was a tense and muted atmosphere at the Hammerson Shaw offices this morning, what with investigators poking around the place, and throwing guilty looks at everyone.

Sherry Hill tapped on the door. She had been running late this morning, and Mike wanted to see her. He wanted to try to start the ball rolling again and get some semblance in the office, it had lost its momentum due to the recent dreadful event. Mike was looking to kick start the team again and move on. Someone had to take the place of Christina. He thought Morgan would be the obvious choice, or he would just take both roles up himself for the interim. He wanted to speak to his staff, starting firstly with Sherry. He knew that she was close to Rebecca workwise - and wanted more information on the young girl.

Sherry sat down, only to hear another knock on the door. Not waiting for an answer, DCI Richards pushed it open and wandered into the room, as if he owned it.

'Sorry, I'm not intruding, am I?' Not caring if he was. He was directed to the office by a staff member.

'No. Do come in inspector, we were just about to discuss company issues, and how we would move on under the recent dreadful circumstances, do come in.'

'Thank you, Sir. This is my colleague, DI Sutton,' he turned and introduced a tall male, five feet-ten in height, with black hair, with a side parting. He was in his mid-forties. His roving eyes were scouring the room as if he were doing some of his bosses work for him, being nosey, and looking for clues.

Mike smiled at them.

'And when would you like to commence the interviews with my staff?' Mike said politely.

Detective Chief Inspector Richards was a tall figure of a man. He had a prominent nose, his age was hovering just above the half-century. He had dark hair. His eyebrows were thick, and he had a distinctive pointed beard, and a chin strap, similar to the character, D'Artagnan. He had been in the Met all his working life, working his way up through the ranks. He started off life in the cadets. He'd probably got picked on in school and wanted to get his own back on a few people, and society, so he joined the force. He was a typical copper, inquisitive, regimental, spoke in short syllables, and he was on his second marriage. He loved the force, he loved his job, he was the type who would write out a parking ticket to his granny. He didn't answer Mike's question. He smiled at Sherry, and then looked at both of them.

'Do you know a Mr Turner, a Mr Jeff Turner. He works in the construction industry.' Mike and Sherry looked at each other with minor bemusement. Mike shook his head.

'No, I can't say I do, Sherry, do you know of him?'

'No, sorry, I've never heard of him,' she said thinking if she did.

'Well, he said that he had met three, or maybe four people that work for this company,' Richards peered at them.

'He's six feet two tall, a good-looking chap, olive skin and in his late thirties, no?' Richards said, waiting for an answer.

'It doesn't appear that we know this chap that you mention. So, are you going to let us know who this person is? I don't think either of us know this—Mr Turner?'

'Well, I'll get to the point,' Richards said. 'We brought Mr Jeff Turner into the station yesterday afternoon at six forty-two p.m.' he glanced at his colleague. 'In connection with the murder of Christina Zabrinski.' He took two steps to his left as he looked at the two of them. Sherry looked at Mike who in turn was engrossed in what the DCI was explaining. 'We questioned Mr Turner for several hours. I have told you first Mr Schreiber, seeing that you are in charge, but I will have to question the people whose names he has mentioned to us.' There was a slight feeling of culpability. 'And one of those names is Sherry Hill.' He looked at her with a gaze of guilt. He had a slight Scottish accent.

'Me?' Sherry said with a startled voice, pushing a finger at her chest. 'I have never met a Mr Turner in my life.' She turned and looked defensively at Mike, the man with the pointed beard had a smug look on his face.

'So. You are Sherry Hill?'

'Are you sure that you have this right, Detective? Sherry is saying that she hasn't met this man before, she seems to be confident of that,' Mike said in defence of his employee.

'Mr Schreiber.' the detective said in a governing voice. 'Mr Turner has described Ms Hill's details, her hair, her height, and her eye colour.' He looked at Sherry, 'And he has got most things correct.'

'I have never met this man, err, Richards, I can assure you of that. Where does he come from?'

'Detective will do please.' He stared at her. 'Well, he appears to know you Ms Hill,' he said, in an insinuating tone.

'Mrs Hill, actually!' Mike glanced at Sherry, slightly surprised at her abrupt attitude towards the detective.

'Yes, well, as I said, I'm here to find out what's going on between you both, so I can rule you out of our enquiries - Mrs Hill.' He glanced at her ring finger, the tone of his voice increasing, 'And we need to work on any leads that we have at this point.'

'Who is this—Jeff Turner person? Is he a friend of Christina's? What connection does he have with her? Detective Richards, you appeared to have picked him up quite quickly, is he a boyfriend of hers?' Mike was in a challenging mood, plus he wanted to find out why this person wanted to kill a work colleague of his. Again, he ignored Mike's question.

'Does she have many boyfriends, Mr Schreiber?' DI Sutton said walking around the office and staring at them both.

'What sort of derogative question is that supposed to be, Detective?' Mike said, snapping at him. 'It's a question that we need to ask Mr Schreiber,' Sutton waited for his reply. Richards stood with his hands in the pockets of his black leather jacket, pushing downwards, 'What has this—Mr Turner been telling you?'

'Only that, he told us that Christina had found it difficult to hold down a relationship. We are just approaching the names mentioned to us at the moment Mr Schreiber,' said Richards.

'OK,' said Mike, calming down and trying not to start a potential flair-up. He sensed that there was a dislike between both Sherry and the DCI.

'Mr Turner also mentioned that he had met a female by the name of... Mars? Do you have a Mars working here Mr Schreiber?' he said, the way that only a detective could, knowing full well that there was a girl with that name employed by Mike.

'Yes, we do, she's head of sales and strategy, and she's worked here for some time, Detective.'

'Is she in today, as we tried to speak to her yesterday, Mr Schreiber?' he said in a blunt tone.

'Yes, she is. She's downstairs.'

'Strange name for a woman isn't it, Mr Schreiber, isn't Mars the red planet?'

'Sorry, Detective?'

'Is it a pseudonym by any chance?' he said in a mocking tone.

'Well not really,' Sherry butted in, she didn't like his attitude, or the sound of his voice. The detective's head turned towards her. 'Her name is Helen Marshall, Mars is a nickname inspector, and it's stuck with her. We like it, most people like it,' Sherry said tartly. 'You don't seem to have a sense of humour do you, Detective?'

'I tend to lose my sense of humour when someone has been murdered... Mrs—Hill,' he said with his grey sturdy eyes, staring at her as if she were the culprit.

'What about her boyfriend, Antonio, have you spoken to him yet?' Sherry forced out her words.

'Ah yes, indeed, Mr Garcia. Yes, we have spoken to him,' he said that he was in Portsmouth on the night of the 31st, at a business conference. He has an alibi. He said that he was at a restaurant, with a female client. We are checking up on this.' Richards peered at Sherry.

The detectives found a business card of Jeff Turner's in one of Christina's handbags. They also found court letters in one of her cupboards. They presumed that Jeff could have murdered her to rid of his large debt that he was being chased for.

Christina was last seen leaving her office on Friday October 31st around seven p.m. by a female cleaner, and then discovered on Monday November 3rd at eleven fifty-two a.m. Forensics said she had been dead for around three days. Jeff tried to explain his whereabouts at the time of the murder. He went missing on Friday, for about an hour and a half, between six-thirty and 8:05 p.m. He'd left the Crown Public House in Chiswick High Road at around six-thirty p.m. This had been confirmed by the mate of his, who he went for a drink with after work. He had said as a joke that it was his round, so that's why he left. One of the barmaids confirmed seeing Jeff in the pub, telling the police that he was "boyfriend material".

Jeff said that he had had to meet a lady friend of his who lived nearby at six forty-five p.m.

On his way to her, he had received a text message from Shabina saying that she was running late - and would be at least another hour. He said that he had turned up on a road near where she lived, as there was no parking outside her house. He sat there and waited for her to return and caught up on some paperwork. He told the detectives that he spoke to an elderly chap in his sixties that evening. The man was out walking his dog. He said that the man's dog relieved itself on the rear tyre of his truck. The elderly man mentioned that one of his tyres was bald. He said that they had spoken for about fifteen minutes about the vehicle, as the man once worked for the company that made some parts for it. The man said that his dog had feared the noise of the fireworks going off. But this man had never been traced, making the detectives suspicious of Jeff's whereabouts that evening. Shabina had arrived home at 8:05 p.m. texting him at 8:06. So, Jeff had a void in his evening.

He had protested his innocence to the police. He had told them where he was on the evening. But at this moment in time, they just didn't have enough evidence on him, for the murder of Christina Zabrinski.

Thirty-eight

'Mr Baxter, I am asking you. Where did you get your TV from?' There was a knock on the door. 'One second please.' Richards got up and left the room.

'Chief. Sherry Hill, she has an alibi.' Richards scratched a cheek. 'She was around on the evening of the 31st, her husband was out, she walked to a friend's house, about half a mile away. We've tracked the friend down and spoken to her. They had a drink and a chat with each other at the house, at the time of the murder, while the friend's son was out, trick or treating, so everything adds up.'

'Right.'

'On another note, we have found some CCTV footage from a camera, three streets away from Christina's house, in Fletcher Road. We did some routine door knocking, and the neighbour, well the almost neighbour had some film.'

'And, tell me more.' He sounded excited. 'We ran it, and we found a figure. It looks like a woman. It's a bit grainy, it looks around five foot six tall, and carrying a rucksack on it's back. It was walking in the road, near to parked cars, probably to avoid cameras, I guess? The film at eight-forty-three p.m. showed the figure heading in the direction of Bollo Lane. And then, what looked like the same figure walking in the opposite direction, down Fletcher Road, away from Bollo Lane at ten-thirty-nine p.m. It looked more agitated this time.' He went on. 'Another neighbour, a man who lives in the same road, said he saw what he thought to be a woman. It had the hood of its fleece up covering its face and was carrying a rucksack on its back. This was around the same time. He thought it was around ten-thirty?'

'Thanks James,' he smiled.

'Mr Baxter, you have a TV in your lounge, yes?'

'Aye, sure, I do.'

'So, where did you get it from?' DI Sutton said, pushing the point home.

'I, I bought it from the retail park in Greenford Road, I think,' his answer was hesitant, as he fidgeted in his seat.

'Are you positive?'

'Er, sure I am.'

'Don't make it up as you go along, will you?'

'I'm not.'

'Well, Mr Baxter, I have news for you, we have checked the serial number on your, TV, and found that it was purchased from a store in Oxford Street, west one, and paid for with a credit card, belonging to a, Ms Christina Zabrinski. So did you steal the credit card from Ms Zabrinski?'

'No, I didn't.' He began to perspire.

'So, you're lying then, aren't you!' The Scottish builder looked at the table. He became fixated on it.

Richards entered the room and sat down.

'You do realise Mr Baxter, we are investigating a murder, don't you?' Donal looked shaken. 'And, at the moment, you have a motive for the murder.'

'It wasn't me!' He sounded worried. 'I have no reason to kill the woman. I, I was at home that night, with my girlfriend, I've told you before, go and check with her.'

'We will. Don't you worry.' He moved his chair, to try and approach his suspect from a different angle.

'We found the receipt for a new TV, a replacement that Christina bought. We found it in a box in a cupboard on her landing, at her home. We also found a receipt from a glazing company, stating that they'd "refitted a pane of glass in her kitchen patio doors". We spoke to the glass company, and they said that it looked as if someone had purposely removed the pane, to gain entry to the house. The date on the receipt of her new TV was two days after the glazing receipt. We guess that her house had been burgled. So, your alibi is brittle Mr Baxter.' Sutton scrutinised his face. 'So, was it you that burgled the home of Ms Zabrinski was it? And stole the TV set, seeing that it is in your lounge?' He leaned back. The room was quiet.

'She, she owed me money.' Donal rubbed a hand over his face, hiding a deceitful expression.

'How much?' came a blunt reply from Sutton.

'It was four hundred pounds!'

'What for?' There was a pause.

'I got her some drugs, some coke. She said that she would pay me in a few days' time, I trusted her... then she refused to give me the money, she said that it wasn't a good quality, she expected better, and she was disappointed with it. She said that it was only worth about a hundred quid. We argued about it. I desperately needed the money to pay my supplier for the gear. I'd borrowed the money from my girlfriend for the stuff. Then Christina wouldn't budge on the money.' He put his cupped hands over his face. 'So, so I broke into her home... and stole the TV, to repay my debt. These suppliers are bloody ruthless, if you don't pay them, then, they threaten to shoot your kneecaps off.' He leaned his head on the table, thinking that if he confessed to the drug deal, hopefully they would back off with the murder charge, which they were trying to pin on him.

'Do they now?' Sutton said, gritting his teeth.

The detectives looked at each other. Richards looked at Donal. He then summoned an officer into the interview room.

'Take him away, officer, and book him for burglary... and the possession of class A drugs... with the intent to supply.' Richards looked tired.

'What do you think, guv?' Richards rubbed his eyes.

'Nah, we just don't have enough on him. He wouldn't know how to murder someone in that fashion, he hasn't got the intelligence to tie up his shoelaces, let alone a body from a bannister. We'll check over his phone records again.' He stood up. 'So, who does that leave us with Sam?'

'Well, Sherry is clean. There's nothing on Mike's phone connecting him with Christina.'

'Rebecca Ansell?' Richards retorted.

'Interesting, guv. She doesn't appear to have any friends. We've looked into her movements that night. DI Lambert spoke to her about her whereabouts that Friday evening and her face went bright red. She said that she went to Christina's house, just to look at it. Lambert thought that was strange. She said that she then went back home by bus. She said that she just needed to get out and get some fresh air. Lambert asked, did she murder Christine, she just said "no". She then said that she wanted a legal representative. The solicitor then said that she wouldn't be answering any more questions, simply because "she has never killed anyone".'

'It can't be her? I think we are looking for someone with intelligence. This is a well-planned, and a well-calculated murder, it's bloody well thought out, that's for sure. And I'm not too sure that our Ms Ansell could have held her nerves enough to see it through, not with that form of depression she has. Speak to her again, she may have seen something that Friday.' There was silence.

'Oh. What about our Miss Remington then?' Sutton flicked through his notes.

'We checked her bank statements. She was in a grocery store in Tooting Broadway at six-forty-four p.m. and she spent ten pounds eighty on her bank card. She also found her rail ticket for Friday evening, which we looked at, and it all matches up with what she told us.'

'Well, I suppose, that leaves us with... Jeff Turner and Helen Marshall.'

Thirty-nine

'Detective!' came a voice from what sounded like a young woman standing behind him. He turned, only to see Kathy Berberian waving an arm. Kathy was from the Hammersmith and Fulham Gazette, they had met briefly before and had spoken at a distance, at a press conference on his last murder case. A local drug baron shot a rival through the head, on Ealing common, and then got his cronies to do his dirty work. Drive the body up to Scotland and dump it in a forest, outside Pitlochry, hoping that the wild animals would digest it for their lunch, but it had been discovered by two Norwegian hikers. The body was identified, and the druggie was eventually put behind bars.

Ms Berberian again wanted to pick his brains on this case, the case of the "dangling lady", as the press are calling it. Richards didn't have the time for this rather energetic, slim upstart of a girl. Kathy was in her mid-twenties and wanted to move quickly through the ranks of the newspaper world. She aimed to become a journalist with a Fleet Street newspaper. But first, she wanted to cut her teeth with the local gazette.

'Why don't you have a suspect Detective? I hear that you haven't made an arrest yet for the murder of this poor innocent woman. Is that correct? Do you know when you might have a suspect Detective, will it be soon?' said the pesky auburn-haired girl. She was trying to pick away at him, and slightly intimidate his intellect.

'No, Miss. No' we don't have a suspect yet, we are working hard though.' He avoided using her name as he didn't want to get friendly with this young wannabe of a woman. She was pressing herself up against the yellow tape with her mobile at arm's length, which was probably on voice record, aimed in his direction.

'Are you close to getting one Detective Richards? The local community really want their minds put at ease on this, there are some frightened people out there.'

The words "piss off" and "why don't you just leave me alone" came to mind, but she would probably use that against him, saying that the police were ignoring their right to keep the public informed.

'I'm sure they are. We have lines that we are working on, but that's all,' he replied in a somewhat drained voice.

'Do you believe that it is someone who knows her? I've heard that she had enemies.'

'What do you think, you've clearly been speaking to influential people?'

'You're answering a question with a question, Detective?'

'That is my prerogative. Miss,' he said, murmuring his reply.

'Sorry, I didn't quite catch that, Detective?'

'I said that I have to go inside now.' Just then his mobile started making a ringing sound. Great, saved, he thought. He ignored the prickly reporter. Richards answered the call. It was a detective investigating the case.

'Hi Stuart. How are things? Any news?' he said, standing at the doorway outside number fourteen Bollo Lane.

'I've just come out of forensics, guv.'

'Are there any updates?' Richards sounded upbeat.

'Well, the two beer cans that were retrieved from the kitchen at fourteen Bollo Lane, were bone dry inside. Nothing, not a drop of fluid to be found. Dr Waide said he found it to be strange, especially as the house had been cold all over the weekend, and you would expect at least something in one of them, some moisture at least?'

'Yes, you're right you would,' replied Richards.

'And the footprints on the carpets were a size six.'

'What are Ms Marshall's, Stuart?'

'A five mate.'

'Bollocks,' Richards replied, as he moved his mobile to his other ear.

'Oh, and guv, we've located that fella, the one that Jeff Turner said that he spoke to that evening on the thirty-first, while he sat in his truck.

'Oh. Where?' He looked thoughtful.

'Well, Mr Turner's lady friend phoned in, Shabina, she tracked him down. I went straight over and met the bloke. He said that he took his dog out for a walk a seven in the evening, he said that it was a ritual of his, he takes it out every evening at that time, while his wife cooks dinner. He said that he spoke to a man in a black truck. He described Jeff Turner to a tee. He also read out the last three digits of the registration plate.'

'Right. Carry on, tell me more.' Richards stroked his chin.

'Well, he said that he had spoken to him for around fifteen minutes, and he then left him, to continue to walk his dog. On the way back to his house he saw Jeff's truck was still there, he walked past it and noticed he was still sitting inside. He said that he looked like he was doing some paperwork. He said that he got back to his house at around seven-thirty-five. He knew this because EastEnders had started, and he said that he had missed the first five minutes.'

'Well, I never. So, they have located this man then, and he's vouched for Jeff's times on Friday.'

'I then spoke to his friend, Shabina Rahman,' Stuart said. 'She said that she and Jeff spent the evening together, she made him something to eat, and he left hers at around ten-thirty pm.'

'But how do you know that this girl is telling the truth and that she's not sticking up for him?'

'Well guv, her son popped in, with his girlfriend, for around ten minutes or so, at eight-thirty, to pick up some trainers that he had left there. I spoke to the son, and the girlfriend, and they confirmed that Jeff was at their mum's house. The son said that it was the first time that they had met.' Richards looked thoughtful.

'He got home to Chesham at around 11:20, his wife vouched for the time. And the next-door neighbour saw him get out of his truck.' There was silence.

'Guv?'

'I'm listening, mate.'

'We're searching through Christina's phone records. There are some numbers that keep coming up, the boys at the station are working on it.'

'Great, thanks, Stuart.'

'It doesn't make sense,' Richards said to himself. He looked pale. He thought that he had his murderer in his grasp.

'So, we are missing something,' he thought. 'Well, now let's think, who the bloody hell murdered Christina Zabrinski. She must have had enemies, someone that we've missed. We need to go back to Hammerson Shaw and speak to the staff again.' He pushed the door open and went inside. Ignoring the reporter's next question that he heard coming in his direction.

Richards had to tell his wife, Gill, that their upcoming long weekend away to the Cotswolds was off, for the second time, as this case took priority. He was just in the wrong place at the wrong time, he was coming to the end of his shift when he got the call to attend this murder. His diary was then wiped clean. Gill was annoyed, and only mildly understanding towards him, but not to the force, for not allowing him to have such valuable and much-needed time off, deserved time off. She had phoned his boss, the detective super attendant, who she knew, to tell him of her frustration. She had booked the hotel only recently, and when she was told the news that he couldn't attend, she threw a strop and sulked for a few days.

Richards stood in the hallway of fourteen Bollo Lane. He looked up at the first floor. He then looked at the wooden flooring in the hallway.

He laid down on its polished surface, his face level with the floorboards. He smelt the wood. He looked for any marks that the forensics may have missed. He was looking for anything heavy that may have dropped from the first floor, a mark, possibly a dent, anything the culprit may have used in assisting in raising this heavy body to the position it was found in. He looked around at the furniture, it appeared to be in its rightful place. The house felt uncomfortable. He opened a cupboard door. He went to check the bag of the vacuum cleaner. It was missing. he would have to speak to forensics to see if they had taken it, or had it been taken by the perpetrator?

He made his way upstairs to the landing on the first floor. He walked in an orderly and careful manner, studying the staircase for any marks, blemishes, or scuffs maybe. When he reached the landing, he studied the base of the balustrades. He ran a hand around the bottom of the wood, feeling it with detail for any indentations. He stood and scratched his head. He felt all along the top of the handrail.

He started to construct a noose from some rope that he had brought along, it resembled the one used to dangle Christina. He made the noose the size of her ankle. It was also the same length that was used on the deceased.

He thought.

He eased it over the bannister and lowered it down to the position where Christina would have had it tied around her ankle. He held the other end of the rope and made a knot around the handrail, the same as what the culprit had tied. He then cut off the excess. He was now left with thirteen inches of rope.

He thought, 'So, how would the murderer then have been able to pull up a weight of 138 pounds, and form a knot, it would have been problematic, seeing that the piece that was left, would have given the perpetrator a small amount of leverage, their muscles would have had to have been powerful. They could conceivably have pulled the body up with both hands, but then how would they have been able to form a knot around It? At some stage of constructing this knot, they would have had to let go of it with one hand, and then hold on to it with the other. They would have had to have taken the weight of a woman weighing 138 pounds with one hand.

He ran a hand down the balustrades, to see if these had been used and if they had any marks. He pondered for a while.

He lay on the carpet and looked for any imperfections. He was looking to see if a heavy foot had dug into the carpet and had made an obvious mark. Forensics said they hadn't found any. But he checked again.

Opposite the area where he stood was Christina's bedroom. The door was open.

He pulled at his thin moustache. Could the rope have been longer at one stage, and maybe it had been cut in the house? Dr Waide said they found no fragments of the rope, anywhere inside the house. If it were longer, it would have made a difference, it would have made it easier to have then tied a knot. With a longer rope, it would have certainly made the task simpler in hauling up the body to where it was left. But still, at some stage, they would have had to have held the rope with one hand. He knew a woman could not have performed this task, but he doubted himself. Maybe, just maybe, she could have.

He still had uncertainty in his mind, and it wasn't going away.

Were there two people involved? Did Mars and Jeff collaborate in this act together? Both had the motive to kill Christina, but Jeff now had an alibi. Could Mars have had an assistant? Who does she know that would help her, and be prepared to be an accomplice to murder? He would have to keep an open mind.

He stood at the threshold of the bedroom door. His eyes wandered over the room.

He walked around the bedroom, scrutinising the surrounding area. He paced over the floor several times. Did anything go on in this room on the night of the murder? There were no obvious signs, forensics found nothing to substantiate this.

He looked at the walls and the ceiling. He removed a picture from the wall, it was a watercolour, painted in red, orange and yellow, it could have been anywhere in the world. He turned it around; the label said it was painted in Barcelona. He replaced it. He started to pull out the drawers of a very large and well-made oak chest. The top drawer housed only jumpers. The one below was full of underwear, black, white, red and pink. He ran a hand to the back of the drawer, hoping that something was hidden, out of sight, maybe something secretive.

Another drawer below was full of T-shirts. There was also a dildo, it was purple. He held it up, hoping that no one would walk into the room. Lambert was on her way over to meet him. He was unsure what time she would arrive, hoping that it wasn't right now. He rattled it to see if it had batteries inside, he grinned and put it back. The fourth drawer down had an old black radio in it, with its battery cover missing. There were some pens, and some photos. He looked through them. They were of Christina with her parents, many years ago, all were happy and smiling. They were on holiday together, and a palm tree was in the background. Some of what looked like ex-boyfriends, and some of friends, which looked like they were taken at work. There was a thin white belt, some picture hooks, an empty three-year-old brown diary, and a three-pin plug.

He turned and took two steps towards the bed. He ran a hand over the duvet. He removed the small wooden toy block from his pocket and put it on the bed. It didn't seem to match anything in the room.

He blinked. He noticed that the heavy-framed wooden bed was at a slight angle. One end of the headboard was further away from the wall, than the other end. The bed was opposite and faced the bedroom door, and the hallway. The angle of the bed was tilting towards the door. He removed a small torch from a pocket and shone it under the bed. He stood up and pushed a heavy hand over his forehead. He felt his wrinkles.

He held the wooden block between a finger and thumb and studied it. 'Is it linked to the crime?' he wondered. 'Or has it always been here, had it been put here as a red herring, to fool someone, to throw us off of our tracks?' He lined it up, and it fitted in the gap between the back of the headboard which was furthest from the wall, and the wall itself. It was the same measurement. But why? What was the significance of it? This enigma. Was this object involved in the murder of Christina Zabrinski? His questions remained unanswered.

Forty

September 2008

Jeff looked at his mobile, he had just received a text message. He pressed a button, opened it up and read it.

"Hi Jeff, I hope you are well. I hope you don't mind me texting you, but I have a customer who would like a new kitchen fitted. She lives in Amersham. Would you be interested? Let me know thanks Mars xx." Jeff welcomed the work. He somehow couldn't help feeling that it felt slightly odd that she would contact him, due to the animosity between them. He wasn't going to turn down a date with a good-looking girl either, especially one who could put some local work his way.

Mars walked into the Half Moon Public House, a little resignedly, hoping that her date had already arrived. She got some noticeable looks from the clientele, who were all men eager to take advantage of the inexpensive alcohol on sale. It was that time of the evening when the drinks were cheaper for a couple of hours to get the punters in, and try to get the profits up.

She noticed Jeff sitting down and engrossed in some paperwork on the table in front of him. He looked oblivious to all that was going on around him, and had only noticed Mars when she approached the table.

'Hello again, and how are you? Good to see you. You're looking good, as always,' he said standing and leaning towards her, holding out a hand.

'Thank you, Jeff. You're as charming as ever,' Mars replied acrimoniously.

'I'm always charming when you're around Mars, you know that.' He looked her up and down, 'bloody gorgeous,' he thought.

'Huh,' she remarked. 'Thank you for taking time out to meet up, anyway. You look busy, what are you up to?' she said, not caring.

'Oh, I got here early, so I'm doing an estimate for a good customer of mine. It's a lot of work, and they want it started ASAP.'

'Is that going to be possible?' she said pretending to be interested and looking around the slightly seedy environment. There was a menu written in chalk on a board, on a wall close to them, advertising lunches at bargain prices. A dartboard was on another wall. The brown and tan carpet was fraying in one corner of the room.

'Maybe. Anyway, how's life treating you nowadays, Mars?'

'Life is good, Jeff.'

'Oh.'

'Yes, I have a lovely man in my life now, he's gorgeous and he takes care of me... he doesn't strangle me, Jeff, like some blokes can do.' she said making a statement, grinning, and looking down at the paperwork sprawled across the table.

'Please Mars, spare me the gory details, I don't want to know too much.' he laughed at his joke and thought it would probably be best if he didn't continue with that particular line of conversation.

'Although perhaps this new guy in Mars's life doesn't know what he's missing, maybe I need to meet up with him and give him a few tips,' he thought to himself sardonically, but with humour.

'Very funny!' Mars quipped.

'So, you've finally blown me out then, and found yourself a new love, have you?'

'What do you mean "blown you out"? There was never any love between us, and besides, you're a married man now, with a lovely wife, Jeff.'

She thought back to the time when she thought that she was in love with this man, soon after they met. She found him charming, attentive, witty and fantastic company, and good to have on her arm, 'Although he did fleece me financially when we first met.' But she put that down to his work and soon got over it. 'Besides, he made me laugh.' The feelings were never mutual enough between them, under the circumstances at the time. They just didn't get close enough, their meeting was a roller coaster ride. Life moved like a runaway freight train when they met. Jeff had always had a crush on Mars, but was never in a position to commit himself to her. She had been married before, and was now looking for

Mr Right, he knew deep down that he wasn't that guy, he was too involved in his escort work. He enjoyed the attention too much from his various wealthy clients. He enjoyed the challenge, and the thrill that it gave him. He craved the attention he got, and the gifts that came with it. It was a drug, and he wasn't about to give it up at the time of meeting Mars.

'So, who is the lucky guy then, who's this lucky man who has swept you off your feet?' he said taking off his jacket, she stared at the blue zip up top with readiness.

'His name is Matt, he's a company director,' she said, flicking at an imaginary hair.

'Is he a local lad?'

'You're nosey, aren't you?' She never answered Jeff's question. 'Anyway, like the gentleman you are Jeff, can you get me a drink please? It would make a change, wouldn't it?' She smiled. 'Seeing that I may put some work your way, coffee please Jeff, with a shot of brandy would be really nice,' she said, pulling a face of delight and taking her seat. Jeff rose and headed towards the counter. Mars looked around the bar. It wouldn't be a place that she would like to visit again any time soon. It had a sweet musty smell. The floor looked sticky. She felt slightly uncomfortable, she shivered. She then looked over at the paperwork on the table.

'Regular or large, Mars?' came a voice that made her jump.

'Regular, please.'

She then looked at the collar on the blue top, that was draped over the back of Jeff's chair. She pulled out a small plastic transparent bag.

Forty-one

September 2009

'I'm going to get that bastard.' Her eyes were flickering, she was trying to keep them open. Mars had been awake for what seemed to have been half the night. She had too much on her mind, plus that bloody noisy canine, barking all the way through it, well most of it anyway. 'Where were its owners? Yap bloody yap. What was it doing outside all that time? Don't they have any respect for their neighbours, we need to sleep, don't they think about things like that? It's so disrespectful of them. This is our weekend away, and we want to enjoy it.'

She lay on her bed. She ran a hand over the creases of the sheet on the empty side of it. Mars twisted her body and pointed towards the window, looking at a blue sky, and wishing that it was warm outside.

The white cotton sheet covered the lower part of her legs, her smooth silken body was bare.

She thought about her future, her past, and where she should be. Was it here? Was Matt the one for her? He was an amazing guy, and he thought the world of her. He would do anything for her, he was tangible, and he adored her son Tom. Plus, he was financially well off.

She was beginning to settle into her new job, and the new surroundings that it brought and living with a man again.

The tedious arguments had returned; she remembered them all too well from when she was married. The silly habits which annoyed each other. There was less space in the bed now, and beers in the fridge. She now had to answer to someone. "Where shall we go tonight? I don't know, I'm not bothered. Why didn't you call me? Where were you"? There were too many questions all of a sudden. 'Why does he keep watching football? It's full of overpaid prima donnas. Still, the plug on the iron is now fixed, and it's not down to me any more to get rid of the spiders in the bathroom or pump up my car tyres. I hate getting my fingers dirty from that tyre valve thingy.' she thought.

'Have I done the right thing?' She turned and laid on her back and looked at the ceiling. 'I've seen that a few times.' She turned back and faced the window, and wondered what the day outside was like, should she get up now, no. She pulled the sheets up to her shoulder. 'I don't like it when he blows off and doesn't admit to it, or when he subtly leaves his shirts around to be ironed, it's not down to me to do his bloody dirty work. Still, he is lovely. I love the way he holds me, and buys me gifts, no matter what they are, and he shows real empathy. I don't like his loud rock music though. He plays it too loud in his car, and how can he enjoy that noise? I can't understand most of the words, and I don't think they do either, it's so flipping raucous, maybe I'm being cynical, if he likes it then, well… but I prefer my Lionel Ritchie, and I'm going to stick with it, it's much easier on the ears. More easy listening,' she thought. 'Even Neil Diamond even has to be better than that rubbish.' She looked out the window.

'Still, he treats me well, like a princess. I enjoy it when he cooks for me, when I get in late from work, and when he runs me a bath.' She looked at her empty index finger. 'Maybe he'll furnish it with gold one day?'

'His mum's a bit bloody interfering though, always telling me what to do, how I put too much make-up around my eyes, and why is my skirt too short. "It was a bloody hot day! That's why". What's she like, why doesn't she keep her mouth shut. I'm old enough to make my own decisions, thank you Mrs Robson for your comments, but I'm not interested. She's not even my mum. She's full of scepticism, far too conservative for me, maybe I'll tell her one day.

I do miss Sherry and Jenny, for their warmth and vivaciousness. Moving away makes you see less of them. I must phone them and catch up with the gossip, perhaps meet up for a drink. I can't say I miss anyone else, far too illicit they are. I'm not bothered if I see any of the others again. Dave was okay. All they have done is throw those obscene innuendos and accusations at me. Their friendship with me diminished when that bastard detective, with the D'Artagnan-looking beard, turned around and acrimoniously said,' "The female of the species can be more deadly than the male." Huh!'

'We will be keeping an eye on you.' 'That comment was overheard by Hayley, who then pertinently spread it around the office, and it moved like a flame running along a fuel line, and, because Christina's murderer was still on the loose, all the attention then became focussed on me.'

She turned slowly in her bed, and she was now looking at the opposite wall. 'Although, the whole world and its dog, had blamed Jeff for Christina's murder?

How the hell he had got away with it was a travesty of justice. When the police found evidence in the way of Jeff's hair on Christina's sofa, one of his business cards, and the court letters, he had some serious explaining to do.'

Jeff had said that he left the pub in Chiswick high street at around six-thirty on the evening of the 31st. According to his wife, Annabelle, she said that he arrived home that evening at around eleven-twenty p.m.

'But that flipping cow friend of his, Shabina, went out hunting for the man, the elderly chap, and finally tracked him down, and found Jeff his alibi. The man had indeed lived in the area for almost thirty years.

Jeff had a good motive to kill Christina, he had a debt to pay to this woman. Over sixteen grand, or more.

There were no fingerprints and no footprints. Jeff had always remonstrated to the police that he was set up. That I had committed the crime, as I too had a very good motive, in the way of Christina promising me her job on a plate, and then pulling the rug from under my feet, making a massive U-turn, only to offer the job to a rival, infuriating me and mocking my intelligence. And when the same job came open again, I was not going to be inferior anymore. They questioned me. They found no trace of evidence, I was always accountable for my whereabouts, at the time that forensics had stated the time of Christina's death. The Friday evening, I was at home with my son. Friday during the day, I was at work, and at the weekend, again I was with Tom, Tom's friends, and Matt. I always had an alibi.'

'Darling, do you want a coffee,' came Matt's voice from downstairs.

Forty-two

'Who's that at the door, Matt?' Mars shouted from the bathroom, as she was just finishing applying her lipstick.

'I don't know sweetheart, but I'll get it.'

Matt opened the door. He was fronted by a man he had never seen before. He had a guilty look and a dubious stance. He was of a medium build, with black hair. Matt felt that he was in trouble, that's the impression this person gave out to him. He was accompanied by a woman, a colleague maybe, a mate, a friend. Perhaps?

The man was tall, and he was holding a notepad. He instantly started to peer past Matt, and into the house, as if Matt was not the person he was looking for at the address, as if he was looking for someone else. He was being curious, too intrusive for Matt's liking. Matt couldn't think who they were after, maybe they had the wrong address, maybe they would realise this, and move on.

'Hello, can I help you guys?' he said, moving in front of the man's selfish introduction.

'I'm, Detective Inspector Sam Sutton, Sir,' came his answer. He removed his identification, and pointed it at Matt. 'This is my colleague, DC Patricia Leung,' he said, turning halfway around to introduce his partner. She nodded, and grinned at Matt, she was of Asian descent and wore her hair in a ponytail. She wore a cream cotton jumper, and navy coloured chino trousers.

'The police! Oh,' said a bewildered-looking Matt. 'And what can I do for you, I don't think that I've committed any crime, have I?'

'It's not you that we need to speak to Sir, you're OK.' His words were drawn out.

'Sorry, your name is?' He pulled a false smile, still trying to peer down the hallway of the house.

'Mr Robson. Matt.'

'Mr Robson,' came back a sharp reply.

'Is there anyone else in the house, apart from yourself?' Just then Mars appeared, leaning over the shoulder of her boyfriend. She looked somewhat alarmed at the presence of these strange people standing on her doorstep, her stomach churned.

'Oh. Hello, can we help you?' she said, sounding startled.

'I'm Detective Inspector Sutton,' he said. 'And this is my colleague, DC Patricia Leung.'

'Do I know you, and what are you doing here?' she showed a strong annoyance to these intruders.

'We were just passing by Ms Marshall, and I thought that I would like to ask you both some questions, if I may?' She knew that they had not just "Passed by"! She knew they made the trip especially to meet her. She didn't appreciate their visit or the man's tone of voice. She showed hostility towards them.

'Oh, it's a surprise.' she said.

'And about what? what's this all about?' Matt butted in, he looked confusingly at the detectives. Without answering Matt's question, Sam Sutton said,

'Could we come in please? You probably wouldn't want your neighbours to know that the police are at your front door. Besides, the questions and looks you would receive may be unfavourable.'

The four of them stood in the hallway. Mars was determined not to let the two detectives' pry around her house. She didn't like these two people.

'Were you both at number two, Heather Cottage Harrogate, Yorkshire, on the night of August 20th? It was a Saturday.' Sutton looked closely at the two of them.

'Er, yes we were.' said Matt, turning to Mars. 'We were there weren't we, darling.' Mars grinned at Matt, wishing that he hadn't been too hasty in giving the detective that reply.

'Why is that?' Matt said.

'Your weekend retreat, was it?' DC Leung said.

'Yes, well, just a break for a few days.'

'Were you there, Ms Marshall,' said DI Sutton, standing patiently and waiting for her answer.

'Yes. Yes, I was there. We were both there together. Why are you asking us these questions, about our weekend away? It's private, isn't it?'

'Just routine, Ms Marshall. Just routine. Did you ever speak to your neighbours, Mr Griffin, and a Ms Edge?' He looked at his notes.

There was a muted response.

'We spoke to our neighbours. Yes, yes we did. We didn't catch anyone's names though, or their first names, as a matter of fact, they were not our most favourite people to get on with, they kept themselves to themselves. We said hello to them, is there a problem?' she said unhappily.

'Well, Ms Marshall.' Sutton calmly looked at her.

'Their dog was found hanging from a tree, their tree, in their garden, on Sunday morning.' Mars sniggered.

'Do you find that amusing, Ms Marshall?' Sutton said. At that moment DC Leung moved towards the lounge door and stretched out her neck to peer inside.

'I beg your pardon, Miss, excuse me. There is nothing in my lounge of any interest to you. Constable.' She moved to the door, standing in DC Leung's view. She shot her a malicious look.

'Remember, you are invited.' Leung stayed silent.

'Ms Marshall, did you ever speak to your neighbours during your stay at number two Heather cottage Harrogate, did you?' He looked cumulatively at them.

'You've just asked that question, Detective.'

'I'm asking the question to you again, Ms Marshall, seeing that I didn't get a reply the first time.' he said with intent. The atmosphere thickened.

'Yes, we did inspector, and we found them both odd characters. I knocked on their door once to kindly ask them if they could keep their dog quiet in the evening. It made a lot of noise, it kept barking most days that we were there, and it disturbed our peace and our long weekend. He opened the door, and looked at me, and just said "yes, OK." and quickly closed the door in my face as if he wasn't interested. That was about the nearest either of us ever got to them, they seemed out of character for that place,' Mars said with a grin.

'So, is that why you tied the dog up then?'

'I'm sorry! That's a bit of a bloody strange thing to do, isn't it?'

'Our job has taught us that people do strange things, Ms Marshall.'

The detective turned away from Mars and looked around the hallway, and sharply turned back, his head twisting, he looked at her, their eyes met, and he paused.

'Well, you see the dog was found hanging from its left leg. And remember, we are also investigating the murder of Ms Christina Zabrinski, she too was found hanging, from her left leg, a coincidence, don't you think?' he said with delight.

'Excuse me. So, Inspector, are you going to arrest us for the murder of this, this dog?' Mars folded her arms. Matt stared at her as their conversation gathered momentum. Sutton took a breath.

'No, we are not going to arrest you, Ms Marshall.'

'So, why are you here then? It's a bit of a derogative question, isn't it?'

'Your name came up on the radar, and we then became interested,' he said impassively.

'Interested, interested in what, Inspector may I ask?' she retorted.

'Interested with your whereabouts at the time of a crime, seeing that you were neighbours of the owners' dog. And, that you have been interviewed about a more serious crime. It's called a pattern Ms Marshall,' he waited for her reply.

Matt turned and looked at Mars but couldn't get in on the conversation. She could feel him staring at her. She hadn't told him that she had been questioned on a second occasion, over the murder of Christina Zabrinski, although he knew of the ongoing case involving Christina.

Mars felt Matt's stare. She didn't look at him, as she swiftly moved on to answer the detective's question.

'Are you insinuating, Inspector, that we were involved somehow in the death of this, this poor creature?'

'You don't seem to show any remorse, do you? Seeing that you once owned a dog yourself.'

'What's showing remorse got to do with me owning a dog for, and how did you know that I once owed a pet, Detective.'

'It's all on record Ms, a black Labrador, wasn't it?' Sutton said looking content.

'Huh, so, I suggest that you either arrest us both or leave us alone… Mr Sutton.' She glanced fiercely at DC Leung.

'How do you know that the dog in question was murdered? It wasn't mentioned that it was dead, we just said that it was found hanging,' replied Leung.

Mars twisted her arms, her composure deserted her.

'I doubt very much that you would be standing here, if this poor little canine was at this moment in time running around happily, yapping in the garden of those ghastly people's house, and keeping its new neighbours awake at night. Will that be all?' she said, in a foul mood, staring at Sutton.

The detective was tolerant of her attitude towards him.

'Did you kill that dog, Ms Marshall?' He peered into her eyes, as a chill ran down her spine, she felt coldness spread over her body.

'I beg your pardon, are you accusing me?'

'We inspected the area briefly, and when I glanced over the garden wall, to number two Heather cottage, where you stayed. I noticed that the washing line from your garden airer matched the line around the dog's neck and leg. Your washing line seemed to be interfered with.' Mars gulped.

'And Detective, to what are you implying?' came her obstinate reply. He stood patiently. He was trying to trip her up, trying to look for a slip in her vocabulary. He was looking for movements in her face, but she stood her ground. This woman was not for turning. She was hard, and would be a tough nut to crack.

'Did you tie up the dog, Ms Marshall, with the cord from your washing line in your garden? You know what I am getting at, don't you? It appears coincidental, doesn't it? I like coincidences, it makes my job a bit easier.' He looked her deep into her sea-blue eyes, and into her soul, he was looking to catch her out.

'No, I don't know what you're getting at? And do you have a warrant to be on my premises, Detective. Inspector, Sutton?' He looked down at the ground he was standing on.

'What shall I take that answer to be then, a yes or a no? Because It's difficult to answer a question when you are hiding something, and a whole lot easier when you're not,' he said, waiting and knowing that she would come back with an answer. Mars snapped.

'Have you interviewed the neighbours at number six, next door to them Inspector?' Her voice became agitated.

'Oh, we certainly have.'

'And what did they have to say? I'm fascinated to know.'

'The elderly couple you mean? They were not at the premises the night of the crime. They were at their son's house, twenty miles away, in Appletreewick. A very apt name, don't you think?' He smiled at her. Matt looked on, wondering what was going on between the two of them. They were constantly in opposition to each other.

'We spoke to their son, a, Mr Paul Benson,' he glanced at his notes, and he confirmed that his parents were with him at the time in question. It was his birthday, they had had a little get-together, and their son cooked for them that evening.'

'If you are not going to arrest us both, Inspector, then I suggest that you leave our premises and leave us alone. We have things that we need to get on with.' She pursed her lips and ushered them in the direction of the front door. There was animosity between them. Mars didn't want to hear any more questions from these people, they had no warrant for her arrest, so she had decided that the questioning had to end.

'We have no further questions to answer for you, thank you.' Mars threw the inspector an insouciant look. She put her hand on the door and began to close it.

'OK, Ms Marshall, we will leave you both in peace now, but you will be receiving a visit from the RSPCA in the next day or so.' She had a guarded look.

'The suspense will kill me, Detective.' She scowled at him, as she firmly closed the door.

'You were quite aggressive towards him weren't you, Mars?' said Matt. He looked at her with a mixture of suspicion and support. He pulled a face.

'What's going on? Were you involved in the hanging of this dog? I didn't notice anything darling, I'm confused, and furthermore, were… you involved in…' Mars turned and growled at him before he finished his sentence, she knew what he was about to say.

'Don't you, don't you, bloody start!' She huffed and walked away from him. 'I've had enough of bloody Doctor Watson out there.' she said pointing towards the front door of their house. Her eyes appeared to turn a green colour, the perimeter was black. For a split second, her face changed to one of fury. She shook her head hysterically. And then stopped, all of a sudden, as if nothing had happened. She stood tall, she had a look of steel in her eyes as she waited for his next question.

'Well!'

Matt looked startled. He had a bemused look about him.

'Are you OK, darling?'

'What is your next question going to be?' she snarled.

'I, I know you weren't involved Mars, darling.' Matt was trying to be sympathetic towards her, but at the same time, he wanted to know exactly what was going on. Why were the police at their door asking her incriminating questions, looking at her in a devious way, and trying to sound her out?

'But what does he mean, a pattern? I'm only asking, sweetheart.' He wanted to know what the police were talking about, and why they were questioning his girlfriend. He knew of the murder of Christina Zabrinski and was convinced by what Mars had told him, that Jeff was the culprit, even if he had got off with it. He wasn't going to doubt his beautiful girlfriend.

'I don't know, Matt, they are all getting on my bloody nerves. I've had all this before.'

'I'm confused.' He rubbed his head. 'He said a minute ago that the crimes were linked. I know that you weren't involved in the murder of Christina. I know you didn't commit the crime,' he said. 'Is that true honey, what's going on?'

She turned her back on him. He leant over and he put a hand on her shoulder, to turn her around and face him. She rejected him, flicking her shoulder sharply, and ignoring his affection.

'Mars, turn around and talk, please, I'm on your side, darling.' His voice was challenging. She slowly moved her body; her head was tilting down.

'Look at me Mars! What's this all about? You never said anything about this? You didn't mention anything to me about this hanging dog. You never said anything to me, this is the first I've heard of it.' She went into a momentary lapse in concentration. 'Is this why we left the cottage early? What's going on Mars? Are you OK?' He held his arms out.

'No Matt, no I'm actually not OK. I need a drink, can you get me one please, a Bacardi would be great.' She grimaced at him, 'You are pissing me off Matt, stop asking me all these awkward questions please, I don't want them.' He looked at her, as he headed towards the kitchen.

'OK. The police questioned me a second time, about Christina. And no, I didn't tell you, yes, I should have done, and yes, they suspected me, and they questioned me in detail for a lengthy period in fact.' She swished her glass around, looking at the drink inside it, as she returned it to the kitchen table where they were now sitting, discussing the visit of the two officers. Matt looked at her drink. He was lost in thought as he listened intensively. He didn't quite know what to say at this moment.

'The police said that I was their person of interest for some time, it was horrible. It's because I didn't get on with Christina, we were always at odds with each other, all the time, and we had so many differences. She promised me her position at work, it was a position that I really wanted, I suppose everyone in the office knew this. I was so looking forward to it, she then pulled the rug from my feet. Metaphorically speaking I wanted to kill her. This got around to various chinwaggers at work, so they pulled me in. They had nothing on me though. I was at home with Tom, at the time of the murder.' She grinned. 'In the end, the police arrested Jeff Turner.' She took another large gulp of her Cuban salvation.

'Christy was found, strangled by a rope, and was found hanging from the bannisters of her stairs.' Her voice slowed. 'She was tied up by her ankle, dangling upside down. The rope was tied around her left ankle. It must have been a gruesome scene. It appears that the dog in the garden next to us was tied up in the same manner, with something, so that's why they were here. They never once listened to me when I told them that deep down inside Christina liked the way that I stood up to her and that I was the only one in the company who did?' Matt leaned forward; his face was perplexed.

He stood up and walked around. He rubbed a hand down the side of his arm. He stared at the large bunch of red and pink roses he recently bought her.

'So, the dog, hanging from our neighbour's tree. Who killed that then? I didn't know anything about it, until those two turned up?' said, Matt.

'How the hell do I bloody know?' she snapped at him.

'Well, now I can see why he said there's a pattern.' He held out a hand in comfort towards her. Mars rejected it.

'Whose side are you on, Matt?' she sneered. She rose from her chair, pushing it back with the rear of her legs.

'I'm on your side darling, I told you, but…' Mars interrupted.

'Well, you have a strange way of showing it Robson!' Her voice sounded agitated.

'Why are you getting so upset? I'm just asking a couple of questions sweetheart, why are you so defensive?'

Mars headed towards the bottle of rum sitting on the kitchen worktop. Matt looked on.

'So, you think, I killed.' There was a slight pause in her voice. 'the wretched dog, do you? Or are you thinking more along the lines of, I was involved in Christina's death?'

She grabbed the bottle and tilted it towards her empty glass.

'OK, I'm sorry. I wouldn't have thought that you would have got so upset over the issue darling. It's just that I didn't realise that a dead dog was hanging in the garden next to where we were staying.' Matt had some other questions to ask Mars, his mind was still not at ease. He looked over at her, as she stood, perched against a cabinet. Her figure was curvaceous, her blonde hair was immaculate. She was a classy girl and she knew it, she was the kind of woman who would turn heads when she walked down the street. Men would follow her, chat with her, and ogle at her. Mars was a woman that you would like to walk into a room with. Men would look at her, then at you, then back to her, wishing that they were you. They would be envious, she was that good. Above all she was gifted and intellectual, she was clever and articulate. Matt loved her from the moment he set eyes on her in the car park at work. He was gob-smacked when she agreed to him asking her out on a date. He felt for the first time in his life that he was in love, and he was happy, really happy. She was like a drug to him, she's addictive. This was the first confrontation they had had with each other, the first time their voices had been raised in anger between them.

She poured another drink and added some coke from the fridge. But his conscience wasn't clear. 'Why did she mention the dog was dead? He couldn't remember the detective saying that it was. Why did we leave the cottage earlier that morning, we didn't need to check out until ten?

Why was she so defensive towards his questions? It's like the detective said, it's easy to answer a question if you're innocent, and harder if you're guilty.'

He looked at the clock on the wall and counted the number of drinks she had downed. The level in the bottle she had attacked during their heated debate had diminished somewhat. He was in no position to lose this beautiful woman, he was in awe of her. He decided, for the time being, not to ask any more questions regarding the matter. She was obviously under pressure, she looked stressed with the arrival of the two officers. For what reason he didn't know, but he thought he would cool it with her. Go along with her and agree with her every word.

'You not having a drink, Matt?' She threw a slice of lemon into the mixture.

'Er, no, no not for me, sweetheart, I'll give it a miss for now. I must make a phone call.' Matt walked over to her and kissed her on the cheek. She turned and grabbed his arm with a hand, forcing him towards her. She smiled and she ran her other hand over his chest, her nails digging into his T-shirt. He was caught off guard.

She scratched him. He moved his lips towards her, he heard her glass of alcohol bang on the worktop.

They were lying on the bed together, Matt was panting with pleasure, as he lay on his front. His back was grazed with the scratches from her amorous advances, there were blood marks on the sheet.

'Who were you going to call, darling?'

'Pardon, sorry, phone who?' replied Matt.

'You said that you had a call to make… when we were downstairs in the kitchen earlier.'

'Oh. Er, I had to call work, I had to arrange a meeting for Monday with accounts.' Matt was lying. The phone call reply had been an excuse to get away from Mars and defuse the heated conversation that was building between them.

Forty-three

December wasn't a good one for Rebecca Ansell. It came and went in the blink of an eye. Christmas Eve consisted of a couple of bus journeys that started at Ealing and ending at her mum's house in Twickenham.

There was the usual argument with her elder brother. This year's consisted of who owned the   remote control. It resulted in Rebecca screaming at her sibling, as she lost the battle for television rights. And so, she hid in the spare bedroom for twenty-four hours. All means of negotiation tactics from Mrs Ansell to prise her daughter out of the cramped area, failed miserably. And come Boxing Day when she rose from her lay-in at one-thirty in the afternoon, she left her family, and headed west, back to Ealing. New Year's Eve wasn't any better, but she finally persuaded a cousin to go bowling with her, at the Royale Leisure Park. This was an activity that she was polished in, and duly defeated her opponent. And the hamburger and fries, also went down a treat, which was the main pulling point for her to book up a lane.

New Year's Day started for Rebecca at twelve forty-five, with a headache. Nevertheless, she said to herself that her resolution was going to be to tidy up her bedroom, come what may. Besides, she had sod-all else to do until she went back to work on the fourth of January.

She had emptied the paper contents from a large glass bowl that had made its home on a chest of drawers since she had moved into the flat, around three years ago. Rebecca being the hoarder that she was, not much got thrown away. She unravelled a receipt and she stared at it. She recognised the venue. It was for two coffees, paid for in cash. It stirred fond memories for her, she reminisced about the day that they had spent together, just the two of them.

Rebecca removed a drawer from a bedside cabinet in frustration and turned it upside down. She emptied the guts onto her bed, next to the two others that had just received the same violent treatment. She tilted her head backwards, and took a long draw of her cigarette, the smoke wafted into the air, adding to the discolouration of her ceiling. She looked up. Rebecca wasn't the tidiest of girls in the world. She had become more depressed recently since her part-time lover, friend, and compatriot, had been brutally murdered, in cold blood. Rebecca felt there was now a hollow void in her life. Her mood now was very prosaic. Gone were the little gifts she used to receive, the spontaneous text messages, "How's your day been? Hope you are well darling", and asking, "When can we meet up?" She missed the dishonesty, the fun it used to give her, her favourite hobby was missing from her life, and her meal ticket had been taken away, gone for good. And so, her social life had gone into a decline. It had been a downhill spiral since Christy left her.

Rebecca felt that there was not much left in her world anymore. She had taken to drinking in the evening when she arrived home from work. She was buying a bottle of vodka, or Bacardi, mixing it with a fizzy drink, and downing a few large measures each evening. The sort that would cost you quite a few pounds at a bar or pub. It washed away the hurt and pain. She wanted to be on another planet, when she was lonely. She wanted to be somewhere else, and she wanted the demons to take over her soul in the evenings.

She didn't have much else in her life apart from her work, which she enjoyed, but outside of that, there wasn't much else to put a smile on her face. She realised she needed another interest, what though? Plus, she really couldn't be bothered. And for now, this was her pastime, and for the time being this hobby suited her.

There were a couple of squashed beer cans on the side cabinet next to Rebecca's bed. Her ashtray was full, in contrast to when she was with Christy, the ashtray was always clean and shiny.

A bottle of water stood on the carpet, which had condensation forming from the inside.

She half-heartedly flicked through some old paperwork which was strewn across her unmade bed. Rebecca kept most items that she bought, she had a fear of getting rid of things. She had to keep almost everything. Her wardrobe was full to the rafters, and it looked like the makings of a jumble sale. The doors had to be forced closed to shut it correctly. You had to lean against it. Her bedside cabinets were the same, they housed bank statements in no uncertain order, her gas and electric bills, and receipts from Tesco and Lidl. But she couldn't find the one receipt she was hunting down, one piece of precious paper eluded her, it was out of her grasp.

She took a sip of her tea, which had now gone cold. She gathered up the debris from her bed and returned it to the drawers.

She left the bedroom, disgruntled that the small piece of paper she longed to find was missing. She went to the lounge of her small one-bedroomed first-floor flat. She poured herself the remnants of her bottle of supermarket wine. There wasn't much of it left, it hardly covered the bottom of her glass. She relaxed in front of the TV and pressed a button on the remote.

She was stirred by the sound on her television. She slowly opened her eyes and looked at her clock. She was laying on her sofa, and it was three o'clock in the morning. She decided to make her way back to her bedroom where she finished her night's sleep.

'Where the crap is it! Maybe I've thrown it away, maybe it's gone forever?' she thought.

It was Friday morning but it seemed like a Sunday. She didn't do much on Sundays, just lazed around, took it easy, and maybe phoned a few friends. She looked out of her lounge window and into a car parking area below. There was a young couple, they were kissing each other, and the girl looked as if she had spent the night with her new boyfriend, Rebecca recognised the boy as being local. 'Lucky bastards,' were her thoughts. She stood and looked around. She wandered into her kitchen in her pink dressing gown and glanced up at some boxes that nestled on top of her units. She climbed onto the worktop and grabbed at one of them. She placed the box down and immediately opened it up. It was full of paper, rubbish, and items that you don't know whether you should throw away or keep. So, you keep them and put them somewhere where you think they will solve that problem itself. There were batteries in partly opened packets. She flicked through small pieces of paper - they were creased and folded. She straightened one out, the paper sounded crumbly, but it was music to her ears. It was headed. "Harrods". It had the date on it, method of payment and a serial number. It had the time of purchase. It's one that you just want to keep, a memento. One that you feel proud of having, especially because of the price you paid for it, a special handbag for your lover. And a designer handbag from a top Italian manufacturer. It was the receipt for the Gucci handbag she had bought for Christina Zabrinski, from one of the leading department stores in the world, for her birthday. She had thought it was quite exclusive when she purchased it until she noticed that Helen Marshall appeared to have one dangling from her shoulder, the Monday after the weekend that Christina had been murdered. She thought something was odd but just couldn't get her head around it, the penny didn't drop. She couldn't recall seeing it in Mars's company before that, otherwise, she would have surely noticed it. She never saw both girls displaying the bag at the same time. She pondered for a while.

If Mars had noticed Christina with the bag, and Christina had used it on numerous occasions since it was bought for her, it would have been the last thing that Mars would have purchased, seeing that there was resentment between them. Mars would have purchased something of a complete and opposite style to it. 'So, why then has she got this bag? Was it the same one?' she questioned herself. 'And more importantly, where did Mars get it from?'

Forty-four

'Not you again Richards? Persistent, aren't you? I've told you before that I have nothing more to say, and I can't assist you any further with your enquiries,' Mars said, standing in the doorway of her house.

He took in the stricken look on her face. He exchanged glances with his colleague.

'That's correct, Ms Marshall, it's me again, your worst nightmare,' he said, his face carrying a sneer.

'And what's that Inspector?' she said, looking at the warrant as he held it up to her.

'It's a search warrant, Ms Marshall.' She looked in between Richards and Lambert. Two uniformed officers were standing at the end of the path to her house. There was also a smartly dressed female, in a suit. Mars began to realise the seriousness of the situation. 'We have permission to search your premises... Ms Marshall, so, could we please come in?' he said, looking pleased with himself, with his mild north-of-the-border accent

'A warrant officer? And for what reason? What gives you the right to search my premises? I have nothing of interest that concerns you,' she said, sounding indignant. 'You have no reason to be here.' There was animosity between them, there has been dislike between them since their first meeting.

'There has been some new evidence in the case of the murdered Christina Zabrinski. You do remember Christina, don't you Ms Marshall?' he said, sounding corrosive, as he looked her in the eyes. Her face was vacant, as he stared at her. 'We have been given some fresh leads, new information. And some of the leads that we have, have led us to you.'

'What!'

'Yes. We understand that you may be able to help us in some way with our fresh enquiries. Is there anyone else in the house?' His voice was tiresome.

'I don't know what you are talking about, and I don't see how I possibly can help you in any way, Inspector.' came her impertinent reply. She ignored his question. She felt a tingle run down her spine.

'Well, Ms Marshall, that's what we are here for, to find out.' he said, turning to his colleagues, and then back to Mars again. 'So, that's why we have this warrant to search your premises.'

'And if I refuse your invitation to search my premises, then what?'

'Then that's your prerogative. It would then denote that you are hiding something. May we please come in, Ms Marshall?' He squinted his eyes at her, eagerly waiting for her next move and her reply. DCI Richards was listening to her answers for any mistakes in her dialogue.

'You sound like a tape recorder Inspector, repeating the same things over and over again.' she said in a mocking reply.

'Thank you, Ms Marshall. I appreciate your views on my vocabulary. So, do we go in, or do I arrest you, and have you taken down to the station by my colleagues, while I take care of the search, without you around?' he said, with a hint of narcissism.

'There is nothing in my possession, Detective, that I have of interest to you.'

'Ms Marshall, I will ask you once more, do we come into your premises, or do you jump into the cars with the officers, and drive down to the station? It is as simple as that.'

Mars stood in the doorway, and feeling slightly uneasy with the situation, she had no one to turn to, had no support at hand, Matt was away on business. DCI Richards was standing three feet away from her. She looked at the three other officers as they stood impassively. Things looked serious.

The officers wandered around the house, but Richards made his way straight to where he thought the item he was looking for might be.

He slid back a wardrobe door, which housed an oblong mirror. The cupboard was full of clothes, dresses, skirts, and jackets of all descriptions, denim and leather. Belts were thrown onto coat hangers which were already taken up by some other garments. There wasn't an empty hanger in the cupboard, and there was certainly no more space for another dress to fit in. On the floor were shoes. Open-back sandals, boots, high-heeled shoes, flip flops, all kinds of colours and shapes, mauve, leopard skinned, white, shiny gold, from all kinds of different manufacturers.

On the shelf above, bundled into an unorganised pile was what the detective was looking for. His eyes lit up.

Forty-five

The room had a cold feeling. It smelt of bodies and anxiety. Mars sat on a government iron-framed regulation chair. In front of her was a square laminated table. The four walls were white, going on grey, and nondescript.

Thoughts were racing through her head. She didn't want to be here. She had been in a custody cell overnight whilst the police downloaded information from her phone. They had searched her house, pulling it apart, looking through cupboards and drawers for the tiniest piece of information, searching the loft and the garden shed. Removing and taking away vital information in plastic bags, in an attempt to put a charge of murder on to her. She slept on a narrow thin blue mattress, which sat on a sturdy concrete block. She was covered with a grey woollen blanket, which had probably been used to cover many criminals before her.

She felt alone and cut off from the world and isolated. Her privacy had been stripped from her. She put her arms around herself to drum up some warmth as she looked around the dingy room. There were no windows and there were no views to take in. There were no pictures to occupy her mind. Mars felt that she was being spied on.

There was a creek, as the only door to the room opened. She looked up. In walked a familiar face, a face she didn't like or welcome to. Her face looked strained.

'Afternoon, Ms Marshall.' DCI Richards said, a serious look was on his face. She glanced at the tall woman standing next to him. He noticed her do this, he introduced the woman. 'This is my colleague, DI Lambert Ms Marshall. She will be assisting me in this interview today.' Lambert threw Mars a routine smile. She had short dark hair, wore black-rimmed spectacles and looked clean-cut. She didn't look like she should be in the police force, she looked more like a schoolteacher. She was clutching a folder, holding it to her chest with her arms crossed, protecting it, like it was an expensive manuscript. The two detectives sat on the chairs opposite her.

'What do you want from me Inspector? I hope this interview can be concluded quickly so I can be on my way, I have a meeting to attend to later.' Richards shuffled on his seat.

'I will do my best, but it depends on your cooperation with our enquiries today Ms Marshall. I have some important questions to ask you, that's why you are here.'

'What sort of questions may I ask?' Her veneer of composure cracked a little.

'Well, let me ask you. Where were you on the evening of October 31st, 2008? It was a Friday night, it was quite misty and it was Halloween night to be precise. It was the night that Christina Zabrinski was murdered.'

'What is this all about Inspector?' She looked expressionless.

'It's really a simple question to answer. It isn't difficult. Where were you that night, the night in question?' She looked at the detectives.

'I was at home with my son, Tom, I've told you all this before in our previous meetings.'

'Were you there all night, Ms Marshall?'

'Yes, of course I was, he's my son. I'm hardly going to leave my son by himself Inspector, am I? Why?' she said defensively.

Richards laid out on the table a selection of paperwork. Mars stared at it, and then at Richards.

'I have obtained your records from your mobile phone company, Ms Marshall.'

'Pardon?'

'I have checked through them, and they have revealed that your mother tried to contact you on that evening, at…' He looked at a piece of paper on the desk, 'At 8:54 p.m. and again at 9:13 p.m.' She looked taken aback by his delving into her private life. Richards scribbled some notes on a pad of paper.

'I must have been in the bath, it's a Friday night thing you know.' She smiled smugly at him.

'You also had two missed phone calls on your mobile from your boyfriend, Matt Robson, one was at 9:01 p.m. and again at 9:26 p.m. and then a text message at 9:28 p.m. and another from Jenny Ross at 8:49. That's a lot of calls to have missed, is it not? Do you have any reason as to have not answered these calls Ms Marshall? I would have thought that if you were relaxing, on your Friday night off, as you said you were, you would have had the decency to return the calls to these people, who are your friends, family, and boyfriend, but you didn't. Was there a reason that you didn't return your boyfriend's calls, or his text message,' he said in a drawn voice.

'Well, my phone must have been on silent Inspector, it was my night off, I'm entitled to have one occasionally, and besides, you have no right to go through my private calls.'

'Oh, but we do Ms Marshall, especially when we are investigating a murder.' He looked her in the eyes.

'Like I said, it was my night off, and I was going to enjoy it by relaxing.'

'Really.' replied an inquisitive Richards.

'Why have you given up attending "Harper's Gymnasium", suddenly, after joining it in October 2007, and being a member for twelve months? Can you answer that one for me please?' She groaned.

'It was boring, I was hoping to meet a man there, but it didn't happen. Still, I have since found a man, does that answer your question?' He didn't comment.

'Indeed.' He quickly moved on. He looked at his notes.

'Your ex-husband Rick tells me that when he first met you, you were a fan of Alice Cooper, the rock singer.' She looked bitterly at him. 'He told me that you both went to a fancy dress party, where you dressed up as Alice Cooper, is that true Ms Marshall?'

'What the fuck is all this about Inspector.' She wriggled around in her chair.

'Just answer the question Ms Marshall, did you go to this party dressed as… Alice Cooper.' She looked at Lambert, then back to DCI Richards.

'I really cannot remember, it was too long ago, too many things have happened in my life since then. Besides what are you doing talking to my ex for?'

'Mr Marshall was only helping us with some of our enquiries, and these are steps that we have to take.'

'Right,' she replied. looking uninterested.

'And Alice Cooper carried out an imitation act on stage at one time, where he hanged himself, did he not?' She squinted at him.

'Where is this all leading to, it's all so boring.' Richards picked up his pen.

'Can you ask me why Christina Zabrinski sent you a text message at 6:22 p.m. on Friday, October 31st, 2008, stating that she was looking forward to… I quote, "our private meeting"?' She looked unrepentantly at him.

'The message ended with two x's.' He flicked his pen on the table. 'I don't want to sit here for hours on end fishing, I'm looking for the truth, so no games please, no lies. Do you know where I'm coming from?' His voice was forceful.

DCI Richards had interviewed Mars twice in the past about the murder of Ms Zabrinski, all to no avail. But he still had his suspicions about her. He knew that he had the culprit, but just didn't have enough to charge her. This time he had better lines of enquiries, better questions to open her up with. He felt this time was his final attempt, he had to nail this woman today. He leaned forward in his chair.

'What time did this private meeting commence then? And where did it take place? Just the facts, and please come to the point, Ms Marshall.'

His face was serious, and he wanted the truth. She didn't like what she was being asked.

'We were' she breathed heavily, she began to feel an ounce of pressure as he scrutinized her. 'I want an answer, now.' He said.

'Well. We were going out together, in the week, just the two of us, to a bar. A bar uptown.'

'What sort of bar,' snapped Richards.

'A gay bar,' she replied.

'Are you gay?'

'Huh, no I'm not Inspector, no.'

'What's the name of this gay bar, Ms Marshall?'

'I don't know, it was Christina's idea, it wasn't mine, she had made all the arrangements for the evening, she's like that, she loves organising things, she's very exuberant.' She looked at him. 'Was.' She pursed her lips.

'I'm trying to catch you lying Ms Marshall, and at the moment I think you are lying to me.' He looked suspiciously at her.

'We were going out to have some fun, that's all, nothing else, just a laugh.'

'Quit—the bullshit, Ms Marshall,' he snapped at her.

'You didn't get on with Ms Zabrinski, did you? You were virtually enemies at work. We have spoken to your work colleagues. They said that you were recently offered Christina's job, then she took it away from you, is that correct?' His voice was serious. She didn't answer him.

'Well…'

'Well, what,' she snapped.

'You're not telling me the truth, are you?' Richards stared intensely at her, his face looked warm and humid.

'I am telling you the truth. We were going out for a laugh, it's not a crime is it Inspector, to have a laugh, is it, you should try it yourself one day?' she replied arrogantly, as she glanced at Lambert. Richards sighed and looked at his colleague.

'Where did you get the green Gucci bag from, Ms Marshall?' Lambert said.

'What bag?' came a humble reply.

'The bag that we found in your bedroom wardrobe, on the top shelf.' Lambert paused.

'Er, from a boyfriend, why?'

'What's his name?' The reply was quick.

'Er, Jonathan.' Her voice sounded unsure.

'And where does this Jonathan person live, do you have his address?'

'I don't know where he lives, I only saw him two or three times, why should I know where he lives? I wasn't involved with the guy.'

'It's a very expensive bag to be bought by a boyfriend you've only seen two or three times, don't you think, Ms Marshall?' Lambert adjusted her glasses. Her face was expressionless.

'I'm worth it.' She gives a thin smile that even she thinks may not be entirely convincing. 'I have expensive tastes and he knew it. Perhaps he wanted to see me again, and that's the reason for the present. It's what blokes do you know, they buy you things when they want to get you into bed. Maybe that's what he was after Inspector?'

'Really.' Richards leaned forwards taking over the conversation. He stared at her. He moved around in his chair. He then dug a hand into his pocket and retrieved a small wooden object. He put it on the table in front of her, making sure it made a tapping sound. She looked broodingly at it.

'Any idea where this wooden toy-like implement comes from, Ms Marshall?' He leaned back on his chair, waiting for an answer. There was a pause.

'No officer, I haven't got a clue,' she said, not removing her eyes from the oblong block.

'Well, Ms Marshall, we found this under Ms Zabrinski's bed, at fourteen Bollo Lane. It's a strange object for Ms Zabrinski to have in her house, and let alone, under her bed, it doesn't match anything else in her home, we find it odd.' She ignored his question. She felt that he was playing devil's advocate with her, he was trying to provoke her. It wasn't working for him. This woman was like ice.

'On our search of your premises we went into your son Tom's room. We found four of these on a shelf. Three of them were stood upright, and another was laid across two of them, making what looked like a bridge, the piece that was to make the second part of the bridge, was missing or removed. Any ideas Ms Marshall as to how a piece of your son's building block found its way into fourteen Bollo Lane?' He stroked his moustache.

'This object, a toy as you call it, is probably made in its thousands. You cannot pin this thing down on me. You have no proof this came from my house Inspector, so please don't put your misdemeanours of your poor search on to me please.' She sipped at the cup of water on the table.

'Why are you asking me these ludicrous questions Mr Richards?'

He didn't like being called Mr when he was a detective chief inspector. He leaned forward in his chair, it was balancing on two of its legs. Frown lines appeared between his eyes. In a lowered tone, he said.

'Because. I'm the sheriff, and you're just a Marshall, Miss Marshall.' She narrowed her eyes at him. He stood.

'Ms Marshall, have you ever been strangled by someone, with a rope?'

'Excuse me!'

'Can you answer the question for me please, have you ever been strangled with a rope?' Mars looked at Richards, she glanced at his colleague Lambert. She felt that she had to be very careful with answering his questions now.

'Er... No, I haven't.' She looked nervously at Richards. He was aware of every nuance in her voice.

'Have you ever strangled anyone, Ms Marshall?'

'It's a question of immense juxtaposition isn't it, Detective?' Richards stroked his spiky chin.

'Would you care answering the question please?'

'No, I haven't Detective.' The DCI sat down, he methodically thought about his next question.

'I'm going to take an educated guess Ms Marshall... I think you killed Christina Zabrinski.'

'Rubbish,' she snapped back at him. 'You have the wrong person Detective, you are clutching at straws.'

'You had a motive to murder Ms Zabrinski, and your alibi is thin.' He looked her in the eyes.

'Once I find out why, which I have, I then go onto—whom.' She crossed her legs.

'I think you left your house that Friday, the 31st, October 2008, maybe around eight-thirtyish. You left your son Tom on his own, you may have told him not to take any calls, or you disconnected the phone line, that's the reason you missed your mother's phone calls, and your boyfriend Matt's phone calls. You had bought your son a DVD, it lasted for eighty-eight minutes, which takes it up to around ten o'clock, about the time a nine-year-old goes to bed, isn't it?' He leered at her. 'You took public transport, leaving your vehicle outside your house so the neighbours could see it, and if questioned they would say that "your car was outside your house that night". He went on. 'You then arrived at the home of Ms Zabrinski at around 9 p.m.'

'It just isn't true, and you know it Detective,' Mars remarked.

'We found Ms Zabrinski's diary.' She breathed in. 'And there was an entry in it on October 31st, 2008.' There was silence. 'It read. "Private meeting. Nine". She looked at both detectives. They both looked smug.

'I'm guessing how you got there we are still not sure, probably by private taxi. We have spoken to numerous people, cab drivers, bus drivers, and neighbours, and we have built up your intended route to the address. We think you jogged part of the way, being the fit person that you are, and a member of a gym. And you took a cab part of the way.' He stared at her waiting for a reaction, but it never came. She sat silently.

'You were invited into the house by Christina because you had an invitation. Hence the text message from her, "looking forward to our private meeting".'

'You are on the wrong track, Inspector,' Mars butted in.

'You have the wrong candidate for your position sitting here.' retorted an agitated Mars.

'Please, let me continue with what I am saying to you, your turn will come later.'

'I have every right to challenge your mistakes, detective. You are talking to the wrong person,' she growled.

'Please, this is a formal interview, and I intend to see it through. So if you would let me continue please.' Mars grappled nervously at her cup of water on the table and took a firm swig of it as if it were a large vodka and coke. Her face betrayed a minor panic.

'OK, I will carry on Ms Marshall, thank you.' Again, he leaned forward in his chair, he glanced at the paperwork on the desk. 'I will continue. You purposely set up a meeting with Ms Zabrinski, at her home on Friday 31st. Maybe it was a joint meeting with her, but I think you callously set up this rendezvous, you enticed Ms Zabrinski into believing she was going to engage with you in a sexual act.'

'Rubbish!' She stormed.

'Your strength—then took hold of you; you may have coaxed Ms Zabrinski to lay on her front, we found traces of Clonazepam inside her body, maybe you fed this to her. I doubt that she would have taken it herself, do you, Ms Marshall? There was no sign of it in her house, and it was not a medicine she took or a medicine that was prescribed to her.'

'Ha!' she retorted.

'And when she became weak, you then possibly pushed her face down on the sofa.'

Mars sat stationary as she listened intensively to

 Richards' words unable to defend herself.

'You then managed to find your way on top of her back. You then placed a piece of rope around her neck, pulled it together and then began to strangle her with it, convincing her that an act of sex was going to take place, as she was face down, and pointing to the cushions on the sofa.' Mars folded her arms for comfort and let out an audible sigh at him. 'You then tightened the rope and continued tightening it as you squeezed the life from her and you were, possibly kneeling on her back at this time.'

'Bullshit, Inspector,' she raged at him.

'It's the truth, isn't it Ms Marshall?'

'No! Inspector, no it isn't the truth. You have it all wrong.' She scoffed at him.

'I will continue, please... Somewhere during this confrontation her hands then became loose, and she scratched at the only thing she could reach for, the cushions. As she became unable to defend herself against you, you fought with her as her arms flapped around in defence. You then hit her on the head with what we believe to be an ashtray, and you then continued to strangle her as she weakened. We never found an ashtray in her lounge, and being that Christina was a smoker, we found it somewhat strange that she never had one laying around. Forensic tests stated that she had smoked that evening. But we never found a cigarette butt, just a small dusting of cigarette ash, strange, don't you think?' She glanced at the female detective. Lambert sat observing Mars.

'And then after you'd killed her, I believe you pulled her along the carpet of the lounge, and then dragged her limp, dead body out and onto the wooden surface of the hallway floor. You then tied her left leg with some of the rope that you'd brought along with you.' Mars sat still. She felt frozen.

'You then threw the rope up to the first floor or took it up with you as you walked up the stairs. And then with the strength which you had gained from going to the gym, which you joined twelve months before the murder of Ms Zabrinski,' he said as he stared at Mars looking for a reaction to his question.

'You then commenced pulling her body upwards, again with your strength you managed to tie the rope around the bannister.' Richards stared at her, trying to call her bluff, hoping that she would slip up in saying that she was not strong enough to hold a dead weight and tie a knot around the wooden post. Mars didn't flinch.

'You then left Ms Zabrinski dangling in mid-air.' He waited for an answer from her. There wasn't one.

'And as she dangled, you then carried out an act of mockery, by painting her eyes with black mascara. Like your girlhood hero. Then, as she dangled upside down, dead, in her hallway, you possibly removed her right stocking from her leg, we haven't yet got to why you carried out this act. And you callously forced an apple into the dead Ms Zabrinski's mouth, maybe to say to yourself, "at last, shut up will you! And listen to me for once". You then went back into the lounge and proceeded to scatter some of Jeff Turner's hair onto the sofa. We spoke to Mr Turner, and he confirmed that you had had a meeting with him at the Half Moon Pub in September 2008, you offered him some work, but he never heard from you again. We believe that you gained some of his hairs, maybe from his clothing in that meeting. A witness in the pub said that you were acting strange when Jeff was at the bar getting you a drink. You took some of them and placed them on the deceased, to make it look like he was there, that Jeff Turner had carried out the murder. He told us that you hugged him goodbye when you were leaving the meeting with him at the public house. He said he found it bizarre, wanting to meet him, seeing that there was animosity between the two of you. He said that he thought he would never see you again.'

Mars sat there, rigid, like a statue, she was unrepentant. Her eyes welled up. She sat motionless in her chair, she leaned forward and picked up the almost empty plastic cup of water. She found it difficult to hold the cup without shaking. Fear was now evident in her, and she tried to hide it from the detective. He fixed on her with his cold gaze.

'The green Gucci bag Ms Marshall.'

'Yes, well?' She breathed heavily.

'It wasn't bought for you, was it?'

'Yes, it was, I told you where it came from!'

'You stole it from Ms Zabrinski, didn't you?'

'No, I told you it was bought for me by a boyfriend of mine.'

'What's his name?'

'I've already told you that.'

'His surname, what is it?' She didn't answer him.

'Forensics examined the inside of the bag, and they found the DNA of Ms Zabrinski on it. Yes, it had wash marks on the inside, but the cleaning process failed to get rid of all of Ms Zabrinski's DNA.' There was silence.

'Ms Marshall, do you have anything to say on the points that I have gone through with you?'

'I most certainly do Mr Richards, your claims are without any validity, all your evidence detective, what there is of it, is purely circumstantial, and you are drawing on your own conclusions.'

'Strong, circumstantial evidence, Ms Marshall,' said Richards. She went on.

'You have no evidence whatsoever to prove that I was your killer, or that I was at the house on the evening the murder took place. Your evidence is raw, and it will not hold up in a court of law. You are speculating Inspector. You cannot put me at that house at the times you are mentioning, you are clutching at straws because you haven't caught the person who carried out this, this horrific crime, so you have decided to put the blame onto me. It will be ridiculed by a lawyer, and he will embarrass you Mr Richards.' She glanced at Lambert, looking for a reaction.

DCI Richards turned and flicked his eyes at Lambert. Mars sat impassively. Lambert removed a plastic transparent bag from a folder, she held it in a hand. Mars looked ambiguously at DCI Richards and the folder, Detective Lambert held the folder proud of herself.

'Do you know what this is Ms Marshall?' His stare ran through her.

'What, the plastic folder, or the contents inside Inspector?' She threw a pointed look.

'The rope inside the plastic folder Ms Marshall. Do you recognise the rope inside the folder?' She hesitated, she knew that she had killed Christina with a rope, but was the detective going to try and bluff her into submission? Mars had foolishly kept the rope that she killed Christina with, as a prize, and now wished she hadn't done so. It looked like the

261

same rope which she took from Jeff Turner on the night he strangled her, in his sister's flat. But was this the same rope?

'They had interviewed Jeff, so they knew that he had strangled me. He must have told them that the rope had then gone missing.' She now wondered, does it contain any samples of DNA? It looked the same colour as what she had used around Christina's neck, and looked the same length and texture. 'What was he holding and how did he obtain it? It must have been by luck that he found it in my bedroom when he searched my house, as I'd hidden it in a bag at the back of a drawer. Or had I?'

'So, these detectives are smarter than I thought. What's my next move going to be, come on Mars, think!' She pondered for a while. 'If it's the rope he found in my house, then it contains DNA, Christina's DNA, and Jeff Turner's DNA. It still doesn't put me at the murder scene, so how do I answer his question? He will ask me what I am doing with this rope in my house, with the dead Christina Zabrinski's DNA on it.' The skin on her cheek had become itchy with anxiety. She wanted to scratch it, but she didn't want to let on to the detectives that she was feeling nervous. She began to fidget and squirm, unable to find a comfortable position on her seat.

'Well, Ms Marshall, we found it in your house, after a thorough search of the premises.' She looked stunned and began to feel cold inside. He went on.

'So, have you seen this rope before?'

'Yes, I have.' The detectives looked at each other.

'Also, Inspector, I need some more water please, cold water that is. Thanks.' She was looking wan, and bleary-eyed.

The interview paused. It was a plan for Mars to have some time to think things out. It was becoming a game of cat and mouse. Richards was hoping that she would crack, and request a lawyer at some point, or go onto, "no comment" answers, but she didn't. Either of these would be the start of her downfall, admitting that she needed some kind of help with their questioning. Mars knew this. They could then begin to corner her. Some of their questions were awkward, some telling. She was a smart woman. She stood strong.

There was a brief hiatus.

Richards and Lambert marched out of the room. Lambert went outside for some fresh air.

Richards could feel tension in his body as he stood, exhaling slowly whilst staring down the corridor. He felt the dampness in his armpits, mild aching at the foot of his skull. He had her on the back foot, but she still refused to crack.

'I'm going to need something to eat when I get away from here, I hope I can nail this woman, fast.' he said to Lambert as she returned.

'You nearly had her boss, you were moments away.'

'She's as guilty as sin,' he replied. 'She continually hides behind her eyelids when a problematic question is asked.' Lambert disappeared to grab what she could from the canteen.

'Last throw of the dice, guv,' she said, handing him a bag of Maltesers. He ripped at the packet.

She looked at her new plastic cup, her lips were dry. 'What do I say now?'

'So, have you ever seen this rope before, Ms Marshall?' He observed her calculating her next move.

'Yes, I have seen it before.'

'So, the middle section of the rope contains yours, and Ms Zabrinski's DNA and the outside of the rope contains fibres, probably from gloves... and Jeff Turner's DNA. So, I'm thinking that this rope had to have been used twice,' Richards said. 'What is confusing me is... why does it contain Christina's DNA? And why was it found in your house? Could you answer that question Ms Marshall?' He sat tapping the edge of the paperwork on the table, waiting patiently for her answer, with a smug look.

'We recently spoke to Mr Jeff Turner, and he told us that he had strangled you in a game that you both participated in at his flat with a rope. You must have then taken it from his flat, as he said that he couldn't find it. And you then used it to strangle Ms Zabrinski, replicating what he did to you, in bitterness, didn't you? That's why it contains Ms Zabrinski's DNA. So, you're lying, aren't you? You killed Christina

Zabrinski, didn't you Ms Marshall?' She looked into the eyes of the detective.

'You have missed a point Detective.' She paused. 'Have you not thought that Jeff Turner could have also used it to strangle Christina in one of his sick games, that he plays, detective, with that rope.' She gazed at it. 'You see, she had a huge crush on Jeff. I have proof that I gave Christina Jeff's mobile number, so she could contact him, she was desperate to go out with him, and get him into bed. A few people at Hammerson Shaw would also agree with me on that point. I thought, Inspector, that this is a point that you would have investigated, and not left it for this interview?' She smirked at him. He stopped tapping the paper. Lambert sighed.

'He's a bit of a chameleon, isn't he, Detective Richards?' She rammed the question home to him. Richards twisted in his seat. He was hoping that Mars would have missed that fundamental point. And that he would finally have nailed her for the murder. He looked pissed off. He tapped a finger on the table.

'We know that he may have used it on Ms Zabrinski, but we still need to know why we found it in your house… Ms Marshall?' He leaned back in his chair, waiting for her answer. He twisted his wedding ring around its finger.

'I, I took it from Jeff, hoping that it would never be used again,' she was hesitant. 'I was going to destroy it, but somehow, I ended up keeping it, still, it doesn't prove anything does it?' Her voice was forgiving.

He looked at her, he was pondering his next move.

'Can I go now Detective, this is becoming ever so tedious, you have nothing on me.' She got up out of her chair, 'I have things to do you know.'

'Sit down please Ms Marshall, the interview is not over yet.'

'Pardon!'

'You do not have a credible alibi for the Friday evening, do you?' He searched her eyes for an answer. She sat down and looked at the detective.

'You cannot put me at the scene of the crime Detective, on the 31st.'

'Oh yes I can.' He fixed his gaze on her.

'You are forgetting one basic point.'

'And what bloody point is that!' she growled.

'The figure in the garden Ms Marshall, aren't you? Who was staring at you whilst you stood next to the dangling body of your victim?' She coughed. Mars sat paralysed she was stuck to her chair. This time she held her tongue, she thought back to that evening. She thought back to the time when she stood motionless, looking and wondering who the hazy figure in the garden was, who was that looking at her? The figure who she'd thought was possibly a burglar. Her muscles tightened as her world was turning upside down.

'The figure in the garden Ms Marshall is a credible witness. The figure in the garden bought the green leather handbag for the victim.' Richards was pushing his index finger on the table in the direction of her, as he was putting his point across. 'The shape that you saw and looked at whilst you had just completed your vindictive act, was someone that you know very well, and it was someone who knows you, very well. The figure is a fundamental witness and will testify against you in court.' She sat on the small uncomfortable chair, lifeless as she now believed she didn't have any answers for the detective's questions or have the energy to put up any kind of defence. It had gone. Her lips were parched, and her tongue was tired. The room was silent. Richards looked down at his notes.

'Do you have anything to say Ms Marshall?' She gulped. The room was quiet.

'Ms Helen Marshall, I am charging you with the murder of Ms Christina Zabrinski.' She scowled at him.

'My lawyer will have suspicions about your decision, Mr Richards.'

Forty-six

The four women from the five from the jury sat on small wooden chairs on the cramped mezzanine landing. Helen Marshall also sat on a small chair; their seats looked like they were made for school children. Mars looked thoughtful as she sat flanked by a court officer.

The judge for the case stood on the first stair that led up to the first floor. He had decided that he didn't want to sit for the show. Near to him stood a barrister for the prosecution, holding a folder to his chest. There were also two court clerks and a reporter.

Richards and Lambert stood on the first-floor landing, along with the male contingency from the jury. Richards' beady eyes were glued towards the front door of the house. The air was tense.

In front of all of them and on show for all to view dangled some heavy metal weights in the hallway of the house, tied together with brown rope. The other end of the rope was tied to a wooden balustrade on the first floor.

Mars's lawyer, a Mr Jeremy Rice-Evans took centre stage. He stood in the hallway on the ground floor. He was a wily character, he measured five feet ten in height and was a master of ruling the minds of people. Mr Rice-Evans was in his early sixties; he enjoyed the attention and craved the limelight and the publicity of these somewhat testing cases. He was not only a lawyer of immense experience, but a well-known figure in the circles of justice. Law was in his blood; it was his craft.

He fought cases in defence and nothing else. He had a statue of "the scales of justice" in his lounge at home.

He stood with his half-framed glasses perched on the bridge of his hawk like nose holding a wad of papers in his hand like the conductor of the London symphonic orchestra held his baton.

His smile came from the confidence of always being right. He didn't the fear wrong.

He had convinced the judge, Mr Justice Bicknell, that he be allowed to demonstrate to the jury that it was impossible for his client to have pulled up a weight of 138 pounds and suspended it. And that she was categorically and unequivocally not guilty of the horrific murder of Christina Zabrinski. And that Ms Helen Marshall was the innocent party in this case.

They had previously been at the Central Criminal Court in London for two and a half weeks, thrashing out the evidence in the case of Regina Vs Helen Marshall.

The judge had allowed Mr Rice-Evans to prove a significant point and take the jury to fourteen Bollo Lane, London – a point that Mars's lawyer insisted that this could be the only way to prove her innocence.

Yes, the body could have been pulled up with two hands, but this would mean that at some stage of the procedure, the assailant would have to have released one hand from the rope, meaning that one hand would be holding all the weight of the body, all nine and a half stone.

Then the other hand would have been left to weave the rope through the underside of the handrail, then manoeuvre it around the length holding the weight, and then try to get the end of it through the gap to begin to form a knot.

'Ms Lauren Haskins has the characteristics as my client; she weighs the same, and is of a similar height, five feet seven inches tall.' He had chosen Lauren for these comparisons. She had said that she was willing to take part in this demonstration. Lauren was the second woman to take on the role. The first participant had failed.

Ms Haskins was dressed in trousers and trainers. She looked anxious - there wasn't much of a grip for her, as there wasn't ample enough rope to get to pull on to get any momentum going.

The end of the rope sat on top of the handrail waiting for her. The participant leaned her arms over it to try to get a grip on it in order to proceed with the pulling up of the weights. She took the rope with both hands to start the process. She took a breath. Lauren shuffled her feet, trying to get a feel for the floor and to work out how she could best use her feet in this important demonstration.

She looped the rope around one hand, then began to pull the rope over the wooden rail, and then held it as she walked away from the wooden bannister. A strain came over her face, and she puffed as she stepped backwards, heading away from the bannisters. Her trainers dug into the carpet. A court official stood downstairs and indicated to her when the weights had reached around four feet from the ground, the same height which Christina Zabrinski's head had dangled. She stopped when the man told her to.

Lauren, a reasonably fit thirty-eight-year-old stood wondering what to do next as she felt the heaviness. She eased open the hand which was wrapped around the rope in preparation for carrying out the second part, which was to get it wrapped around the wooden bannister and create a knot.

The rope moved over the edge of the handrail and began to edge its way downwards as the weight got the better of her. She slipped forwards sharply as she was tugged forward but managed to stay upright. There was a gasp from some of the onlookers. She regained her composure and pulled the rope back towards her.

She started the procedure again, taking more time in gripping the rope around her hand. She pulled at it, as she walked backwards.

She released a hand and slid it down the rope, but she was not strong enough to hold the mass with the other hand. The weight began to get the better of her. She ran out of ideas. Lauren stood, clutching the rope, staring at the crowd around her, looking for clues, and speculating what her next move should be.

Rice-Evans peered at Detective Richards, his face was pale, who in turn was absorbed in the movements of the rope.

Lauren let go, and the rope raced through the palms of her hands, burning them. The end of it flicked upwards, like the tail of an angry animal, before it swiftly disappeared. The weights crashed to the ground. She looked lost. Her face was red and clammy. She looked at her fellow jury members.

The room was high-ceilinged. The upper section of the walls were painted beige, or they had once been white and hadn't been decorated for years. Wood panelling decorated the bottom half of the large arena. It is typically simple and unadorned, with a white tiled floor.

She had hardly slept the previous night. Pacing the floor back and forth, when she had laid down on the bed, she just tossed and turned, and perspired. At one stage her head throbbed uncontrollably.

Mars sat anxiously behind the glass screen; it made her feel guilty even before the verdict was read out. It made her feel lonely and shut off from the world. It was intimidating knowing that everyone was staring at you, you the murderer. You, the evil person, who had taken the life of an innocent woman. You, the one who should be sentenced to the maximum amount of time the judge could hand out. She could now just do with a cup of tea.

She swivelled her head towards the public gallery. Some of her friends were there to supporter her. Jenny, Dave Palmer, and her next-door neighbour Marion Saunders. She gave them a fleeting smile. It was good to see them here, it gave her encouragement knowing that they were rooting for her. Mars was astonished to see her ex-husband Richard Sean Marshall sitting nearby. What the hell was he doing here. Why has he suddenly appeared, on the last day of the trial? Perhaps to give some form of moral support. Not that she needed it from him. Maybe if she went down the steps he would then take custody of Tom? Why hadn't he attended on the other days? Mars didn't even smile at the self-centred, self-righteous person that had lured her into marrying him, and then divorced her when she preferred to stay in west London rather than move to a rural village in Suffolk and live on a small holding that he wanted to buy. Well, there were other issues - his controlling nature was one, his blatant flirting with his secretary, Jane "the tart" Pinkham.

She remembered when they had first met, in Acton. He took her down the Thames on a boat trip, sweeping her off her feet with his charm and endearments. They had laughed together and holidayed at places they hadn't been to before. They had bought a flat in Uxbridge together and lived a comfortable life. She had felt lonely for the first time in her life when he wasn't around and couldn't wait for him to get home from work. He was the first person that she had missed. She had felt so privileged when he walked into her life. They used to send each other silly text messages in the beginning. She couldn't sleep properly, and neither could he. They used to get drunk and lay in bed on the Sunday after until midday. They had done all the things that young lovers did.

The relationship went smoothly until Mars found a text on his phone, from her. His lies were pitiful, and from then on the relationship went downhill. They argued, they raised their voices at each other, and then he stayed out on weekends. On his return, he gave ludicrous excuses. So, she picked up Tom and left.

Mars moved her head half a degree to notice Mr and Mrs Zabrinski sitting next to their family support officer. They both looked stoic and grey. Their faces were forlorn and fearful. Mars had met Mr Zabrinski once when he came to the office to see Christina, and she had introduced him to Mars. He was an intelligent guy, and told her that he had persuaded his daughter to go to university and study economics. He said that he came over from Poland at the age of twelve and had gone on to study it himself in London. He later worked for a biopharmaceutical company before working abroad. Mars liked John Zabrinski and wondered where his daughter got her selfishness from - it didn't appear to have come from him. He was enjoyable to talk to, and he had time for you, unlike Christina. Mars bet he couldn't believe seeing her in the dock. Christina had been his only child.

Mars tried to make out the jury. Where they worked, what they went home to at night, and were they intelligent enough to understand what they had heard over the past few weeks of this trial? Had they been influenced by her Barristers act at Christina's house? Had it swayed them?

And then the door finally opened, and in walked the judge. Everyone stood up.

The jury deliberated the outcome of the case for almost three days before returning to the courtroom. Mars looked over at Richards and saw that he had a pensive look as he stared at the door of the court. There were people in the room that were entirely unknown to her. Journalists, and day trippers eager for a free day out. She avoided locking eyes with anyone.

A member of the jury stood, and when asked what their verdict was, the woman said. 'Not guilty.'

There was a squeal from where the spectators sat. Richards buried his face in his hands, looking bereft. DI Lambert grimaced and crossed her legs.

Mars shrieked in a high-pitched voice; she hugged her lawyer when they met.

Ms Helen Marshall walked from the courtroom, not looking once at the detectives. She walked outside, flanked by her mother Ruth, and her boyfriend Matt Robson, with her lawyer in close attendance. Mars was a free woman.

They were met outside by a reporter and a photographer. Questions rained down on her, a camera was pointed close to her face, but she wasn't at all interested in being part of an interview.

Matt managed to flag down a black cab in the busy London Street. The brakes on the vehicle screeched as it whizzed past them, then the cab reversed back to where they stood.

The four of them jumped in the back. Mars flopped onto the rear bench seat, excitement oozed from her face, relief drained from her body, and she wiped away an emotional tear. Her mother sat beside her; their arms entwined with each other's. The two men sat opposite them on the pull-down seats. Mars remembered the time when she had first sat on a cab bench seat with Jeff Divine, when they met for the first time, on that dark January night, travelling to fourteen Bollo Lane, to Christina's party.

She looked out of the rear window. Their taxi was stationary, stuck behind a car in front. Only then did she notice Rebecca Ansell standing on the opposite side of the busy street. She stood alone and had an odd look about her – she looked like an effigy. As Mars focused on her, people jostled with each other, as they moved around the busy and vibrant capital. Rebecca looked in Mars's direction.

The cab finally pulled away after Matt had told the driver their destination. She turned and looked out of the rear window again. Rebecca was heading towards another black cab, and the driver looked like he was expecting his next fare. Mars watched as Rebecca jumped into the back of the cab.

Rebecca was the one witness that the prosecution had been desperately hoping would turn up to give evidence against Mars. She was the one that Richards had eagerly depended on, the one who could have sealed Mars's fate. The golden nugget.

Forty-seven

October 31st 2008

The alarm went off, making a high-pitched buzzing sound with breaks in between. It was the last sound that she wanted to hear, and she was unaware of what time it was, but it didn't wake her - she had been awake now for some time. In fact, she thought she'd been awake for most of the night, stirring constantly in the middle of it, and had felt restless and unable to settle, twisting and turning in a futile effort to get a good night's sleep. On one occasion she had got out of bed, and gone downstairs and turned on the TV to see what was happening in the world in the middle of the night as she tried to settle her mind.

She felt tired as she grappled with the clock to switch the alarm off. She wandered into the bathroom and pulled the cord to turn on the light. It made an echoing sound in the empty room.

The shower felt good as she turned the chrome control. It felt uplifting and invigorating, and she felt a tingling sensation as the water cascaded over her body.

She stepped out feeling refreshed and headed back to her bedroom. On the way, Mars opened Tom's bedroom door and walked over to wake him. He stirred and grumbled as she leaned over and opened the curtains to let some light in, hoping it would put some life into him.

'Come on, darling, it's morning time. Wakey-wakey!' she said in a cheerful voice.

Mars brushed her blonde hair as she looked at herself in her dressing table mirror. She looked at the holdall next to her feet, looked inside it and then pushed it together to close it. It was going to be a long day, probably one of the longest she would face in her life. She had spent the last couple of months preparing for this day, and now it was here.

The toaster made a muffled click and popped up two slices of burnt bread. She threw them onto a plate, and then turned around to see her young son, Tom, waddle into the kitchen, holding a plastic mask.

'Morning, Tom.' There was a half-hearted "morning" in reply.

His Rice Krispies stood where they always did, there each morning next to the jug of milk. He poured the milk over his cereal and crunched his breakfast, making a chomping sound as he enjoyed his start to the day. Mars scraped a knife full of butter over a slice of her toast, and bit rapidly into it, feeling that time was beginning to go against her. She left the kitchen, went into the lounge and turned on the TV. She watched it very briefly, as her nerves began to get to her. Then she returned to the kitchen to check on her son.

She slurped at her tea as she heard the front doorbell chime.

'Tom, it's time to go. Silvia's at the door.' Tom's nanny had arrived at the house a couple of minutes late to whisk him off to school.

Tom kissed his mum goodbye and disappeared out of the kitchen, heading towards the front door and picking up his satchel from the floor on the way. Mars followed, only to catch the pair of them already down the pathway and out through the gate.

'Bye,' Mars said as she waved to the pair of them as they played out their ritual of heading, somewhat late today, down the pavement towards the road and off to school.

'Bye, Ms Marshall,' returned a distant-sounding voice from her au pair. Tom quickly turned around to his mum.

'Don't forget to get the Transformers DVD for me tonight, Mum.'

'I won't, darling,' she replied. 'I won't,' she muttered to herself.

Mars had promised Tom a special treat. It was something that he wanted to watch as some of his friends at school had already seen it and he wanted to catch up on the action as well.

Mars looked ponderously at the morning sky unfolding in front of her. Clouds were swirling around. It was a damp October morning with a hint of sunshine. She had thought that summer and autumn had gone weeks ago, but today there was a touch of sun in the sky. Crisp brown leaves were falling gently from the trees. Conker shells lay on the pavement, the treasure inside having been plundered by the local kids. And the frost on the windscreens of the parked cars was beginning to melt. Nevertheless, there was a chill in the air as she closed the wooden front door of her house. She leaned with her back against it. As she listened to the silence for a while, the sense of peace she felt seemed priceless. She had no thoughts in her head apart from what the next fifteen or so hours were going to bring her, and they could possibly change her life. Forever. Perhaps…

Mid-morning at Hammerson Shaw had a boisterous atmosphere about it. The phones appeared to be more active and there was more vocal noise than usual. Mars was slightly oblivious to what was going on around her.

She was emailing an auction house in Manchester, trying to finalise a piece of land they had purchased in view of getting planning permission to build offices on the site for a client that they had lined up. And today it was taking an unusually long time. She had half a cup of cold tea sitting next to her for company. Dave Palmer walked by.

'Morning, Mars! What's up, cat got your tongue this morning?' She jolted slightly.

'No, not really Dave, I didn't sleep too well last night. Too much on my mind. You look happy, though,' she replied, probably regretting what she had just said.

'I'm always happy, Mars, when it's payday. It means that the missus will be happy as well, thank God.'

'What are you getting up to this weekend, Dave, much?'

'It's supposed to be a good weekend weather-wise, hopefully, so we're going down to Croydon to see the wicked witch, I mean the mother-in-law. It's got to be done occasionally, got to show your face, and it keeps Bev happy. Besides, give the mother-in-law her due, she does a lovely roast dinner, nice crispy potatoes, so she's not all that bad, I suppose. She has got some good points about her.'

'What about yourself, Mars, what are you up to? You have a man in your life, haven't you?'

'Er… yes, Dave, I do - Matt, he's coming over tomorrow. We're going over to see some friends to celebrate Halloween with some drinks and nibbles. Should be fun.' She smiled, feeling somewhat tired.

She turned and looked out of the window to hide the pang of guilt on her face.

'Talking about witches, Dave, where's Christina today?' He grinned.

'Oh, she's out, at a meeting. She'll be back in the office about three, I think?'

'I just wondered; I thought I hadn't seen her around this morning.'

Dave disappeared as the conversation petered out. Just then a bleep came from her handbag. She retrieved her phone and pushed two buttons to read the message. It was from Sherry. It read,

"What about lunch today, 12:30?"

Mars looked at her watch. It told her it was now four-thirty-one. She felt a headache coming on as she rubbed her temple and remembered she had some shopping to get on her way home. And she couldn't forget Tom's DVD, or she would be toast.

She picked up her belongings and headed towards the stairs and home as the office cleaners took her place. She decided to walk home as much of the way as possible until her legs could take no more. She needed the time to contemplate the forthcoming hours ahead.

The afternoon air was still, and the trees were motionless. It was a mild late afternoon and darkness had already fallen. She texted Silvia to say that she was running late and asked if she could stay around a while longer.

Tom was happy. He had his new DVD, his warm glass of fresh milk beside him, and a plate of popcorn for extra company this evening. Mars looked ominously at the glass and wondered if the mixture of brandy and milk was the correct potion.

She checked the items that were laid out on the bed before putting them into her zipped holdall, then picked up a small white towel and put it in the rucksack, followed by a pair of high-heeled shoes. Next, she put in a thick pair of socks, and then a plastic bag containing two used beer cans, a sharp knife, a large sheet of newspaper and a pair of Latex-gloves. She wiggled in a pair of oversized trainers, and one of Tom's toy bricks, a handbag, and then finally the large roll of twisted brown rope.

She kissed Tom on the forehead, and told him that she wouldn't be long, she just needed to go for a jog and that he should enjoy the movie, watch what he liked on the TV, and try to settle down no later than 10:00pm.

She picked up an apple from her fruit bowl and threw it into the bag. She looked at her watch, zipped up her hooded fleece, and checked that a small plastic bag was in one of the pockets. She flung back her head, donned the brown wig, and made some adjustments to her hair. She crept out of the house, shutting the door gently behind her. She stood in a shadow and listened for any noises; the air was murky.

Helen Marshall moved into the darkness of the night.

She walked a mile until she flagged down a black cab. The driver had a warm smile, and she jumped in.

'Where to, Miss?'

'King Street, please,' she said.

The four-and-a-half-mile trip took fifteen minutes. She paid the driver and gave him a tip.

She got out and walked to a phone box in Stamford Brook.

She then got a second cab to Acton Lane, West Three. She got out and walked the remainder of her journey to her destination.

She slowly looked around, as she stood in an unlit area of the street. There were crackling noises in the air. She saw someone wandering down the road on the opposite side to where she was standing. At first the figure looked blurry until it got nearer. It was a man wearing a red sweatshirt. He took no notice of Mars, acting as if she wasn't there, like she didn't even exist. He was too busy chatting on his mobile phone and seemed far too engrossed in his conversation to take notice of what was going on around him. When he disappeared, she looked around her for a second time. In the distance, she heard the noise of people enjoying the evening. A firework went off in the sky. Mars scanned the area like an eagle looking for its prey, then made her way to number fourteen.

She gently pushed open the garden gate and walked up the path. She heard classical music coming from inside the house, she paused for a moment. She changed into her black high-heeled shoes, removed her wig and put it into a side pocket of the rucksack. She held her handbag and hid the holdall behind a bush. She pushed the doorbell.

Forty-eight

She leaned on her victim, her knee pushed into her back, trapping her. Mars pulled the rope tighter and tighter. She twisted it to make sure that it squeezed into her skin. Christina's arms flapped around like the wings of a baby duck that had just taken its first plunge into the air. Her fingers dug into the cushions making a scratching sound on the fabric as she writhed in agony. But she had been placed in a position where she was powerless to defend herself and fight back.

Mars had to work harder than she had thought. She had plied her victim with alcohol to relax her and make her weak, while she herself had only sipped water, claiming that it contained vodka.

Her prey was putting up a good fight. Mars had assumed that the task of looping a rope around an intoxicated Christina's neck and forcing the life from her would go smoothly and quickly, but her victim was putting up a good defence against her attacker. Mars was struggling to end the life of her arch-enemy and needed an extra weapon to get rid of this woman.

Mars grabbed at a large glass ashtray, raised it and thrust it down with venom against the back of Christina's head. She raised it again, ready for the next onslaught before she realised that her victim's flapping arms had slowed. She then returned and continued pulling and twisting the rope in fury until Christina gave up the fight to save her own life and her arms went limp.

Mars lifted her head and tilted it back. She was panting as she watched Christina's body twitch below her.

The life had finally drained from Christina as she began to turn into a corpse. Mars looked unrepentant as she felt the spirit leave the body. She gazed at what she had just undertaken, and what she had achieved. She had now finally stopped the overbearing Christina Zabrinski from controlling her, telling her what to do, and bossing her around. It wouldn't happen again. But was this the way it should have been? Could there have been another way? She pondered as she looked at the picture of the Earl of Leicester on the wall. Mars remembered Christina telling her that Robert had bought it for her birthday boasting how large the picture was, how much time he must have spent on finding such an opulent present for her, and how expensive it must have been. She had gone on for days reminding her about it as if Christina was the only person who received lavish gifts. It had pissed her off.

The room had become discomfortingly silent. She took in the stillness for a moment. She smelt the air and detected the scent of peach. Mars relished the supremacy she now had over her former nemesis. Kneeling on her body gave her an overwhelming feeling of fulfilment, knowing that she now finally had control over her victim.

She slowly got off from Christina and stood up, looking at the scene. The body was still. The music had ended. Christina's clothes were ruffled and creased. The once fashion-proud woman was now laying in a tangled mess, the rope still around her neck. Mars went into a reverie for a moment, realising what had just happened, as reality started to set in. She realised now that she was a murderer. And now someone would be after her.

Mars took hold of Christina's ankles and dragged the lifeless body off the sofa, and onto the lounge floor. The head thumped face down onto the carpet, and she squirmed. She turned it over. Blood trickled from the corpse's nose. She then dragged Christina outside by the ankles and into the hallway. The floor became smoother as she slid the body to its position.

She then went outside and collected her rucksack and came back in. She changed into her thick socks and the other set of trainers; they were a size larger than she regularly wore. She then removed a short piece of rope, turned the body over, and tied Christina's hands together behind her back.

She had practised for this for weeks. She borrowed a book from the library on tying knots. She had practised tying a piece of rope in her house, around her bannisters. Perfecting the art. She looked around, then went upstairs, carrying the rucksack with her over her shoulder. She removed some of its contents.

Mars unravelled the bale of rope. She made a noose with one end, then placed it through the balustrades and dropped it downstairs to where Christina lay. She then went back downstairs and tied the white towel around the right ankle, then put the noose around the towel and tied it tight, pulling at the knot to make sure that it wouldn't come loose.

She returned upstairs, unravelled the coil of rope, and slid it through one hand while opening it up with the other. She headed towards the bedroom as far as the threshold. About five feet away from the bed, she put the rope down and stood gazing at it laying on the carpet, calculating how much would be needed for the first stage of the plan.

She checked her position. She spread out the newspaper and laid it on the carpet, then removed a sharp knife from her rucksack and cut the rope over the paper. She then formed a noose of around eighteen inches in diameter in the length of rope that led downstairs.

Mars removed the toy wooden block from the rucksack. She went over to the bed and squatted down, her chin rested on the corner of the bedspread. She breathed heavily as she lifted the bed. She fumbled with her vital tool as she placed the wooden block, lengthways, between the underside of the wooden bed leg and the carpet, using it to raise and support the heavy bed slightly from the floor. She moved it into place, positioning the wider part of the oblong so it faced the bedroom door. She knew that she had to get everything exactly right in order for her plan to succeed.

Mars went to look over the bannister and down at Christina, frowning at the sight of her. She returned to the rope near the bedroom and sat on the floor. She then wrapped some of it around her leg. She gripped the section that led to the bannister with both hands.

Mars breathed deeply as she pulled the rope, her back toward the bedroom. She tugged until she felt the weight of the dead body move and until it began to rise off the floor. She listened to the sound of the body as it moved into a different position on the floor below. It made a crumbling sound as if someone was picking up a large, half-full heavy fabric bag. She heard Christina's head slide over the floorboards, her earring making a scratching sound on the polished wood until it stopped. She gathered that it was now raised fully away from the ground.

Her feet dug into the carpet as she gathered momentum. The rope squeaked as it strained over the wooden base plate and she could feel the tension in her face as she continued hauling Christina's lifeless body from the floor.

She turned her own body around towards the bed, the rope biting into her leg as she edged herself along the carpet. She then moved her thumbs into the centre of the noose, making a triangle shape. She felt her legs straining. She had to work fast.

She rested her other foot on the bedroom door frame for support and leverage. With her leg bent, she forced the noose towards the toy block, her legs taking most of the weight as she twisted her head to take a look at it. Her arms were taut, her face tense, and her thumbs around the rope reddened as the blood rose to the surface. She edged a leg forward to a new position, and at the same time pushed the rope forward as she felt Christina move slowly. She took another step, her foot gripping the carpet, as she felt the weight now rising gradually towards the landing. She forced the rope towards the bed with all her strength. She groaned heavily with the strain, as she felt the ascent of the body slow down. Mars continued to guide the rope forwards to its intended position. She knew in her mind that failure was not an option. She concentrated on only one thing - getting the rope to its intended location.

It now came to within an inch of the wooden pivot. The rope stopped moving as she stared at the lacquered finish on the toy block. It was close to her face now, she was so near, yet still so far. She could almost see her reflection in its sheen. She forced her bent leg outwards as her foot gripped the door frame, her calf muscles beginning to pull and twitch as they worked hard.

She then let out a wild scream as she thrust the rope against the wooden brick. It gave way. The bed thumped down onto the carpet, the wooden bed leg fell into the middle of the noose, and the brick disappeared. She released her hands from the rope, and it immediately stretched, as it turned into a loop. The noose stayed wrapped around the bed leg, and a section of the rope bit into her leg. She twisted and unravelled it, and the weight of the body moved. She waited for a second, and then breathed a sigh of relief.

She had achieved her main objective. She exhaled and groaned.

She rolled over and lay sprawled on the floor, her aching arms draped over the carpet as she felt a mixture of pain and reprieve flow over her body. She shivered as she felt a sense of anxiety take hold of her. She wondered for a moment about the consequences of her plan. She thought about her son, Tom… If this all went wrong, where would he end up? Would he be taken away from her? Would he be looked after? Would Matt ever believe her if she were to be found guilty of this crime? Would he stand by her? Her thoughts had to be brief. She had to move on. Her mouth was dry and sticky.

She looked at the ceiling and wondered what the hell she was doing exactly. She wondered if she had done the right thing. Was this going to solve her issues with this woman? Would this really advance her promotion through the company? She no longer cared where she would end up, but right now she felt a sense of total relief. She finally felt liberated from her arch-rival. The silence around her was golden, but she also felt like an intruder. She felt that she was trespassing. And she knew that she shouldn't be where she was.

She slowly eased her back up off the carpet. She flicked at the stiff rope like it was a string on a guitar. She looked at the thin strands sprouting proudly from it. She stood up, clutching at the door frame. She could see the top of Christina's foot.

Mars looked over the wooden handrail, not knowing what to expect. The site she saw was pitiful. She then walked over to the coil of rope and formed another noose, draping the rope over the top of the wooden handrail on the landing and lowering it down.

She knew that she still had a mountain of work to undertake as she hurried down the stairs.

She heard a groan. Mars turned around. She was certain that the rope had moved. She stood still, thinking that it had now stretched to its natural form, through holding its new weight. She had checked and calculated how much weight the rope she had purchased would support.

She thought about the remaining steps that she had to get through. She simply had to forget about the noise she heard and move on.

The head of the body dangled around four feet from the ground. She bitterly ripped off the stocking from its left leg. She then tied the noose of the rope around the left ankle, went back upstairs, and tugged at the other end of the rope until it felt tight. She held it in her hands and jerked it. It was going to be an easier task than her first exercise. She walked backwards. She passed the rope under the handrail and formed a knot around it.

She studied how much surplus rope she was going to leave from the knot - it had to be enough for someone to be able to haul up nine and a half stone. It had to be convincing and believable. She cut off the excess with the knife over the paper.

She looked at the first rope as it hovered above the carpet, and she cut that. The rope flipped up as it vanished down to the hall below. The second rope then made a creaking sound as it tightened itself on the handrail.

She then went to the bedroom and untied the knot on the noose around the leg of the bed. She looked at her watch, removed a business card of Jeff Turner's from a pocket of her trousers and put it into one of Christina's handbags.

She then headed towards the stairs. She stopped and turned around looking at the wooden area where the first rope had slid over. Mars went to the bathroom, grabbed a face towel, wet it under a tap, and at the same time splashed her face with water, returned to the wooden base rail and wiped it over. She also wiped the door frame where the sole of her trainer had pushed against it.

Forty-nine

She let out a moan. She began to feel some pressure as she thought about what she may have missed or would possibly miss once she left the house. She pulled at the skin on her forehead. 'Have I covered everything?' If she hadn't, she now certainly didn't have the time to go back. She returned to the bedroom and picked up some black mascara from the dressing table.

She finally went downstairs and undid her well-tied slip knot, which was around the white towel wrapped around Christina's right ankle. She then callously stuffed the apple into the gaping mouth of the suspended deceased body.

The body swayed slightly. She stood for a second and looked around. She went into the kitchen and removed the empty beer cans from a plastic bag, sat them on the worktop and looked at them. Something worried her, something just wasn't right…But she couldn't put her finger on what was bothering her. Was she thinking too much? She knew that she had to move on.

She headed towards the lounge. Removing the small plastic bag from her fleece pocket, she opened it up and scattered a couple of human hairs and pieces of cotton fibres onto the sofa. She had already dispensed the business card.

She brushed the ash and cigarette butts from the small glass table into her holdall, having earlier emptied the ashtray in order to pound it against Christina's skull. The cleaning up of this mess was not on her "to-do" list. She hoped that there wasn't anything else that would slow her down.

She picked up the heavy ashtray from the floor and threw it into her bag. Again, she scrutinised the room for any clues that she may have left. She looked to see if she had given anything away. She picked up her glass and put it into her holdall. She then looked around the room. She took a final look at the sofa, remembering the earlier event. She found herself begin to shake.

Mars returned to the hall and looked up at the first-floor landing, wondering if the rope would continue to hold her victim. Her face was one of relief and anger rolled into one.

Suddenly, she heard a snap, a kind of click… It came from the direction at the rear of the kitchen. Her eyes flickered faster than a reporters camera shutter. Mars stood frozen. In a split second, her body turned from a relative calm to one of sheer terror. Fear entered her. All the methodical planning she had undertaken over the previous weeks and months seemed to have vanished. Every inch of her skin appeared to tense up and turn cold. Goose pimples made her flesh prickle.

She found herself glued to the spot. Rooted. She was unable to move from where she stood. She was too scared to. She felt like stone. She was staring at where her eyes led her, looking into the kitchen. Mars was standing in the hallway. Her breathing became heavy, and her heart was pumping at an alarming rate. What was it?

Mars stood still, with Christina Zabrinski beside her dangling upside down from the rope that she had tied to her ankle. Christina's face looked sinister.

But Mars had company.

There was a figure looking at her from afar. A profile that she couldn't make out, its face and most of its body hidden by the pillar in the middle of the kitchen patio doors.

The figure was standing in the garden of Christina Zabrinski's house and it was facing towards her. And it was looking at her.

Thirty seconds passed, but it seemed like an hour. She looked at this figure and wondered who the hell it could be. Why wasn't it doing anything, why was it just staring at her? Her scalp felt as if it was shrinking. She tried to make out who it could be. It was somebody shorter than herself, around five-feet-two.

The figure was plump and dressed in dark clothing. Mars was thinking, her mind racing.

'For Christ's sake, why is it not moving?' she muttered. It looked as if it were just as scared as she was. 'Who knows that I'm here tonight anyway? Hopefully no one.' Most people would be out, seeing that it was a Friday. They would be enjoying themselves, letting off bloody fireworks, especially on a night like this.

'Can it see me?' She looked around briefly at the light. The only light sources were a softly lit lamp in the front lounge of the house and the glare from the bathroom light that had been left on, on the first floor. She was feeling exposed to this person, this thing. She thought that there was probably enough light in the hallway shining on her to be seen. Her face was not covered, and she knew that the figure would be able to recognise her. She lifted her hood from her fleece and covered her head.

She thought hard as her temples throbbed with more pressure than she had ever felt in her life. She felt a force on the wall of her brain as if it was trying to escape. It was becoming too much for her to take.

So, who the bloody hell was standing in the garden, standing still, and looking at her?

She turned around very quickly to look at the front door behind her. She looked through the small opaque window to see if she could make out any shadowy figures. Maybe this person had an accomplice, and they were just a decoy.

But there was no-one at the door as far as she could tell. She then spun her head back towards the figure in the garden… It had gone, it was no longer there. Mars looked shocked.

She no longer knew what her next move should be. She felt that she now had to get away, quickly, but also stick to her plans.

Mars stood in the hallway, perplexed, unsure as to what to do next. Where had this figure gone to? Had it gone to get assistance? Would it, they, be back soon? Why did it disappear? 'I didn't do anything to scare it.'

She now had to think quickly, quicker than her plans allowed her to.

She looked nervously again towards the patio doors to see if the figure was there, and thought, who was it? Where is it now? Is it coming back?

She then picked up the rucksack, put it on her back and headed towards the front door. She turned and looked at the body suspended in mid-air. It was a pathetic gruesome sight, morbid and surreal. A sight that she could have never imagined seeing in her lifetime. It was only something that she saw in the movies, yet it was in front of her, it was a sight that she had created. A work of art, maybe? She appeared pleased with her evening's effort. She had a cynical smile.

Once outside in the still of the night she breathed heavily. She retrieved her wig from her bag, pushed up her blonde hair, and pulled on the new headwear.

She walked three streets away from the house constantly looking behind her. Was the figure following her? She flagged down a cab.

She inserted her key into the lock, slowly turned it and gently opened the front door. She eased artfully inside, removed her wig and shook her head. Her holdall was missing most of the items that she had taken with her earlier. She had dumped some of its contents in various dustbins before getting her ride back. She had left the high-heeled shoes and the expensive trainers outside a charity shop. She knew that they would be snatched up almost instantly, taking her DNA with them. She had kept one item and would dump the wig and rucksack somewhere else tomorrow.

She retched as she leant over, a hand from her outstretched arm resting on the wall as she spewed out very little, bile dripping from her mouth like a piece of white string as she thought about what she had just gone through. Her mouth was arid, and her breath was foul. She wiped it with her hand. The picture of the body was stuck in her mind. She would have to snap out of it and move on with her plan.

She locked the door. Mars stood motionless in the hallway and listened to the peace and calm of the evening. It was a lovely sound. She looked at the darkness around her as she gathered her senses, then let out a long, audible sigh of relief. She rubbed the nape of her neck with a hand, and then pulled out a piece of scrunched-up paper from a pocket of her trousers. She looked at the list, and it told her that she had a couple more things to do. She walked into the lounge and clicked the phone jack back into its socket. She took her mobile phone off silent. She then returned to the kitchen, turned on a ring of the gas cooker, and burnt the piece of paper.

She crept up the stairs and headed immediately to Tom's bedroom, hoping and wishing that all had gone to plan and that he would be fast asleep. As she opened the door to check if he was there, she heard the reassuring sounds of her snoring son and the television making a mild hissing noise. It was a lovely sound. She went into the bathroom and downed a couple of painkillers.

She lay in the bath as deep thoughts pervaded her head. It was finally over, all done, she could not go back now. She had to stick rigorously to her story. There would be questioning, interrogating, and interviewing. Sly innuendoes, gossip and pressure heaped upon her, but she knew that she could cope with what was to come in the next few days. She had got her revenge. She had meticulously planned this evening for months, going over the finer details time and time again to get it correct. She had rehearsed some of this evening. Yet she couldn't help thinking that she had missed something. She felt that all had gone well, except for the figure in the garden who just stared at her silently. Mars wasn't sure if the person could have seen the body next to her because of the angle which it stood. Mars thought that, because Christina's body was to her left when she was looking towards the figure, it should have been out of sight, obscured by the wall in the hallway. She hoped that her theory was correct. Maybe just a part of Christina's body had been visible but, from where it was standing, could the figure have made out what it was? And there was also the issue of the light in the hallway… Was it bright enough for her face to have been seen? Just who was it out there and why were they there? What happens if I get a knock on the door from the police tonight, what should I say? Surely if it had been reported, and they knew me, they would be here by now. Mars continued to fret as she looked out of the dark window.

She closed her eyes and sunk into the bath until the water was level with her nose. Her knees pointed upwards, and the bubbles were dissipating.

It could have been a burglar who, by sheer coincidence, had come to burgle the house at the same time Mars had been there, and then become equally scared and not knowing what to do, froze and gave up on its mission.

It had the shape of a girl, she thought. Or could it have been a young man? She just didn't have a clear idea of who the mystery person could be. It was certainly playing heavily on her mind.

She jolted sharply as if someone had thrown a live wire into the bath. Water shot into the air like a fountain. 'Oh fuck!'

287

Fifty

Friday was finally here, at last. She couldn't wait to get home. Tom was at a sleepover nearby at a friend's house, and Matt had said that he would cook for her this evening. What could be better?

Mars left work and headed towards Bookham and home.

She enjoyed her new job. There were new faces, new friends, and fresh challenges. And there were no domineering vice-presidents looking over her to shove her around.

Yes, she had targets to meet. She had to deliver, and she had to answer to her boss. And she had for now, for the time being, given up chasing her superior's position.

Under a cloudless blue sky, she turned off the Lower Road and into Pine Close.

She put a foot on the brake pedal in surprise and breathed heavily. Rebecca Ansell sat on a wooden bench, oblivious to what was happening around her, and had not noticed the car heading towards her into the cul-de-sac.

Mars drove past her and parked away from her house. She looked in a wing mirror. Rebecca was still in sight.

'So, she now knows where I live, but why is she here?' Mars thought. She sat in her car, worried. 'I'm going to have to get out sooner or later and face her, as she now knows my address. What is she doing here and what does she want?' Two minutes passed. Mars pulled out some make-up from her bag and applied some blusher to her cheeks. She looked thoughtful.

She got out, wearily, and closed the door, she continued to look towards Rebecca, who heard the noise and looked up. Rebecca wore brown frumpy flowery slacks and a blue woollen buttoned jacket with a collar, neither of which complimented the other. Her plastic shoes were purple. Mars walked resignedly in her direction and stopped near the bench. Rebecca had a wayward look about her, and her body language was unresponsive. An empty crisp wrapper was wedged between two of the flaky wooden bench slates. She looked up and smiled at Mars.

'Hi,' she said, sounding unconvincing.

'Hello Rebecca, how are you?' She looked around, 'What brings you here, then?' she said in a gentle tone, sounding like she was her liaison officer.

'Nice evening, isn't it?' Rebecca said, appearing to be agitated and nervous. She sounded out of her comfort zone. A bird whistled in a nearby bush.

Mars sat down on the bench next to her. A large tree branch draped over them. She felt tension from the young girl.

'What brings you here then, Becks?'

Rebecca looked thoughtful and didn't immediately answer.

'You followed me, didn't you, from the court? That's how you know where I live, isn't it?'

'Maybe.' She gulped. 'Nice house.' She looked in its direction.

'Thanks, but you're not here about my house, are you?' Mars had an inkling as to why she was there. She knew that she hadn't travelled from her house in west London for a chat. There was a pause. Mars waited patiently.

'I could have been in that courtroom that day. I could have been in there. I was asked to attend by that bloke, Richards. I also received a summons. I should have turned up, but maybe it was the fear of standing in front of a crowd of people, having to answer their questions, and in a packed room, with all those faces looking at me.' She breathed out from her nose a couple of times. 'I just don't think that I could have handled it. It would have felt like I was being interrogated. I've seen it on the telly, on programmes and in films. I got a doctor's medical certificate excusing me, but Lambert still phoned me a few times when I didn't show up. She texted me as well, but I didn't answer her calls.'

Mars sighed. Rebecca turned and looked at her, her complexion changing.

'They questioned me soon after the murder. They asked me where I was on the night that Christina was murdered.' Mars stared at her. 'I told them that I went over to Christina's house that night. I told them that I stood outside and just looked at it. But I didn't, I went into the garden, and looked into the house.'

Mars shifted her position on the bench.

'It was you inside Christina's house, wasn't it?' Her voice was uncertain.

'I don't know what you mean, Rebecca. I don't understand what you are saying. It wasn't me that murdered Christina…'

'But it was, and you know it!' She looked bluntly at Mars.

'I could have been in that courtroom, and if I was, they would have asked me questions. One would have been, "Is the person that you saw at fourteen Bollo Lane, on the night of the 31st, October, in this room?"' Mars waited intensely for her to finish what she was saying.

'I would have had to say yes.' Rebecca looked up to the sky. There was a silence between them. 'You have to tell the truth in court, don't you?'

'So why didn't you, then? Why didn't you turn up at the court?' Mars said with apprehension.

'I don't think that I could have handled the pressure. It would have scared me.' She sounded solemn.

'You see, it was you inside the house on Halloween night.' She looked ahead; she had a distant look. Mars stayed silent, waiting for what she was going to say next.

'Did you kill Christina?' Mars looked at a nervous Rebecca.

'No, Becks, no I didn't.'

'But you see Mars, I'm just not sure of that.' She turned and looked at her for a reaction, her fingers playing with her lips. Mars sat, thoughtful.

'You see, I've come here to ask you for some money. Well, maybe a few thousand pounds.'

'I'm sorry?' Mars said, looking shocked. 'Whatever for, Rebecca? Did I hear you correctly?'

'I want some money, Helen. I could go back to Richards and tell him that my nerves got the better of me on that day, and I was too scared to go to court, you see. I have Asperger's. I have difficulty mixing with people, interacting, you know. It's a social thing.'

'Has anyone put you up to this, Rebecca? Have you spoken to anyone about this?' asked Mars, her voice sounding as if to console her. She knew Rebecca was not a strong-willed person, and that she could be easily led.

'No,' came a forthright reply.

Mars mused over the outrageous demand that Rebecca had made and wondered what figure she had in mind.

'I'm sure Richards would be pleased to hear what I would have to say to him, seeing that the murder of Christina is still unsolved, don't you think so?' She sounded nervous.

'Do you know that this is a form of blackmail, and that blackmail is a criminal offence? You could go to prison for it - you do know that - don't you, Rebecca? And it could be a long sentence.'

Mars then saw a figure in the distance. She leaned down, opened her handbag and removed a small notebook. Rebecca glanced at her movements.

'It's your choice, would you really want to go to court and go through all that trauma, all those questions, all those prying eyes? They will dissect your every word and drag your private life out into the open in front of a watching crowd. You have to be prepared for your whole life to be opened up and scrutinised. It's horrific, Rebecca, it really is. If you were to go ahead, then I'd have to testify against you this time.' Rebecca looked uneasy at what she heard.

'Pardon?'

'You do know, Rebecca, that you cannot be tried for the same crime twice, don't you? Even if new evidence emerges. It's called the "double jeopardy law".' Rebecca looked confused and unsure about what she was being told. Mars knew that this was not entirely correct though.

The figure approached the two girls.

'Hi Judy, how are you?'

'I'm fine, Helen, I'm just heading up to the shops to get some bits. You always need something, don't you?'

'You do, you're right, Judy.' Mars held out a hand. 'This is a friend of mine, Rebecca Ansell. We're just having a little chat together.' Mars introduced her. Judy was short and had brown hair, it was tied in a ponytail. She smiled at Rebecca but got a blank look in return.

'I'll see you later, Helen, you look busy.'

Mars started to scribble in her notebook.

'What are you doing?' Rebecca asked as she moved uncomfortably on the bench.

'Well, Rebecca… if you think that you can blackmail me,' she scribbled away. 'Then I'm writing down the contents of our conversation… and our meeting today, here. I am writing that you have followed me to find out where I live, because I certainly didn't give you my address, and I never invited you here.' She looked at Rebecca, waiting for a reaction, Rebecca stared blankly at her. 'I'm also writing down that you have asked for a sum of money from me, and if agreed, promised not to go to DCI Richards.' Rebecca looked concerned. Anxiety and fear came over her. She looked stone-faced.

'I have also included that Judy Hamlin was a witness to our sitting here at…' She looked at her watch. 'At 6:49 pm. And when she returns, I'll ask her to sign it.'

She grinned at her foe.

Acknowledgements

The seeds that grew into the idea for this book started when I was young and attended a fair in Borehamwood, it then came back to me when I heard the group Steely Dan sing the line bobbing for apples in their song, 'Everyone's gone to the movies.' That was in Shoreditch. Then I entered (for me) this world.

They say writing a book is like running a marathon – two marathons if you possess something that hampers your creativity. You shouldn't hold back and allow it to stop you from having that dream, come what may and fulfil it. Be it difficult, hard or bordering on the impossible. The story turned out more horrific than when I first started it. I was in that courtroom, in a real case that I enjoyed being in and it added to the intensity to write this book.

My thanks go out to Sarah Cardwell and Martin Dowsing for their grammar. Carol Green for your reads. Linda Tovey for your help. Ew for your advice about advice. And for the woman that didn't turn up at our court case (I never remembered her name).